Nightingale
Wedding Bells

Donna Douglas

arrow books

1 3 5 7 9 10 8 6 4 2

Arrow Books
20 Vauxhall Bridge Road
London SW1V 2SA

Arrow Books is part of the Penguin Random House group of companies
whose addresses can be found at global.penguinrandomhouse.com.

Penguin
Random House
UK

First published in Great Britain by Arrow Books in 2019

www.penguin.co.uk

A CIP catalogue record for this book is available from the British Library

ISBN 9781784757168

Typeset in 10.75/13.5 pt Palatino by Jouve (UK), Milton Keynes
Printed and bound in Great Britain by Clays Ltd, Elcograf S.p.A.

Nightingale
Wedding Bells

Donna Douglas lives in York with her husband and two cats. They have a grown-up daughter. When she is not busy writing, she is generally reading, watching Netflix or drinking cocktails. Sometimes all at the same time.

To my beautiful grandson, Sebastian

Acknowledgements

Big thanks to Emily Griffin and the amazing team at Arrow for all of your hard work and dedication. Producing a book is much more than putting words on the page. It has to be edited and proof read, a beguiling cover has to be created and enticing copy has to be written, and then last but by no means least someone has to go out there and sell it. It has been great working with you all to create and develop the Nightingale series. I owe so much to you guys.

And let's not forget my wonderful agent, Caroline Sheldon – who has championed me through thick and thin – and my family, who must at times have wondered whether it would be easier if I just went out and got 'A Proper Job'.

Finally, a big thank-you to all the readers who have followed the Nightingales' journey from the first book. What a journey it's been! I'm so grateful for all of your support and enthusiasm for the series. I hope you've enjoyed reading the stories as much as I've enjoyed telling them. And I hope you will stay with me and enjoy all of the stories that are still to come.

Chapter One

1917

'Look out, lads. Here comes the Agony Wagon!'

There was a grin on the young corporal's face as he called out, but Anna could see the fear in his eyes as he watched her push the dressings trolley down the ward.

All the men dreaded the dressings round. Some would start screaming as soon as they saw the trolley. Others would wait, white-faced and mute with terror, knowing their turn would soon come.

Others, like Corporal Bennett, would crack feeble jokes to hide their nerves.

'Has it grown back, Nurse?' he asked, as Anna tentatively peeled the bloody dressing from the raw stump where his left arm had once been.

'I'm afraid not, Corporal.' Anna tried her best to smile back at him. Corporal Bennett was one of her favourites on the ward. He had arrived with the latest convoy, sent over from France a few days earlier. He was twenty-seven, two years older than her and the same age as her fiancé Edward.

Corporal Bennett grinned. 'Oh, well, I s'pose I'd best write to my pals in France and ask 'em to look for my old one, eh? I seem to recall I left it in a dugout somewhere near Passchendaele.'

Beside her, Staff Nurse Hanley tutted. 'Do get on with it, Nurse! That poultice will be stone cold by the time you put it on!'

Anna sent her a sideways glance. She dreaded doing the dressings round, but she dreaded doing it with Staff Nurse

1

Hanley even more. The older woman towered over her, as big and strong as a man, not an ounce of compassion or sympathy in her square-jawed face.

'Best do as she says, Nurse.' Corporal Bennett was gritting his teeth now, his whole body tensing, ready for what was to come. 'Get it over with.'

Anna removed the cloth covering the enamel dish and took out the steaming poultice. She took a deep breath, gave the young soldier a quick nod to make sure he was ready, then pressed the hot poultice to his raw wound.

Corporal Bennett hissed with pain, tears springing to his eyes. It was for his own good, Anna told herself over and over again. The poultice would keep the wound clean and fresh, to give it the best chance to heal properly.

She turned her gaze away from the young man's anguished face and looked towards the window instead. It was late-September and the rain was still coming down as it had for the past week. A dreary curtain of water streamed down the glass, blurring her view of the world outside. Even though it was ten o'clock in the morning, the sun still hadn't emerged. It lurked behind a dense pall of grey cloud, draining the life and colour from the streets of London's East End.

But it was worse in France, Anna thought. Edward had written to tell her that it hadn't stopped raining there all summer. The near-constant drizzle had filled the craters with muddy slime. The field drains had been shattered by the weight of the constant bombardment, and even when the rain did stop there was never enough sunshine to dry out the ground. His letters made her weep, with their stories of living and sleeping knee-deep in icy water, and the men he knew who had died in the man-made swamp.

Please, God, don't let Edward die. Anna sent up the same silent, beseeching prayer she had said for him every day for the past three years.

'That's enough, Nurse!'

The rasp of Staff Nurse Hanley's voice made Anna jump. She looked up at the woman's unsmiling face, her thick brows drawn over glacial grey eyes. Then she looked down at her own hand, still pressing the poultice to Corporal Bennett's wound. He was managing to still smile but his teeth were gritted in agony, and beads of perspiration had formed on his brow.

'Oh, Lord, I'm sorry.' Anna snatched the poultice away, dropping it back in the enamel bowl.

'You were away with the fairies, Nurse!' Corporal Bennett joked feebly.

'She had no business to be,' Nurse Hanley snapped. 'Her attention should be on what she is doing.'

'Oh, I dunno.' The soldier winked at Anna. 'I don't blame you for being miles away. I would be too, if I could.'

Anna looked at the raw stump of his shoulder and felt a pang of guilt. 'Nurse Hanley is right,' she said. 'I could have hurt you, and I'm sorry.'

'Don't suppose you could do worse than those bloody Huns, Nurse. Pardon my French!'

Anna quickly set about dressing the corporal's wound. All the time she was aware of Staff Nurse Hanley's severe gaze on her, making her fumble nervously.

You're a qualified nurse, just the same as she is, Anna reminded herself. But ten years her senior as she was, Veronica Hanley still treated her like a probationer.

'Duffield! What do you think you're doing?'

Sister's voice rang down the ward. Nurse Hanley rolled her eyes heavenwards.

'Not again!' she murmured.

Corporal Bennett grinned. 'What's she done this time?'

Anna risked a glance down the ward at her friend and fellow nurse Grace Duffield. She stood by the door to the linen store, her hands clasped in front of her, being told off by the ward sister. Even with her head hanging, Grace's lanky frame still towered over the much shorter and rounder outline of Miss Sutton.

'That girl is a menace,' Veronica Hanley muttered.

'Don't be so hard on her. She's got a heart of gold,' Corporal Bennett said.

Anna shot him a quick, grateful look. She'd wanted to say the same thing, but she knew better than to answer Nurse Hanley back.

'It takes more than a good heart to make a good nurse,' Hanley snapped.

What would you know about that? Anna thought. So far as she could tell, Nurse Hanley barely had a heart at all.

Anna looked back over her shoulder at Grace, lolloping away towards the sluice, her head still down. Poor girl, she couldn't help being so clumsy. They had trained together and Anna knew it was a constant struggle for her friend, keeping those long, angular limbs of hers in check.

Anna finished dressing Corporal Bennett's shoulder, and stepped back.

'There, all done. Now, can I get you anything else?'

She saw the cheeky glint in the young man's eye and knew what was coming next.

'A kiss would be nice.' Corporal Bennett puckered his lips.

Once upon a time she might have blushed and fled. But after three years on the wards, Anna was quite used to the men's sense of humour.

She straightened his bedclothes. 'Now, Corporal,' she said primly. 'You know very well I'm spoken for.'

'You can't blame a fellow for trying, can you?' Corporal Bennett turned to Nurse Hanley. 'How about you, Nurse? Or are you spoken for, too?'

4

'Certainly not!' Nurse Hanley retorted, turning crimson. She turned on her heel and walked away, pushing the trolley before her like a chariot.

Corporal Bennett winked at Anna. 'Thank the Lord for that,' he whispered. 'For a minute there, I thought she was going to say yes. It would have been like kissing my old sergeant major!'

Anna laughed, then quickly straightened her face as Staff Nurse Hanley summoned her.

'When you're quite ready, Nurse?' she snapped.

Anna scurried to join her at the foot of the next bed, where another young soldier was already whimpering in fear.

This time Nurse Hanley took charge. Anna watched as the senior nurse set about removing the man's dressings. His screams went right through Anna and she looked away as the dressings tore further skin from the raw flesh. But Nurse Hanley did not even flinch.

'The Dakin's Solution, Nurse, if you please.'

Anna jumped to attention and handed her the dark brown bottle from the trolley. But she was clearly not quick enough for Staff Nurse Hanley, who regarded her through narrowed eyes.

'Are you all right, Nurse?' she said.

'Yes, Staff.'

'Only you don't seem to be very with it.' Nurse Hanley peered at her. 'And you look tired. Are you tired, Nurse?'

'No, Staff.' Anna straightened her shoulders.

'Don't lie to me, Nurse, I can see it in your face. You're pale and drawn, and you have dark circles under your eyes.' Nurse Hanley snorted. 'I suppose you've been out dancing and gallivanting with the other girls until all hours? It won't do, you know,' she went on, not waiting for an answer. 'You must exercise some self-control in future and put a stop to all these late nights. You are responsible

5

for looking after these men, and they deserve your full attention.'

'Yes, Staff.' There was no point in arguing with her. Nurse Hanley always knew best. She was as bad as any ward sister for that.

Besides, she wasn't completely wrong. Anna *was* tired. It had been nearly three in the morning before she'd crawled back into bed that morning in the nurses' home, and barely three hours later Miss Williams the Home Sister had been knocking on their doors to rouse them.

But there was certainly no dancing or gallivanting involved, whatever Nurse Hanley seemed to think. Anna wondered what the senior nurse would make of it if she knew where Anna had been the previous night. And almost every night before that.

She wouldn't understand, Anna thought. Nursing was Veronica Hanley's whole life. At thirty-five years old, she had no husband, no sweetheart, and no family either from what Anna could tell. She had a few friends among the ward sisters and senior nurses, but most of her life was dedicated to her job.

She wouldn't be able to comprehend that Anna had another life, one outside the hospital walls that was just as important to her.

When the dressings round was finished, Anna joined Grace Duffield in the sluice. She was standing at the big stone sink, disconsolately scrubbing bedpans. She was tall and gawky, with a country girl's flushed pink cheeks and warm hazel eyes. Wisps of light brown hair escaped from beneath her lopsided cap.

'Why on earth are you doing that?' Anna asked her. 'Surely one of the VADs should be on bedpans?'

'I know, but she asked me to help her. She seemed so overwhelmed, poor thing.'

Anna thought about where she had last seen the little VAD, puffing away on a cigarette in the kitchen. She hadn't looked particularly overwhelmed.

'They're here to help us, not the other way round,' she pointed out.

'Oh, I don't mind,' Grace said. 'Besides,' she added cheerfully, 'I can't get into any trouble in here!'

'I saw Sister taking you to task again earlier on. What was she ranting about this time?'

Grace's rosy cheeks darkened. 'I dropped a thermometer,' she mumbled. 'And then, when I was rushing to pick it up before Sister noticed, I accidentally stepped on it.'

'Poor Duffield!' Anna couldn't help smiling.

'I know. I'm so clumsy.' Grace stared mournfully down at her large feet, encased in stout black lace-up shoes. 'If ever anyone was misnamed, eh?'

Anna looked at her friend's open, smiling face. Grace was the butt of everyone's jokes, but she always took it in good part. Anna sometimes wished she wouldn't be so quick to make fun of herself.

'It's only because you get nervous,' she said. 'You're a good nurse really.'

'That's not what Sister wrote in the ward book yesterday. Now, what was it she said?' Grace paused for a moment, remembering. ' "Duffield has a tendency to be like a bull in a china shop." '

'Corporal Bennett reckons you have a heart of gold.'

Grace's face brightened. 'Does he? That's nice of him.' She turned on the tap to rinse a bedpan. Water gushed everywhere, and Anna had to jump back to avoid a soaking.

'Did you hear the news?' Grace carried on, apparently unconcerned by the puddle around her feet.

'What news?' Anna picked up a mop and started cleaning up.

7

'Sylvia Saunders is engaged to Roger Wallace.'

'No!' Anna instantly stopped mopping. 'That was quick. They've only been courting a few months.'

'I know. Saunders reckons they're head over heels in love. They're planning a summer wedding, apparently.'

'Good for her.' Without thinking, Anna twisted the engagement ring on her own left hand. She hadn't realised she was even doing it until she saw Grace's sympathetic smile.

'It'll be your turn soon,' she said. 'When Edward comes home.'

If he comes home.

Anna pushed the thought determinedly from her mind. She did her best to stay positive and tell herself that everything would be all right. But they had been engaged for nearly four years now. And the longer the wretched war dragged on, and the more injured men arrived every day, the harder it was for her to believe her dream would come true.

But she couldn't allow herself to give up hope, for Edward's sake.

'I know.' She smiled, then changed the subject. 'We'll have to celebrate Saunders' good news.'

'I think everyone's meeting in the nurses' home tonight.' Grace glanced around the empty sluice, then lowered her voice. 'There's talk of Hilda Wharton smuggling in a bottle of sherry, if she can get hold of one.'

'That sounds like fun.' Anna went back to her mopping. 'It's a pity I won't be able to stay long.'

Grace looked over her shoulder at her. 'Surely your mother wouldn't mind if you missed one night?'

Anna shook her head. 'She relies on me to help her. She can't manage without me.' She looked at Grace. 'Will you cover for me?'

8

'Of course.'

'I'm sorry to have to keep asking you. I know you could get into as much trouble as me if we're caught—'

'I'm hardly a stranger to Matron's office, am I?' Grace looked rueful. 'Besides, that's what friends are for. And I'm sure you'd do the same for me, if I ever found myself coming home after lights out!'

She gave a self-deprecating smile as she said it. Nearly every nurse stayed out late at some time, and the other girls usually helped by leaving windows unlocked so they could sneak back in after the front doors were locked. But no young man had ever enticed Grace Duffield to flirt with the Home Sister's wrath.

It was such a shame, Anna thought. Under that gawky exterior, Grace was the kindest, sweetest girl she knew.

Then another thought occurred to her. 'Does Dulcie Moore know that Saunders is engaged?' she asked.

Grace swung round so fast she knocked into a teetering pile of bedpans with her elbow. Anna dropped her broom and rushed to catch them before they crashed to the ground.

'Oh, gosh, I never thought of that,' Grace said, as they steadied the pans to stop them toppling over. 'Poor girl. I wonder if she does know?'

At that moment the doors to the sluice swung open and Dulcie Moore herself stalked in, her pretty face thunderous under her starched white cap. She thrust a cloth-covered bedpan into Grace's hands and stomped out again, letting the door crash to behind her.

Anna and Grace stared at each other.

'I think that's our answer, don't you?' Anna said.

Chapter Two

'I was thinking about roses. I do love roses, especially pale pink ones, and they're perfectly in season in June, aren't they? Or perhaps a posy of violets? I love violets, too. Such a lovely fragrance . . .'

Spare me! Sitting at the other end of the couch, Dulcie Moore took a long swig from the sherry bottle Hilda Wharton had just passed to her.

Sylvia Saunders had only been engaged a matter of hours, and Dulcie was already sick and tired of hearing about it. To make matters worse, earlier on Sister had given them both the task of making up beds for the latest convoy of military patients. Dulcie had been stuck in the linen store with Sylvia as she bored on with the details of the family church where she intended to hold the service, and the hymns she had chosen. Then, as they made up the beds, Dulcie had been forced to listen to her pondering every detail of her dress, and whether or not she planned to have pearl trimming on the lace: 'I know it's pretty, but pearls can be rather old-fashioned, don't you think?'

At supper, Dulcie had positioned herself at the far end of the long dining-room table, but she could still hear Sylvia's excited little squeaks over the clatter of plates and cutlery, talking about the reception party.

And now, Dulcie found herself trapped in the common room at the nurses' house, listening to the bride-to-be going on and on about flowers.

'I mean, anemones are pretty too, I suppose. But they're rather a showy flower, don't you think?'

'Lord help us.'

Dulcie hadn't realised she had uttered the words aloud until Miriam Trott, who was sitting next to her, turned and said, 'Did you say something, Moore?'

Her tone was innocent, but the malicious glint in those keen brown eyes told Dulcie she had heard every word.

'I was just wondering if this is all Saunders is going to talk about for the next six months,' she muttered.

'I daresay she's just excited,' Miriam said. 'Anyone would be. I'm sure *you'd* be excited too, if you'd just got engaged.'

There was something about the way she said it that made Dulcie's hackles rise. There had never been any love lost between her and Miriam Trott, from the day they started training together three years earlier. Miriam was a tiny, bird-like creature, with mouse-brown hair, beady eyes and a beaky nose she was always sticking where it didn't belong. She had a very unkind streak and seemed to take pleasure in other people's suffering.

She was taking a lot of pleasure in the present situation, Dulcie thought.

'Yes, but I wouldn't bore everyone to tears with it,' she replied, taking another swig from the sherry bottle.

'That remains to be seen, doesn't it?' Miriam nodded towards the bottle. 'Aren't you going to pass that round?'

Dulcie passed it to her, and glared as Miriam took a gulp.

I hope it chokes you, she thought.

'Anyway, I like hearing about Saunders' wedding plans,' Miriam said. 'Although it must be rather difficult for *you*, I suppose,' she added as an afterthought.

'I'm sure I don't know what you mean,' Dulcie lied, snatching the bottle back from her.

'Oh, come on! Everyone knows you expected to be the one walking down the aisle with Roger Wallace!'

The whole room seemed to fall uncomfortably silent. Dulcie felt everyone's eyes swivelling curiously in her direction.

'It was a long time ago and it wasn't serious,' she dismissed.

'Really?' Miriam said. 'I seem to remember you telling everyone you were practically engaged. You even chose your bridesmaids. You were so sure he was going to pop the question, and then—' She shrugged. 'But that's just the way it seems to go with you, isn't it? Men are only interested for five minutes.'

Dulcie's hand closed around the bottle; she was fighting the urge to throw its contents in Miriam's smug little face.

'At least they *are* interested in me,' she murmured.

Miriam turned a deep shade of scarlet. 'And we all know why, don't we?' she hissed back.

'May I see the ring again?' Grace broke the uneasy silence. Sylvia was immediately distracted and smugly proffered her left hand for all to see.

As Grace stepped forward eagerly to get a closer look, Miriam let out a yelp of pain.

'Ow! Careful, you clumsy oaf, don't trample me!'

'Sorry,' Grace mumbled.

'I should think so, too.' Miriam theatrically examined her stockinged foot. 'You might have broken my toes.'

'Pity she didn't break your neck,' Dulcie muttered.

It was too much to hope Sylvia had not overheard her conversation with Miriam. Dulcie could see the bride-to-be watching her uncertainly throughout the rest of the evening. And when she finally decided she couldn't bear any more wedding talk and got up to leave, Sylvia followed her into the hall.

'May I have a word with you, Moore?' she asked quietly.

Dulcie's gaze drifted towards the stairs. She was fighting the urge to run away. 'What about?' she said.

As if I didn't know.

'About Roger and me.'

Dulcie faced Sylvia. She was a few inches taller than her, slender and graceful-looking, her long, pale face framed with straight, silvery-blonde hair. Her eyes were a limpid grey colour.

Roger had always told Dulcie he preferred brown eyes, like hers.

'What about you and Roger?'

'You don't mind, do you?'

'Why should I mind?'

Sylvia's cheeks flushed the palest of pinks and she averted her gaze delicately to the ring on her finger. 'I know you were – fond of him once.'

I was fond of *him*? Dulcie pressed her lips together to stop the words from spilling out. Roger had declared his love for her a million times, sworn she was the only girl for him as he kissed her and fumbled with her blouse in the back row of the Old Ford Picture Palace.

And Dulcie had allowed him to do it because she was certain that this time was different, that he would be the one to keep his promise to her.

She looked at Sylvia, so cool and perfect, her starched collar fastened tightly around her long, elegant throat. She didn't look like the type of girl to allow any man liberties.

Mustering all her pride, Dulcie managed a light laugh. 'As I said to Trott, it was nothing serious. And it was a long time ago.'

This time last year, a voice inside her head whispered. Last September they had walked hand in hand through the fallen leaves in Victoria Park, and made plans for their future.

But by summer it was all over. And exactly four months later, he had chosen the very same spot to propose to Sylvia Saunders.

'Anyway, I'm thrilled for you,' Dulcie added with a forced smile.

'Oh. Oh, well, that's all right then.' Sylvia's face brightened. 'I'm so glad there are no hard feelings. You know I've always thought of you as such a good friend. Which is why I wanted to ask you a very special favour . . .'

'Me, a bridesmaid! Can you imagine? Honestly, the cheek of her.'

Dulcie was still fuming about it when she sat down in Grace and Anna's room later. She was trying to darn a pair of stockings but her hands were shaking with so much anger she could barely get the stitches in the black wool.

'I mean, it's bad enough that she's stolen my boyfriend, without expecting me to trail up the aisle after them,' Dulcie went on. '*I've always thought of you as such a good friend,*' she mimicked Sylvia's girlish voice. 'Good friends don't steal each other's men, do they?'

Anna and Grace looked at one another. Anna was getting ready to go out, pulling on her coat and winding a muffler around her neck. Dulcie could see the doubt in their faces. They didn't understand what she and Roger had meant to each other before Sylvia had sneaked in.

'Of course, I know she's only doing it to be spiteful,' Dulcie said.

'Spiteful?' Grace said.

'She wants to make a fool of me. She wants everyone to see that she got the man and I didn't.'

'Perhaps she just wants to be nice?'

Dulcie glared at Grace. Duffield drove her mad sometimes, she was always so determined to see the good in everyone.

She wished she had someone else to talk to about it. Her best friend Sadie Sedgewick would have understood, but Sadie had decided to do her district nurse training, so now she was living out in one of the district houses in Mile End.

Since she had gone, Dulcie had grown closer to Grace, mainly because she had fallen out with most of the other girls. Either she had been catty to them, or they had been spiteful to her. But it was impossible to offend Grace.

'Nice? I doubt it,' Dulcie scoffed. 'No, she's got a plan, I know she has.' She considered for a moment. 'She'll probably make me wear a horrible dress. Although I daresay I'll still look better than her . . . I've a good mind to do it, just so I can outshine her.'

'I'm going now,' Anna interrupted her.

Grace went to the window and peered out. 'It's still raining hard,' she said. 'And the gutter's overflowing again. That drainpipe will be treacherous to climb—'

'Stop worrying,' Anna said. 'It's not as if I haven't done it before.'

She put on her hat, tucking her dark hair under the brim then reaching for her gloves. 'Don't forget to leave the window open a bit for me, will you?'

Grace nodded. 'I'll listen out. And I'll be sure to leave the lamp on so you can see where you're going.'

'Say hello to your fancy man for me,' Dulcie called after her as she clambered through the window. Anna shot her a dark look but said nothing.

A moment later she was gone. Grace leaned out, watching her until they heard the crunch of feet landing on the gravel path below. Then she ducked back inside, brushing the rain off her light brown hair.

'I wish you wouldn't say things like that,' she reproached Dulcie. 'You know she doesn't have a fancy man. She has to go off and help her mother run the bakery. She's managing it all on her own, and Beck's worried that it's too much for her.' She pressed her face to the glass, peering into the darkness. 'If you ask me, it's too much for Beck, too, working here all day and at the bakery all night.'

'She should close the place down, in that case.' Dulcie stifled a yawn with the back of her hand.

'She'd never do that!' Grace looked shocked. 'You know how devoted she is to that place. Her father built it up from nothing, she wants to keep it going for him. Besides, she wants something for Edward when he comes home.'

'That's her problem, isn't it?' Dulcie shrugged, already bored with the subject. 'So, do you think I should do it?' she asked.

'Do what?' Grace said absently, still looking out of the window.

Dulcie sighed. 'Be a bridesmaid, silly! Actually, I don't think I will,' she answered her own question.

'Won't Saunders be disappointed?'

'Hardly. She won't even notice, I'm sure, since she's asked practically everyone in the set to be a bridesmaid. Honestly, there'll be more bridesmaids than there will be congregation.'

'She hasn't asked me.'

Dulcie felt a brief stab of guilt. There she was, going on and on, not realising that poor Grace had been left out yet again.

'You can take my place if you like,' she said.

'Oh, no, Saunders wouldn't want that. Can you imagine it? I'd probably step on her dress and rip it, or drop my flowers or something!'

Dulcie looked at her friend's open, smiling face. 'You're not that bad,' she said. 'I'd let you be my bridesmaid.'

A blush rose in Grace's cheeks. 'Gosh, thanks.'

'Don't get too excited. I'll have to find someone to marry me first. And the way I'm going, I'll probably be the last in our set to get engaged.' Dulcie shuddered. 'God, imagine if Trott got married before me. She'd be utterly unbearable, wouldn't she? Even worse than she is already.'

She could hardly bear the thought of Trott's smug face, grinning at her from under a wedding veil.

It was so galling, Dulcie thought. The only reason she had come to train as a nurse at the Nightingale was to find herself a wealthy doctor to marry. She had announced as much to the rest of the set the day she arrived.

And yet here she was three years later, with a nursing qualification but no ring on her finger.

And as Miriam Trott had so unkindly pointed out, it wasn't for want of trying. Dulcie had no trouble getting men interested. It was keeping them that was the real problem.

In her agitation she jabbed herself in the finger with her darning needle and cursed under her breath.

'It's no good, I can't mend these wretched things any-more.' She threw down her sewing in defeat. 'They're already more darn than stocking!'

'Why don't you buy yourself a new pair?'

'I would if I had the money, but I don't have a bean until the end of the week.' Dulcie picked up her sewing again reluctantly and stabbed at it with the needle. 'I hate being poor,' she muttered. 'I'll bet Saunders will never have to mend her stockings once she's married to Roger Wallace.'

Not that she needed to mend them anyway, Dulcie thought. Sylvia Saunders' father managed a bank, and the family lived in great comfort in a leafy London suburb. Sylvia had gone to boarding school and rode ponies and played tennis and all kinds of other things that wealthy, well-bred young women did. She had certainly never had

17

to travel around in her father's cart at harvest time, looking for work, or sleep in a hay loft in the middle of winter.

No, Sylvia probably threw out her stockings at the first sign of a hole.

'Why do you think Roger chose her?' She asked the question that had been bothering her ever since she had heard the news.

'What?' Grace looked startled. 'Goodness, I don't know. He fell in love with her, I suppose.'

'Yes, but why? She's not even pretty.'

'I think she is.'

Dulcie frowned. Grace was a loyal friend, but she didn't always say the things friends should say.

'All right, I suppose she is, in an insipid sort of way.' She put her hand up and touched the brown curls that framed her own face. No one could ever call *her* insipid.

Roger used to love her curls. He used to try and count them, winding them around his fingers. She couldn't imagine him doing that with Sylvia's fine, silvery hair.

'I wonder if it's because she's rich?' Dulcie mused. Sylvia seemed to have that self-satisfied sheen about her, the kind that people with money always had.

Roger Wallace had it too, which was what had first attracted Dulcie to him.

'I don't know why people fall in love with each other,' Grace said. 'They just do, don't they? They can't help themselves.'

'What utter nonsense,' Dulcie said, attacking her sewing more vigorously. She had already made up her mind that she was going to make Roger fall in love with her.

Now all she had to do was win him back from Sylvia Saunders.

Chapter Three

Anna reached Chambord Street just as the pubs were turning out. Men spilled onto the pavement, laughing and jostling each other and complaining about the rain. They loomed out of the darkness towards her, but Anna wasn't afraid. She had grown up in Bethnal Green, she knew every cobbled alleyway and gas-lit street.

She knew most of the people, too. As she turned the corner, Anna saw Mr Hudson, who owned the butcher's next door to their shop, leaning against a lamp post outside the Angel and Crown. He was trying to light a cigarette but seemed to be having a lot of trouble finding his mouth with the match. Anna watched him struggling for a moment, then she approached him.

'All right, Mr Hudson? Can I help you with that?' She took the matchbox from him and lit another one, shielding it from the rain with her hand as she held it steady. Mr Hudson took a long drag on it until the tip glowed. Then he took a step back, staggering slightly to regain his balance.

'Ta, love.' He exhaled slowly and squinted at her through the stream of smoke. 'What you doing out on a filthy night like this?'

'I've come to see my mother, Mr Hudson.'

'At this hour? Bit late to go visiting, ain't it?'

Anna said nothing. The neighbours knew enough about their business, without her telling them any more.

Finally, Mr Hudson said, 'I'll walk with you, shall I? Make sure you're all right.'

'If you like.' They started down Chambord Street, Mr Hudson weaving unsteadily beside her. After he'd veered off the kerb and into the gutter twice, Anna took his arm.

'How's your dad, then?' Mr Hudson asked as they walked. 'Seen him lately?'

'I visited him at the internment camp last month. He seemed very well.'

Mr Hudson shook his head. 'Such a bad business. You'd think they would have let him out by now, wouldn't you? How long has it been?'

'Three years.' *You should know,* Anna thought. *You were there when they came to take him away.*

'That long, is it? Terrible shame, I call it.' Mr Hudson took another drag on his cigarette. The rain dripped steadily off the brim of his hat, splashing on the shoulders of his overcoat. 'I mean, don't get me wrong. I've no love for the Germans, any more than the next man. But your father . . . well, you only have to look at him to know he's a good man. One of the best.' He shook his head, spattering raindrops all around. 'Someone should do something about it.'

Like you did? Anna thought bitterly. She would never forget how Mr Hudson and their other neighbours had stood by and watched her father being marched off to the internment camp with the other German-born men who were living locally. None of them had spoken up for him, and no one had lifted a finger to help Anna and her family afterwards, either.

In fact, their old friends and neighbours had all turned their backs on the Becks. They had boycotted the bakery, taken their business elsewhere, watched and done nothing when marauders smashed their windows and terrorised them.

Things had changed since then, however. Somehow over the years, the war had exhausted them all so much that they'd had no choice but to mellow towards each other. Customers began returning to the bakery, and the neighbours no longer turned their backs on Anna and her family.

Papa had said she mustn't bear a grudge, so she tried her best not to say anything. But even though they were cordial with each other now, Anna knew she would never forgive them for what they had done.

They reached the short parade of shops, all in darkness, then turned down the narrow alleyway that led to the rear of the shops. Lights glowed in a couple of the windows, casting shadows across the cobbled yards.

'Looks like your mother's waiting for you,' Mr Hudson said.

'Looks like your wife's waiting for you, too.' Anna nodded towards the light coming from the window next door.

'With a rolling pin, I daresay!' Mr Hudson gave a long-suffering sigh. 'Oh, well, I'll be seeing you, love.'

'Goodnight, Mr Hudson.'

I mustn't bear a grudge, Anna told herself. But she couldn't help a little smile when Mr Hudson slithered on the wet cobbles and ended up sprawled face down on his doorstep.

Anna let herself in her own back gate, lowering the latch quietly. When she looked through the window she could see her mother at the kitchen counter, kneading a batch of bread dough, her shoulders hunched over the task.

She looks tired, Anna thought, as her mother straightened up to tuck a lock of fair hair under her headscarf. Years of strain had taken their toll on her beautiful face, leaving it lined, grey and exhausted.

Dorothy Beck turned as Anna let herself in through the back door.

'Hello, love.' she greeted her with a weary smile. 'I wasn't expecting you.'

'I told you I'd come.' Anna shrugged off her coat. The

21

kitchen was bright and blissfully cosy from the ovens, the warm air fragrant with the smell of baking bread.

'Yes, but not in this weather.' Her mother's gaze moved towards the rain streaming down the window pane. 'You'll catch your death.'

'It's you I'm worried about.' Anna put her coat over the chair closest to the fire. 'You look exhausted. Why don't you sit down and rest?'

'I can't, there's too much to do.' Her mother looked down at the mound of bread dough on the wooden counter in front of her. 'I've only just got the first batch in.'

'That's why I'm here.' Anna rolled up her sleeves and reached for her apron, hanging on a hook on the back door.

'But you've had a long day too,' her mother protested. 'It's not fair to ask you to come here after your shift and help with the baking.'

'You're not asking, I'm offering.' Anna went to the big stone sink to wash her hands. The cold water stung her skin, and the scent of the red carbolic soap reminded her of the Nightingale Hospital. 'We all have to work together to keep this place going. And since Liesel went off to be a Land Girl . . .' Anna pulled a face. She still hadn't forgiven her younger sister for abandoning them and going off to work on a farm in the wilds of Essex three months earlier, leaving their mother to cope on her own.

Dorothy seemed to read her thoughts. 'You mustn't blame her,' she said. 'She's young, it's only fair that she should be allowed to spread her wings—'

'She should be here, helping you, not muck-raking and milking cows! This is supposed to be a family business, after all,' Anna said bitterly.

'You know your sister has never been suited to working in the bakery. Not like you.' Her mother smiled. 'You were the one who inherited your father's gift for baking.'

Anna unhooked the towel from the nail to dry her hands. 'Then why won't you let me give up nursing and come back to work here full-time? I could run the kitchen and you could—'

But her mother was already shaking her head. 'We've been through all this, Anna,' she said. 'I don't want you to give up nursing.'

'But I never wanted to be a nurse!' she protested. 'Papa always meant for Edward and me to run this place together . . .'

'I said no!' She started at her mother's sharp tone. 'I won't hear of it, Anna. Now stop talking about it, please.'

'All right.' Anna retreated into sulky silence. She had never known her mother to speak so abruptly to her. She must be very tired indeed, she decided.

As she stooped to take the lid off the earthenware flour tub under the table, she heard her mother sigh.

'I'm sorry, my dear. I didn't mean to snap at you. It's been a rather trying day, that's all. I'll go and put the kettle on, shall I? Make us both a cup of tea.'

Anna looked at her mother, the tired smile that didn't quite reach her faded blue eyes. 'That would be lovely,' she said. 'I – what's this?'

She straightened up, the flour scoop in her hand. It was heaped, not with the usual pure white flour, but with something else. It was greyish-brown, coarse, and when Anna sifted it between her fingers it felt gritty.

Dorothy Beck turned, taking off her apron. 'It arrived this morning. It's all we could get,' she said. 'You know what it's been like recently, what with the German block-ades in the North Sea, and no food getting through? Well, the Government has issued us with this flour instead.'

'You call this flour?' Anna sniffed it. 'It smells like sawdust.'

'It might well be, for all we know. But it's supposed to be very nutritious.'

Anna frowned. 'I don't know what Papa would make of it.'

'I don't know what the customers will make of it, either. But I suppose we'll all just have to get used to it, like everything else about this war.'

Dorothy went to make the tea, leaving Anna to finish off kneading the dough. But no sooner had she put the bowl to prove than her mother returned with two letters in her hand.

'Before I forget, these arrived for you this morning.'

Anna took the two thin blue envelopes. One bore Edward's even, looped handwriting; the other an equally familiar spidery scrawl.

'You're still writing to Tom Franklin, then?' said her mother, looking over her shoulder.

'I promised I would.' Anna looked back at her. 'We owe him so much.'

Dorothy nodded. 'We do.'

Three years ago, Anna could never have imagined how much Tom Franklin would mean to her. Up until then, he had been nothing more than her father's delivery boy, a scowling, surly young man from a bad family. No one else would have given him the time of day, let alone a job, but typically, Papa had seen something in him that none of the rest of them had.

And, as usual, he had been proved right. When someone, supposedly in the name of British patriotism, had decided to set fire to the bakery with Anna and her family inside, it was Tom who had risked his life to rescue them. He had then set about rebuilding the bakery on his own, carefully restoring it to the way it had once been. That Anna, her mother and her sister were alive and had a roof over their heads was all due to him.

So when Tom was called up and asked her to write to

24

him, Anna agreed. Tom had no family of his own – or none who cared about him. The least she could do was to help him feel less alone.

Her mother patted her shoulder. 'You're a good girl,' she said. 'I'll go and make that tea.'

She went off, and Anna looked down at the letters in her hand. She wondered what her mother would say if she knew how much Anna looked forward to receiving Tom's letters. Somehow, over the years, what had started off as a duty had become a pleasure. She and Tom had formed a close friendship through their correspondence. Whether it was the years of war, or just because he found it easier to put his feelings down on paper than to say them out loud, somehow Anna had discovered a different side to Tom through his writing. A warm, genuine, caring, funny side that she had never imagined existed.

Of course, he would never replace Edward in her affections. Edward was her first love, she adored him with all her heart and couldn't wait for him to come home so that she could spend the rest of her life with him.

But unlike Tom, Edward found writing letters very difficult. His, when they arrived, were short, light-hearted, full of jokes. He complained when Anna was too emotional. 'It's depressing,' he said. 'Do you think I need to hear how miserable you are? Cheer me up, sweetheart, for heaven's sake!'

So Anna tried to keep her letters to him light and entertaining. It was only to Tom that she was able to open her heart, to share her deepest, darkest fears. And he did the same.

Anna tested the envelopes. Edward's was thin, barely substantial. She couldn't blame him for that, but she dearly wished he would allow her more than a few hastily written lines now and again.

She slipped the letters into her apron pocket and set about her work again.

Chapter Four

Mixing and kneading the dough, Anna could feel the tension in her shoulders relaxing, and the flutter of fear in her stomach ebbing away. The warm fug of the kitchen, the delicious smell of baking, transported her back to a time when she was young and carefree, when she and Edward worked side by side with her father, learning their trade. How they all used to laugh together, so content in their little world of bread and pastry and sugarwork. Even though her father could be an exacting task master when he wanted to be, he always delivered his lessons with a twinkle in his dark brown eyes. Anna could see him now, busy in the kitchen, his slight figure so precise in his movements, his white toque perched on his sleek dark head.

Oh, Papa. Anna blinked back the tears that blurred her eyes. She had to be strong, for everyone's sake. She had to keep the bakery going, so that Papa and Edward would have a place to come back to when they both returned home. And then they could all be together again.

She had taken the last batch of loaves from the oven when she remembered the tea her mother had promised her two hours earlier. Anna had been too busy to think about it, but now her throat was parched from breathing in the dreadful grey-brown stuff that was more dust than flour. Surely the kettle should have boiled by now?

She took off her apron and went down the hall to the small scullery that served as the family's kitchen.

'What is it they say about a watched pot?' she started to

say. But the scullery was empty. The kettle was on the stove, but when Anna put her hand on it, it was stone cold.

She went next door to the sitting room. There was her mother, sitting on the couch fast sleep, her chin on her chest.

Anna smiled. Poor Mother, she must be exhausted to drop off like that. She didn't even stir when Anna fetched a shawl from her bedroom and draped it over her to keep her warm.

As an afterthought, Anna sat down on the couch beside her. Almost immediately the wave of weariness she had been fighting overcame her. Surely it wouldn't hurt to close her eyes for a couple of minutes, she thought, nestling against her mother and pulling the shawl up over her shoulder.

She was woken by the sound of a whistling kettle. Anna sat bolt upright, startled into wakefulness.

'Morning, Miss Anna.'

Ida Church stood in the doorway, taking off her coat. She had been a customer at the shop for years, but since Liesel had left, she had been helping behind the counter. She had lost her husband at the Somme and struggled to survive on her widow's allowance, so the money came in useful.

Anna blinked in confusion at the sight of her. What was she doing there in the middle of the night?

Then her tired brain registered the crack of pale light creeping through the drawn curtains. 'What time is it?'

'Nearly six. Your mother's in the kitchen, making tea.' Ida went to the window and pulled the curtains back. 'And the rain's stopped at last, which is a blessing. I was beginning to think we might need the Ark!'

But Anna was scarcely listening. She was already on her feet, heading for the kitchen, hastily gathering up her shoes and coat.

Her mother appeared in the scullery doorway. 'Don't you want a cup of tea?'

'I can't.' Anna hopped on one leg, pulling on her shoe. 'I'm late as it is. I'm due on duty in an hour. If the Home Sister sees my bed hasn't been slept in she'll have my guts for garters.' And poor Grace's, too, she thought.

'I'm sorry, I shouldn't have let you sleep. But I've only just woken up myself when Mrs Church arrived.'

'Like a right pair of Sleeping Beauties, you were.' Ida Church beamed. 'I hardly liked to disturb you. Mind, I'm sure it did you both the world of good.'

Anna looked at her mother. At least she looked more rested now. Some of the grey pallor had gone from her face.

'It's no good for you, coming here to work as well as your nursing.' Ida Church shook her head. 'I dunno how you do it, I really don't.'

'It's got to be done, Mrs Church.' Anna shrugged on her coat. Even after a night in the warm kitchen, the damp cold seeped through to her skin.

'I wonder why you're bothering.'

Anna turned on her. 'Because it's Papa's business, and we need to keep it going for him.'

'Yes, but surely—'

'You'd best be going, hadn't you, Anna?' Dorothy cut in before Ida Church could finish her sentence. 'Don't want you to be late, do we?'

'I'll see you tonight.' Anna planted a quick kiss on her mother's cheek.

At least Mrs Church was right about one thing: the rain had finally stopped. But it was bitterly cold, and the sun was still shrouded behind cloud, the pale sky reflected in ice-laced puddles.

Anna hurried up the alley into Chambord Street. Mrs Hudson was opening up the shop next door, her husband nowhere to be seen. She waved at Anna as she swept bloody sawdust from the doorway into the street.

Anna looked up at the sign above her father's shop. *Beck's Bakery*, it said, the curling gold letters cracked and faded with age. She remembered her father telling her how proud he was as he had stood on that very same spot as a young man, watching the sign writer painting those letters.

I wonder why you're bothering. Mrs Church's words came back to her.

Anna shook her head. *Oh, Papa*, she thought. *Ida Church would never understand.*

Dorothy Beck stood at the shop window, her teacup in her hand, and watched her daughter going up the street. Anna was so like her father, small and slight, with her dark colouring and lively face.

'I dunno where she gets her energy from,' Mrs Church commented, coming to stand behind Dorothy.

'She's determined, like her father.' They were so similar, it made Dorothy's heart ache.

Mrs Church was silent for a moment. Then in a quiet voice she said, 'She doesn't know, does she?'

Dorothy shook her head. 'No.'

'When are you going to tell her?'

'I don't know. Soon, I suppose.'

'She'll have to find out sometime.'

'I know.' Dorothy dragged her gaze from the window. But she also knew it would break Anna's heart.

Chapter Five

They had barely finished making up the last bed before the new convoy of war wounded began to arrive.

They knew they were on their way because crowds started to form beyond the hospital gates. They pressed against the railings, watching as the string of ambulances made their way up the gravel drive and circled around the main hospital building to the Casualty block.

Another crowd had gathered there to watch the wounded being brought out. Some of the men hobbled on crutches, others were brought out on stretchers. They were still in their khaki uniforms, filthy and mud-caked, their wounds wrapped in crude dressings. They blinked in the pale light, squinting into the sky in dazed disbelief. The onlookers cheered and threw cigarettes and chocolate, but only a couple of the men stopped to pick up the gifts. Most shuffled on, heads down, shoulders hunched.

'They look so tired,' Anna said.

'I hope they're not all lice-infested like the last lot.' Dulcie shuddered. 'I hate lice.'

'I don't suppose the poor men like them much, either,' Anna snapped back.

Grace sent them both a sidelong look. As usual, she was standing between them, caught in the middle.

'Do stop gawping, Nurses!' Sister's voice rang out behind them. 'Look sharp, there is work to be done. Duffield and Beck, go down to the Admissions ward and do what you can to help. Take Parrish with you,' she added as an afterthought. 'I'm sure they will welcome an extra pair of hands.'

As Miss Sutton had predicted, the Admissions ward was desperately busy. Nurses hurried back and forth between the closely packed white beds, wheeling trolleys of dressings and medications and endless amounts of hot soapy water. But even the strong scent of carbolic was not enough to overcome the stench of filth and sweat coming off the men.

They heard them before they saw them. Their screams, moans and rasping coughs echoed up the long corridor.

Grace looked across at Anna. Her face was white, bloodless lips pressed together. She looked as if she might be sick.

'What do we have to do, Nurse?' a trembling voice beside her asked. Grace turned to see Eliza Parrish, the newest VAD. She had only started on the ward the previous day, fresh from her Red Cross training. She was terribly young, and very afraid, by the look of her. The poor girl had probably joined the Voluntary Aid Detachment imagining she would be doing nothing more than fetching bedpans, making beds and reading the men's letters from home.

This must look like hell to her, Grace thought.

'We have to get their uniforms off, get them washed and dress their wounds, and generally make them as comfortable as we can,' she said, picking her way over the line of stretchers waiting in the passageway outside the ward. Then, seeing the young girl's apprehensive look, she smiled and said, 'Stay with me, I'll help you.'

Grace showed her how to bundle up the filthy uniforms for the orderlies to take away and burn. She also showed her how to cut off the men's field tickets, the labels bearing their names and their injuries.

It wasn't an easy job. The wounded were in a dreadful state, their uniforms crusted with days of dirt and blood, and crawling with lice. Dulcie would be pleased, Grace thought. They screamed and cursed as she and Eliza carefully peeled them off and washed their wounds. Grace could feel the young VAD shaking with nerves beside her, but to the girl's credit she carried on doggedly.

Some of the injuries were truly dreadful. Most were from artillery shell damage, as usual, but there were also gunshot and bayonet wounds, skin blistered from mustard gas, and the persistent, hacking cough of trench fever.

One of the young men swore and tried to lash out at Grace as she peeled the bandages off his feet.

'Don't mind him, he doesn't know what he's saying,' she said to Eliza, whose round blue eyes had filled with tears. She was obviously a well brought up young lady, not used to such language.

'I bloody do!' The young man let fly with another stream of obscenities, some of which even Grace hadn't heard before.

As she peeled off the last of the filthy bandages, she heard Eliza Parrish gasp with horror.

'Sod off if you don't want to look!' the young man snarled.

'Why don't you go into the ward and ask Sister if there's anything she wants you to do?' Grace nodded towards the double doors. Eliza fled gratefully.

Grace turned back to the young man. 'Now then, let's see what we can do with these feet of yours, shall we?' she said bracingly. But even she could scarcely bring herself to look at them. They hardly seemed like feet at all, more like swollen, misshapen lumps, the skin blackened and blistered, half the toes already rotted away. And the smell . . . That awful, sweet, decaying smell that came from trench foot.

Eliza was still trembling when Grace went to check on her later in the scullery. She was bundling up the last of the uniforms, ready for burning.

'I don't understand why they're so angry,' she said in a quiet voice. 'You'd think they'd be pleased to be safe . . .'

'They don't realise they are,' Grace said. 'They've spent so long in the trenches, feeling very afraid, expecting to die at any moment. They've seen some awful things – things we couldn't even imagine. It's going to take a long time for their minds to accept that they're not in danger any more.'

Eliza Parrish stared back at her with wide, frightened eyes. Grace understood that, like the men, the VAD had also seen some things today that she couldn't possibly have imagined.

'I don't like it when they cry,' Eliza said slowly. 'And the ones who stare at you, as if they don't know where they are. –'

'Shell shock,' Grace said.

'It just seems – unmanly to be like that, don't you think?'

Grace stared at the girl's pert, pretty little face, and it was all she could do not to take Eliza Parrish by the shoulders and shake her.

She decided to walk away before her temper got the better of her. As she went, Eliza said, 'What will happen to him?'

'Who?'

'That boy . . . The one with the trench feet?'

'We'll have to see what the doctor says. But I expect they'll have to amputate.'

'So he'll never walk again?'

Eliza's face crumpled and she started to sob. Grace glanced nervously over her shoulder, then quickly took a handkerchief out of her pocket and stuffed it into the girl's hand.

'Here,' she said. 'You'd better not let Sister see you crying. She can't bear tears on the ward.'

Finally, when all the men were clean and comfortable, they were seen by the doctors who assessed their injuries and sent them up to the various wards.

Grace and Anna brought eight patients back to Monaghan ward with them, with another three to follow after
surgery. Once in bed, the men were offered a cup of tea
and a cigarette. Most were relaxed and smiling now, but
some still kept their backs to Grace, ignoring her as she put
their teacups down on their bedside locker. She knew they
wouldn't turn around until she had gone.

Later on, the orderlies started bringing back the men
after their operations. They were still groggy from the
anaesthetic, and each was assigned a nurse whose job it
was to sit with them until they regained consciousness.

Grace's patient was in a particularly bad way. He had taken
an artillery shell blast that had blown a huge hole in his torso.

Roger Wallace came up with him. He was the junior surgical registrar, and had assisted with the long and complex
operation.

'We've done our best with him, but I shouldn't think
he'll live,' he told Grace matter-of-factly. 'Frankly, I'm
amazed he's even made it this long. There aren't many men
who'd survive the journey back from France in that condition, let alone the operation.'

'Sergeant Samuel Trevelyan.' Grace read the name on his
notes. 'You never know, he might survive. He's obviously a
fighter.'

Roger shook his head. 'I doubt it. But sit with him anyway, just until—'

He stopped speaking abruptly, his gaze fixed beyond
Grace's shoulder. Turning round, she saw Dulcie standing
a few feet away from them.

'Hello, Roger,' she said.

Roger cleared his throat nervously. 'Nurse Moore.' His
voice came out as a high-pitched squeak.

Grace looked from one to the other, her heart sinking. It

34

was inevitable they would come face-to-face sooner or later. She willed Dulcie not to say anything that would land her in trouble with Sister.

For a moment no one spoke, and Grace could feel tension sizzling in the air. Then Dulcie said, 'Sister wondered if you'd come and look at one of the post-op patients, since you're here? She's worried his breathing is rather shallow.'

'Right. Yes, of course.' Roger hurried off, looking flustered.

'Doctor?' Dulcie called after him.

Roger stopped. 'Yes?'

'Don't you want to know which patient?'

'Oh. Yes, of course.' A deep blush crept up from beneath his collar. 'Um – where is he?'

'Bed three, Doctor.'

'Thank you.'

They watched him hurrying away, his head down. Then Dulcie giggled.

'Someone seems a bit flustered!'

'Can you blame him? Poor man.'

'Poor man, indeed!' Dulcie looked back over her shoulder, then whispered. 'Did you notice the way he looked at me?'

Grace had noticed, but she didn't want to say anything encouraging. 'He looked terrified,' she said. 'I daresay he thought you were going to slap his face.'

'No, it was more than that.' Dulcie looked thoughtful. 'He still likes me, I can tell.'

'But he's engaged!'

'I can't help that, can I?'

Grace eyed her warily. 'You're not going to – do anything, are you?' she said.

'I'm sure I don't know what you mean,' Dulcie said. But her face told a different story.

'Yes, you do. Oh, Moore, please tell me you're not going to try to get him back?'

'As I said, I can't help it if he likes me.' Dulcie shrugged carelessly.

'But he's engaged to Sylvia.'

'He was nearly engaged to me before she stole him from me. I'd only be taking back what's rightfully mine.' Dulcie sent her a pitying look. 'Oh, don't look so horrified, Duffield. You saw the way he looked at me. He's still in love with me, I'm sure of it. He just needs a little . . . nudge in the right direction, that's all.'

'Well, I don't want any part of it,' Grace said.

'I'm not asking you to help me. I can manage very well by myself, thank you very much,' Dulcie said pertly.

And with that she was gone. Grace turned to watch her as she strutted down the ward, her head held high, a new spring in her step. As Grace turned back, she caught the edge of an enamel kidney dish with her elbow and sent it clattering to the floor.

'Duffield! Is that you making a racket again?' Sister's voice rang out down the ward.

Chapter Six

'*Dear Mother, Please excuse the poor handwriting. My fingers are still a bit sore from where a calf stood on my hand this morning. I don't think there are any bones broken but I have a nasty bruise . . .*'

Anna grinned as she read aloud from her sister's letter. 'Trust Liesel!' she said. 'What on earth was she doing to have a calf stand on her hand, I wonder? I can't imagine it.'

It was a bitterly cold Saturday afternoon, and since Anna had the rare luxury of a day off, she was spending it with her mother. Saturday was half-day closing at the bakery, and Anna could hear Mrs Church bustling about in the shop, clearing the shelves and sweeping the floor before she locked up for the day.

Outside, the October weather had turned fiercely cold, but the crackling fire suffused the cosy sitting room with a welcoming warmth.

Anna went back to reading the letter. '*But at least the calf was friendly. Not like last week, when I was chased by an old sow who took a dislike to me as I was hauling a sack of potatoes up the field.*' Anna paused again, trying to picture it. Just the thought of her sister trying to out-run a pig was enough to make her giggle.

'*Of course, I ran away as fast as I could, but she kept up with me until I backed through a hedge. I managed to get away, but I tore my trousers on a piece of barbed wire. It was very embarrassing, having to walk all the way back down the lane with my bloomers on show . . .*'

Anna let the letter drop into her lap. She was laughing so much she could hardly read the words. Tears streamed down her face.

'Oh, Mother, did you ever hear anything so funny?'

Her mother looked up from her knitting and smiled. But there was something strained about her expression, as if she hadn't been listening at all.

Anna picked up Liesel's letter and read on. *'Anyway, I had the last laugh in the end. Yesterday I went to the market with the farmer and his wife, and they sold the animal for nine pounds ten shillings. I hope by the time you read this that horrible old sow has ended up in Mr Hudson's shop . . .'*

'At least she seems to be enjoying herself,' Dorothy commented absently.

'When she's not being trampled by cows and chased by pigs!' Anna shook her head. 'Honestly, I never thought I'd see the day Liesel went to work on a farm. She's never liked getting her hands dirty. But I suppose that's this wretched war for you. It's changed everything, hasn't it?'

Dorothy lowered her knitting and looked up. 'Anna—'

'What else does she say?' Anna scanned the letter again. 'She thanks you for the socks and the cake you sent her . . . oh, and she goes on about her latest day out with Davy.' Her mouth curled over the name. It seemed to crop up more and more in her sister's letters. 'She's seeing rather a lot of him, isn't she?'

'They're courting, I suppose. He seems like a decent enough young man.'

'If he's that decent, why hasn't he enlisted?'

'He's in a reserved occupation.'

Anna said nothing as she folded up her sister's letter and slipped it back into the envelope. She understood that there were certain jobs that required men to be spared from going to war, but it seemed unfair that Liesel's young man should be free to drive a train while Edward was away, risking his life for his country.

She looked across at her mother. Dorothy Beck was staring into the fire, a faraway look on her face. Seeing her expression gave Anna an uneasy feeling.

'Are you all right, Mother?' she asked.

She expected her mother to smile and say she was fine, just tired. But when Dorothy raised her eyes to hers, Anna saw an intent expression in them that gave her a surge of sudden panic.

'Anna,' her mother's voice was gentle, 'I need to talk to you.'

She jumped to her feet. 'I'll just close the curtains first. There's a draught blowing in from somewhere.'

'Anna—'

She went to the window. 'The weather's so cold now, isn't it?' She put her hand to the icy glass. 'I knew it. There's cold air blowing in here. The last raid must have shaken the pane loose. We'll need to get that fixed before the winter sets in . . .'

'Anna, please. Come and sit down.'

She stared out of the window at the street below. Next door, Mr Hudson was pulling down the shutters of his shop, stopping to exchange a few words with Mrs Church as she locked up. Mr Hudson said something, and she heard Mrs Church's shrill laughter. A horse pulling a coal cart clopped slowly down the middle of the street, the coal-man muffled so deep inside layers of scarves and coats that only his long nose could be seen poking out under the brim of his hat.

Anna stayed still, watching them, her hands curled around the thick chenille curtains. *If I just stand here*, she thought. *If I stand here and don't turn around, then Mother won't say anything, and nothing bad will happen.*

'Anna, there's something I need to tell you.'

She pulled the curtains, shutting out the ordinary world, then took a deep breath and turned to face her mother.

'What is it?' she asked.

Anna bent double in the armchair, her arms wrapped protectively around herself. She felt winded, as if someone had punched her in the pit of her stomach.

Her mother was still speaking, but Anna couldn't take in the words.

'I wanted to tell you . . . I know I should have said something sooner . . . I didn't want you to be upset,' she was saying softly. 'Anna, I'm so sorry.'

'But I don't understand. Isn't it bad enough that they've locked him up all these years, without sending him back to Germany?'

'It's the Government's decision.' In the dim glow of the firelight, Anna could see tears shimmering in her mother's eyes.

Anger flared inside her, pushing out the pain. 'But Papa hasn't set foot in Germany for thirty years! It's not his home anymore. He's lived in England longer than he ever lived there.'

'I know, my dear. But that's what the authorities have decided. They're repatriating the whole of your father's camp, so they can turn it into a military hospital.'

'But there must be something we can do about it? Surely there's someone we can write to? Our Member of Parliament, or the newspapers . . .'

'Don't you think I've tried?' Dorothy's mother's voice was short. 'I've written letters, begging everyone I can think of for help. But they all say there's nothing they can do. And as for the newspapers – do you really think they'd take up the case of a German?'

Anna thought about the newspapers that were delivered

to the men on the ward. How they gleefully described the atrocities the Germans had carried out on the brave British, and declared: 'The only Good Hun is a Dead Hun.'

'We have to face the fact, your father isn't welcome here anymore,' Dorothy said quietly.

Anna wanted to scream at the unfairness of it, but she could see her mother was already upset enough. Flying into a rage wouldn't help anyone.

Her gaze fell on the envelope lying on the hearth. 'Does Liesel know?'

Dorothy shook her head. 'Not yet. I wanted to go and see her, to tell her myself.'

'When is he leaving?'

'Next month.'

Anna looked up sharply. 'Before Christmas?'

'I think so.'

Anna looked around the sitting room. It no longer seemed cosy or welcoming. It suddenly felt too hot and stuffy to breathe. The walls appeared to be closing in on her, the heat from the fire scorching her face.

She couldn't cope with it. So much in her life had changed: her father going away, then Edward, then nearly losing their home, then Tom leaving, even Liesel . . . Anna wasn't sure how much more she could take. Every little change, every departure, seemed to take a piece of her with it, until she hardly knew who she was anymore.

'Papa must be heartbroken,' she whispered. 'He loved this place so much. He always said the East End was his real home.' Then another thought occurred to her, and she turned to her mother. 'Will you go with him?'

Dorothy looked away. 'Your father thinks I should stay here, with you and Liesel.'

Yes, Anna wanted to cry out. *Stay with us. Let me keep one fragment of my life, please.*

But then she saw her mother's forlorn expression and realised how selfish she was being.

'You want to go, don't you?'

'I don't want to leave you.' Her mother turned back to her, her eyes pleading for understanding. 'But my place is with your father . . .'

Anna nodded. 'You can't let him go by himself, it wouldn't be right.' She could only imagine how scared and alone he would feel, going back to his home country after all these years. He should not have to face that alone. 'Perhaps we could go with you?' she said.

Her mother shook her head. 'It wouldn't be allowed. Anyway, you and Liesel have your own lives here.'

'That doesn't matter!' Anna insisted. 'We're a family, we should be together.'

'But we might not stay together. Don't forget, you and your sister would be treated as foreigners in Germany, just like your father has been over here . . .'

'You mean, they might lock us up like they did Papa?' Anna said. 'How do you know they won't lock you up, too?'

Dorothy lifted her chin. 'That is a chance I'm willing to take, if it means being with your father.'

Anna looked across at her mother. She'd always known her parents loved each other, but hadn't realised how much until this moment.

'Oh, Mother,' she said. 'Of course you must go.'

They spent the rest of the afternoon talking and crying and hugging each other.

'We will see you and Papa again, won't we?' Anna sobbed.

'Of course. This war surely can't go on forever.' Her mother put her arms around Anna, drawing her close. The soft wool of her cardigan smelled of lavender soap. 'We'll all be together again one day, I'm sure of it.'

Anna nodded. 'You're right. This war will be over soon. And then you and Papa can come home, and take over this place . . .'

Her mother pulled away from her, holding her at arms' length. 'No, Anna,' she said gently. 'We will see each other again one day, I'm sure of it. But you must understand, your father will never run the bakery again.'

Anna stared at her, aghast. They had been talking about her father leaving for hours, turning it all this way and that. But until that moment it had never occurred to her that somehow, sometime, he wouldn't be here again, standing in his kitchen, testing the trays of loaves to see if they were baked, or working on one of his artful spun-sugar creations.

'But what will happen to this place?'

'I don't know . . . I suppose we'll have to sell it.'

Pain lanced her, like a knife deep in her heart. 'We can't! Not Papa's bakery. It's his life.'

'His family is his life. This is just bricks and mortar, Anna.'

She wrenched herself free from her mother's grasp, suddenly furious. 'How can you say that? It's more than that. It's what Papa worked all his life for. It was – is – his pride and joy.' She shook her head. 'We can't allow the bakery to close. I won't let it happen.'

Her mother looked helpless. 'I can't see another way . . .'

'Edward will run it,' Anna said. 'You know Papa always meant for him to take over the business one day? He can do it when he comes home.'

'That might – be a long time.' She could see her mother choosing her words carefully. But Anna still understood what she really meant. And she couldn't allow herself to think that way.

'He will come home,' she insisted quietly. *And so will Papa*, she added silently. One day she would have her loved ones all back together again, and everything would be just as it always was.

And until then, she had to keep everything going for them.

Chapter Seven

Grace never approached Sergeant Trevelyan's bed without expecting him to be dead.

It had been three weeks since he survived his operation, defying all the doctors' worst predictions. His recovery had been agonisingly slow since then, and every time Grace had to go to his bedside to feed him, or wash him, or administer his painkillers, she did it with dread, thinking that this would surely be the day she found his lifeless corpse lying there.

She was sure of it now, as she and Dulcie did the dressings round together. Grace had been keeping her eye on his bed while they attended to the other patients. He was lying on his back, perfectly still. It was hard for her to tell if he was breathing, but she was certain he hadn't moved in all the time she had been observing him.

When the time came, Grace found herself approaching Sergeant Trevelyan's bed on tiptoe, wincing at the trolley's squeaky wheel.

'What do you think you're doing?' Dulcie asked.

'Shhh!' Grace turned to her, finger to her lips. 'I think Sergeant Trevelyan might be – you know.'

'What?'

Grace mouthed the word silently. 'Dead.'

Dulcie frowned. 'Why are you whispering, if he's dead? He won't hear you.' She peered over Grace's shoulder. 'Come to think of it, he does look a bit blue,' she said.

'Do you think so?' As Grace edged closer to check, a

pair of cold green eyes snapped open. Grace jumped back with a yelp, colliding with the dressings trolley and sending a bowl of swabs clattering to the floor.

Dulcie laughed. 'Look, Duffield, you've woken the dead!'

Grace quickly gathered up the scattered swabs and put them in the bowl ready for burning. Then she turned back to Sergeant Trevelyan with a smile.

'Good morning, Sergeant,' she greeted him brightly. 'How are you today?'

'Still alive.'

He looked quite angry about it. But then, Sergeant Trevelyan was remarkably bitter for someone who had been snatched from the jaws of death. His square face was a mask, his mouth a permanently unsmiling line. When he spoke at all, his deep voice was clipped and gruff, as if he could hardly spare the words.

Most of the other men on the ward had lost their anger now, but not Sam Trevelyan. His guard was still up, his gaze cold and watchful under permanently frowning brows.

'Well, that's good news, isn't it?' Grace said. 'Now, let's take a look at you, shall we?'

As she removed the dressings to reveal the wound, she noticed Dulcie out of the corner of her eye, averting her gaze.

Grace couldn't blame her. Three weeks on, Sergeant Trevelyan's wound still wasn't a pretty sight. Even Grace had to brace herself as she carefully peeled away the bloodied gauze that packed the gaping crater in his side. Raw flesh glistened under the hospital lights.

How had he ever survived it? she wondered. Most men would have died on the battlefield.

As tenderly as she could, Grace removed the last of the gauze packing, and started to wash out the wound with saline.

'Now, you know this is going to sting,' she warned.

It was an understatement. Usually the men started screaming at this point, unable to stand the agony. But Sergeant Trevelyan endured it in absolute silence. Only his gritted teeth and the sweat standing out on his temples gave him away. Grace could see the powerful muscles bunched in his arms and shoulders, the sinews standing out under his skin as he braced himself against the pain.

'There, all finished.' Grace heard Sam Trevelyan's slow exhalation as she put away the saline and started to repack the wound. 'How does that feel?'

'How do you think?'

Grace looked up at his face. He had the flat, broken nose of a prize fighter, his firm jaw bristling with sandy-coloured stubble. He had obviously refused to allow the VAD to shave him again. His obstinacy annoyed Sister no end. She liked all the men under her care to be turned out smartly. But even she did not care to tussle with Sergeant Trevelyan.

'It's turned even colder, hasn't it?' Grace tried again to make conversation. 'They say it's going to be one of the worst winters we've ever had. Still, it's nice and cosy in here, isn't it? Although I reckon those poor VADs will have their work cut out for them, keeping the fires going . . .'

She chattered on, trying not to look into his face. *Talk to him*, Dr Carlyle had said. *Try to draw him out.*

She would have had more luck getting blood out of a stone.

She tried again. 'Trevelyan,' she said. 'That's a Cornish name, isn't it?' He didn't reply, but his green gaze sharpened. 'I thought so. I'm from Devon, you see. The West Country, just like you.'

He looked away, his blank mask back in place.

'My father has a dairy farm, just outside Tiverton,' Grace

ploughed on. 'There have been Duffields there for at least six generations, Pa says. He reckons our family might even go back to William the Conqueror . . .'

'Jesus Christ!' Sam Trevelyan's pained curse cut her off.

'I'm sorry,' Grace said. 'Did I hurt you?'

He flashed her a murderous look. 'I'm not interested in your family, or where you come from, or bloody William the Conqueror for that matter!' he hissed. 'Just concentrate on what you're doing, will you?'

Before Grace could reply, Dulcie joined in.

'Leave her alone, she's doing her best,' she said. 'Anyway, she's only trying to be nice.'

'I don't want her to be nice,' Sam Trevelyan snarled back. 'I just want her to do her job properly!'

'It was my fault,' Grace put in quickly. 'He's right, I wasn't thinking about what I was doing. I – I'm sorry.'

As she blundered to her feet, she crashed into the dressings trolley, sending another bowl of swabs flying and splashing Dulcie with saline.

'Careful, you clumsy oaf!' Dulcie gasped, mopping at her apron.

'Leave her alone, she's doing her best,' Sam Trevelyan parroted in a low voice.

Grace swung round to look at him. His face was impassive as ever, but she wondered if she had imagined the glint of amusement in his green eyes.

Chapter Eight

'I don't know why you bother trying to be nice to him,' Dulcie said later, after she had changed her apron and they were continuing with the dressings round. 'He's so rude.'

'Dr Carlyle says I should try to talk to him,' Grace replied. 'She's worried about how withdrawn he is.'

'Oh, Dr Carlyle!' Dulcie said scornfully. 'I suppose she's decided he's to be another of her pet shell shock cases?'

'Don't say it like that. Dr Carlyle says neurasthenia is a real medical condition.'

'Neurasthenia now, is it? I suppose Dr Carlyle taught you that word, too? Giving it a fancy name doesn't make it real, you know.'

'There are psychiatric hospitals where they offer specialist treatment—'

'I wonder Dr Carlyle doesn't go and work there, then.'

'Dr Carlyle is a physician, not a psychiatrist,' Grace reminded her.

'Why should that stop her? Since she's so wonderful, I would have thought she could do anything.'

Dulcie's voice was bitter with jealousy, and Grace knew why. Years ago, while they were students, Dulcie and Kate Carlyle had fallen out over a man. Dulcie had ended up humiliated and she had never forgiven Dr Carlyle for it.

It was such a pity, Grace thought. As far as she was concerned, Kate Carlyle was an inspiration. As the first female medical student at the Nightingale, she had fearlessly taken on the men and beaten them at their own game. She had overcome all kinds of obstacles and prejudices to qualify as a doctor, and also to work on the male wards, somewhere female doctors were generally not allowed.

She had blazed a trail for other women. Ten more girls had since studied at the Nightingale, but so far as Grace was concerned, Kate Carlyle was the bravest of them all.

'Did Sergeant Trevelyan's wound look all right to you?' Dulcie changed the subject.

Grace frowned. 'Yes, why?'

'I don't know . . . I just thought it looked a bit – inflamed.'

Grace was surprised Dulcie could tell, from the wary distance she had kept. 'Do you think so?'

Dulcie nodded. 'Perhaps we should get the doctor to look at it.'

'I'll mention it to Dr Carlyle when she does her rounds later.'

'Dr Wallace is the surgical registrar. Surely he should be the one to look at it?'

Grace glared at her friend. Dulcie's innocent tone did not fool her for a minute.

'If you think I'm going to summon Dr Wallace just so you can flirt with him again, you've got another think coming!' she said.

'I'm sure I don't know what you mean.'

'Don't you?'

For the past three weeks, Grace had watched Dulcie shamelessly throwing herself at Roger Wallace. Fortunately he seemed more bemused by the situation than anything else, but poor Sylvia Saunders was taking it rather badly.

'I was just concerned about a patient, that's all,' Dulcie said. 'But if you don't think it's worth mentioning to a doctor . . .'

'I'll talk to Dr Carlyle,' Grace said firmly.

Dulcie was still sulking as they approached their final patients.

The two young men had arrived in the same ambulance just before Grace went off duty the previous night; a head wound who was able to walk on crutches, the other man on a stretcher.

The stretcher case still looked pale and terrified, but his friend with the head wound had cheered up immensely. He sat up in bed, a broad grin on his face as they approached.

'Here, Gordon lad, look what we've got here,' he called out to his friend in a broad cockney accent. 'Two lovely ladies. One for each of us, eh? You can have the tall one, though. No offence, miss,' he said to Grace. 'But I'm a bit on the short side myself, and I can't have my girlfriend towering over me, can I?'

'I quite understand, Corporal –' Grace consulted his notes '– Sallis.'

'Albert, please. But you can call me Albie, love.' The young man winked at Dulcie.

'And you can call me Nurse!' she snapped back.

'Ooh, get her! Your pal's not very friendly, is she?' Albie Sallis pulled a face. He was a stocky boy, nineteen years old according to his notes, with a freckled face and a squashed pug nose. The close-cropped hair around his bandaged wound was coppery red. 'Don't suppose you'll give me a kiss, either?'

'Certainly not!' Dulcie looked so indignant, Grace almost laughed.

She knew very well that Dulcie didn't mind giving a soldier the odd peck on the cheek if she liked the look of him. Poor Albie had obviously got on the wrong side of her.

'I think she prefers you, lad.' Albie looked at the young man in the next bed. 'Gordon's more the strong, silent type,' he said. 'Ain't that right?'

Private Gordon gave them a wavering smile.

'See what I mean?' Albie said. 'Lucky he's got me to do all his talking for him, eh?'

'You seem like good friends,' Grace said.

'Would you believe, we only met on the ambulance train coming over from France? But we're best pals now, ain't we, Gordon? Albie leaned closer to the nurses. 'I've taken him under my wing, so to speak,' he whispered to Grace. 'Poor blighter's lost the use of his legs. Reckons his back's broken.' Albie shook his head. 'Terrible business. And him only twenty, too.'

'And what about you, Corporal Sallis?' Grace said. 'It says here you have a shrapnel wound.'

'I'll say I have, Nurse. A right corker, it is.'

'Let's have a look at it, shall we?'

Grace wasn't sure what to expect as she unwound the dressing around Albie's head. But the wound was surprisingly small and clean.

'Hardly a mark there, eh?' he said proudly. 'I would scarcely have believed it myself, but the doctor showed me the X-ray last night, and there's still a bloody great lump of shrapnel in there. If you'll pardon my French,' he added quickly.

'Can they get it out?' Grace asked.

'Don't reckon they can, Nurse. Not without killing me, at any rate.' Albie sounded remarkably cheerful at the prospect. 'No, all they can do is leave it there and hope it don't decide to shift one way or the other. If it does . . .' He shrugged. 'And to think, if that shrapnel had gone in an inch to the left or the right – well, I wouldn't be here now. I'm a walking miracle, that's what I am!'

'I should think you are, Corporal Sallis,' Grace agreed, as she set about cleaning his wound.

Grace and Dulcie finished the dressings round just as Dr Carlyle arrived on the ward.

Dulcie saw her first. 'Now we'll be for it,' she muttered. 'You know Sister likes to have everything done before the doctor arrives. We should have finished doing the dressings ages ago. That's your fault for stopping to chat all the time – oh, Lord, she's coming this way!'

They both stood to attention, adjusting their caps and smoothing their aprons like soldiers on parade as Dr Carlyle approached, carrying a large buff envelope tucked under her arm. Grace noticed how her gaze slid past Dulcie as she greeted them with a nod.

'And who's this?' Albie immediately turned on his boyish charm. 'Another pretty nurse? Reckon we're spoiled, Gordon lad.'

'Good morning, Corporal Sallis. My name is Dr Carlyle.' She turned to the young man in the next bed. 'And you must be Private Gordon?'

'Dr Carlyle?' The look of astonishment on Albie's face made Grace smile. But Kate Carlyle seemed coolly unaware of it as she picked up Gordon's notes and started to write on them.

She finished finally and put them aside. 'I would like to test your reflexes, Private Gordon, if I may?'

Grace and Dulcie glanced at each other, then slowly they began to back away, inching the trolley between them. But as they turned to go, Dr Carlyle said, 'Please stay, Nurse Duffield. I may need your help. You may go,' she dismissed Dulcie curtly.

Grace couldn't look at Dulcie as she left. But the rattle and squeak of the dressings trolley as it was shoved down the ward told her how angry the other nurse was.

Grace pulled back the covers on Gordon's bed and

carefully adjusted the folds of his voluminous hospital gown to expose his white, bony knees, covered with a smattering of coarse dark hairs. His calf muscles were already starting to wither, she noticed.

She stood back as Dr Carlyle tested the young man's reflexes. As Grace had expected, there was no response. Dr Carlyle tested them again, striking his knees harder this time with her tiny metal hammer, until even Grace winced. But still Private Gordon did not twitch.

Grace watched Dr Carlyle's face. Her expression was impassive but there was concern in her dark eyes.

She put her hammer away. 'Can you stand up for me?' she asked.

Private Gordon glared at her. 'C–c–can't.' Spittle flew from his slack lips as he struggled over the word.

'If you could just try.' She turned to Grace. 'Help him, Nurse, if you please.'

Grace froze, not knowing what to do. Gordon's face was working, his eyes filling with tears, mouth moving, trying to frame words that would not emerge. She went to move his legs, but he pushed her away, his hands flailing.

'C–c–ca—'

'For pity's sake, can't you leave him alone?' Albie shouted. 'How do you expect the poor sod to walk in his condition?'

The ward fell silent, his words hanging in the air. Dr Carlyle said nothing as she added a few more lines to the private's notes.

'That's enough for now,' she said finally. 'Get him back into bed, Nurse.'

She walked off without another word.

'Well, I can't say I thought much of her!' Albie said.

'She isn't always like that, I promise you.' Grace re-arranged Gordon's hospital gown around his knees. His legs were heavy and lifeless as a puppet's as she moved

54

them back under the bedclothes and tucked him in carefully. 'She's a very good doctor.'

'I don't know about that!' Albie did not look convinced. 'If that's lady doctors for you, give me a man any day. What do you say, pal?' he called over to the next bed. But Gordon did not reply. He lay still, a hunched, curled shape under the bedclothes.

'Reckon she's upset him good and proper,' Albie muttered. 'We won't get a word out of him for the rest of the day, I'll bet.'

'I'll bring you both a cup of tea later, if I can,' Grace promised. As she turned to go, she spotted the buff envelope Dr Carlyle had been carrying. It was lying on top of Gordon's bedside locker. 'Oh, dear, the doctor has left the X-rays behind. I'll take them back to her . . .'

She went to pick up the envelope, but it slipped from her fingers and a couple of sheets of celluloid slid out on to the floor. As Grace hurried to gather them up, she couldn't help taking a quick peek. X-rays always fascinated her, especially the ones of the wounded men. Seeing those tell-tale black shapes standing out against the white bones . . .

She frowned, looking closer. Then she shuffled the sheets and looked at the next one, and the next. They all told the same story.

'What's up, Nurse?'

Albie's voice behind her made her start guiltily. 'Nothing, Corporal Sallis.' She quickly shoved the celluloid sheets back into the envelope.

'There ain't nothing badly wrong with him, is there?'

Grace shot a panicked glance at Gordon, but Albie said, 'Don't worry, he can't hear us if he's on that side. The bombs have sent him deaf in one ear.' He looked at her considering. 'I'm right, aren't I? His back's not broken.'

Grace opened her mouth to deny it, but the words wouldn't

come. 'I can't see any damage on the X-ray,' she admitted slowly. 'But I'm no expert,' she added. 'There might be something I've missed, or there could be another reason why he can't walk.'

'Oh, there's another reason, all right.' Albie nodded wisely. 'I've seen lads like him before: can't speak a word, tottering around the trenches like newborn lambs. Yet the doctors can't find anything wrong with 'em. Because it's all up here.' He tapped his temple.

'It's not in his imagination!' Grace started to defend him, but Albie shook his head.

'Oh, no, Nurse, you don't have to convince me of that. I'm not one of them ignorant so-and-sos as reckon they're putting it on, believe me.' He looked back at Gordon who was snoring softly now, his breath rising and falling steadily. 'No, as far as I'm concerned, his injuries are as real as mine. And I'll batter anyone that says different!'

'I hope it won't come to that, Corporal. Sister wouldn't approve of fisticuffs on her ward.' Grace smiled at him. 'But Private Gordon is lucky to have a friend like you.'

'Aye, he is.' Albie grinned. 'I reckon there was a reason we ended up on that ambulance train together. I'll look after him, Nurse. Don't you worry about that.'

Chapter Nine

Dulcie had barely got the men on to the terrace when the air raid started.

It was a crisp October day, and Sister had decreed that the men's beds should be wheeled outside to make the most of the sunshine, even though it was bitterly cold.

'Have a heart, Nurse. It's blooming freezing!' a burly sergeant complained, pulling his blankets up to his chin.

'Don't blame me, it's Sister's idea. She thinks you'll benefit from the sun.'

'We'll get bloody frostbite and lose our toes. No offence, lad,' he added to the young man in the next bed, who had had one of his feet amputated through trench foot.

No sooner had Dulcie, Anna and Sylvia wheeled the last bed out and lined it up on the terrace as Sister had instructed than the air-raid klaxon started up.

Private Gordon started like a frightened rabbit, looking around him with wide, terrified eyes.

'It's only an air raid, pal. They won't be coming for us, don't worry.' Albie Sallis leaned over and patted his friend's hand. 'And on a Sunday morning, too,' he tutted. 'I ask you, is nothing sacred to those bloody Germans?'

Sylvia looked around nervously. 'Perhaps we should bring the men back in?'

'But we've only just got them out!' Dulcie sighed. 'Anyway, it's probably just a false alarm.'

'I don't think so – look!' Anna pointed towards the sky,

where a scattering of dark dots were approaching over the distant horizon.

The men craned their necks to see. One of the soldiers, a pale young Lance Corporal called Frost, began to hum under his breath as he always did when he was nervous.

' "*It's a long way to Tipperary, it's a long way to go. It's a long, long way to Tipperary . . .*" '

'He's off again!' Dulcie sighed to Anna. 'He'll be singing that wretched song for hours now.'

'They're coming this way, I think. This should be rather good.' George Jeffers, a young captain in the Royal Fusiliers, lit up a cigarette and leaned back to enjoy the show.

'Take no notice of him, Nurse,' Albie said. 'They're miles away. There's no need to be afraid.' But even as he said it, he was shaking so much his iron bed frame rattled.

'Oh, don't worry about me.' Dulcie turned round to tell him she was not in the least bit afraid, that in fact she found the distant sound of the aeroplanes quite exhilarating, when she saw Roger Wallace in the doorway.

Immediately she dissolved into a fit of nervous trembling. 'Oh!' she squealed. 'Oh, I can't bear it. Make it stop, please!'

'What's going on?' Roger said.

'Nurse Moore seems to be having hysterics,' Anna said in a flat voice. 'They came on suddenly.'

'Very suddenly,' Sylvia said.

'I can't help it if I'm terrified, can I?' Dulcie launched herself at Roger, burying her face in his chest. 'It's the planes, I can't stand the sound of them,' she whimpered. 'What if they bomb us?'

'Perhaps we should slap her face?' Sylvia suggested.

'Really, Nurse Moore. You must try and collect yourself. Remember the men . . .' Roger gave her a half-hearted pat on the shoulder. He was holding himself far too rigid for

Dulcie's liking. She threw her arms around his neck and burrowed her face deeper into his white coat, breathing in the antiseptic smell of him. She pressed her face against his chest, hoping to hear his heart skittering at the nearness of her, but all she could feel was a disappointingly steady thud against her cheek. Meanwhile, all around them, the patients cat-called and whistled.

'Come on, let's get you inside.' To Dulcie's annoyance, Anna stepped in briskly, pulling her away from Roger. 'I'll make you a cup of hot sweet tea. That'll sort you out.'

'Good idea.' Roger stepped aside smartly.

Once back inside the ward, Anna closed the French doors and hissed, 'It won't work, you know.'

'I beg your pardon?'

'This silly game you're playing, trying to win Roger Wallace back. We can all see it, we know what's going on.'

'I'm sure I have no idea what you're talking about,' Dulcie said.

'Suit yourself. As long as you know, we're all watching you. And we won't let you ruin things for Sylvia.'

She turned on her heel and started to walk away. 'What about my hot sweet tea?' Dulcie called after her.

'Make it yourself, I'm not your servant!' Anna threw over her shoulder.

As Dulcie watched her go, a deep voice suddenly said, 'She's right, you know.'

She swung round. Sam Trevelyan was the only patient within earshot. But he had his eyes closed. And besides, he never spoke to anyone.

Grace was always trying to draw him out, to coax him into conversation. But Dulcie never bothered. It suited her to treat him in silence. When he did speak, he was always so angry and bitter, she could not be doing with it.

'Did you say something?' she asked.

59

'I said, she's right.' Still his eyes didn't open. 'You're never going to get him back. You're just making a fool of yourself.'

Dulcie gasped. 'How dare you!' And then, because she couldn't help herself, she added, 'What makes you say that?'

But it seemed Sam Trevelyan had done all the speaking he was going to do for that day. Dulcie stared at him for a moment, then she said, 'I don't care about your opinion, anyway. You know nothing about it.'

She flounced off to the kitchen, where Grace was making Miss Sutton's afternoon tea.

'What a ghastly, infuriating man!' she fumed.

'Which one?'

'Sergeant Trevelyan.' She spat out the name like poison.

Grace smiled over her shoulder. 'Oh, dear, what's he done now?'

Dulcie opened her mouth to tell her, then decided against it. 'Nothing. I just don't care for him, that's all.'

'He can be very difficult,' Grace agreed. 'But I'm sure he's all right when you get to know him.'

'I'm not sure I'd ever want to.'

Grace finished pouring the tea into a bone china cup, then arranged it carefully on a tray with a plate of biscuits. 'Have you heard the news?' she said.

'What news?'

As Grace turned around with the tray, Dulcie snatched the teacup off it and took a quick sip.

'Moore!' Grace stared at her in horror. 'Sister will go mad.'

'She'll have to catch me first, won't she?' Dulcie swiped a biscuit off the plate. 'Go on. What news?'

'Dr Carlyle is setting up a new ward, just for shell shock patients.' Grace nervously eyed the fragile cup in Dulcie's hands.

'You call that news? I was expecting some exciting gossip.'

'It is exciting,' Grace insisted. 'Dr Carlyle will be in charge, and they're going to get a psychiatrist in to help, too.'

'Dr Carlyle and a whole ward of shell shock patients? Sounds like my idea of hell.' Dulcie took a bite of her biscuit. 'The mentally disturbed patients give me the shivers, all those wobbly limbs and glassy eyes.'

'They can't help it. They're ill.'

Dulcie brushed crumbs off the bib of her apron. 'I suppose you're going to volunteer to join this new ward?'

Grace turned away, blushing. 'Oh, no. I don't suppose Dr Carlyle would want me. I'm far too hopeless.'

Before Dulcie could reply, the door to the kitchen swung open. Thinking it was Sister, Dulcie thrust the teacup back at Grace, who promptly dropped it. It hit the tiled floor and shattered.

'Oh, no!' Grace stared down at the tiny fragments. 'What am I going to do? That was Sister's favourite cup. There'll be murders over this. Quickly, help me clear it up . . .'

But Dulcie didn't move. She was too transfixed by the vision standing in the kitchen doorway.

He was simply the most beautiful man she had ever seen in her life. Tall, dark-haired and immaculately dressed, even his horn-rimmed spectacles only seemed to emphasise his high cheekbones, perfect features and deep blue eyes.

'Excuse me,' he said, in a voice like melted chocolate. 'I'm looking for Miss Sutton?'

Grace spoke up. 'She'll be in her sitting room, waiting for her afternoon tea.' Dulcie felt the weight of her accusing gaze, but she didn't care. All she could do was stare in silence at the man before her, taking in every perfect inch of him. 'I'll show you—'

'No, I'll show you.' Dulcie found her voice at last. 'You'd best clear up this mess,' she said to Grace.

She led the way down the passageway and back to the

ward. 'Sister's sitting room is on the other end of the ward, near the private rooms,' she said.

'Thanks. This place is like a rabbit warren, isn't it? It's taken me half an hour to find the right ward.'

He walked with a slight limp, Dulcie noticed.

'I take it you're not a patient?' she said.

'Good Lord, no. Although I suppose you could be forgiven for thinking that.' He patted his leg. 'My name is Robert Logan, and I'm the new doctor here.'

'Oh!' Dulcie's heart skipped with delight. 'That is good news. I mean – we're a bit short of doctors at the moment. Ours keep enlisting.'

'I've done my bit. I was invalided out six months ago. They decided I was more of a hindrance than a help with my gammy leg, so they sent me back to Civvy Street.'

As they headed down the ward, Dulcie was aware of Roger Wallace watching them. But she barely spared him a glance.

'Well, here we are.' She stopped at the door to Sister's sitting room. 'I'll leave you here. Sister will go mad if I'm not polishing or scrubbing something.'

'Thank you, Nurse—?'

'Moore. Dulcie Moore.' She could feel the heat rising in her face. She never blushed.

He smiled. He had a beautifully shaped mouth, she thought. 'I daresay we'll be seeing each other again, Nurse Moore.'

Oh, we will. I'll make sure of that, Dulcie thought as she walked away.

She hurried back to the kitchen, where Grace was on her hands and knees, sweeping up the last fragments of bone china.

'Sister is going to be furious,' she said gloomily. 'And I'll get the blame as usual.'

'Never mind that! What did you think of him?'

'Who?'

'Him! The new doctor! Oh, Duffield, he was here not a minute ago. Surely you couldn't forget *him*?'

'I don't know, I only caught a fleeting glimpse of him.' Grace clambered to her feet. 'He's a doctor, you say?'

'Dr Robert Logan.' Dulcie said the name slowly, savouring it.

'He seemed nice enough, I suppose.'

'Nice? He was the most perfect man I've ever seen in my life!'

Grace laughed. 'How do you know that? You know nothing about him.'

'I know he's a war hero, and he's very handsome. I also know he's a doctor, so he's bound to be rich.'

'Not necessarily! The medical students are always trying to borrow money from us, in case you hadn't noticed?'

'Yes, but once they qualify and become consultants, they have lots of money.' Dulcie pressed her hands together. Her palms had gone very clammy, she noticed. 'Do you know? I think I might be in love.'

Grace laughed. 'What about Roger Wallace?'

'What about him?' Roger had already faded into the back of her mind, with his weak chin and his flat-footed walk. Sylvia was welcome to him, she decided.

She had already found the new object of her affections. And this time nothing was going to stop her from getting her man.

Chapter Ten

On a cold afternoon in late October, Anna and Liesel travelled to the internment camp in Holloway to see their father one last time. Liesel's boyfriend Davy went with them.

The sisters had been visiting the camp every month for the past three years, but Anna didn't think she would ever get used to the grim surroundings: the featureless slabs of grey single-storey accommodation blocks surrounded by guard posts, high walls and savage barbed wire.

'At least Papa will be free from this place soon,' she said quietly.

'He should be coming home,' Liesel said. 'He's done nothing wrong, and they're sending him away. It's not fair.'

She started to cry again. Anna took out her handkerchief and stuffed it into her sister's hand.

'Do stop it,' she snapped. 'Papa will feel wretched enough without you making it worse.'

'Leave her be.' Davy put his arms protectively around Liesel. 'She can't help it if she's sensitive. She's upset.'

'We're all upset,' Anna snapped. 'But that won't help our father, will it?'

Davy ignored her, burying his face in Liesel's fair hair. 'There, there,' he soothed her. 'Don't upset yourself. I know it's hard for you, but we'll get through this, I promise. You've got me. I'll look after you.'

Anna watched her sister nestling in his arms, fighting down a feeling of annoyance. She didn't know why Liesel had insisted on bringing Davy with her, he wasn't even family. This should have been a day for just the two of them, and Papa.

But Liesel never seemed to go anywhere without him these days. His stocky, swaggering figure was always at her side, giving his opinion, sticking his nose in where it wasn't wanted.

And he'd made her late. The train he'd been driving to get here had ended up stuck in a siding, and instead of going on without him, Liesel had insisted on waiting. So Anna had been kept waiting too, a precious half an hour that she could have been spending with Papa.

They reached the gates and waited in line with the other families for the guard to search their belongings and issue them with a ticket to go inside.

'Are you family?' he asked Davy.

'No,' Anna said.

'Yes,' Liesel replied at the same moment. 'Nearly,' she added, shooting a sideways look at Anna. 'We're practically engaged.'

'Practically engaged ain't good enough. He'll have to wait outside,' the guard said.

'But I want him with me!' Liesel protested, her pretty face screwing up as it always did when she was on the verge of a tantrum. She would be stamping her foot any minute, Anna thought.

'For heaven's sake, let's go in,' she sighed.

'But I want—'

'Don't make a fuss, Liesel! We're late enough as it is. Do you want to waste even more time?'

She half dragged her sister through the gates, ignoring the longing looks she sent back over her shoulder at Davy.

'Practically engaged, indeed!' Anna snorted.

'Well, we are!'

'You're barely twenty!'

'I'm exactly the same age Mother was when she married Papa, so there.'

Anna thought her heart would break when she saw her father standing waiting for them. Friedrich Beck was smiling as usual, but she could sense the deep sadness in him.

'Look at you both. What beautiful young ladies you are!' he greeted them in his usual way, kissing them on both cheeks and holding them at arms' length to look at them.

'I'm not beautiful, Papa. Look at my hands. They're so rough and red, like an old woman's.' Liesel held them out for him to inspect.

'Nonsense, the outdoor life suits you. You have quite a bloom in your cheeks.' He stroked Liesel's face, then turned to Anna, his features softening. 'And you, *Liebling* . . . Your mother has told me how you have been helping her in the bakery as well as doing your own work. It is very kind of you.'

'I did it for you, Papa.'

'My sweet girl . . .' Friedrich turned away, but not before Anna saw the tears glistening in his dark eyes.

They spent the next hour or so as they usually did, walking in the grounds, then drinking tea in the recreation room. They played cards, and chatted, talking about anything but what was to come. They all talked too fast and laughed too loud to try to keep it at bay. But it was there all the same, casting its dark, heavy shadow over all of them.

And all the time, Anna's gaze kept straying to the clock on the wall, its ponderous ticking measuring away the precious time she had left with her father.

Finally, Friedrich said, 'I'm sorry, my girls, but we must talk about the practicalities of what is to come.'

He sat very still, his thin hands resting on his knees. The skin on the back of them was wrinkled and spotted with age. He was barely fifty but his shoulders were stooped like an old man's, Anna noticed.

'Now,' he said. 'I want you to know that you will be well looked after, even though I cannot be here myself to take care of you. I have written to a solicitor and made arrangements for you both.'

'Papa, please. Don't,' Anna begged, but her father held up his hand.

'No, *Liebling*, this is something I must say. I need you both to listen.' He looked from one to the other. 'Liesel, I have arranged for you to have some money. It is not a fortune – as you know, I am not a rich man – but it will be enough to make sure you are reasonably comfortable until you get married.'

For once Liesel didn't seem to be able to speak. She could only nod, her head bowed.

Friedrich turned to Anna. 'And you, my dear,' he reached for her hands, 'I am giving you my bakery.'

'Papa!'

'I would have divided everything between you both equally, but I know Anna has always been more interested in the business than you are, Liesel.' He looked anxiously at them both. 'What do you say? Do you agree it is fair for your sister to take over the bakery?'

Anna held her breath as she waited for her sister to speak.

'Yes, Papa,' Liesel replied.

'But I don't want you to think you have to keep the business going,' he said to Anna. 'You may sell it if you wish, use the money to make a life for yourself. But as you know, I have always said I would pass it on to you and Edward, so – I wish to keep my promise.'

'Thank you, Papa.'

The words didn't seem enough to express the emotions

welling up inside her. This was all so enormous, she could barely take it in.

She was still in a daze when they came to say goodbye. After warning Liesel not to make a fuss, when Anna fell into her father's arms for a final hug she could not stop the tears flooding out of her.

'There, my *Liebling*. Don't cry. This is the start of a new adventure for us all.' Friedrich held her face between his hands and stroked away her tears with his thumbs. He stared at her, his dark eyes holding hers, as if trying to imprint the memory of her in his mind forever. 'Take care of yourself, and your little sister for me,' he whispered. 'I'm sorry I can't be there to dry your tears forever, my precious girl . . .'

'You'll come home one day, Papa.'

'Oh, Anna.' He pulled her into his arms for a final embrace, pressing her to his heart.

Davy was waiting for them by the gates. Anna felt a jolt of jealousy as she saw Liesel run to his waiting arms. She desperately wished Edward could be there to hold her and tell her everything would be all right. She suddenly felt very alone.

As they trudged back to the station, they discussed what her father had said to them. Of course, Davy had an opinion about it.

'I think it's very sensible, under the circumstances,' he said loftily. 'And very fair, too. I'm sure Anna will get a good price for the bakery.'

'I'm not selling it,' she said.

She kept walking, facing straight ahead, aware that they had both stopped in their tracks.

'But why?' Liesel wanted to know.

'Because it's what Papa would want.'

'No, it isn't. You heard what he said, he doesn't mind if you—'

'I heard what he said.' But she had also seen the look of yearning in his eyes. There was only one reason why he had left her the bakery: because he knew it would be in safe hands.

'And how do you propose to run it?' Davy said.

Anna fought the urge to tell him to mind his own business.

'I'll take on some help,' she said. 'Mrs Church's nephew used to work at a bakery in Hackney before he got called up. Now he's been discharged he's looking for a job. I'm sure he can run the place until Edward comes home.'

'Hmm.' Davy pulled a face. 'I wonder if I should meet this young man before you take him on?'

'Why?' Anna looked at him. 'What do you know about baking?'

Davy's face flushed. 'Well, nothing, but—'

'So mind your own business, and I'll mind mine.'

'I was only trying to help,' he protested, but Liesel shook her head.

'Leave her be,' she warned. 'My sister can be very stubborn when she wants to be.'

As Anna marched on ahead, she heard Davy mutter, 'We can only hope this Edward comes home, then.'

Oh, he will, Anna thought. And then everything would be all right again.

Chapter Eleven

It was early November when the nightmares started again.

It was the first time it had happened since he came home. In France, before the artillery shell hit him, he had woken up screaming nearly every night. But since returning to England – nothing.

Perhaps it was the physical shock of his injuries that did it, but Sam Trevelyan had finally dared to believe that the nightmares were over for good. Until the night he woke up, bathed in a pool of his own sweat, gasping and crying and fending off unseen horrors with flailing hands.

Now, in the pale light of the morning, Sam felt queasy and ashamed. He could see the ward sister with her nurses gathered around her, and he knew immediately she was talking about him, passing on the night sister's report, telling them to keep an eye on him, as if he were a helpless child.

Anger surged inside him, scorching through his veins. God, how he wanted to get away from here, never to have another nurse around him, to see the pity in their eyes and hear the cloying sympathy in their voices. He wanted to stand on his own two feet again, not suffer the humiliation of having to beg for a bottle to pee in, of having a young girl washing him like an overgrown baby.

Most of all, he wanted to go home.

He turned his gaze to the window, its panes rimmed with frost. His father would be bringing the cows down from the fields by now, if he hadn't already done it. If Sam closed his eyes, he could almost see John Trevelyan, a battered old hat perched on his grizzled head, pushing through the heavy cattle, herding them into the byres. He had turned sixty but no one would ever think it to see him, strong and wiry as he was, his skin baked brown from years of working outside. He toiled every bit as hard as the young farmhands, and could even give Sam a run for his money when they worked side by side . . .

He flinched, turning away from the window, shutting out the memory. He could never allow himself to go back there, not even in his mind.

Not after what had happened.

At the far end of the ward the nurses started to disperse, ready to start their various daily tasks. Soon they would be busying themselves, sweeping and dusting and polishing every surface in sight, pushing their clanking trolleys up and down the ward, laden with dressings and medicines. They would bustle about with fresh sheets, haul him and the others out of their beds, set about them with soap and flannels, comb their hair and lift them on to bedpans. No humiliation would be spared.

It was the curly-haired girl's turn to do the washing round today. Sam didn't know whether to be relieved or not. At least she didn't bother to try and talk to him like the tall one did. She barely spared any of the men a second look most of the time, let alone a kind word.

She seemed so completely indifferent, Sam couldn't help admiring her for it.

The only person who roused her interest was the new doctor, Logan. Sam noticed how she looked out for him every morning. How disappointed she was when he wasn't there! And if he was, she would follow him like a puppy, inventing excuses to talk to him. Watching her was the only amusement Sam ever got on the ward.

71

But at least it meant she left the other one, Dr Wallace, alone. The poor sap still looked quite bewildered about it, although his fiancée was clearly relieved . . .

He checked himself angrily. What was he thinking, letting himself get carried away by the petty dramas going on around him? It was none of his damn business.

But he had to have something to occupy his mind while he was trapped in here. Either that or go slowly mad.

Finally, it was his turn. Nurse Moore appeared with her trolley at the foot of his bed.

'Good morning,' she greeted him in her usual offhand way. 'How are you today?'

Sam didn't reply. She wasn't listening anyway as she briskly pulled the curtains around his bed.

Sam eyed the bowl of water on the trolley, the soap, flannel, combs and razor lined up neatly beside it.

'I'll wash myself, if you don't mind,' he said.

She did not object like so many of the other nurses did. The earnest-looking VADs always looked positively offended, as if he had questioned the very purpose of their existence.

But not Nurse Moore. She simply lifted her shoulders in a little shrug and said, 'If you want. But I'll have to help you off with your gown.'

He had no choice but to allow her to help him; the wound made it nearly impossible for him to lift his arms. He was conscious of his once-powerful limbs, now so heavy and useless, as she eased off his sleeves, pulling the gown down around his waist.

He saw her avert her eyes from his wound, the way she always did. He didn't blame her; he hated looking at it himself.

She arranged the soap, water and flannel within his reach, then stood back as he started to wash.

He was conscious of her watching him, and hated himself

72

for his stiff, clumsy movements. He tried to shave himself, dipping his chin and turning his head awkwardly this way and that to reach. But he grew impatient with his slow efforts, tried to rush and nicked his jaw. Nurse Moore did not fuss over him, but silently handed him a cotton swab to wipe away the blood.

'You've missed a bit,' was all she said. 'Up there, near your left ear.'

'Thanks.'

He was rinsing away the last of the soap when she suddenly said, 'I heard you had a nightmare last night?'

The question surprised him. But then he remembered Sister's huddled pow-wow with the night nurse around her desk that morning. Of course, she would have told her every detail.

'What's it to you?' he growled.

Another nurse might have blushed, but Nurse Moore didn't have that delicacy.

'Nothing.' She shrugged. 'But Sister told me to ask you about it.'

He didn't reply, groping blindly for the towel. Nurse Moore handed it to him.

'So what was it about?' she asked.

'I dreamed I was stuck here forever and you were the only nurse.'

'That would be a nightmare for both of us, wouldn't it?'

Sam buried his face in the towel so she wouldn't see him smile.

Later, as she was helping him back into his gown, she asked, 'Did it hurt?'

'What?'

'When the artillery shell hit you. Did it hurt?'

He looked down at the bloodstained dressing that bound his left side from his chest to his hip. Half his ribcage

73

had been shattered, blown away by the blast, along with the lateral muscles, his spleen, and part of his stomach.

What do you think? he wanted to say. But what came out was, 'If you want to know the truth, I have no recollection of anything until I woke up here, after the operation.'

Nurse Moore nodded, taking it in. 'So that wasn't what your nightmare was about?'

A picture filled Sam's mind. Looking down the barrel of his gun, that face in his sights, white with fear. His finger curling, squeezing the trigger, then the recoil of his rifle butt against his shoulder, and the sound – sometimes a volley, sometimes a single shot – and the thud of a body, dropping like a stone . . .

'No,' he said.

'What, then?'

He stared at her. She was tidying away the washing things, piling them up on the trolley, her head down. Not listening.

He changed the subject deliberately. 'I haven't seen much of Dr Logan on the ward recently.'

That got her attention. Nurse Moore looked up sharply, her eyes flaring. 'What makes you say that?'

'Just an observation, that's all. I suppose he's busy on the new ward.'

'What are you talking about?'

'That new ward. You know, the one for the shell shock patients.'

'What's that got to do with Dr Logan?'

'He's going to be running it, isn't he? Or that's what I heard.'

He enjoyed a brief moment of satisfaction, seeing the surprise on her face. Nurse Moore's hands stilled for a moment, then she carried on briskly.

'You've got it wrong. Dr Carlyle is running the new ward.'

'With Dr Logan. Turns out he's a qualified psychiatrist as well as a physician. I'm surprised you didn't know that, since you take such a close interest in him?'

He saw her mouth purse with annoyance. Then, without another word, she yanked back the curtains and was off, her trolley clattering down the ward.

Sam felt slightly ashamed of himself as he watched her go. What kind of man had he become, he wondered, that his only enjoyment came from baiting Nurse Moore? She was just a kid, a vain, self-centred little girl. It was none of his business if she became infatuated with a man.

He shifted his weight, and flinched as pain lanced through him, like a red-hot bayonet blade. A sudden and shocking reminder that he had more important things to occupy him.

Chapter Twelve

A week later, Grace was packing up the contents of Lance Corporal Frost's bedside locker. He watched her from the chair, fingers gripping the arms for dear life.

' "It's a long way to Tipperary . . ." ' he sang through chattering teeth.

In between snatches of song, he asked the same question, over and over again. 'Why are they s–sending me away, Nurse?'

'No one's sending you away, Lance Corporal,' Grace explained patiently yet again. 'You're just being moved to a different ward, that's all.'

'B–but why? Wh–what have I done?'

Grace paused in her packing, a pair of socks in her hand. 'It's a special place, for men with shell shock.'

'B–but I–I'm all r–right—' He gave up trying to speak and retreated to singing, to calm himself down.

' "It's a long way to Tipperary, it's a long way to go . . . It's a long way to Tipperary . . ." ' He rocked back and forth in time to the tune.

'Of course you are, old man. You're as sane as the rest of us.' In the bed opposite, Captain Jeffers lit up a cigarette and settled back against the pillows, a mocking smile on his face. 'But let's look on it as a bit of a holiday, shall we? A chance to get away from all these ghastly wounded chaps.'

Grace looked across at him. He was a handsome young man, fair-haired with an aristocratic, high-cheekboned face. He liked to present a louche, untroubled demeanour

76

to the world. But Grace had changed too many of his damp, soiled sheets every morning to be fooled. He was being transferred to Wilson ward with the rest of them.

Most of the men who were being transferred were too far gone to understand or care what was happening to them. They submitted like lambs, their faces and limbs twitching, looking up at the orderlies with vacant eyes.

At the other end of the ward, Private Gordon was as agitated as Lance Corporal Frost. But at least he had Albie Sallis to help him.

'Calm down, mate. They're sending you next door, not to Timbuktu!' Albie joked. But Grace could see his smile was strained with worry as he looked at his friend.

'It's not that he minds going,' he explained to Grace. 'The silly sod's just upset I won't be with him. Isn't that right, pal?' He turned to Gordon, who nodded. 'I've tried telling him, it's not a place for the likes of us common folk!' He grinned. 'And it's not like I won't see you again, is it? I'll come and visit you as soon as I'm up and about. I'll come and play whist with you, how about that? That is, if you can take another beating!'

Gordon laughed, a strange, gurgling sound deep in his throat.

Just then, the orderly arrived with a wheelchair.

'Look, your chariot awaits! Talk about travelling in style.'

As the orderly started to lift Gordon off the bed, Albie turned to Grace and said in a low voice, 'You will take care of him for me, won't you, Nurse?'

'I wish I could, Corporal Sallis. But I'm afraid I won't be moving to the new ward.' Then, seeing his stricken face, she went on, 'But I'm sure Dr Carlyle and Dr Logan will take good care of him. And I'll try to pop in as much as I can to make sure he's all right.'

'Thanks, Nurse.' Albie sent Gordon an affectionate look. 'I'll miss him, y'know. Still, at least I can get a good night's sleep now, without him whooping and hollering all the time!'

Gordon was very subdued as the orderly helped him into the wheelchair. But when they went to wheel him away he broke into noisy sobs.

'Aw, Jesus, will you look at the fuss he's making?' Sergeant McCray shouted out in exasperation. He had come in a week earlier, a loud-mouthed Scottish sergeant who had had his right leg amputated below the knee. 'He ought to be ashamed of himself!'

'Oi!' Albie shouted back. 'You watch what you're saying. That's my pal you're talking about.'

'Then you ought to be ashamed, too!' Sergeant McCray called back. 'Look at him, blubbering like a great baby. I didn't make all that fuss when they were sawing my bloody leg off! You want to act like a man, son. Get out of that bloody wheelchair and walk!'

Grace saw Gordon's shoulders stiffen, his head go down.

'He can't walk, in case you haven't noticed,' Albie said.

'Can't walk? Won't walk, you mean! We all know he's putting it on. Shell shock, indeed!' Sergeant McCray shook his head, mouth curling in disgust. 'A lot of fuss over nothing, I call it. Any of my men started sobbing like a lass, I'd give 'em a swift kick up the backside and tell them to get on with it. Look at him,' he sneered, 'hunched up in that wheelchair. You know what I'm saying is right, don't you, Gordon? That's why you can't meet my eye. You might be able to fool your daft friend over there, but I'm not afraid to call you what you are – a bloody coward!'

Grace saw Albie start to throw back his bedclothes, and moved to stop him. 'No,' she said. 'Leave him, it's not good for you to upset yourself.'

'But he's—'

'I said, leave him.' Grace turned away from him to face the Scottish sergeant. He was sitting up in bed, his angry face as red as a side of beef.

But Grace was angry too. She could feel it simmering inside her, bubbling through her veins. It was a rare feeling for her.

'You can still feel your leg, can't you, Sergeant McCray?' she said.

He stared at her, blankly. 'What's that got to do with anything?'

'It's true, isn't it? You're convinced it's still there. I've heard you telling Dr Carlyle how much it's hurting you.'

A couple of the other men muttered in agreement. 'I get that too,' Corporal Bennett agreed. 'I could swear my arm is still there sometimes. The doctor reckons it's just my mind playing tricks on me.'

'Exactly, Corporal,' Grace said. 'Your mind is a very powerful thing. It can make you believe all kinds of things, like your arm's not missing, or there are German snipers hiding on the ward, or that you can't walk . . .'

She was aware that a hush had fallen over the men. At first Grace thought it might be her impassioned speech that had stunned all of them into silence – until she turned round and saw Miss Sutton standing there, bristling in her grey uniform. Dr Carlyle was with her.

'Nurse Duffield,' Miss Sutton shook her head, jowls wobbling. 'I might have known it would be you, causing a commotion as usual.'

'It's my fault, Sister,' Sergeant McCray spoke up, breaking the silence. 'I was the one who started it.'

'Be that as it may, Sergeant, Nurse Duffield should know better than to join in.' Miss Sutton turned her beady eyes to Grace. 'I'm surprised at you, Nurse.' She shook her head.

'What have I always told you about maintaining a calm, cheerful disposition?'

'Sorry, Sister.' Grace studied the toes of her stout black shoes. She had forgotten to polish them the previous night. She hoped Sister didn't notice the scuff marks.

There was no point trying to defend herself. All Grace could do was stand there, cheeks burning with humiliation, and hope that the storm of Miss Sutton's anger blew itself out sooner rather than later.

But the worst of it was that Dr Carlyle was watching her with those shrewd dark eyes of hers. God only knew what she made of it all.

Finally, after five minutes of hearing how incompetent, irresponsible and utterly unsuited to nursing she was, and with a few dark threats about sending her to Matron, Grace was allowed to escape.

To her relief, Miss Sutton dismissed her to the new ward to help settle the patients.

Private Gordon was still in his wheelchair, beside his freshly made bed. The orderly was trying to chat to him, but Gordon had turned his head away, staring listlessly out of the French windows.

'What a lovely spot you have, Private Gordon. Talk about a room with a view!' Grace went to the French windows and peered out. 'And, look, you can see your old ward from here. You and Corporal Sallis can wave to each other.'

Gordon sent her a gloomy look, but said nothing. His eyes were still red-rimmed from crying.

'He's had a bit of an accident, Nurse.' The orderly nodded towards the dark stain in the lap of Gordon's hospital gown.

'Oh. Well, never mind. You wait there, Private Gordon,

and I'll fetch some water to get you washed. We'll soon have you nice and comfortable again.'

As Grace was returning with the washing trolley, she nearly collided with Kate Carlyle emerging from one of the side rooms. Fortunately, Grace just managed to pull the trolley to a stop before she mowed the doctor down.

'Sorry, Doctor, I wasn't looking where I was going.'

'No, Nurse, it was I who should have been paying attention.' Dr Carlyle eyed the trolley. 'Where are you off to with that?'

'Private Gordon needs cleaning up, Doctor.'

'Oh. I see.'

'He's just a bit unsettled,' Grace said.

'Right. Yes.'

'I'll get on with it then . . .'

Grace had started to push the trolley away when Dr Carlyle called out, 'I heard what you said to that patient – the amputee?'

Grace gave her an embarrassed smile. 'You couldn't really miss it, could you?'

'Indeed. I had no idea you could shout so loud, Nurse Duffield.'

'Oh, you'd be surprised, Doctor. I grew up with eleven brothers and sisters. You have to be able to shout just to be heard among that lot!'

Dr Carlyle's brows rose, and Grace wondered why she had spoken so freely to her. Most doctors barely knew the nurses' names, they certainly wouldn't care about their families.

'Anyway, I've told Sister it won't happen again,' she mumbled.

'I should hope not, Nurse. The last thing the men on a shell shock ward need is someone shouting at them like a sergeant major.'

Grace frowned. 'I'm sorry, Doctor, I don't think I understand?'

'It's quite simple, Nurse.' Kate Carlyle smiled at her. 'I'm asking you if you would come and work with Dr Logan and me on Wilson ward?'

Grace's mouth fell open. 'Me? Oh, no, I couldn't possibly!'

Dr Carlyle's smile hardened. 'I'm sorry,' she said. 'After hearing what you said, I was under the impression you might enjoy the work . . .'

'Oh, I would,' Grace said in a rush. 'I'd like nothing more. It's just – I don't think I'm up to the job.'

'Why not?'

Grace felt herself blushing again. 'You must have seen how clumsy and accident-prone I can be?'

'I've also seen how compassionate you are,' Kate Carlyle said. 'That's what we need on this ward, Nurse. Someone who will take the trouble to get to know the men, to understand them. I believe you would be perfect.'

Grace stared at her. No one had ever called her perfect before.

'In that case, I would very much like to work here,' she said. 'Thank you, Doctor.'

'That's settled then. Now, I'll leave you to get on with Private Gordon.'

As Dr Carlyle walked away, Grace looked down at her hands, gripping the handle of the washing trolley.

'Dr Carlyle?'

Kate Carlyle stopped and turned to face her. 'Yes?'

'About Private Gordon . . . I wonder, would it be possible for Corporal Sallis to move to Wilson ward, too? I know his injuries are only physical,' she went on in a rush, 'but I really think it would do Private Gordon the world of good to have him here. They've become such good friends . . .'

Her voice trailed off. Kate Carlyle was staring at her with

that inscrutable dark gaze, and for a terrible moment Grace felt sure she was going to tell her that she had made a mistake and would not be moving her to Wilson ward after all.

But then, suddenly, she smiled. 'I knew there was a reason why I chose you for this work, Nurse. Yes, I do believe transferring Corporal Sallis would be an excellent idea. I'll talk to Sister and make the arrangements.'

'Thank you, Doctor.'

As Grace had imagined, finding out that he was to be reunited with his friend did wonders for Private Gordon's sagging spirits, and he seemed quite happy once she had washed him and got him into a fresh gown.

She left the orderly to get him into bed, and hurried back to the other ward. It was already dark outside, and there were still several men to be transferred before teatime.

She had barely got through the double doors before Miss Sutton bore down angrily on her.

'Nurse Duffield?'

I am not going to miss that voice, Grace thought as she turned around, pinning a smile to her face.

'Yes, Sister?' Even the carping ward sister could not destroy her sunny mood.

'Where have you been all this time?'

'One of the patients on Wilson needed cleaning up, Sister.'

Miss Sutton's mouth pursed. 'Dr Carlyle has informed me you're moving,' she snapped. 'I can't say I'll be sorry to see you go.'

I can't say I will, either, Grace thought.

'But you're still here now, and there is work to be done.' The ward sister's beady eyes were narrowed under the doughy folds of her face. 'There is a new patient on their way up from Admissions. See to him, please, and put him in Private Gordon's old bed.'

'Yes, Sister.'

'And do stop smiling, Nurse. It's one thing for a nurse to look cheerful, but you seem positively manic.'

I don't care, Grace thought, as Miss Sutton plodded away. Dr Carlyle's warm praise still glowed inside her, and not even Sister could take that away from her.

The double doors swung open and two orderlies appeared, bearing a stretcher with a hunched shape covered in a blanket. Grace went over to them.

'He's to go over there, bed three,' she instructed. She picked up his notes. 'It's all right, we'll soon have you nice and comfortable, Private—' She saw the name on the notes, and the words died on her lips.

Chapter Thirteen

Dear Tom,

Thank you for your letter. As you can see, my knitting has not improved since the last pair of socks I sent you! But they will help keep your feet nice and dry, and that is the main thing. It has barely stopped raining here, and every time I see it, I think about you and Edward and all the poor men out there in your trenches. I do hope the weather will improve for you soon.

It was so nice of you to remember Papa, and to include a letter for him. I'm sure he will appreciate it. As it happens, I received a letter from Mother only this morning, giving their new address. She says she and Papa are settling in well in Germany. They are staying with some distant cousins, but are hoping to find a place of their own soon. Mother says everyone has been very kind to them, but I fear she's putting on a brave face for my sake. As she says, we must make the best of the situation. But I do miss her and Papa dreadfully, even though it has only been a couple of weeks since they left. I can still scarcely allow myself to think that I might never see them again . . .

A tear splashed on to the paper, and Anna blotted it carefully to stop it smudging the writing. She wished she could stop crying. Sister had commented on her red-rimmed eyes that morning.

'Really, Nurse Beck, don't you think the men have enough

problems of their own without seeing your long face?' she had scolded. 'Cheerfulness is what they need.'

Anna wiped her running nose on her handkerchief and continued writing.

No, I wasn't really surprised when Papa told me he was giving me the bakery. He knows I love the place as much as he does, and that I will take care of it. I look forward to the day Edward comes home, when we can run the place together, just like Mother and Papa did for all those years. We'll fill the place with love and laughter and happiness again, just as they did.

She paused for a moment, her pen hovering over the paper. Writing Edward's name brought a rush of guilt.

What would he say if he knew she was writing to Tom Franklin? There had been no love lost between Tom and Edward when they'd worked together at the bakery. As far as Edward was concerned, the Franklins were criminal scum.

He was right, too. All the Franklin boys, including Tom, had spent their lives in and out of jail. But unlike his brothers, Tom had managed to turn his back on a life of crime, thanks to Anna's father giving him a job and the chance to go straight. He had changed his life, but Edward would never give him credit for it.

'Once a Franklin, always a Franklin,' he would say. 'Your father doesn't know what kind of a viper he's invited into his nest.'

But Tom had proved himself when he saved Anna and her family from the fire that had swept through the bakery and the rooms above. And he had been a loyal friend ever since, helping to rebuild their home and business for them.

Not that Edward would ever understand that. Anna had tried to explain everything that Tom had done for them, but Edward had made it clear he didn't even like to hear his name mentioned, so in the end she had given up.

It was strange that Edward wouldn't give Tom a chance, she thought, especially when the paths of their lives had been so similar. As an orphan, straight out of the children's home, Edward had fallen in with the Franklin boys and nearly ended up in prison himself. Like Tom, her father had been Edward's salvation, taking him on as an apprentice and giving him a fresh start in life.

But for some reason, Edward seemed to resent Tom being given the same opportunity. It was something Anna could never understand.

Tom seemed just as antagonistic towards Edward, too. Anna was usually careful not to mention the other's name in her letters to both men. But Tom knew that Edward was her fiancé, so why shouldn't she mention their future together?

She put pen to paper again, and went on writing.

In the meantime, I have taken on someone to help in the kitchen. His name is Charlie, and he's Mrs Church's nephew. He trained at another bakery in Hackney before he enlisted, but since he was discharged he's been looking for work. He seems to know what he's doing, and he's bright and willing enough, so I hope he'll do.

Not that he would ever have met her father's standards, Anna thought. But at least the bread was getting made every morning, and he was willing to work for the pittance she could afford to pay him. All the same, she wished Papa or Edward could be there to keep an eye on him. A day under Friedrich Beck's watchful eye would have knocked him into shape.

She finished her letter to Tom, then tucked it carefully inside the parcel of chocolate and cigarettes she had wrapped for him. She placed it on the mantelpiece next to the identical package she had prepared for Edward.

She sat back and stretched out her arms, then glanced at the clock. It was twenty-five-past four, and she was due on duty at five o'clock. She was already dreading the thought of heading out in the rain again. She had barely dried out from her last soaking.

She was in the common room, trying to dry her shoes out in front of the fire, when she heard the front door open. The next moment she caught sight of a flurry of navy blue cap through the open common-room doorway as Grace rushed past, heading for the stairs.

'I hope you're not running, Duffield?' Anna laughed. 'You know what Sister says. Only in the case of fire or haemorrhage—'

She broke off at the sight of Grace turning round to stand in the common-room doorway. She looked even more dishevelled than usual. Most of her hair had managed to escape its restraining pins and now hung in damp strands around her face. There were holes in both knees of her black woollen stockings, exposing grazed, dirty skin. She had tripped and fallen again. It was nothing unusual for Duffield. The knees of her stockings were permanently darned.

But it was her ashen face that stopped Anna in her tracks.

'Duffield, what is it? You look as if you've seen a ghost.'

She saw the sympathy in her friend's hazel eyes and dread settled in her stomach like a cold, hard stone.

'What is it?' she said. 'Tell me!'

'Oh, Anna,' Grace whispered. 'It's Edward . . .'

Gas poisoning.

They were the only two words Anna heard. She saw Miss Sutton's mouth moving, but didn't take in the rest of what she said.

She had run all the way back to the hospital, not even stopping to put on her cape. By the time she arrived on the ward she was a soaking mess, her hair hanging loose, starched cuffs missing and collar unbuttoned.

Miss Sutton met her in the doorway. 'Good God, Beck, what do you think you're doing? You can't come on duty dressed like that.' She pointed a stubby finger back towards the doors. 'Go and explain to Matron why you—'

'Edward Stanning,' Anna cut across her. 'Where is he?'

Miss Sutton's tiny raisin eyes blinked at her in disbelief. 'I beg your pardon?'

'Edward Stanning.' She craned her neck to see past Sister's shoulder. 'He's my fiancé.'

A look of realisation gradually settled on the ward sister's features. She reached out and planted her plump hands on Anna's shaking shoulders.

'Come into my sitting room,' she said.

'But I—'

'My sitting room,' Miss Sutton said firmly. 'Now.'

Anna had never been in the ward sister's sitting room. It was her inner sanctum, a place the nurses were forbidden to enter. And yet Anna now found herself perched on the edge of the overstuffed sofa, staring at an assortment of china ornaments on the mantelpiece, a cup of hot sweet tea laced with brandy in her hands.

And all the while, Miss Sutton was talking, her voice gentler than Anna had ever heard it, explaining how Edward's battalion had been caught up in a mustard gas attack.

Anna heard the words and stopped listening. She knew all about mustard gas. She had washed it off blackened, blistered skin often enough. She had seen its victims coughing and choking, fighting to breathe through burned throats . . .

'Is – will he—'

'Will he live?' Miss Sutton finished the sentence that Anna could not. She paused a moment too long, and Anna could see her weighing up her words.

'He has sustained some superficial injuries, but most of the damage was to his lungs,' she said at last. 'And, as you know, that can make it rather difficult to assess the long-term damage . . .'

Anna understood. A patient who had inhaled mustard gas might seem to recover at first, only to succumb to respiratory failure a couple of weeks later.

'However, Mr Stanning is young and strong, and Dr Logan has every reason to believe he will recover,' Miss Sutton went on. 'Would you like to see him?'

Anna looked up at her sharply. For once, the ward sister's broad face seemed soft, her eyes kind.

'Yes – yes, please,' she whispered.

Anna felt a surge of panic as she approached the figure in the bed. She forced herself to walk slowly down the ward, clasping her hands together to stop her reaching out for Miss Sutton beside her.

Superficial injuries, the ward sister had said. But that could mean anything. Anna had seen men so disfigured by war that their own mothers wouldn't have recognised them. Their flesh melted by the gas, features blurred and formless like dripping candle wax . . .

Anna pressed her lips together. She hoped her expression didn't give her away too much. The last thing she wanted was to upset Edward.

She saw his fair head resting on the pillow, and her heart shot into her mouth. She wanted to stop, but she forced her feet to move forward, closer and closer . . .

Relief rushed through her. Thank God, he looked the same. Older, of course, and his handsome face was more gaunt than the last time she had seen him. But he was still her Edward.

He was sleeping, but as Anna crept closer he suddenly

jerked awake. He stared straight at her, and for a second his face twisted with fear and hostility. But then he seemed to recognise her and the warmth came into his blue eyes.

'Anna?' His voice was a hoarse whisper.

'Edward!' Anna promptly forgot all Miss Sutton's warnings about being gentle with him, and rushed into his arms. 'Oh, Edward!'

He hissed with pain, and she pulled away. 'I'm sorry, did I hurt you?'

'It doesn't matter.' He held her at arms' length. 'Is it really you?' he said. 'Only I've had this dream so many times, and every time I wake up, you're gone . . .'

'It's not a dream. I'm really here.'

'So where am I?' He looked around him, confused and disorientated.

'The Nightingale Hospital, Bethnal Green.'

'The Nightingale?' His gaze flicked back to her. 'I'm home, then?'

'Yes,' Anna said. 'Yes, you're home.'

It was nothing short of a miracle that had brought him to her, she thought. Injured men were usually hospitalised as close to their homes as possible, but it was just as likely Edward could have ended up at one of the military hospitals on the coast, or out in a far-flung part of Essex.

And if it had been a day or two earlier, the wards would have been full and there would have been no room for him. It might have been weeks or months before she heard any news . . .

'Thank God.' He released her hand, and slid his fingers under his hospital gown, wincing as they found the dressing over his damaged skin. 'Is it – very bad?' he whispered.

'You're safe,' Anna replied. 'That's all that matters.'

He managed the smallest of smiles. 'Yes,' he said. 'That's all that matters.'

Chapter Fourteen

'I have considered your request, Nurse Moore, and the answer is no.'

Dulcie stared at Matron across her polished mahogany desk. She couldn't look at her elaborate starched white headdress without thinking of a galleon in full sail.

'But why, Matron? I don't understand.'

Matron bristled, her mouth pursing in disapproval. Dulcie knew it wasn't the done thing to question her judgement, but she couldn't help herself.

Matron's stiff grey uniform crackled as she pulled herself upright. 'I have spoken to Sister and consulted the ward reports, and I do not believe you are cut out to work with the neurasthenia patients.' Her eyes met Dulcie's. 'Quite frankly, Nurse, I am surprised you would even put yourself forward for such work.'

'But I'm very interested in shell shock, Matron,' Dulcie insisted.

'Are you, Nurse? From what I've read in the ward reports, it seems to me you are hardly interested in the patients at all, shell shocked or otherwise.'

She opened the drawer on her left and drew out a heavy ledger, which she placed on the desk in front of her. Dulcie's heart sank as she recognised the dreaded ward book, where the various ward sisters wrote all their comments about the nurses' conduct and behaviour.

'Let's see, shall we?' Matron opened the ledger and ran her finger down the page. 'Ah, here we are. "Twenty-seventh of

June, nineteen seventeen . . . Nurse Dulcie Moore left a patient unattended in the bathroom today. Sister has told her that she must not be so ready to make excuses for her mistakes."' She flicked over a few pages. 'Or this one, from the seventh of July . . . "Sister found Nurse Dulcie Moore smoking in the sluice today, when she should have been with the patients outside. She has been warned."' She turned over more pages. 'And here is one from the nineteenth of September. "Nurse Dulcie Moore requires keeping up to the mark, as she is inclined to get slack if left unsupervised . . ."'

Matron looked up, her pinched face framed by white linen. 'It all makes for rather depressing reading, doesn't it, Nurse?'

'I can do better,' Dulcie said. 'If you just give me a chance to prove myself?'

'You have had ample opportunity to do that, Nurse. And you have failed every time.' Matron closed the ledger and put it back in her desk drawer. 'May I ask why you are so determined to work on Wilson ward?'

Dulcie lowered her gaze and tried to look suitably humble.

'I believe men's minds can be broken just as badly as their bodies,' she said. 'I am interested in helping them to heal.'

Risking a quick glance, she saw Matron's expression soften, and was glad she had listened for once when Grace Duffield was explaining it to Eliza Parrish on the ward earlier.

'Very well,' Matron said at last. 'I will give you a chance to prove yourself, Nurse Moore.' Then, before Dulcie could respond, added, 'But not on Wilson ward. Not yet, anyway. I want you to demonstrate to me that you can show compassion to all our patients before I agree to your moving.'

Dulcie frowned. 'And how long will that take, Matron?'

Matron's gaze was every bit as unforgiving as the November frost outside. 'That really depends on you, Nurse Moore, don't you think?'

'"That really depends on you, Nurse Moore,"' Dulcie mimicked to Grace later on as she watched her scrubbing a mackintosh sheet. 'Honestly, she was so high-handed, I'm surprised I didn't walk out.'

'That wouldn't have done you a lot of good,' Grace pointed out mildly.

'It could be weeks or months before I'm finally transferred to Wilson,' Dulcie went on, ignoring her. 'Some other girl is bound to have snapped up Dr Logan by then. It's so unfair!'

'You'll just have to do as she says then, won't you?'

Dulcie sighed. 'That's easier said than done, isn't it? Especially with Sister on at me all the time for the slightest thing, just waiting to write my name in those wretched ward reports of hers.' She still burned with indignation, thinking about how Matron had produced those pages so smugly, reading each damning line aloud. How Dulcie would love to throw that wretched book in the stoke hole! 'Anyway, I daresay whatever I did, I could never become as perfect as those paragons they'll have on Wilson ward.'

Grace, who was trying to manoeuvre the mackintosh over the rack to dry, suddenly lost her grip. The sheet flapped like a wild, wet sail, showering Dulcie in soapy water.

'Watch it!' she cried out.

'Sorry.' Grace wrapped her arms around the sheet, man-handling it over the rack.

'I should think so.' Dulcie brushed at the wet spots on the bib of her apron. 'Do you know who's going to be working there?'

'Where?'

'Wilson ward!' Dulcie stared at her, exasperated. Really, Duffield could be very obtuse sometimes. 'Come on, you must have heard some gossip?'

'No.'

The mackintosh slithered off the rack, soaking Grace's apron.

Dulcie sighed. 'Here, let me help you.' She stooped to lift the edge of the mackintosh. 'I daresay it's some absolute angel, anyway.' She laughed as Grace's blushing face emerged from the other end of the mackintosh. 'Duffield . . . are you all right? You've gone positively puce.'

And then it dawned on her.

'It's you, isn't it? You're moving to Wilson.'

Grace's blush deepened to an unflattering crimson. 'I didn't ask to go,' she gabbled. 'I don't even know why they picked me. I'll probably only last a day before they get rid of me . . .'

Dulcie watched her, open-mouthed. 'You mean to tell me last week, you were asked to move? You didn't even have to put your name forward?'

Grace looked away awkwardly. 'Dr Carlyle approached me,' she mumbled.

'Oh, her!' Dulcie rolled her eyes. 'Well, that's it, then. I'll never be moved to Wilson now, not while Dr Carlyle is in charge. She hates me.'

'I'm sure that's not true.'

'You know it is. She's never forgiven me for all that business with Dr Latimer.'

As if it was her fault that the senior houseman had made a play for her! Dulcie hadn't even known he was courting Kate too. She had tried to do the right thing and end it with Charlie Latimer as soon as she found out – Dulcie had no time for deceivers. She had also tried to warn Kate Carlyle what he was really like, but it had all backfired on her.

She didn't know why Dr Carlyle still bore such a grudge, especially as she was now madly in love with another doctor, Rufus French. If anything, Dulcie had helped her to a lucky escape.

She looked at Grace, still struggling with the mackintosh sheet. She was such a blushing, clumsy mess, it was hard to imagine how Dr Carlyle could have decided she was a better bet than Dulcie. It could only be jealousy, she thought.

But then again, there was a way it could all work in her favour.

'At least you can keep an eye on him for me,' she said.

Grace looked up, startled. 'Me? Keep an eye on Dr Logan?'

'Why not? You'll be working together. You can keep all the other nurses at bay.' Dulcie nudged her. 'And you might even put in a good word for me, too.'

'I can't!' Grace was horrified. 'I can barely speak to him, he makes me so nervous.'

'Go on,' Dulcie wheedled. 'You are supposed to be my friend, after all. You can turn on the charm for my sake, can't you?'

'Oh, my.' Grace looked faint at the prospect. Friend or not, Dulcie didn't hold out much hope for the chances of either of them.

Chapter Fifteen

Dulcie returned to the ward, still simmering over Matron's words. It was completely unfair, she decided. She was every bit as good as the other nurses, and better than some. Miriam Trott, for instance, could be positively callous at times.

And besides, didn't Sister always say nurses had to learn to keep themselves distant from their patients? It didn't always do to be as soft-hearted as Grace Duffield, letting herself get so emotional over the men's troubles.

'Nurse? Nurse, can you help me?'

Dulcie turned at the sound of a man's voice coming from the bed opposite. She was just about to go over to him when she realised he was calling out to Anna Beck at the other end of the ward.

Dulcie stopped in her tracks as Anna approached him. 'Yes, Private Garrett? What seems to be the matter?'

'My splint's giving me a bit of gyp. You couldn't loosen it off for me a bit, could you?'

'Let's have a look at it, shall we?'

Dulcie watched Anna as she unfastened her starched cuffs and slipped them into her apron pocket.

'I daresay he didn't want to bother you, Nurse,' Sergeant McCray answered Dulcie's unspoken question. 'We know you're always so busy.'

She turned to look at him. There was a mocking glint in the sergeant's eye she didn't like.

An orderly appeared, carrying a bundle of newspapers. Dulcie hurried over.

'I'll have one of those, please.' She took it from him and made her way purposefully up the ward, to where Sam Trevelyan was sitting propped up in bed, scowling into space as usual.

He sent her a wary look as she approached. 'What do you want?' he growled.

Dulcie determinedly ignored his ferocious mood. 'Good morning, Sergeant Trevelyan,' she said. 'I've brought you a newspaper.'

He looked at the paper in her hands, then turned away. 'I don't want it.'

'Don't you want to know what's going on in the world?'

'Not particularly.'

'I'll leave it here on your locker for you anyway. Just in case you change your mind.'

'I won't.'

Dulcie stared at him, at a loss for a moment. 'Some of the other men are setting up a game of whist,' she said. 'Don't you want to join them?'

He looked up at her with those cold green eyes of his. 'Any reason why I should?'

'I just thought you'd enjoy some company, that's all.'

'I'd rather be on my own.'

He sent her a meaningful look, which Dulcie ignored. 'Here, let me plump up your pillows.'

'There's no need,' he started to say, but she was already punching them into shape.

'What's all this in aid of?' Sam Trevelyan wanted to know. 'Are you in Sister's bad books again?'

'Certainly not!' Dulcie said, but all the same she couldn't help glancing around, hoping that Miss Sutton would witness her being busy and compassionate. But she was busy behind the screens around bed four.

'You'll punch all the life out of that pillow if you're not careful.'

Dulcie stuffed it quickly back into place. 'There, that's better, isn't it?'

'If you say so.'

She was about to walk away when the screens around bed four were suddenly pushed back, and Sister emerged. Dulcie immediately turned back to Sam Trevelyan.

'So,' she said. 'You come from Cornwall, do you?'

He looked up at her sharply. 'Who told you that?'

'I heard you telling Nurse Duffield.' She glanced sideways. Sister was still deep in conversation with Dr French. 'I'm from the west country myself.'

'You're a long way from home.'

'Yes, and that's just how I like it.' The words came out without her thinking. Then, seeing Sam's look of surprise, Dulcie said, 'I much prefer the city. That's why I became a nurse, so I could move to London.'

'And there was me, thinking it was your caring nature.'

Sister was coming, her flat feet plodding down the ward. Dulcie swung round, searching for something purposeful to do.

'I'll tidy your locker, shall I?'

'There's no need . . .'

'It's no trouble.' She bent down to open the door.

'I said, leave it!'

But by then she had already found the flat leather box. 'What's this?'

'Put it back.'

'But what is it?'

She heard Sam's angry sigh as she started to lift the lid. Inside the box was a gleaming silver medal bearing an image of King George, on a crimson, white and blue ribbon.

'Oh, my goodness, where did you get this?'

He didn't reply. Dulcie removed the medal from its box. It felt cool and heavy in her palm.

She turned it over to read the inscription on the back.

'For bravery in the field . . .'

No sooner had the words left her lips than Sam snatched the medal out of her hands. He shut it back in the box and tossed it carelessly to the back of his locker.

'Why did they give you a medal?' Dulcie asked.

'I don't want to talk about it.' He slammed the locker door.

'Why are you hiding it away? You should be proud.'

'What do you know about it?' For a brief second, Dulcie caught a look of unguarded pain in his green eyes, before the mask descended again. 'I'm tired,' he said. 'Go away and bother someone else.'

'But—' Dulcie started to say. But Sam's eyes were already closed.

For the rest of the day Dulcie couldn't stop thinking about the medal in Sam Trevelyan's locker. In the end, she decided to ask Staff Nurse Hanley about it. The senior staff nurse came from a military family and took a great interest in such things.

'It sounds like the Military Medal,' said Nurse Hanley, when Dulcie described it to her. 'It's a gallantry award, given to NCOs for particular acts of bravery. It's really quite an honour to receive one.'

Dulcie thought of the medal, thrown carelessly into the back of Sam Trevelyan's locker.

'What kind of bravery?' she asked.

'Well, it depends . . . They usually publish the information in the *London Gazette*, if that's any help?' Staff Nurse Hanley frowned. 'Why are you so interested, Nurse?'

Dulcie glanced back at Sam Trevelyan. He was awake again now, his eyes fixed unseeingly on the ceiling. His face was a set mask.

'No reason, Staff,' she said.

Chapter Sixteen

'Nurse Beck, will you pay attention?'

Anna looked round sharply at the sound of Nurse Hanley's stern voice. The senior staff nurse stood facing her, a length of rubber tubing in one hand and a catheter in the other.

'You're supposed to be keeping an eye on the patient's pulse,' she snapped. 'How can you be ready with the stimulant if you're miles away?'

'Yes, Staff. Sorry.'

Anna gave the patient in the bed a quick, apologetic look, and checked his pulse. It was a good, steady beat, forceful enough to tell her he was suffering no ill effects from the abdominal drainage procedure.

She allowed her gaze to travel stealthily back to the far end of the ward, where the curtains were pulled around Edward's bed. Dr French had been in there a long time, she thought.

Today was the day they decided whether to ship Edward back to France. Officially, he would have to go before a Medical Board who would decide his future, but Anna knew they nearly always took the advice of the doctor in charge of the soldier's case.

She kept telling herself not to think the worst, but it was difficult after everything that had happened. She tried to keep up a brave face for Edward's sake, but every night she would pray that God would not take him away from her, too. She wasn't sure she would be able to bear it if she were left alone again.

'Nurse Beck, I am about to suture the wound,' Nurse Hanley's voice rapped out.

'Yes, Staff.' Anna got to work, administering the local anaesthetic. But as she watched Nurse Hanley carefully stitching, her mind was elsewhere.

Suddenly the screens around Edward's bed were pushed back and Dr French emerged with Miss Sutton. Anna watched them talking together, trying to work out what they might be saying. They both looked very solemn, she thought.

Nurse Hanley finished her sutures and Anna was allowed to apply the many-tailed binder and then dress the wound. She settled the patient and made sure he was comfortable, then hurried off to see Edward.

He was listlessly doing a crossword when she approached. Anna took one look at his subdued face and her heart sank.

'Oh, Edward, what did the doctor say?'

He shook his head. 'It's bad news, love.' Then, before Anna could reply, he went on, 'It looks like those Germans will have to find someone else for their target practice!'

It took a moment for the news to sink in. 'You – you mean, they're not going to send you back?'

Edward shook his head. 'The doctor reckons my lungs are too damaged. Another gas attack could kill me, he says. I'll have to go in front of the Board to make it all official, but Dr French says he'll be recommending light duties at home. Or you never know, I might even get a complete discharge!' His face brightened.

Anna stared at him, scarcely able to take this in. She had seen so many other men, often in a worse state than Edward, shipped off back to France. He must be very lucky, she thought.

Or perhaps God had decided to answer her prayers for once.

'You'll be coming home.' Her dazed mind could scarcely take it in. She had longed for this moment for so long, part of her wondered if it was still a dream. It seemed too good to be true.

'Yes.' He turned his head away from her, a faraway look on his face.

'Edward, what is it? What's wrong?' Anna asked.

'Nothing. Only – well, I don't know where home is anymore, do I? I've been away so long, I'm not really sure what I'll do once I'm in Civvy Street again. I mean, where will I live for a start?'

Anna stared at him. 'Why do you have to ask that? Of course you'll come and live at the bakery.'

'Yes, but it's not really my home, is it?'

'It will be once we're married.'

He looked up at her, his face so full of hope and uncertainty, Anna felt as if her heart would break.

'Do you mean it?' he said. 'You still want to marry me?'

'Of course I do, you daft ha'porth. It's all I've ever wanted.'

'I wasn't sure if you'd changed your mind after all this time?'

Anna laughed. 'As if I would!' Then a thought struck her. 'Unless – you're the one who's changed their mind?'

'What do you think?'

Edward reached for her hand just as Miss Sutton came stomping down the corridor. Anna quickly drew away from his grasp, hiding her hands in the folds of her voluminous blue dress.

'Don't,' she whispered. 'Sister might see.'

'I don't care.' Edward grinned. 'You'll be Mrs Edward Stanning soon, and then I can hold your hand as much as I like!'

Anna was still blushing as she hurried away. For the rest

of the afternoon, she went about her work, unable to keep a smile off her face.

Edward was coming home. If he did not receive a complete discharge, at least she would know he wasn't in danger anymore. And even if his light duties took him to another part of the country, they would still be married.

And one day, when this wretched war was over, he would come home to her and they could be together again, in the bakery, just like old times.

'Nurse? Could you do me a favour?'

Anna looked over to where Corporal Mason was sitting up in bed against a bank of pillows. He had a serious heart condition that meant he had to remain propped up at all times.

'What is it, Corporal?'

'You couldn't give these pillows a bit of a shake for me, could you? One's slipped down a bit, and it's ever so uncomfortable.'

'Of course.'

She should have known, Anna thought. As she approached the soldier's bed, she could hear the muffled snorts of laughter. She should have realised then that something was up. But she was so carried away with her own daydreams that she barely noticed the grins on the faces of the men in the surrounding beds.

'Now, let's see, shall we?' She reached for the pillow, and immediately felt the Corporal's arms go around her middle, pulling her off balance. He was surprisingly strong for a wiry little man, and Anna fell into his lap as the other men whooped and cheered around them.

Corporal Mason's face filled her vision, leering cheekily down at her. 'Give us a kiss, Nurse!' he cried. The next minute his wet lips had descended on hers.

As Anna struggled to fend him off, she heard Miss Sutton crying out, 'What is going on here?' This was followed quickly by another cry of, 'No, Nurse, don't fight him off. He might die! Give in, give in!'

'You heard her, Nurse. Give in!' The other men joined in the chorus in delight.

It was so funny, even Anna was helpless with laughter as she tried to twist from the man's grasp. But then she heard Sister's shout of dismay, and the next thing she knew she was being hauled roughly away by a pair of strong hands.

Anna looked round, laughing, expecting to see Sister, and found herself staring instead into Edward's icy blue gaze.

'Corporal Mason, are you all right?' Miss Sutton pushed Anna out of the way to get to the soldier, who had collapsed back against the pillows, gasping for air. 'Fetch Dr French, Nurse, quickly. And you –' she turned angrily to Edward '– get back into bed.'

For a moment Edward stood his ground, his hands balling into fists. Then, to Anna's relief, he turned on his heel and stomped away.

Thankfully, Corporal Mason survived his attack. But Edward was simmering with anger when Anna went to see him later.

'He's still alive, then?' Edward nodded over to where Miss Sutton was fussing over the hapless soldier. 'Shame.'

'You mustn't say that, Edward. He didn't mean any harm by it.'

'He had no right to paw at you like that.'

'It was just a bit of fun.'

Edward turned on her, coldly accusing. 'You sound as if you enjoyed it?'

It was so ridiculous, Anna couldn't help laughing. 'You really think I enjoyed kissing Corporal Mason? He's over forty, and he's only got three teeth!'

'I don't know, do I?' Edward's chin jutted. 'You're always very friendly to the other men.'

'It's my job.'

'Well, I don't have to like it.'

She stared at his face, surprised to see anger clouding his eyes. She had never known Edward so jealous before. But before she could say any more, Sister summoned her to help with a patient's bath.

All through the afternoon, Anna was aware of Edward sulking as she went about her work. Whenever she tried to catch his eye he would look away.

Meanwhile, Corporal Mason had recovered and was feeling thoroughly ashamed of himself.

'It was only a bit of fun, Nurse. A few of the other lads egged me on to do it,' he said. 'I hope I ain't caused you any offence?'

'Not at all, Corporal,' Anna replied.

'I'm not sure your young man feels the same.' Corporal Mason nodded over towards Edward. 'D'you reckon I should apologise to him, too?'

Anna glanced back at Edward. 'I'd leave him be if I were you,' she said. 'He'll soon calm down.'

'I hope so.' Corporal Mason grimaced. 'I wouldn't fancy being on the end of that right hook of his. Finish me right off, I reckon!'

It wasn't until she was serving the teas before she went off duty that Anna found herself face-to-face with Edward again.

'I'm sorry,' he said quietly as she put his teacup down on the locker beside him.

Anna looked at him but said nothing.

'It was stupid of me to get so jealous,' Edward went on. 'But I couldn't help it. When I saw him pawing you like that . . .'

'I told you, he didn't mean anything by it.'

'All the same, it's not easy for me to sit here and watch some other man kissing the girl I love. I mean, how would you feel if you caught me kissing one of the other nurses?'

'I don't suppose I'd like it,' Anna admitted slowly.

'So I'd better not kiss Staff Nurse Hanley, then?'

Anna looked up into Edward's face, and the next minute they both burst out laughing.

'Definitely not!' Anna said.

Edward reached for her hand again. 'Do you forgive me?' he said softly.

'I suppose so. But don't go trying to murder any more of the patients!' Anna warned him.

'I promise.' He ran his thumb over the engagement ring on her left hand. 'I can't wait until you're properly mine, Anna Beck. Then I'll have no reason to be jealous again.'

Anna thought about her latest letter from Tom, lying on the bedside table at the nurses' home.

'No,' she said. 'No, you won't.'

Chapter Seventeen

At the end of November, Miss Parker, ward sister on Wilson, was due to take a week's holiday. Matron had arranged for one of the other ward sisters, Miss Collins, to take over from her, but on the morning Miss Parker was due to leave, Miss Collins was admitted to the sick bay with suspected laryngitis.

'She can barely speak, poor thing,' Florence Parker said when she called Grace into her office that morning. She looked odd out of her stiff grey uniform, dressed in an old-fashioned fitted coat that nearly reached her ankles. An elaborate feathered hat sat on the desk between them, beside a pair of grey kid gloves. In the corner of the room was a leather suitcase. Miss Parker must have been on her way to catch her train when she was summoned back, Grace thought.

'I'm sorry to hear that, Sister,' Grace said. 'I suppose you will have to postpone your holiday until she recovers?'

'Och, no, I'm still going home to Edinburgh.' Florence Parker shook her head. She was a slightly built, energetic woman, whose keen blue eyes radiated a fierce intelligence. 'Matron has promised to find another ward sister by this afternoon. Until then, she has agreed I am to put you in charge, Nurse Duffield.'

'Me, Sister?' Panic washed over her. 'But—'

'Now, I don't want to hear any arguments,' Miss Parker cut her off briskly. 'It really isn't that difficult, Nurse. All you have to do is make sure the ward is kept tidy and the men looked after. I have already taken report from the night sister and given out the work lists, so everyone knows what they are supposed to be doing. You just have to make sure they do it.'

But Grace was hardly listening. Her mind was racing ahead, thinking of everything that could possibly go wrong.

'It will only be for a few hours, Nurse Duffield.' Amusement gleamed in Miss Parker's eyes. 'I'm sure even you could not bring the place to calamity by teatime.'

'I hope not, Sister.' But Grace's palms were already clammy with the possibility.

She watched as Miss Parker put her hat on before the mirror, turning her head this way and that to check every angle. All the while, she went on issuing instructions.

'Now, make sure everyone knows you are in charge, and don't take any nonsense from anyone. Especially not the VADs. And particularly not Marchant. She is rather full of herself and inclined to take over if she is not kept in check.'

'Yes, Sister.'

'And don't take any nonsense from the men, either. You must make sure that they are all in bed and the ward is tidy before Dr Logan does his round at ten o'clock. They're bound to be in the middle of a card game, but you must tell them to stop. Confiscate their cards if you must.'

'I will, Sister.' Grace's downcast expression must have given her away, because Miss Parker turned from the mirror and said in a kindly voice, 'It will only be for a few hours, Duffield. Just do the best you can, and make sure you don't lose anyone.'

She made it sound very simple. But Grace's knees were still knocking underneath her voluminous skirt as she returned to Wilson ward. She felt sure that her fellow nurses would have something to say about her being in charge.

Surprisingly, they didn't seem to mind.

'Of course you should be in charge,' Sylvia Saunders

said, as if it was the most obvious idea in the world. 'You're so good with the patients, far better than we are.'

'But I've never been in charge before,' Grace said anxiously.

'We'll help you, don't worry,' Mary Finnegan said kindly. She was a pretty Irish girl, with dark hair and bright blue eyes.

'And we'll keep the VADs in check for you,' Sylvia offered.

'Except for Marchant,' Mary Finnegan said, rolling her eyes. 'No one can keep her in check, not even Matron.'

'Speaking of which, Matron will be doing her rounds soon.' Sylvia looked at the clock. 'We'd better get this place tidy before she arrives, or it'll be a black mark for all of us.'

They worked together, dusting and polishing and straightening the bed castors so they all faced in the same direction. Grace sat at Sister's desk in the centre of the ward and surveyed the rows of neatly made beds with satisfaction. Perhaps this wasn't so bad after all?

Then the double doors swung open and Matron arrived, gliding in with great ceremony in her long black dress and snowy headdress. Grace shot to her feet so quickly, she knocked over the chair with a resounding clatter.

Matron winced delicately. 'Good morning, Nurse,' she greeted her. 'Are you ready for my inspection?'

'I think so, Matron.'

'You *think* so?' Matron's brows rose under her elaborate headdress. 'That doesn't sound very promising, Nurse. Let's see, shall we?'

Grace prayed silently to herself as she followed Matron up the ward. All the while, her gaze darted around. It would be just her luck for one of the men to start screeching, or a VAD suddenly to appear with a trolley full of dirty laundry.

Matron seemed particularly determined to find fault. She moved from bed to bed, wielding a wooden ruler which she used to measure the turned down top sheets. She ran her finger along windowsills and the tops of lockers, then leaned down and tapped the bedsprings from underneath, looking for dust. Grace, Sylvia and Mary exchanged nervous glances as they followed in her wake.

The only difficult moment was when she reached the bed of Captain Jeffers.

'And how are you today?' she asked her usual question.

'Dying for a cigarette, since you ask,' the young officer replied. 'I don't suppose you've got one on you, have you?'

Grace and the other nurses froze. Mary looked as if she might burst from suppressed laughter.

Thankfully, Matron didn't seem too ruffled. 'I'm afraid not,' she said, before gliding on to inspect the next bed.

By the time they reached the end of the ward, Grace's heart was wedged so firmly in her throat she could scarcely breathe.

'Yes, well, that seems to be in order,' Matron said. 'Although I notice the fire at the far end of the ward has not been lit, and it's rather chilly.'

'I'll see to it at once, Matron.'

Grace waited, still holding her breath, until the double doors had closed behind Matron, then she allowed herself to exhale. Mary and Sylvia did the same.

'Thank the Lord!' Mary said. 'I thought she'd never go.'

'Did you see her inspecting those castors?' Sylvia said. 'I'm so glad Sister made me scrub them with a toothbrush yesterday!'

'We can't relax yet. We've still got Dr Logan's round to come.' Grace looked up at the clock. It was only half-past nine, but it felt as if she had been on duty for several hours. 'I'd better see to that fire before he gets here.'

'Get Marchant to do it,' Sylvia said. 'That's what the VADs are here for, to do the menial tasks.'

'I don't think anyone has told Marchant that!' Mary laughed.

'No one would dare.' Grace said.

Most of the VADs lived in absolute terror of the nurses, but not Vivienne Marchant. She was a terribly grand lady in her fifties, the wife of one of the hospital's Board of Trustees, who had decided it would be rather fun to do her bit and join the Voluntary Aid Detachment.

Unfortunately, she had never quite grasped what it meant to be a VAD. Or rather, she chose not to. She was very good at reading and writing letters for the men, and she always took a great deal of trouble serving tea, although not all the men appreciated her wafer-thin cucumber sandwiches. Once she had even had her piano brought in from home so she could entertain the patients with her singing, until Matron tactfully suggested they could all do without her tremulous soprano.

But when it came to getting her hands dirty, Mrs Marchant was decidedly unforthcoming.

'Nurse, I simply don't have the first idea how to make up a fire,' she insisted, as she and Grace stood in front of the fireplace. 'We have a girl to do it at home.'

'It's quite simple,' Grace said. 'You just have to clean out the grate, then take some paper and some kindling, and—'

'So many instructions! I'll never remember them all.' Vivienne Marchant looked flustered. 'I really think it would be easier if you showed me, Nurse. Then I'll know what to do next time.'

There was a point at which she could have said no, Grace reflected later, as she kneeled down before the fireplace, sweeping ashes out of the grate on to a sheet of newspaper. There was a moment when she could have straightened her shoulders, looked Mrs Marchant in the eyes and told her just to get on with it. But she couldn't for the life of her think when it had been. In fact, Mrs Marchant had long since lost interest in watching her demonstration and had disappeared off to the kitchen to gossip with the other VADs.

Grace tried to tell herself she didn't really mind, that it was probably quicker and easier for her just to do it herself. But inside she felt foolish.

She was still trying to coax some life into the fire when Sylvia came up behind her and said, 'Duffield, it's ten o'clock. Shouldn't we be outside, waiting for the doctor?'

'Oh, Lord!' Grace jumped to her feet and gathered up the newspaper, sending up a cloud of ash. 'He's probably out there waiting now. Go outside with Finnegan and keep him occupied, will you? I'll be with you as soon as I've cleaned this lot up.'

It was a little ceremony all the doctors expected on their round, to be greeted at the doors by the ward sister and nurses, who would then follow him like handmaidens from bed to bed.

As Sylvia and Mary left, Grace stuffed the newspaper bundle in a metal bucket, and scuffed the drift of ash into the polished floor with the toe of her shoe. Hopefully Dr Logan would not be quite so meticulous in his inspection as Matron had been.

Then she hurried down the ward, jabbing a loose pin back into her cap as she went.

Just as she had feared, Dr Logan was already waiting in the corridor, frowning ostentatiously at his watch. Sylvia Saunders and Mary Finnegan stood awkwardly beside him, shuffling their feet.

The nurses both stared at Grace in horror as she threw herself through the double doors. Sylvia's eyes were as round as saucers, while Mary looked as if she had accidentally swallowed a frog.

What were they staring at? Grace wondered. She put her hand up to check the pin in her cap.

'There you are, Nurse. I must say, I'm—' Dr Logan looked up from his watch and instantly fell silent.

Grace followed his gaze and immediately realised why Sylvia and Mary had looked so horrified. Her once spotless white apron was streaked grey with ash. Her hands were grimy with it, under her nails and between her fingers.

'I'm terribly sorry, I . . .'

'Shall we go?' Dr Logan cut her off. 'We're already nearly five minutes late as it is.'

They followed him through the double doors, Grace trailing behind.

'Oh, Duffield, what have you done? You look as if you've been sweeping the chimney, never mind making the fire!' Mary gave a muffled snort of laughter.

'Is it that bad?'

'Your apron and your hands are filthy, and you've got a smudge on the end of your nose,' Sylvia said.

Grace scrubbed at her face with the corner of her apron. 'Is that better?'

'Not really.' Sylvia looked pained. 'Just be glad it's only Dr Logan doing the rounds, and not one of the consultants.'

'Dr Logan is bad enough.' Grace looked at the doctor's broad back. He did not turn around, but she could tell from the rigid set of his shoulders that he was bristling with outrage. 'I'm going to have to sneak off and change my apron, at least.'

'You can't!' Mary looked panicked. 'You've got to be here to answer his questions.'

'She's right,' Sylvia said. 'You'll only annoy him more if you disappear.'

114

'But it'll only be for a minute,' Grace said. 'Surely he won't even notice if—'

'Nurse?' Dr Logan's voice rang out, stopping her in her tracks. 'Would you mind telling me what has happened to the patient in bed five?'

Grace stared at Captain Jeffers' empty bed. 'He's gone,' she said.

'I can see that, Nurse,' Dr Logan said impatiently. 'But where has he gone, that's the question?'

Grace went on staring at the rumpled bedclothes, as if they could somehow yield a clue. 'I – I don't know.'

Just do the best you can and make sure you don't lose anyone. Sister had meant it as a joke, but it didn't seem so funny anymore.

Dr Logan cleared his throat, startling her back to attention. 'Don't you think you should look for him?'

'Yes. Yes, of course.' Grace turned to Sylvia and Mary. 'Saunders, go and check the kitchen. And Finnegan, have a look in the bathroom.' Please God he had taken himself off there, she thought.

She looked at the patients to either side of Captain Jeffers' bed. They stared vacantly back at her. There was no point her asking where he had gone. They barely knew what was going on from one moment to the next.

She turned back to Dr Logan. 'I'm sorry,' she mumbled.

He said nothing, but his stony look said it all.

Sylvia and Mary returned to report that there was no sign of Captain Jeffers in the kitchen, the sluice, the scullery, the prep room or either of the bathrooms. Fighting panic, Grace was about to suggest they search the linen cupboard when the doors opened and an orderly came in, pushing a wheelchair with Captain Jeffers in it. He was pale and shivering in his rain-soaked pyjamas, his fair hair dripping.

'Lost someone, have you?' the orderly said cheerfully. 'One of the porters caught him just as he was wandering out of the main gates.'

'I was only going to get some cigarettes,' Captain Jeffers replied in injured tones. 'I told you I'd run out.'

'Lucky the porter spotted him,' the orderly said. 'He would have been halfway to Roman Road by now. And in his pyjamas too!'

'Oh, Captain Jeffers, you're freezing. Let's get you warmed up and out of those wet clothes. Nurse Saunders, run a hot bath for him. And Nurse Finnegan, prepare some hot water bottles for his bed. Oh, and we'll need some extra blankets—'

'What about my cigarettes?' Captain Jeffers complained.

'Here.' Dr Logan took a packet of Woodbines out of the pocket of his white coat and thrust them at him.

'Thank you, Doctor. You're a true gentleman. May I trouble you for a light?'

Grace cringed as Dr Logan took out a box of matches and lit the officer's cigarette. She knew she should say something, but the words wouldn't come.

'Doctor, I—' she began, but Dr Logan interrupted her.

'I'll come back and finish my round when you've sorted out this mess,' he said shortly.

Then he turned on his heel and left the ward.

Captain Jeffers blew a smoke ring into the air. 'Oh, dear. He seems rather miffed. I hope it isn't anything I've done?'

Grace stared down the ward. Dr Logan had barely looked at her since the moment she had come through the double doors.

'No, Captain,' she sighed. 'I think it's me he's miffed with.'

Chapter Eighteen

'The neurasthenia ward? But why?'

'You tell me.'

Edward's voice was flat, but Anna could sense the frustration simmering inside him.

She didn't blame him for it, either. They'd both been expecting him to be discharged at the end of the week, but this morning Dr Carlyle had announced that he was to be moved to Wilson ward.

'Have they said anything to you about it?' he asked Anna.

She shook her head. 'The first I knew was when Sister told me to pack up your things. I asked her why, but she gave me short shrift.'

'You're here to follow the doctors' orders, Nurse, not to question their decisions,' had been her exact words.

Edward sank back against the pillows with an angry sigh. 'I wish I understood why they were moving me to the shell shock ward, of all places. It's not as if I'm a gibbering wreck, is it?'

Anna paused for a moment, her hands stilling as she packed his belongings into a box. 'I suppose they must have their reasons,' she said slowly.

Edward sat up straighter. 'What?' he demanded. 'You do know something, don't you? Come on, tell me!'

Anna hesitated. 'It's just something I saw in your notes,' she said.

Edward stiffened. 'What? What did you see?'

Anna raised her gaze to meet his. 'Dr Carlyle says you've been having nightmares.'

His face lost all expression for a moment, but a tiny muscle flickered in his jaw.

'I don't know what she's talking about,' Edward dismissed. 'Everyone in this place has them. It's the ones who don't wake up screaming that you have to watch out for!'

'Yes, but it's not just screaming, is it? It says in your notes that you sometimes sleep walk, that you've been violent—'

'What rot!' Edward snapped. 'It was one night, if you must know. And I wasn't violent, as she calls it. An orderly tried to get hold of me and I lashed out in my sleep. As soon as I woke up and realised I'd clipped him, I was mortified. That hardly makes me a madman, does it?'

'Well, no, but . . .'

'Oh, so you do think I am mad, do you?' Edward's eyes flashed angrily.

'Of course not,' Anna said.

He went very still, his whole body tense. Then the fight seemed to go out of him and his shoulders slumped.

'I'm sorry. Ignore me, I'm just feeling wretched. I didn't mean to take it out on you. I'm just so disappointed, that's all.'

Anna watched him. He started to gnaw on his thumbnail, a sure sign he was sinking into a black mood. 'Try to look on the bright side,' she urged. 'It might not be for very long.'

'I hope not! The last thing I want is to be locked up with all the lunatics.' He looked at her, and Anna saw the fear and shame in his eyes. 'I'm not like them, really I'm not,' he said quietly.

He looked so scared, it was all Anna could do not to hug him. Shell shock provoked strong feelings among the men on Monaghan ward. Some rejected the very idea, claiming it was nothing more than cowardice. Others, who had witnessed it at close hand, knew better.

And some, like Edward, were terrified at the thought of being rendered weak and unmanly by their own minds.

'I know,' she said.

'Do you?' He smiled warily. 'Do you really?'

'Of course.'

'And you still want to marry me?'

'Why shouldn't I?'

'I don't know ... I can understand why you wouldn't want to, if – if what they say is true.' His gaze shifted towards the double doors and Anna knew he was worried about what awaited him on Wilson ward. Those empty, shambling shells of men, screaming in the night and jumping at shadows.

She knew that wasn't her Edward, no matter how bad his nightmares were. Yes, he might be traumatised by four years of war, but it was nothing that love and patience couldn't cure.

And she couldn't wait to make a start.

'Let's set a date for the wedding,' she said.

Edward turned sharply to face her. 'Do you mean it?'

'Why not? We've waited long enough, don't you think?'

He smiled. 'When?'

'How about Christmas?'

His mouth twisted. 'That's only a couple of weeks away. I might not even be discharged by then.'

'New Year, then. How about New Year's Eve? I'm sure you will be home by then.' Anna reached for his hand. 'Wouldn't it be wonderful to start the New Year as man and wife?'

He looked down at her hand resting in his.

'I can't think of anything I'd like more,' he said.

*

Grace was surprised to hear Edward Stanning had been transferred to Wilson. She had always thought of him as such a strong, steady type. And yet there he was when she reported for night duty, sitting up in the bed next to Corporal Frost's, a sullen expression on his face.

'I'm afraid Private Stanning has not settled in very well,' Miss Parker said when she was going through the patients' notes with Grace. 'He refuses to speak, and wouldn't even look at me earlier when I tried to talk to him. Dr Carlyle has prescribed a sedative for him this evening, but he may well refuse to take it.' She handed over his notes. 'I fear you may have your work cut out with him, Nurse.'

'I'll do my best, Sister.'

'I'm sure you will, Nurse. And at least you'll have Marchant with you. I'm sure she will be a great source of help and comfort.'

Grace caught the gleam of amusement in Miss Parker's blue eyes. 'Thank you, Sister,' she said.

When she had finished taking report from Sister, Grace helped Sylvia Saunders and Mary Finnegan hand out cups of cocoa to the patients, then assisted with the bedpans.

After that it was time for the medication round. As Sister had predicted, Edward refused his sedative.

'I don't need it, Nurse,' he insisted. 'I shall sleep quite well without it.'

'Are you sure, Private Stanning? I see from your notes your nightmares can be—'

'I'm well aware what my notes say, Nurse. But I'm telling you, I don't need a sedative.'

Grace looked at him for a moment, so solid and strong-willed, his mouth set in a stubborn line.

'Very well.' She made a note on his chart. 'But let me know if you change your mind. I'm afraid night-time on this ward can be rather lively.'

'If you can sleep standing up in a dugout, you can sleep anywhere.' He was smiling again, back to his old charming self.

'I don't know why you didn't just force him to take the sedative,' Vivienne Marchant said as she followed Grace and the medications trolley to the next bed.

'How could I?' Grace reasoned. 'Anyway, the men on this ward are fragile enough without being forced into anything.'

'He didn't seem very fragile to me.' Vivienne Marchant sniffed. 'Are you sure he belongs here? He doesn't seem like the other patients.'

'Dr Carlyle must have had her reasons for bringing him here.' Although Grace had to admit, Marchant had a point. Edward seemed far too fit and healthy for Wilson ward.

But there had been something there, the briefest loss of control, that made her feel there was more to Edward Stanning than met the eye.

Once the medication round was finished, Grace prepared to settle the ward for the night. She turned down the lamps over each bed, then placed a green cloth over her desk lamp to dim its light before settling down to make a start on the reports.

She already knew the night would not be a peaceful one. In spite of their sedatives and sleeping draughts, the men were always restless then. They sobbed and moaned in their sleep, or screamed out orders. Even the mute ones, who never spoke a word when they were awake, cried out garbled warnings of 'Fire!' and 'Watch out!' They crawled across the floor, slithering under imaginary barbed wire, or sat bolt upright, arms flailing, fending off invisible missiles. It was awful to watch them coming to life, living out their nightmares in their sleep. Grace barely sat for five minutes without having to get up and coax someone back

121

into bed, or sponge their sweating face, or hold their hands until their terrible, breathless panic subsided.

The only one who made no sound was Edward Stanning. He lay on his back, eyes wide open, staring up at the ceiling.

Grace was about to offer him the sedative again then changed her mind and went quietly back to her desk.

Shortly after midnight, the air-raid warning started. Looking out of the double doors, Grace saw the Head Porter marching down the long corridor that ran the length of the wards, followed by a retinue of porters and orderlies, all ringing bells.

'Gosh, an air raid. How exciting,' Marchant said.

'A nuisance, more like,' Grace muttered. 'I don't know why they bother warning us, when we're not expected to evacuate or anything.'

'Do you think they'll come close this time?' Vivienne Marchant went to open the curtains, but Grace said, 'No, don't. Keep them closed.'

'But I want to look outside. I do love a good air raid.'

'You might, but the men don't.' Grace looked down the ward, where the patients were starting to grow agitated.

'But it's such a thrilling sight when all those bombers pass overhead.'

'Then go down to Monaghan and open their curtains!' Grace snapped.

Vivienne Marchant flounced off, leaving Grace to walk the length of the ward with her lamp held high, checking on all the men and trying to calm them down.

Then she reached Corporal Frost's bed and realised it was empty.

' "It's a long way to Tipperary, it's a long way to go . . ." '

The faint sound, half singing, half whimpering, came from under the bed.

Sadie bent down and found herself staring into a pair of frightened eyes.

'Are you all right, Corporal Frost?' He nodded. 'Why don't you get back into bed? You'd be a lot more comfortable.'

No sooner had she said the words than the boom of the anti-aircraft guns in Victoria Park shook the windows. This was followed by another, and another, making the glasses rattle on the bedside lockers.

Corporal Frost flinched and covered his head with his arms. '*"It's a long way to Tipperary, it's a long way to go . . ."*' his muffled voice sang.

'Can't you shut him up?' Edward complained from the next bed.

'You should have taken that sedative, shouldn't you? I warned you the nights could be lively,' Grace snapped back.

There was another boom from the anti-aircraft guns, making the metal bed frames rattle.

Grace got down on her hands and knees. 'It's all right,' she said. 'They're on our side.'

She wasn't sure if Corporal Frost heard her or not, he was trembling so much.

'*"It's a long . . . It's a long . . . It's . . ."*' Grace saw his Adam's apple bobbing convulsively as he fought to find the words. But he had lost the thread of his song, and she could see his fragile self-control unravelling with it.

She slid under the bed beside him and reached for his hand. His long, bony fingers were slick with sweat.

'*"It's a long way to Tipperary,"*' she sang out. '*"It's a long way to go . . ."*'

He stared at her with wide, terrified eyes. His mouth moved along with the words, but no sound came out.

'Come on, Corporal,' Grace urged. '*"It's a long way to Tipperary . . ."*'

'Doesn't he know another song?' Edward grumbled from somewhere above her.

'Stop complaining, you miserable bugger!' Albie shouted back. 'Come on, lads, let's have a sing-song.'

There weren't many who joined in. Only a few could remember the words, but others clapped along. In the end even Edward joined in. Soon they were all singing and clapping, drowning out the sound of the bombs and the anti-aircraft guns.

Grace looked at Corporal Frost. He was singing too, tears streaming down his face.

Then, gradually, the men stopped singing, their voices fading.

'What have you stopped for?' Grace called out. 'Come on, keep singing!'

She stuck her head out from under the bed to see what was going on, only to find herself staring at a pair of highly polished black shoes. Her gaze moved slowly upwards, past long, pinstripe legs, to settle far above on a bespectacled face looking down at her.

'Hello, Nurse,' Dr Logan said. 'Would you mind telling me what you're doing?'

Grace tried to extricate herself but Corporal Frost gripped her hand tighter, holding her fast.

'I'm singing, Doctor,' she replied.

She saw his features tighten and knew it was the wrong thing to say.

'I heard that, Nurse. You have managed to drown out the noise of the air raid.'

'That was the point, Sir.'

'I beg your pardon?'

'Corporal Frost is finding the air raid quite difficult, Sir.' He was clutching her hand so tightly now, she could feel his nails piercing her skin. 'I thought if we sang, we could drown out the sound of the guns.'

'So you have, Nurse. In fact, you've drowned them out so effectively you've failed to notice they stopped several minutes ago.'

Grace paused to listen. There was only the deep, ringing silence that followed a raid.

'He's right,' she whispered to Corporal Frost. 'We can come out now, it's quite safe.'

Grace clambered out from under the bed, painfully conscious that Dr Logan was watching her every move, and also that she was as ungainly as a newborn colt.

She helped Corporal Frost back into bed and pulled the covers around him.

'I'll make you a nice cup of tea,' she promised. 'You'd like that, wouldn't you?'

Corporal Frost nodded. He had the covers pulled up to his chin so that only his wide eyes and the ruffled top of his head were visible.

Grace made her way to the kitchen, Dr Logan striding behind her. She was in trouble, and she knew it. But for once she didn't really care.

Dr Logan stood in the doorway, watching her as she put the kettle on.

'How often does Corporal Frost end up under his bed?' he asked.

'Every time there's an air raid.'

'And you always get under the bed with him?'

'Sometimes. If he's particularly nervous.'

'And the singing?'

'Mostly he sings by himself, and that's enough to calm him down. But if he's very nervous he forgets the words, and then he gets in a terrible state. I was just helping him.'

She banged the kettle down on the hob. If he was going

to give her a dressing down, she wished he would get on with it.

'Why "It's a Long Way to Tipperary"?'

'Why not?' Grace turned to face him. 'It's a jolly tune and Corporal Frost seems to like it. I did try "Keep the Home Fires Burning" once, but it seemed to make him rather agitated.'

'I see.' Dr Logan looked thoughtful for a moment, as if Grace had said something incredibly wise. Then he nodded and said, 'Good work, Nurse. Carry on.'

'Thank you, Doctor.'

And then he was gone. Grace stared, mystified, at the now empty kitchen doorway. She couldn't quite believe she had escaped another telling-off.

She listened to his footsteps echoing down the ward. He was humming softly to himself, she could hear the faintest sound under his echoing footsteps.

' "It's a long way to Tipperary, it's a long way to go . . ." '

Grace smiled to herself and went back to making the tea.

Chapter Nineteen

Oh, Lord, not again!

Sam Trevelyan saw Nurse Moore heading purposefully down the ward towards him, pushing her trolley, and his heart sank. In the past three weeks, Dulcie Moore had decided to single him out as her pet. She lavished all kinds of unwanted attention on him, bringing him books and newspapers he never read, offering him cups of tea and trying to pester him into conversation when he plainly did not want to talk.

He had tried ignoring her and being offhand with her, but she would not go away.

'Good morning, Sergeant Trevelyan,' she greeted him with that fixed smile of hers. 'How are we this morning?'

'I don't know about you,' he growled back, 'but I'm still stuck in this bed with a hole in my side and a pair of near-useless arms.'

'That's why I'm here. I'm doing your therapeutic massage today.'

Sam watched in dismay as Dulcie set out her cloths and a bottle of oil. 'Nurse Beck usually does the massage.'

'Well, you've got me for a change.' Her smile brightened. 'And I've brought your newspaper.'

'How many more times do I have to tell you, I don't read them?'

Dulcie ignored him, setting the folded paper down on his bedside locker. 'Right, let's make a start, shall we?'

Sam grudgingly allowed her to help him off with his

hospital gown. 'I wish you'd pick on someone else,' he grumbled.

'What do you mean?'

'I know why you're doing this. You're trying to impress Sister so she lets you move to the shell shock ward.'

She blushed, but didn't try to deny it.

'I suppose you want to be closer to Dr Logan?'

'How did you guess?'

'I can't think of any other reason why you'd want to go there. And frankly, I don't really care. Now why don't you go and minister to McCray or Bennett? I'm sure they'd appreciate it more.'

'Perhaps they would, but it has to be you, I'm afraid.' Nurse Moore poured oil into her palms and rubbed her hands together briskly. 'Sister has particular concerns about you, you see. She thinks you need drawing out.'

He had to admire her honesty, if nothing else.

'And what if I don't want to be drawn out?'

'Oh, I don't think you have any choice in the matter. Now, sit up, please.'

Nurse Moore's massage technique left a lot to be desired.

'Ow!' Sam yelped in pain. 'Do you have to be so rough?'

'Do you have to be such a baby?' she shot back. 'Sit forward a bit more, I can't reach your shoulder properly.'

As Sam leaned forward, he spotted something on the bottom of the trolley, half hidden by a cloth.

'Is that a magazine?'

Nurse Moore ducked guiltily, covering it with the cloth. 'Don't tell Sister, will you? One of the VADs brought it in. It's got some pictures I want to cut out.'

'Pictures?'

'Just clothes and hats and things.'

'Can I have a look?'

She pulled a face. 'I thought you didn't like to read?'

'I don't like to read newspapers. Besides, I only want to look at the pictures.'

He held out his hand. Nurse Moore bent down and retrieved the magazine, then handed it to him.

'I suppose you just want to make fun,' she mumbled.

Sam flicked through the pages of *Vogue* magazine. It was full of colourful pages showing slender, aloof women in exotic-looking fashions, alongside advertisements for jewellery from Asprey and handbags from Harrod's.

The prices made him whistle. 'I didn't know nurses were so well paid,' he said.

'Oh, I can't afford them now,' Nurse Moore said. 'But I will when I'm married.'

'And when will that be?'

'When someone asks me.'

He tried not to smile as he looked at the magazine. 'You're going to marry a rich man, then?'

'Of course.' She gave a little shrug, as if it was a foregone conclusion.

'Dr Logan?'

Nurse Moore smiled and carried on with her massaging. Sam flinched as her tensed fingers dug into his shoulder muscles.

'So you're choosing your trousseau before you've chosen your husband?' he said through gritted teeth.

'Something like that.'

'You know what you want, don't you?'

'There's nothing wrong with that.'

Now it was Sam's turn to smile. She was so sure of herself, he couldn't help envying her.

'You think it's funny?' Nurse Moore said sharply.

'Not at all. I'm just wondering what you'll do if you end up accidentally falling in love with someone penniless.'

'I won't.'

'You can't help who you fall in love with.'

Nurse Moore gave a harsh laugh. 'Goodness, Sergeant, what a romantic you are! I would never have thought it. You sound like Nurse Trott. She's always reading her penny novels and going on about true love, too.' She shook her head. 'Of course you can help it. You can choose who you fall in love with, just as you can choose what shoes to put on in the morning or what hat to wear.'

There speaks someone who's never been in love, he thought. A picture of Philippa filled his mind, and he braced himself for the familiar jab of pain.

He looked back at the magazine in his hands. 'So this is the kind of life you want, is it?'

'Why not?' Nurse Moore sounded defensive. 'What's wrong with wanting to better yourself?' She glanced over his shoulder at the magazine. 'I want to live in London, and to be able to go to the music hall and the picture house whenever I please – and to sit in a box, not in the stalls, with opera glasses and violet creams from Fortnum's.' Her words tumbled out in a rush, a faraway look in her eyes. 'And I want to take taxis everywhere, and go into Selfridge's and Harrod's and have the commissionaire open the door for me, and greet me by name. And I want a house overlooking Kensington Gardens, with a girl to do all the fetching and carrying—' She stopped herself, pressing her lips together.

Sam broke the silence. 'It all sounds very grand.'

Nurse Moore dropped her gaze, her cheeks flushing. 'I just want someone who can look after me.'

'You don't need a box at the theatre or an account at Harrod's to love someone,' he said quietly.

'Now you sound like my mother!' Nurse Moore paused, pouring more oil into her palms. 'She always says she married my father for love. Much good it did her.'

The bitterness in her voice made Sam turn and stare at her. 'Why do you say that?'

'Well, she doesn't have an easy life. My father works as a farm labourer, so they're forever moving from place to place, taking whatever jobs he can get. And when he can't find work, she has to take in washing and sewing to make ends meet. It's such a hard, horrible life for her.'

'Is she unhappy?'

'Oh, no, she seems quite content. At least, she says she is. But I don't see how she can be, when they're living hand to mouth.' Nurse Moore was pummelling away at his shoulder, taking out all her pent-up anger on his muscles. 'The point is, she could have done better for herself. She was a vicar's daughter, very well brought up. She could have married a curate and been living in a comfortable rectory now, instead of the muddy, stinking little hovels my father provides for her.'

'And you want better than that for yourself?'

'Of course. Who wouldn't?' Nurse Moore shook her head. 'I'm not going to make the same mistakes she did, that's for sure.'

They both fell silent for a while. While Nurse Moore continued her massage, Sam fought an inner battle with himself.

Don't say anything. He had promised himself he wouldn't reveal anything about himself, he wouldn't be like the other men, handing round photographs of their loved ones and sharing their letters from home. The less anyone knew about him, the better.

And yet, the words bubbled inside him, fighting to get out.

'My wife was like your mother,' he said finally. 'She was a teacher at the local village school when I met her. I suppose she thought she would marry someone with an education, who would bring her up in the world. But she met me.'

'You're married?' Nurse Moore said.

'I was. She died a year before I was called up.'

'Did you have any children?'

Sam paused for a long time. He had already given away far too much about himself.

'Three,' he said reluctantly. 'Two boys and a girl. Have you finished yet?' he demanded impatiently, before she had a chance to ask any more questions. He couldn't talk about his children. Even thinking about them was painful enough. If he had to say their names . . .

Nurse Moore looked taken aback. 'Yes, I have.'

Sam watched her in silence as she gathered up her towels and oil, and helped him back into his gown.

As she walked away, he said, 'You forgot this.'

Nurse Moore looked down at the magazine he was holding out to her. She hesitated for a moment, then snatched it out of his hand, covered it with a cloth and put it on the trolley.

He watched her walking away and smiled to himself. You had to admire Dulcie Moore's determination, if nothing else.

Poor Dr Logan, thought Sam. He had no idea what was about to hit him.

Chapter Twenty

On Christmas Eve, Edward received official notification that he was to go before a Medical Board the following week.

The letter seemed to bring out all his old fears, making him jittery and nervous.

'We knew it was going to happen sometime,' Anna tried to console him. 'And Dr French has already said he's recommending you for light duties. They'll probably just give you a desk job somewhere.'

'Yes, but it's not that simple, is it?' Edward snapped. His thumb worked at a scar on his knuckle, rubbing away at the reddened skin. 'What if they decide to keep me in here?' He looked around him. 'I'm not sure I could stand it much longer, locked away with all the lunatics!'

Anna darted a quick look around her, hoping Miss Parker had not heard. 'They won't,' she said. 'You're making good progress, aren't you?'

'So they say.'

'And you haven't had any more nightmares?'

'Not that I can remember.' He scraped at his knuckle with his thumbnail.

'Well, then. They have no reason not to discharge you.'

'I hope not.' He looked up, meeting her eyes for the first time. 'We're supposed to be getting married this time next week.'

'And we will,' Anna said.

'Yes, but—'

'Edward Stanning, I'm marrying you next week even if we have to do it right here!'

He smiled reluctantly. 'I can just see you walking down the ward in a white dress!'

'I might ask Dr Logan to give me away!'

He sent her a cautious look. 'You'd really do that?'

'What, ask Dr Logan to walk me down the aisle?'

'No! I mean – you'd marry me here? In the hospital?'

'If I had to.' Anna reached for his hand. 'I let you get away from me once, Edward. I'm not letting it happen again.'

He grinned and pulled her hands, dragging her towards him. 'Come here and give your husband-to-be a cuddle!'

'Edward! We can't, not here. What if Sister—'

He silenced her with a kiss, planting his lips firmly against hers. Anna gave in, giggling. From the other end of the ward, she heard Albie Sallis whooping encouragement.

'Look at that, Gordon. Love's young dream, eh?'

'Nurse Beck!' Sister's strident Scottish tones rang down the hall. 'What do you think you're doing?'

Anna pulled herself from Edward's embrace, straightening her cap. 'I'm sorry, Sister.'

'I should think so, too. I know it's nearly Christmas, but surely that's taking the season of goodwill too far?'

But her eyes were twinkling as she said it. Miss Parker was a good sport, unlike her friend Miss Sutton on Monaghan.

'I'd better go,' Anna whispered to Edward.

'She won't be able to stop us this time next week. We'll be married and we can do as we please.'

The way he winked at her made Anna shiver with delight. 'Let's hope you're not still in that hospital bed, then,' she teased.

'Minx! You've put all kinds of thoughts in my head now.

I'll probably have to take one of their wretched sedatives to get to sleep.'

'At least you'll have sweet dreams.'

As Anna was leaving, Edward said, 'I wish I could see you tomorrow.'

'I'd like that too,' she sighed. 'But Liesel's coming to visit, and I'd like to spend Christmas Day with her.'

'And what about spending Christmas Day with me?'

Anna saw his sulky expression and her heart sank.

'Perhaps I could come in and see you, just for an hour.'

'No, it's all right. You spend the day with your sister.'

'Are you sure? Liesel wouldn't mind . . .'

He shook his head. 'No, I'm sure I'll have a delightful day. Think of me, won't you? Stuck in here among this lot while you're enjoying Christmas.' Then he smiled and said, 'I'm joking, love. Believe me, I'd much rather be spending the day here than in the trenches like I did last year!'

But Anna still felt guilty as she trudged home that night. She had been so looking forward to seeing Liesel again; now Edward's comments had dampened her excitement.

It was the middle of the afternoon but already dark. Streetlamps cast dim pools of light on the frozen grey streets of Bethnal Green. In Columbia Road, the coster-mongers were already packing up their wares, huddled inside layers of coats and shawls, stamping their feet on the frosty ground to keep them warm.

There was a group of carol singers clustered outside Wheeler's café on the corner of Chambord Street, their plaintive song filling the cold night air.

'*Silent Night, Holy Night . . .*'

Hot tears stung Anna's eyes. How often had she listened to her father singing that same song in his native German as he worked in the bakery kitchen?

'*Stille Nacht, heilige Nacht . . .*' His light tenor voice would fill the kitchen, and Anna, her mother and Edward would find themselves joining in.

I hope you're singing again now, Papa, she thought, dashing a tear from her cheek.

She was used to seeing a queue outside the bakery on Christmas Eve, but there was no one outside the shop as Anna approached. She paused for a moment to look in the window. Her father always liked to turn the bakery window into a festive wonderland of lebkuchen, stollen and fanciful sugarwork creations at Christmas, but today the window was rather bare, with nothing more than a few dull-looking loaves on display.

She found Mrs Church in the kitchen, smoking and talking to Charlie.

'Miss Anna! We weren't expecting you till teatime.' She jumped and quickly stubbed out her cigarette.

'Sister let me go home early.' Anna looked at Charlie. He seemed unconcerned by her arrival. He lounged in the open back doorway, puffing on a cigarette of his own and blowing leisurely smoke rings out into the yard.

'We were just taking a well-earned break. Poor Charlie's been rushed off his feet all morning, haven't you?'

Charlie shrugged, said nothing.

'There don't seem to be many customers at the moment,' Anna said. 'They used to be queuing halfway down Chambord Street before Christmas.'

'The only queue you'll see now is down the soup kitchen,' Charlie spoke up at last.

'He's right,' Mrs Church said. 'Terrible shame, it is. All those poor women as have lost their husbands, trying to manage on a widow's allowance. And with the shortages, and the prices going up, they can't afford to feed their children.' She shook her head. 'I count myself lucky that my kids were nearly grown up when my Ron was taken, God rest his soul.' She crossed herself. 'Otherwise I reckon we would have ended up in the workhouse, like a lot of the families round here.'

'I didn't realise it was that bad,' Anna said.

'Oh, it's awful. I can't tell you. Some of the stories I hear – well, it'd break your heart.'

'For heaven's sake, don't tell her any stories like that. She'll be giving the bread away.'

Anna swung around. There was Liesel, her arms full of baggage and presents. The winter weather suited her, bringing a rosy flush to her fair skin. She was wrapped up in a fashionably loose woollen coat, a felt hat pulled low over her blonde head.

'Liesel!' Anna rushed to hug her. 'It's so good to see you.'

'Careful, you'll squash my wares.' Her sister dumped the bags down on the ground and wrapped her arms around Anna. 'I come bearing gifts,' she said. 'The farmer's wife insisted on sending me home with a cake, two Christmas puddings and a chicken she killed and plucked this morning.' She pulled a face. 'It smells awful. You can't imagine the looks I got from the other passengers on the train. I swear they thought it was me.'

Anna looked sideways at Charlie. He was staring at Liesel, slack-jawed, cigarette hanging loosely from his lower lip. Anna wasn't surprised. Liesel had inherited their mother's blonde beauty, while Anna was slight, sharp-featured and dark like their father.

But as usual Liesel was heedless of anyone but herself.

'Help me get these things upstairs, will you?' she said, pulling off her gloves. 'I simply must have a rest. That train was packed as tight as a tin of sardines . . .'

And then she was off, leaving Anna to carry her bags.

There was a familiar blue envelope propped on the mantelpiece. Anna spotted it straight away, but Liesel got to it first.

'What's this?' She picked it up. 'A letter for you, from France? Who could that be from? I wonder.' She sent Anna an arch look.

'Give it to me.'

'Does Edward know you're writing to another man?' Liesel asked.

'That's none of your business.'

'I can't imagine he'd be too pleased. I know Davy wouldn't like it at all. And Tom Franklin, of all people. You know how much Edward always loathed him . . .'

'Edward would understand,' Anna insisted firmly.

'If you say so. Well? Aren't you going to open it?'

'I'll open it later.' Anna slipped the letter into her coat pocket.

'Why? What have you got to hide?' Liesel sent her an eager, searching look. 'Are you worried I'll see it's full of sweet nothings?'

'No!' Anna batted her away playfully. 'It's nothing like that. Tom's a friend.'

'How dull.' Liesel looked bored. 'Mind you, I couldn't imagine Tom Franklin spouting love poetry. As I recall, he could barely string three words together!'

You'd be surprised, Anna thought. Tom's letters showed a sensitive, caring side she could never have imagined before. There were no sweet nothings, as Liesel put it, and certainly nothing that could cause Edward any jealousy. They were just good friends, that was all.

Christmas Eve had always been special for the Beck family, the time when they celebrated their father's German traditions.

Even when he was locked up in the internment camp, Dorothy had still cooked fish with potato fritters and sauerkraut on Christmas Eve, and they had opened their presents and sung songs and remembered Papa.

This year, Anna had insisted on carrying on the tradition. But even she had to admit there was a hollow ring to their laughter as they sat in front of the fire, opening their gifts by the light of the Christmas candles.

'It isn't the same, is it?' Liesel said mournfully.

'No,' Anna sighed. 'No, it isn't.'

'Do you remember how lovely it used to be, the four of us together?' Liesel sniffed back her tears. 'I wonder what Mother and Papa are doing now?'

'I expect they're lighting their candles and cooking fish and thinking about us, just as we are them,' Anna said.

'I daresay Papa's singing, as usual.' Liesel smiled through her tears. '"*Ir Kinderlein, kommet, O kommet doch all*,"' she sang in a high, quavering voice.

'"*Zur Krippe her kommet in Bethlehems Stall*,"' Anna joined in.

Liesel dissolved into tears. 'Oh, Anna, I miss them so much,' she sobbed.

'I know, love.' Anna put her arms around her sister, holding her close. 'But we'll be together again one day, I promise. And in the meantime, there's nothing to stop us having a nice Christmas together, just the two of us. Especially as your friend the farmer's wife has been so generous . . .'

Liesel pulled away. 'But – that food isn't for us,' she blurted out. 'It's for Davy's family. His mother has invited me to spend Christmas Day with them.' Her face reddened. 'I'm sorry, I assumed you'd be working tomorrow . . .'

'I took the day off so I could spend it with you.'

'Oh.' Liesel fell silent, biting her lip. 'I don't know what to do.'

'You'll have to tell Davy's mother you've decided to spend Christmas with me instead.'

'But I can't do that!' Liesel looked horrified. 'They're expecting me. And I never see Davy . . .'

'You see more of him than you do me,' Anna pointed out.

Liesel went quiet again and Anna could almost see her sister's mind whirring, trying to work out how to get what she wanted.

'You know, I thought you might be happy for me,' she said in a small, choked voice. 'Davy's parents have been very kind to me since Mother and Papa left. They've welcomed me into their family, made me feel as if I really have somewhere to belong . . .'

'And what about me?'

'You've got Edward,' Liesel said. 'You're going to be married next week, then you'll be off together and I'll be the one left out.'

'I'd never leave you out!'

'No, but you'll have a husband, and that makes everything different.' Liesel pleaded with her for understanding. 'I know you don't like it, Anna, but things change. We can't stay as we are forever, sitting by the fire with our candles and our Christmas presents. Mother and Papa have gone, and now we have to make our own lives too.'

'Fine.' Anna turned away from her, staring into the flickering flames. 'Go and spend Christmas with your precious Davy. I hope they enjoy their chicken and their wretched Christmas cake.'

'They won't,' Liesel said. 'The farmer's wife is a terrible cook. One of the other Land Girls broke her tooth on a mince pie the other day.'

They looked at each other for a moment, and then they both burst out laughing. Honestly, Anna thought, it would

140

be a lot easier if she could stay angry with her sister for more than five minutes.

'Why don't you come with me?' Liesel said. 'I'm sure Davy's mother wouldn't mind.'

'I'm sure she would,' Anna said. 'Besides, I don't want to spend Christmas Day watching you and Davy making sheep's eyes at each other.'

'But I can't bear to think of you being on your own on Christmas Day.'

'I won't. I'll go back to the hospital. I'm sure Sister would welcome an extra pair of hands, especially as most of the VADs have gone home to their families. And I'll be able to see Edward,' she added. That would cheer him up, at least.

Liesel left early on Christmas morning, hurrying off to catch her train in another flurry of bags and luggage. She seemed so grown up, Anna thought as she watched her walking away down the road.

Why did everything have to change so fast? It hardly seemed like any time ago that Liesel was a chubby little toddler, holding tightly to Anna's hand, her fair curls bobbing. Now she was a young woman, and soon she would probably be married too.

The bakery felt too large and too lonely without her sister. Anna couldn't wait to leave and return to the sanctuary of the hospital, where she could be with her friends. The warm, happy atmosphere of Christmas on the ward would soon help melt away her loneliness.

This is the last Christmas I'll be on my own, she reminded herself. This time next year, she and Edward would be celebrating together, and she would never have to feel so alone again.

As she was putting on her coat to leave, she found Tom's

letter in the pocket. Still in her coat and hat, she sat down at the kitchen table to read it.

But there was no letter. Instead Tom had sent her a Christmas card of sorts, a roughly drawn caricature of three soldiers sitting on a hay bale, rifles at their feet and tin helmets at rakish angles on their heads. Each was holding a Christmas pudding in their hands, and underneath were scrawled the words 'Merry Christmas and all the best for 1918 from up the line'.

She recognised the dark curly hair of the figure in the middle: Tom. Seeing him sitting there grinning, made her realise she had never really seen him smile before.

Inside the card, he had scrawled her name and added, *'I hope you are keeping well. I had a couple of days' leave after we took Flesquieres, and I found this in the village shop. I hope you don't mind me sending it to you. Best wishes, your friend Tom.'* Then he'd added, *'P.S. Thank you for the socks. They were most useful.'*

Anna tipped the envelope and a tiny brooch fell into her palm. It was shaped like a bluebell, the petals coloured in deep blue enamel.

Anna stared at it, tears spilling down her cheeks. How typical of Tom to think about her. And how selfish she was, feeling sorry for herself when he and his pals were facing a far worse Christmas than she could ever imagine.

She pinned the brooch to her lapel and set off for the Nightingale.

Chapter Twenty-One

Grace was looking forward to going home for Christmas.

It was so long since she had been down to Devon, she could feel herself relaxing with every mile as the overnight train passed out of the city and rumbled its way west, the houses giving way to rolling green fields.

It was a pity the train was so crowded. Grace had to spend the whole journey wedged between a large woman who smelled of mothballs, and an elderly man who lolled on her shoulder and snored all the way down to Plymouth.

But it more than made up for it when, on Christmas morning, Grace was able to step down on to the platform and breathe in the fresh country air.

There was no one to meet her at the station, but she wasn't surprised. With so many children to think about, her parents could hardly be expected to keep track of them all. Besides, it was only a five-mile walk and the weather was fine, brisk and cold and sunny, just the way Grace liked it.

All the same, after a couple of miles she began to wish she had not brought so many presents with her as she struggled with her bags down the country lane.

She heard the slow, steady clop of horse's hooves on the lane behind her, then a voice called out, 'Miss Grace?'

She swung round, squinting into the sun. Coming towards her, silhouetted again the morning light, was a swaying cart pulled by an elderly piebald horse. As it drew closer, she recognised the man in the driver's seat as Noah Wells, a friend of her father's. He owned the farm that adjoined the Duffields' land. Their families had farmed next to each other for five generations, so her father said.

'Good morning, Mr Wells. Merry Christmas,' Grace called up to him.

'What? Oh, yes. Merry Christmas to you, too. Back from London, are you?' he asked in his thick West Country burr.

'Yes, I've come to spend Christmas with my family.'

'Hop up and I'll give you a lift.' He jerked his head towards the cart. 'You can sling your bags in the back.'

'Thank you, that's very kind.' Grace had no trouble hurling her suitcases over the tailboard of the cart. Her father always said she was as strong as any of her older brothers. 'I don't want to take you out of your way, so if you could drop me at the crossroads—'

'It's not out of my way. I'm going by your place, as it happens. I can drop you at the door.'

He put out a hand to haul her up beside him. He was in his early forties, a couple of years younger than her father, but there was not a thread of grey in his jet-black hair. Her sister-in-law Jessie reckoned he used boot blacking on it.

He jingled the harness and set the horse plodding again. Grace sat next to him, jolting from side to side with the steady sway of the cart. It was all she could do to hold herself upright and stop bumping against his shoulder.

They were both silent. Grace looked around her, admiring how the wintry sun made the frost on the bare tree branches sparkle like diamonds.

'You'll have heard about my wife?' Noah's gruff voice suddenly broke the silence, startling her.

'Yes. Mother wrote to tell me. I was sorry to hear about it.'

'Influenza.' He kept his eyes fixed on the road ahead of him. 'It'll be four months come January.'

Grace nodded. She barely remembered Mrs Wells. She was such a quiet, inoffensive little woman. 'It's a terrible shame.'

'Ah.'

They carried on, the silence stretching awkwardly between them. It was a relief when the cart finally turned off the lane and made its way up the stony track that led to the Duffields' farm.

Grace heard the farm before she saw it. The squawk of the hens mingled with the sound of the dog barking and the low moo of the cows in the byre. Then there were the shrieks of her younger brothers and sisters, and the clatter of metal on cobbles as they chased a hoop around the yard, and the sound of a baby crying.

And rising above it all was the high-pitched sound of her sisters-in-law arguing.

Grace smiled to herself. Anyone who thought the country was a peaceful place had never been to Ezekiel Duffield's farm. But how she had missed it!

Grace's father was proud that his family had lived and worked on the same land for more than two hundred years. But with Grace's brothers away at war, and only her father and younger brothers to take care of the place, the old farm was starting to show its age. The muddy farmyard was edged by an untidy collection of ramshackle barns and outbuildings no one had ever quite got around to fixing. The yard was littered with rusty old bits of farm machinery.

Overlooking the yard was the old farmhouse where Grace had grown up. The whitewashed walls had faded to grey with age, and the thatched roof hung low over the small mullioned windows, thick and untidy.

Grace went to climb down from the cart but Noah was there before her, putting out a callused hand to help her.

The door to the cow barn flew open and her father

145

appeared, tall and burly with a shock of grey hair and beard that seemed to encircle his whole face so only a stubby nose and a pair of bright hazel eyes peeped out.

He gave Grace a curt nod, then said to Noah, 'You've found her, then?'

'We met on the lane.'

The next moment the two dogs ran out to greet her, Patch bounding ahead, followed more sedately by his arthritic mother Jory. Then Grace's brothers and sisters came running around the corner, clamouring to know what was in her bags.

'Have you brought presents? Are they for us?'

'Give your sister room to breathe, for pity's sake!' Ezekiel Duffield swiped left and right with his arm, scattering them. 'Go and see your mother,' he said to Grace. 'I daresay she'll have work for you to do.'

Then he and Noah went off together, shambling past the cow barn towards the fields beyond.

Inside the farmhouse it was bedlam, as usual, with pans bubbling on the stove, clothes horses draped with washing steaming gently in front of the fire, and several small children waddling around. There seemed to be several more than the last time Grace had visited, but she wasn't surprised. If her mother wasn't pregnant, then one or other of her sisters-in-law usually was.

Her mother swept a crawling baby off the stone-flagged floor and dumped him in Grace's arms.

'Here, make yourself useful and change him,' she said. 'He stinks to high heaven.'

Grace looked at her two sisters-in-law, Jessie and Beth. For the moment they seemed to be at peace, standing beside each other, peeling and chopping vegetables. They gave her a sly look over their shoulders, then Jessie whispered something to Beth and they both laughed.

As her mother handed the baby over, Grace noticed the tell-tale bulge under her loose dress.

'You're expecting again?' she said. 'You didn't tell me.'

Her mother shrugged. 'It hardly seemed worth mentioning after so many.'

Grace settled down to change the baby's nappy beside the fire. It had barely been ten minutes since she had arrived, and she had fitted so seamlessly back into the chaos of Duffield family life, she felt as if she had never been away.

Or so she thought.

'You talk funny now, Grace,' Jessie threw over her shoulder accusingly. 'Don't you reckon, Beth? She sounds like a Londoner now.'

'I don't!'

'I don't!' Jessie mimicked.

Grace glared at her. Growing up with nothing but older brothers, there was a time when she had longed for them to marry so she would have a friend. But Jessie and Beth were like a pair of angry cats.

'What's happened while I've been away?' she asked her mother, ignoring Jessie as she mimicked the words to Beth.

'Now, let's see . . . Your father's sold some of the cows at market. Got a good price for them, too. Ned Wibberley – you know, the one up at Tuppers Farm? He bought them.'

'What about Matthew, and Mark and Luke? Any news of them?'

Her mother shook her head. 'We get letters, but they don't say much, really.'

'John's going to join up after Christmas,' Beth said.

'But he's only sixteen!'

Beth shrugged. 'He'll lie about his age like the rest of 'em, I s'pose.'

Grace turned to her mother. 'You can't let him, Mother. He's too young.'

147

'He'll do what he pleases, I daresay. Just like his brothers.'

Grace thought of John, out playing in the yard with his younger brothers and sisters. He was just a kid. She couldn't bear the thought of him going off to fight, maybe ending up like the men she looked after at the Nightingale, hollow-eyed shadows, incapable of laughter.

'You've pinned that nappy too tight.' Jessie's critical voice dragged her out of her reverie.

'Sorry.' Grace unfastened the pin and redid it.

'Now it's too loose.' Jessie tutted. 'Here, let me do it.' She came over and nudged Grace out of the way. 'I would have thought you'd know all about this sort of thing, being a nurse.'

'Yes, but she's not a mother, is she?' Beth said smugly.

'Enough of that, you two. I reckon Gracie's changed more nappies than you two put together, what with all my lot. Take no notice of them,' her mother said to Grace, 'they might seem thick as thieves but the only time they're not bickering is when they've got you to pick on.'

Grace went over to the window, cleared a patch in the grimy glass and peered out. Her father and Noah were trudging back down from the top field.

'What business has Mr Wells got with Father?' she asked.

'Well might you ask!' Beth muttered, and she and Jessie both laughed.

'Noah's buying some of our land,' her mother explained.

Grace looked at her in surprise. 'Father always said he'd never sell an acre of Duffield land!'

'Times are hard,' Beth said. Then she turned to Jessie. 'The way things are going, there won't be anything left of the farm for your Matthew to inherit.'

'At least he'll get something,' Jessie shot back. 'Your

Mark will be a farmhand for the rest of his life, working other people's land.'

'Unless Matthew doesn't come home from the war?'

Jessie turned on her, knife in her hand. 'Beth Duffield! You take that back this minute, you witch! '

The next minute they were at each other, slapping and tugging handfuls of hair. Grace's mother ignored them.

'Your father has also invited Noah to stay for Christmas dinner,' she said to Grace. 'It seems the Christian thing to do, since he'll be on his own otherwise.'

'For now,' Beth said. Jessie immediately stopped fighting her and the pair of them collapsed in a fit of giggles.

Grace stared at them. Sometimes it was as if Jessie and Beth had a secret code that only they understood.

Chapter Twenty-Two

It felt awkward, having a stranger at the Christmas dinner table. But at least Noah Wells helped to fill one of the empty spaces left by Grace's three brothers.

All the same, she wished her mother hadn't insisted on placing her next to him. For once, she was glad of her younger brothers and sisters making their usual din, as it saved her from having to make conversation.

His presence made her nervous, and several times she had managed to slip with the spoon and tip vegetables over the tablecloth. Once, when she was passing him the gravy boat, she had managed to tip its contents into his lap, much to Jessie and Beth's amusement.

She could feel them now, watching her closely from across the table.

'Thank you for inviting me to share your feast, Sarah.' Noah's voice was deep and gruff. He was a lay preacher at the Methodist chapel, and Grace could imagine his voice booming out from the pulpit on Sunday morning. He must strike fear into all the sinners, she thought. 'It's most charitable of you.'

'It's the least we can do, Noah, after your tragic loss.' Grace's mother said demurely. 'She was a good woman, your Matilda.'

'Indeed,' Noah said gravely. 'She is with God now.' He raised his eyes to the ceiling. 'But I must say, the farmhouse is very lonely without her.'

Beth gave a muffled snort, which sounded like a cough.

Only Grace, looking across the table, could see she was laughing.

'Farming is a lonely life, to be sure, unless you have a companion,' her father agreed.

'There's no chance of being lonely in this house!' Grace laughed. 'Not with all these children.'

'Alas, Miss Grace, Matilda and I would have loved children, but we were not blessed.' Noah turned to her, his gaze solemn under his bushy brows. His eyes seemed to be as coal black as his hair. It was difficult to see where his pupils ended and his irises began.

'There is still time, Noah, I'm sure.'

A long silence followed her words, and once again Grace felt as if all eyes were turned to her. She was so confused she dropped her fork with a clatter on the stone-flagged floor.

'How are you enjoying your nursing in London, Miss Grace?' Noah asked when she had retrieved it.

'Very much, thank you, Mr Wells. I'm working on the ward with shell shock patients, which is very interesting and rewarding—'

'But it's only something to do until she gets married,' her father put in.

Grace stared at her father, seated at the head of the table. She wondered why he would ever say such a thing, since it was widely acknowledged that she was the awkward spinster of the family. One of the reasons she had been sent off to London to train as a nurse was because he had been certain no one would ever want to marry her.

'You won't inherit the farm and I can't afford to pay someone to take you, so you might as well learn how to earn your own living and make yourself useful,' were his exact words.

'I'm sure you'll make someone a wonderful wife one

151

day, Miss Grace,' Noah said. His eyes met hers as he wiped his mouth with his napkin.

'I doubt it, Mr Wells,' Grace hooted with laughter.

'You're too modest,' her mother said. 'You have a lot to offer. Your cooking, for instance. She's a wonder in the kitchen,' she said to Noah.

'Am I?' Grace looked at her blankly. This was the first she'd heard of it. Her mother was forever scolding her for burning things.

Sarah Duffield stood up to clear the plates, then winced and put her hand to the small of her back.

'Are you all right, Mother?' Grace asked.

'Stop fussing,' her father dismissed. 'It's not as if she hasn't had a baby before, is it?'

'Eleven children,' Sarah Duffield smiled. 'It's like shelling peas.'

'It's what women were made for,' Grace's father said, kicking out at Patch, who was scrounging under the table for the gravy Grace had spilled.

'I think they were made for more than that, Father,' Grace murmured, staring down at her plate.

'Hark at her!' Jessie mocked. 'Did you hear that, Pa? Our Gracie has turned into a suffragette!'

'Nonsense, Gracie is a good girl. She doesn't hold with all that nonsense.'

'Actually, we have a woman doctor at the hospital now,' Grace started to say, but her mother drowned her out by clattering the plates as she collected them up.

Grace stood to help her, but her father said, 'No, let Beth and Jessie help. You stay here, Gracie.'

She stared helplessly after her mother and sisters-in-law, wishing she could join them. But as it was, she had to sit and listen to Noah and her father discussing stock prices and the various yields of arable acres. Then, much to her horror, her father told her to fetch the tobacco and light Noah's pipe for him, and her hands shook so much she nearly set fire to his shirt front. Luckily, he didn't seem to mind.

It wasn't until Noah Wells had finally gone and her father had disappeared off to do the milking that Grace found out what was going on.

'How do you like Noah Wells?' her mother asked, as she washed up at the big stone sink.

'He's all right.' Grace shrugged, reaching for a plate to dry.

'Do you like him enough to marry him?' Beth asked slyly.

Grace frowned at her. 'What?'

Jessie sighed. 'That's what all this is about, you goose. Why else do you think Pa invited Noah Wells for Christmas dinner?'

Grace swung round to face her mother. But Sarah Duffield's face was implacable as she rinsed off another plate and set it on the draining board.

'Mother, is this true?'

'Noah is keen, and your father thinks it would be a good idea,' she said, her eyes fixed on the greasy water. 'Noah's a good man, and he needs a wife.'

'And he owns a lot of land,' Beth put in. 'If you married him, one day your children might own the whole valley.'

'Not the whole valley,' Jessie muttered.

'More than your Matthew will,' Beth replied, pulling a face.

Grace could hardly take it in. 'You want me to marry Mr Wells? But he's as old as Father!'

'He's very rich,' Beth said.

'Even if he does put boot black on his hair,' Jessie added.

'Imagine trying to scrub that off the pillows!' Beth said, and they both fell about laughing.

'Shut up, you two!' Sarah Duffield snapped. The other two fell into sulky silence.

She turned to Grace. 'How old are you now? Twenty-five? I had six children by the time I was your age. You're not getting any younger, Grace. You need to start thinking about your future.'

'But I thought my future was to be nursing?'

Her mother sighed. 'Surely you don't want to empty bedpans for the rest of your life? Not when you could have a husband and a home of your own. And what about when you're too old for nursing? What will you do then?'

'I – I don't know. I hadn't really thought about it.'

'Well, you should. If you're sensible, you'll marry Noah and be well set up for the rest of your life.'

Grace's fear must have shown on her face because her mother's voice softened. 'Look, he's a good man, a kind man. He'd treat you well. Believe me, there are worse men you could marry.' She wiped her hands on her apron and rested them on Grace's shoulders. 'It would be a weight off my mind, and your father's. To tell you the truth, he's been struggling to make ends meet with the boys gone. That's why he's had to sell off some of the herd, and that field to Noah. But if you married into the Wells family . . . well, think of it as a way to repay your father after everything he's done for you, putting a roof over your head all these years.'

She sent Grace a considering look. 'Promise me you'll think about it, at least?'

Chapter Twenty-Three

Dulcie never minded working on Christmas Day. The ward was always a very festive place, with a huge, glittering tree beside Sister's desk, and paper chains festooned from the light fittings. Sister was usually in a better mood, too, buoyed up on a tot of medicinal brandy. If she was in a really good mood, the nurses would be offered a nip too, or at least some morning coffee. If they were really lucky, Sister would buy them a box of chocolates to share between them.

After breakfast, the chaplain would come to lead prayers, followed by a choir of nurses singing Christmas carols. Then the men's families would arrive for a visit, which was always a very happy time. Later there would be a roast goose served at the long ward table, the bird carved by one of the surgeons while the men jeered and joked grimly about his skills.

And then it would be time for the Christmas show. Any patient who was fit enough would be moved down to the staff dining room, where the nurses and doctors would entertain them with songs and skits and monologues.

This was the part of the day Dulcie was most excited about. Because there she would be able to see Dr Logan again.

Since he had moved full-time to Wilson, Dulcie had only had the briefest of tantalising glimpses of him, not nearly enough for her to work her magic. She had had to rely on Grace Duffield for all the news, and she was utterly hopeless.

'I'm truly sorry, Moore, but I don't know anything,' she had said last time Dulcie pestered her for information. 'Can't you ask someone else? Finnegan or Saunders? I'm sure they're friendlier with him than I am.'

The idea of asking Sylvia Saunders for help made Dulcie shudder.

'But you work with Dr Logan every day. Surely you must speak to him?' she had insisted.

'Not if I can help it,' Grace replied firmly.

Dulcie couldn't understand it. If *she* was working alongside Dr Logan, they would be practically engaged by now. It had all made her even more determined to get herself moved to Wilson ward.

In the meantime, she was pinning all her hopes on the Christmas show. Dr Logan was bound to be there and Dulcie had made sure she was looking her best. She was going to be singing "The Boy I Love Is Up in the Gallery", dressed as Marie Lloyd, complete with an extravagant feathered hat and a parasol.

And she was going to make sure Robert Logan knew she was singing it to him.

Dulcie could hardly wait. But before then, she had to put up with Sylvia Saunders trilling on about the duet she was planning to perform with Roger.

'I'm so nervous about it,' she had confessed with a fluttery little laugh at breakfast that morning. 'I've never performed in public before.'

Then, as all the other nurses fussed around her, reassuring her that her voice was angelic and she would do very well, Dulcie couldn't resist putting in, 'Oh, if you're half as good as Roger and I were last year, you'll be fine. I seem to remember we brought the house down with our duet last Christmas. Not that anyone will be comparing, I'm sure,' she had added with an arch look.

That had shut her up. Sylvia blushed deeply and changed the subject.

'Why did you have to say that?' Anna scolded Dulcie in a whisper.

'Oh, she deserves to be brought down a peg or two,' Dulcie dismissed. 'She's so smug, constantly talking about her fiancé this and her fiancé that.'

'She's just happy,' Anna said, but Dulcie wasn't listening.

'Honestly, I'll be glad when this wretched wedding is over,' she said. 'I don't think I can stand listening to her going on and on about it for another five months!'

'Talking of weddings,' Anna said, looking down at her hands, 'Edward and I are getting married.'

'Well, yes, I know that.' Dulcie buttered another slice of toast. 'You've been engaged for as long as I've known you.'

'No, you don't understand. We're getting married on Monday.'

Dulcie stopped, the piece of toast halfway to her mouth. 'Monday? You mean – next Monday? New Year's Eve?' Anna nodded. 'But that's a bit soon, isn't it?'

'Hardly. You said yourself we've been engaged a long time.'

'But how will you organise it all in such a short time?'

'Oh, there's nothing to organise, really. I've booked the register office and managed to get a special licence. All we really need are the two of us.'

She looked quite happy about it, but Dulcie knew a poky little register office in a back street of Bethnal Green would never do for her.

She was still thinking about it when she reported for duty that morning. It was one of her favourite daydreams, picturing her perfect wedding day. When she married, she wanted a big wedding, the kind that might appear in the society pages of *Tatler*. There would be a host of glamorous guests, but of course none would look more beautiful than the bride, in her stunning white gown.

And Robert Logan would make the perfect bridegroom. An elegantly cut morning suit would really show off his sleek dark good looks. She could just imagine the photographs . . .

'Nurse Moore! You've been cleaning that same patch of floor for the past twenty minutes!'

Sister's harsh voice brought Dulcie sharply back to earth. The beneficial effects of the medicinal brandy had obviously worn off, judging by the scowl on Miss Sutton's face.

'When you've quite finished, kindly take your mop and bucket to the toilets. They'll need to be clean before the visitors come.'

At midday, the visitors began to arrive. They lined up outside the double doors, necks craning, faces pressed against the glass, eager to catch a glimpse of their husbands, sons, fathers and brothers. Inside the ward, the men sat upright, smoothing down their hair and straightening their pyjamas. Most of the men who could get out of bed had changed into hospital uniforms, so as to look their best for their loved ones.

'I do look all right, don't I, Nurse?' Private Anderson looked up at Dulcie as she knotted his tie for him. He was smiling, but the anxious bobbing of his Adam's apple gave him away. 'Don't want to frighten my missus and kids.'

Dulcie looked down at the young soldier, the empty left sleeve of his uniform carefully arranged so as not to draw attention to his missing arm.

'You look very handsome, Private,' she assured him.

Private Anderson blushed. 'I dunno about that,' he mumbled. 'Anyway, you'd better not let my Elsie hear you saying that, or she might get jealous!'

As the bell in the clock tower struck noon, Miss Sutton

gave the nod for the VADs to open the doors, and the families poured in.

'Isn't it wonderful?' Eliza Parrish, the youngest of them, wiped away a tear as she watched them all hugging each other. 'To see them all reunited again – well, it almost makes up for us not being with our own families, doesn't it?'

'Oh, do buck up, Parrish!' Dulcie sent her a withering look. Eliza was barely eighteen, and far too sentimental. She regularly burst into tears while reading the soldiers' letters from home. Sister despaired of her, and Dulcie just found her irritating.

Not all the soldiers had visitors. Some of their families lived too far away, like Sergeant McCray's. Others, like Corporal Stanley's, were too old and infirm themselves to travel. These were the ones who moved Dulcie, far more than the men involved in gushing reunions. It was so hard to watch them acting as if they didn't mind, with forced laughter and fixed smiles. Some played cards or did a crossword, keeping their eyes averted from the visitors clustered around the other beds. But some of the younger ones couldn't keep up the pretence and wept softly into their pillows.

Sergeant Trevelyan did neither. He sat bolt upright in bed as usual, staring around the ward with his usual look of grim determination, as if he was somehow challenging himself not to feel any pain.

'You weren't expecting a visitor, were you, Sergeant?' Dulcie asked when she brought him a cup of tea.

'No.'

'I suppose it is rather a long way to travel up from Cornwall.'

'It would be – if they knew where I was.'

Dulcie stared at him in surprise. 'You haven't told them?'

'They know I've been injured, and that I'm in England.'

'But why don't you want them to know where you are?'

'That's my business.'

Dulcie had heard his sharp tone too often to be put off by it. She placed the teacup on his locker, beside his book. She had managed to coax him into borrowing a copy of *David Copperfield* from the little lending library that came to the hospital wards once a week. But from what she could see he hadn't even opened it.

'It might do you good to see them,' she said.

Sam Trevelyan turned on her, his green eyes cold. 'I really wish you would go and feel sorry for someone else, because I don't need it.'

'I was only saying—'

'Don't.'

She adjusted his bed tray, then placed the cup down in front of him. 'I suppose you haven't told them about your medal, either?' Sam still did not reply. 'I'm sure your sons would love to know their father is a hero—'

'Don't say that,' Sam cut her short. 'I'm no hero.'

'How can you say that? You stayed out in No Man's Land for over an hour, under rifle and bomb fire, bringing in the wounded. Everyone else ran, but you stayed put.'

'There is no medal,' Sam said.

'But I saw it.'

'I threw it away.'

'Why?'

'Because I didn't want it.' He said it in a low voice, not looking at her. 'Anyway, why do I need a piece of metal to remind me when I've got this?' He grimaced down at the dressing on his side.

Dulcie glanced along the ward to where Private Anderson was sitting up in bed, his wife at his side, his one arm curled around both his children. His face was suffused with happiness, all his earlier anxiety forgotten.

'How did you know?' Sam said suddenly.

'What?'

'About – what happened?' He looked up at her. 'I've never told anyone.'

Dulcie felt herself blushing. She wanted to lie, but his steady gaze seemed to draw the truth out of her. 'I looked it up in Staff Nurse Hanley's *London Gazette*,' she confessed.

'Now why would you do something like that?' Sam said softly.

'I was just curious.'

For a moment they looked at each other, then he said, 'Don't look now, but the man of your dreams has just walked in.'

Dulcie glanced over her shoulder. There, in the doorway, stood Dr Logan.

'Well, don't just stand there,' Sam said. 'Go and impress him.'

'I really don't know what you mean,' Dulcie said huffily. But she was already hurrying down the ward, conscious of Sam's cynical gaze on her every step of the way.

'Can I help you, Dr Logan?' Miss Sutton was not on the ward, so Dulcie managed to get to him first.

'I'm looking for Sister. Is she about?' Dr Logan's gaze skimmed past her, searching the crowded ward.

'I'm afraid Sister always takes refuge in her sitting room during visiting time. Was there something I can help you with?'

'Miss Sutton asked me to come and assess a patient. She thinks he might need to be moved to the neurasthenia ward.' He looked around, frowning. 'But I can see I've come at a difficult time. Tell her I'll come back later.'

'No!' Dulcie caught Dr Logan's startled look and realised she had spoken too loudly. 'I mean, I know the patient Sister means. Corporal Kavanagh, bed ten.' She was relieved that for once she had bothered to pay attention during Sister's morning report. 'I'll take you to him, shall I?'

Dr Logan hesitated. 'It might be best if I speak to Sister.'

'I'm sure she would want you to see him as soon as possible,' Dulcie said. 'I know she's rather worried about him. He's very agitated.'

'Is he?' Dr Logan consulted his notes, his dark brows drawing together. 'Sister didn't mention that. Oh, well, in that case, I suppose I'd better take a look straight away.'

Corporal Kavanagh was fast asleep, as usual.

'He doesn't seem very agitated,' Dr Logan remarked.

'You wait until he wakes up. We have a terrible job trying to calm him down.'

It was a slight exaggeration. In fact, Corporal Kavanagh was as docile as a lamb. It was the number of hours he slept that concerned Sister, not his agitation. But Dulcie was prepared to say anything to keep Dr Logan on the ward.

She watched as he examined a rather dazed and sleepy Corporal Kavanagh, all the while trying desperately to think of something to say.

'We don't see you on Monaghan very often,' she finally managed to blurt out.

'No.' Dr Logan paused to scribble some notes. 'I don't have much cause to visit these days. Besides, my work on Wilson keeps me busy.'

'Not too busy to come to the Christmas show, I hope?'

She would never usually have been so forward. But she could tell Dr Logan had nearly finished his examination. Soon he would be gone, and her chance with it.

He blinked at her. 'What Christmas show?'

'You must have heard about the Christmas show? We put it on every year for the patients. They have such fun. I'm Marie Lloyd this year.'

'Really? I'm sorry I won't be there to see it.'

Dulcie's stomach plummeted with disappointment. 'You're not coming?'

'I'm not on call this evening. Are you sure this patient is agitated?' he asked.

'What? Oh, yes. Sometimes. Can't you come anyway?' Dulcie said.

'I have other plans.' He added his signature to the notes and placed them back at the foot on Corporal Kavanagh's bed. 'Please tell Sister I will come back and speak to her about Corporal Kavanagh this afternoon.'

He had turned and was starting to walk away. Dulcie stared after him, helplessly.

She heard a muffled snort to her left. She glanced around to see Sam Trevelyan watching her, almost with a smile.

Then a thought struck her.

'Dr Logan?' she called after him, following him down the ward.

He carried on walking, taking some notes from the pocket of his white coat as he did. 'Yes?'

'May I ask your advice?'

That stopped him in his tracks. 'About what?'

Dulcie caught up with him. 'I just wondered – do you think it benefits patients to get a visit from their families?'

Dr Logan considered the question. 'Well, I suppose it depends on the individual case. Obviously the age of the patient will need to be taken into account, his family situation, his general state of health. But – yes, I suppose in general, patients do benefit greatly from such visits.'

Dulcie let her gaze flick back up the ward to where Sam Trevelyan was still watching her.

'Thank you, Doctor.' She smiled. 'That's exactly what I thought.'

Chapter Twenty-Four

'Just think, Duffield. This time tomorrow I'll be Mrs Edward Stanning!'

Grace could scarcely remember a time when she had seen her friend so happy. Anna whirled about the room, taking her belongings out of the chest of drawers and throwing them into the open suitcase on the bed. Her face was alight with excitement.

Grace smiled at her as she pinned her hair. 'I'm so pleased for you, Beck. But I'll really miss sharing a room with you.'

'I know.' Anna paused, a pile of clothes in her arms. 'I'll miss you and all the other girls, too. It'll seem very odd, not waking up here every morning.'

'I'm sure you won't miss the Home Sister telling you when to get up and when to go to bed,' Grace said. 'Or queuing up for the bathroom on a freezing winter's morning.'

'I suppose not. But we've had some good times here, haven't we?' Anna looked out of the window. 'I won't miss shinning up and down that drainpipe in the dead of night, though. I used to worry every time I came home that you'd be fast asleep and wouldn't hear me tapping on the window.'

'Far from it,' Grace said. 'I used to lie awake at night, worrying you'd break your neck!'

Anna grinned. 'You've been a good friend, Duffield.'

'So have you.' Grace shook her head. 'Listen to us,

getting all sentimental. It's a good thing I'm on night duty tonight, or I'd be in tears by ten o'clock!'

'And it's not as if we won't see each other again, is it?' Anna said. 'I'll be back on duty in a couple of days, once our honeymoon's over.'

'I must say, I'm surprised that Matron agreed to let you stay on.'

'I think she's desperate to keep hold of as many trained nurses as she can.'

It had all worked out very well for her and Edward in the end. Not only had Matron agreed to Anna staying on at the hospital, but today the Medical Board had given him a full discharge.

Grace was surprised. She had seen men in a far worse state than Edward Stanning sent back to the Front. She had expected him to be assigned light duties, probably at a local depot, but instead he had been discharged entirely.

Anna, needless to say, had been delighted by the news. It was more than she had ever dared hope for, that her darling Edward could come home and run the bakery.

'I can't believe it,' she had said to Grace. 'I feel as if I've spent so many years being miserable, watching everyone being taken away from me, and now I've got Edward back. It feels like a dream come true.'

She was still smiling as she dumped the clothes into her suitcase and looked around.

'There, I think that's everything.' She closed the lid of the case. 'It seems rather full,' she said ruefully.

'Here, I'll help you close it.' Grace leaned her weight on the lid while Anna fastened the leather straps. After much pulling and straining, they finally managed to get it done up.

Grace watched as Anna hauled the suitcase off the bed. It landed with a thump on the polished wood floor. Seeing it there made the move seem more real.

She dragged her gaze away and looked at the watch dangling from her apron bib. 'Is that the time? I'd better be off, or the night sister will be wondering where I am.'

'I'll see you tomorrow, at the wedding,' Anna said.

'I'll be there.' Grace seized her friend's hands impulsively. 'I really am so pleased for you,' she said. 'You deserve to be happy.'

Tears brimmed in Anna's eyes. 'Thank you.'

Then, as Grace left, Anna called after her, 'How awful of me, I've been so full of my own plans, we haven't even talked about your Christmas with your family.'

Grace smiled. 'There's really nothing to tell,' she said.

It seemed as if the year was determined to go out with an icy bluster. It was a freezing, bitter night, and flurries of snow swirled and eddied in the icy wind. Grace pulled the hood of her thick cape as far as she could, but the cold still made the bones of her face ache. She picked her way carefully along the path from Walford House to the main hospital building in the dark, her feet slipping on the slushy cobbles. Cold wetness had seeped through the leather of her shoes by the time she reached the hospital building.

Grace stood inside the main doors for a moment, shaking the snow off her cape before making her way down the long corridor to Wilson ward.

There's nothing to tell, she had said to Anna. But the truth was she didn't want to talk about what had happened because she was afraid it would somehow make it more real.

Her father had insisted on Noah taking her back to the station in his cart that morning. He had been very solicitous of her, carefully arranging an old blanket around her shoulders to keep out the cold. Grace had held her breath and tried not to mind that it smelled of old, damp dog.

Noah was a lot more talkative on the way back to the

station than he had been on the way to the farm. He pointed out the land he had harvested earlier that year, and told her about the yield he had had, and the new crops he was planning for the following year.

Grace had the distinct feeling he was trying to impress her, in his own way.

Finally, he said, 'I think your mother's spoken to you?'

'Yes.' Grace felt queasy, and not just because of the lurching of the wagon.

Noah sent her a sideways look. 'What do you reckon?'

'It was – a surprise.'

'Ah. I suppose it might be, at that.'

He was silent for a while, then he said, 'I'd make you a good husband. You'd want for nothing.'

Grace risked a glance at his craggy profile. 'But we hardly know each other, Mr Wells.'

'Noah.' He gave a slight smile.

'Noah.' Even saying it felt wrong, like something sharp in her mouth.

'I reckon we know each other well enough. And we're both steady, sensible sorts, so we'd get along quite nicely, I think.' He paused, then said, 'You'd have a grand place to live. I'm thinking of doing up the farmhouse.' He sent her another quick look. 'You'd have a say, mind. I'd put you in charge of all the alterations, so you could get it just how you wanted it. Even indoor plumbing, if that's what you'd like.'

'Thank you,' Grace looked down at her hands.

Noah grunted. 'I know women are fussy about these things. And I'd want you to feel like it was your home as well as mine.'

The silence stretched between them again until at last the rail halt for the village came into sight.

Grace could hardly scramble off the cart quick enough. As she was gathering her belongings from the back of the

167

wagon, Noah said, 'You just have a think about it anyway. Take your time, I'm in no hurry. You know what it's like, things move slowly down here.'

He leaned forward and Grace realised with horror that he was trying to give her a little peck on the cheek, but she had ducked out of the way just in time.

The train was overcrowded again, but this time Grace scarcely noticed. She didn't even bother to clear a patch on the steamy glass so she could catch a last, lingering look at the countryside. Instead she sat upright, staring at the sagging net of the luggage rack opposite, still trying to take in the events of the past two days.

A few years ago, an offer like this from Noah Wells would have been more than she had ever dared hoped for. From the moment she turned twelve years old and started to sprout taller than her brothers and most of the boys at the village school, it had been made clear to her that she would struggle to attract a husband.

'What man would want a great gangly weed like you?' her mother would say. 'You're all arms and legs, girl, and clumsy with it. You'd break every pot in his house before a week was out.'

As time went on, it seemed as if her mother was right. Gradually the local boys all started to pair up with girls, and the pretty, petite ones like Jessie and Beth went first. Then it was the turn of the girls whose fathers were landowners, and who had no brothers.

Grace took the rejection in good part. She went to all the village weddings, watching as one by one her friends found husbands. After everything she had been told, it simply never occurred to her that she might deserve one too.

Had Noah Wells come along then, with his acres of land and his farmhouse with indoor plumbing, she would have considered herself very fortunate indeed.

But since then she had lived in London and met all the other girls. She had seen them flirt and fall in love. She had seen them giddy with romance; heartbroken when it all ended. From what she could tell, being in love was like being on a carousel at the fairground, going round and round, up and down, caught up in a whirlwind of the most wonderful, exciting highs and lows.

And she dearly wished she could feel some of that heady excitement herself.

Of course, the sensible side of her knew she was being silly, that she might as well wish for the moon. No man had ever shown any interest in her. No young medical student had ever flirted with her, let alone courted her.

No, if she was going to get married then Noah Wells was her best chance.

But then Grace thought about Anna, and how excited she was at the prospect of her wedding. She was so consumed with love, all she could think about was getting married to the man she adored.

Grace could never imagine feeling like that about Noah Wells.

But there was something else to consider besides herself. As her mother had explained, the farm was in trouble and she knew her family was relying on her to help them. This marriage to Noah Wells would solve all their problems.

A steady, sensible sort, Noah had called her. It was hardly the kind of compliment to get a young girl's heart racing. But it was probably the best Grace Duffield was ever going to get.

Chapter Twenty-Five

Grace put her own concerns determinedly to one side as she walked on to Wilson ward.

Sylvia Saunders and Mary Finnegan had already served the bedtime drinks and got the patients settled, and were in the middle of the medications round when she arrived, so she reported to Sister to see if there was anything else to be done.

As Grace approached Miss Parker's office, she heard Dr Carlyle's voice coming from inside.

'A full discharge,' she was saying. 'I really didn't expect that, did you?'

'As a matter of fact, I did,' said Dr Logan. 'I've read his records, and frankly I'm not surprised the army doesn't want him in their ranks anymore.'

'Is he that bad?'

'The man is more lethal than a hand grenade.'

Grace paused, her hand still raised to knock on the door.

'Perhaps we should be keeping him in, if he's so unstable?' she heard Dr Carlyle say.

'I would agree with you, if there was anything we could do to help him.'

'Are you saying he can't be cured?'

'I'm saying,' Dr Logan replied, 'that what we're dealing with is far more than a case of neurasthenia. This particular psychopathy is deep seated and would take a great deal of time and effort to treat. Always assuming Private Stanning is willing, which I believe is highly unlikely, given that he doesn't believe there is anything wrong with him . . .'

Private Stanning?

Grace took a step back, straight into a screen that had been left outside the office. Time seemed to freeze as it fell, crashing to the ground in horrifying slow motion.

She was still standing there, rooted to the spot, as the door to Sister's office opened and Kate Carlyle stuck her head out.

'What the – oh, Nurse Duffield, it's you.' There was no surprise on her face as she looked down at the calamity and then back at Grace. 'What do you want?'

Grace opened her mouth but no sound emerged.

'I – I was looking for Sister,' she finally managed.

'I believe she went down to Matron's office to discuss a new admission.'

'Right. Thank you, Doctor.'

Grace glanced beyond Dr Carlyle's shoulder. Dr Logan was sitting at Miss Parker's desk, his head bent over a sheaf of notes.

'Was there something else, Nurse Duffield?' Dr Carlyle frowned at her.

'No. No, thank you, Doctor.'

The next moment the door closed in her face, shutting her out. Grace stood for a moment, staring at the name plate bearing the words 'Ward Sister's Office'. She could see her shocked face reflected in the polished brass.

'Honestly, Duffield, you could be more careful!'

Grace turned to see Mary Finnegan behind her. 'I'm sorry?' she murmured.

'Trampling around like a baby elephant, knocking things over.' Mary tutted as she went to pick up the fallen screen. 'You know it sets them off. Saunders is still trying to calm Sergeant Flynn down. The poor man is hiding

171

under his bed, convinced he's under enemy fire – are you all right? You look like you've seen a ghost.'

'I – I'm fine.' Grace glanced back at the closed door.

'Then help me with this, would you?'

Grace galvanised herself into action and between them they lifted the heavy screen back in place, just as Miss Parker returned to the ward.

'At last!' Mary Finnegan said. 'Now we can go off duty. Try not to wreck the place overnight, won't you?'

Half an hour later, everyone else had gone, leaving Grace alone on the darkened ward. In the darkness, the sound of snoring mingled with the usual moans, yelps and cries of distress. Some men shouted warnings, while others simply sobbed. One man, Private Hobbs, cackled with laughter in his sleep.

Grace made her way slowly down the ward, checking on them all by the dim light of her lamp. As she approached Edward Stanning's bed, she could see he was sitting up, propped against the pillows.

Grace felt the hairs on the back of her neck prickling. She would have walked by, but Edward called out to her.

'Did you hear my news, Nurse? I'm going home tomorrow.'

Grace paused at the foot of his bed. 'Yes,' she said. 'Nurse Beck told me you'd been discharged.'

'A full discharge, Nurse!' Edward grinned. 'I'll never have to wear a uniform again!'

Frankly I'm not surprised the army doesn't want him in their ranks anymore. I've read his records . . .

Grace swallowed hard. 'That's very good news, Private Stanning.'

'It's more than that, Nurse. It's the start of my new life.' He looked pleased with himself. 'What with that and marrying Anna, I reckon after tomorrow I'll have everything I've ever wanted.'

Outside, the wind sent a sudden squall of sleet rattling against the window like a burst of machine-gun fire. Grace started in fright.

'Blimey, Nurse, what's the matter with you?' Edward said. 'You're as jumpy as these other poor devils!'

Grace smiled uneasily. 'It's just the storm, that's all.'

'It's horrible, ain't it? Mind, the weather had better buck its ideas up by tomorrow. If the sun doesn't shine on my wedding day, I won't be happy about it!'

Grace looked at his open, laughing face. Surely Dr Logan must have got it wrong, she thought. There was no malice in Edward Stanning's expression.

'I'll keep my fingers crossed for you,' she said.

But Grace was still troubled when she returned to her desk in the centre of the ward. She tried to work on the reports, but her mind kept wandering back to the conversation she had overheard.

Was Edward Stanning really dangerous? she wondered. She knew he had a quickfire temper, and his moods could change from day to night in the blink of an eye. But lots of the men on Wilson ward found it difficult to control their emotions. And Edward had always been quite charming to her.

And Anna loved him with all her heart. Surely she would have sensed if there was something dark in him?

More than a case of neurasthenia, Dr Logan had said.

She glanced down the length of the ward. The end of the long gallery was in shadow, but she could hear the soft chorus of moans and sighs as the men finally settled into uneasy sleep. From what she could see, Edward had settled down too.

Grace put down her pen, the page still blank in front of

her. It was no good; she would not be able to concentrate until she knew for sure.

Leaving her lamp on the desk, she crept down the ward to the foot of his bed.

'Private Stanning?' she whispered. 'Edward?'

There was no reply. In the darkness, she could hear Edward sighing in his sleep.

She carefully unhooked his notes from the foot of his bed and scuttled back to Sister's desk.

There was the usual sheaf of medical notes, with details of pulse, respiration, temperature and the results of any samples taken and medication given. But underneath these someone had pinned a large buff envelope marked 'Private' in bold black ink.

For a moment Grace hesitated. Then, with trembling hands, she carefully unfolded the flap on the envelope and took out the sheets of paper within.

There was Edward Stanning's army report, several pages detailing incidents of disciplinary matters, all written in his commanding officer's neat hand. Grace leafed through them, her eyes running down the columns listing various fights, arguments with the other men, and acts of insubordination that had resulted in several field punishments. There was also a note that Edward had been taken away from the front line several months earlier and given a transport job in one of the supply trenches because he was 'seriously affecting morale'.

What did that mean? Grace wondered.

She set the report aside and turned to Dr Logan's carefully typed report. It was difficult to read the close script by the light of the dim lamp, but words popped out at her.

Psychopathy. Constitutional flaws in character. Profound deficit in behaviour, lacking proper feelings, showing tendencies towards delinquency, lying and mania . . .

'Interesting reading, don't you think?'

Grace looked up sharply. Edward's hulking shape loomed over her, his face in shadow.

'I particularly liked the paragraph where he describes me as "having a deeply disturbed nature, masked by superficial charm". If anyone has superficial charm, I reckon it's our Dr Logan. I could have sworn he liked me!'

His harsh laughter echoed around the quiet ward.

Grace rose to her feet. 'You should be in bed,' she said, her voice carefully even.

'And you should mind your own business. Those notes are private, in case you hadn't noticed?'

'You've obviously read them.'

Edward stepped forward. In the dim light of the desk lamp, his face seemed all jutting angles and deep, shaded hollows. 'Of course I did. Don't you think I have the right to know what they're all saying about me? Especially when what they're saying is such nonsense.' He tilted his head to one side. 'It is nonsense. Don't you think, Nurse Duffield?'

'I—' The rest of her words stuck in her dry throat.

'Of course you do. You know me, don't you? Better than Dr Logan, at any rate.' His mouth curled. 'I suppose I should thank him, in a way. He probably helped get me out of the army. But all the same, it's not fair to see lies like that written down. They are lies, Nurse. You know that, don't you?'

There was a fixed quality to his stare that frightened her. But Grace was determined not to betray her fear as she carefully replaced the report in the envelope.

'Let's get you back into bed, shall—'

She gasped as Edward's hand came down on her wrist, trapping it.

'You won't tell Anna, will you?'

Grace looked down at his hand, pinioning her wrist.

175

'Let go of me, please, Private Stanning,' she said in a carefully level voice.

'Promise me, Nurse. Promise me you won't say a word to Anna about that wretched report.'

Grace lifted her chin to meet his gaze. 'She deserves to know what kind of a man she is marrying.'

'But it's all lies!' Edward released her abruptly. He looked down at the buff envelope, the word 'Private' standing out even in the dim light.

'It would break her heart,' he said flatly. 'You're her friend, Nurse Duffield. You've seen how happy she is since I came home. She's so looking forward to us getting married, settling down, building a life together. Do you really want to ruin all that for her – for us?'

Grace thought about Anna, skipping around their room as she packed her belongings. Edward was right, she had been happier since he came home. For the first time in a long time, she was actually looking forward to her future.

'Perhaps that wretched report is right,' Edward interrupted her thoughts. 'Perhaps I'm not the man I once was. God knows, the war has changed me, just like it's changed all these other poor men in here.' He looked around in the shadowy darkness. 'But all I need is a chance,' he said. 'I can be the man I once was. I just need time, a stable home, a purpose in life. I need Anna.' He turned pleading eyes to meet Grace's. 'Please, Nurse Duffield? I know you're a good, kind-hearted person, and I know you want to do the right thing. I wouldn't blame you for a minute if you decided to tell Anna about this. But I'm begging you to give me the chance to prove I can change, that I can be a good man again.' He looked downcast. 'My future is in your hands,' he said.

This particular psychopathy is deep-seated and would take a great deal of time and effort to treat. Always assuming Private

Stanning is willing, which I believe is highly unlikely, given that he doesn't believe there is anything wrong with him . . .

Grace thought about Anna again, the bright smile that lit up her face when she talked about Edward, about her wedding.

Perhaps he was right, that he only needed a chance. Who was she to take that away from him, to ruin two people's happiness?

'It's getting very late, Private Stanning,' she said. 'Let's get you back to bed, shall we?'

Chapter Twenty-Six

New Year's Eve was a dark, depressing day. Wet sleet fell sullenly from a dirty yellowish-grey sky, turning to sloppy slush on the pavements.

But Anna was determined not to allow the miserable weather to dampen her spirits. This was her wedding day and nothing was going to spoil it.

Not even her sister, she thought. She looked at Liesel's reflection in the mirror as she stood behind her at the dressing table, pinning up her hair.

'I really don't know why I'm bothering with this,' she muttered under her breath. 'We'll look like drowned rats by the time we get to the register office.'

'It's only round the corner.'

'But this weather.' Liesel looked mournfully at her dainty kid-leather shoes. 'I wish you could have organised a taxi or something.'

'All right, we'll get a taxi!' Anna said. 'Now will you stop moaning and let me enjoy my day?'

Liesel retreated into sulky silence. She had been in one of her moods since she had arrived that morning.

The first thing she had said was, 'I can't stay long, you know. They're expecting me back for tea.'

'That's a shame,' Anna had said.

'Well, if you will get married at short notice . . . Anyway, it's not as if there's a proper reception, is there?' she'd added pointedly.

As far as Liesel was concerned, the whole wedding was

a mess. It was not just the lack of wedding cars or a reception with music and dancing. She was horrified that there were no flowers or a wedding dress, and that Anna had chosen to marry in Bethnal Green register office and not a proper church.

'I don't know what Papa would say about it.'

'Yes, well, Papa isn't here, is he?' Anna had snapped. She didn't need reminding that her parents couldn't be there to see her wed. It hurt her deeply every time she thought about it. Like every other young girl, Anna had always dreamed of her father walking her down the aisle.

Liesel finished doing her hair and stepped back to admire her handiwork. Anna's fine dark hair was hardly her best feature, but her sister had dressed it beautifully, twisting it up into a knot that showed off Anna's slender neck. Loose tendrils framed her narrow face.

'You look a picture, Miss Anna,' Mrs Church sighed. They had shut up the shop at lunchtime because of the wedding, but Mrs Church had stayed behind to help Anna get ready. 'And that costume really suits you.'

'It does, doesn't it?' Anna ignored her sister's scowling look. The neat skirt and jacket she had borrowed from Dulcie Moore looked quite good on her once she had taken it in at the waist. The rich crimson colour brought out the warm reddish glimmer in her brown hair.

'It's not a wedding dress though, is it?' Liesel said.

'Oh, for heaven's sake!' Anna turned on her sister, fragile nerves snapping. 'I know this is not the wedding you would have chosen, but it'll do for me, all right? I don't care about churches and flowers. All that matters is that I'm marrying the man I love. And that's far more important to me than a white wedding dress!'

Liesel stared back at her, and for a moment Anna thought she saw a glint of amusement in her sister's eyes.

'So I daresay you won't be wanting this then, will you?' she said, reaching down to the carpet bag at her feet. Anna watched as she produced a large parcel wrapped in brown paper.

'What is it?'

'You'd best open it and find out.'

Anna noticed the smiling glance that passed between her sister and Mrs Church as she carefully undid the parcel. Her fingers were trembling so much she could scarcely unfasten the knotted string.

She pulled aside the brown paper and caught sight of a shimmer of delicate, lace-trimmed ivory satin, and her heart leaped.

She looked up at Liesel. 'I – I don't understand?'

'Don't get too excited, it isn't new,' Liesel said. 'One of the Land Girls got married a few weeks ago, and I asked if I could borrow her dress. I'll be on pigsty cleaning duties until Easter,' she grimaced, 'but I daresay it will be worth it.'

'Oh, Liesel!' Anna launched herself into her sister's arms, nearly knocking her off her feet.

'Steady on. You don't even know if it'll fit you yet. The other girl had a lot more curves than you. You're as flat as a board.'

Typical Liesel, Anna thought. She couldn't even do something nice without lacing it with a touch of spite. But Anna was so overcome with happiness her sister's insult barely touched her.

'It'll be perfect,' she declared.

And it was, after a bit of tucking and padding. Anna could scarcely drag her eyes from her reflection as she stared in the mirror.

'You look beautiful, Miss Anna, you really do.' Mrs Church fumbled for a handkerchief before remembering she had used it to pad out Anna's bodice.

'Now you've got something old, something new and something borrowed. But you don't have anything blue . . .' Liesel looked around.

'What about this?'

Anna went to her jewellery box and retrieved the enamelled bluebell brooch Tom had sent her.

'Let me try it.' Liesel pinned it in place, then stepped back again. 'Yes, that looks perfect.'

Anna was glad Liesel had persuaded her to take a taxi to the register office. Heavy splotches of sleet splashed against the steamy car windows, blurring the cold, grey world outside. The streets were deserted and miserable. Even the stallholders on Columbia Road had given up and gone home.

'It's a shame the sun isn't shining,' she sighed.

'That's what happens if you decide to get married in the middle of winter.'

Anna looked at her sister's profile. Liesel's face was expressionless as she fiddled with the lace trim of her gloves. She had opted for a dress in pale ice blue, topped with a fur stole. After her kindness over the wedding dress, she had reverted to being sullen about the rest of the arrangements.

Anna looked away, clearing a patch in the misted glass to peer out. She refused to allow Liesel's sulky mood to spoil her day.

They reached the register office and Anna started to get out, but Liesel didn't move.

Anna looked back at her. 'Are you coming?'

Liesel stared down at her hands, fidgeting at a loose thread in her lace gloves. 'Are you sure about this?' she asked.

It was such a ridiculous question, Anna couldn't help but laugh. 'What are you saying?'

'I'm worried, that's all.' Liesel turned wide blue eyes to meet Anna's. 'Edward has just come out of hospital.'

'I know that.'

'How do you know he's – you know – well enough to get married?'

'He's fine. The doctor says his chest is getting better every day.'

Liesel looked back down at her gloves, plucking at the thread. 'I don't want you to feel as if you've got to rush into anything. You could wait a while.'

'I've already waited for years.'

'Yes, I know, but . . .'

'Liesel, I'm not being rushed into anything. It was my idea to get married, not Edward's. This is what I want.'

'It's not what Papa and Mother would want for you,' Liesel said quietly.

Anna glared at her. 'I'm sure they would want me to be happy.'

'And are you?' Liesel darted a glance at her.

Anna looked out at the grim, grey street.

'Yes,' she said firmly. 'Yes, I'm very happy. Now hurry up, or there won't be a wedding!'

Edward was waiting for her, sheltering in the porch. He looked quite frail, Anna thought with a pang. He was thinner than he used to be, and his face had the ashen pallor of someone who had spent weeks indoors.

'No best man,' Liesel observed, as she followed her sister out of the taxi. 'Isn't it funny how he doesn't have any family or friends?'

'He's an orphan,' Anna reminded her. 'And I daresay all his friends are away fighting.' She hurried to meet Edward before Liesel could make another comment.

He grinned with relief when he saw her.

'Thank the Lord! I thought you'd changed your mind?'

Anna glanced at Liesel. 'Never,' she said.

He held her at arms' length, taking in her appearance. 'You look beautiful.'

'And you look very smart.' Anna looked him up and down. 'But I thought you might wear your uniform?'

'No fear!' Edward shook his head. 'I spent four years wearing it, I don't intend to wear it on my wedding day.' He smiled down at her. 'Besides, this is the start of my new life.'

'Our new lives,' Anna reminded him with a smile.

'Our new lives.' He offered her his arm. 'Shall we go?' he said.

Chapter Twenty-Seven

'Wasn't it a beautiful wedding?' Miriam Trott sighed, as they sat in a café later, discussing it over tea and scones.

'I thought it was a bit disappointing, myself.' Dulcie helped herself to another cup of tea from the china pot. 'You won't catch me getting married in a poky register office wearing a borrowed dress.'

'Oh, yes, of course,' Miriam sneered. 'You want a grand society wedding, don't you?' She rolled her eyes at Grace.

'And what's wrong with that?' Dulcie said.

'You'll have to find someone to marry you first.'

'I bet I find someone before you do!'

It was a spiteful comment, but Miriam deserved it. Dulcie waited for Grace to say something, to tell her off for being mean. But Grace was silent as she stirred her spoon around her cup.

Come to think of it, she had barely spoken a word since the wedding, Dulcie thought.

'I don't think it matters what kind of wedding you have,' Sylvia Saunders piped up. 'I'd marry Roger anywhere, so long as it meant we were together. But that's what true love is all about, isn't it?' She sent Dulcie a meaningful look.

'I agree,' Miriam said. 'Isn't it wonderful to see two people so happy and in love?' she sighed. 'You can see how much they adore each other.'

'I'm not surprised,' Mary Finnegan put in. 'Edward Stanning is a very handsome man.'

'Yes, Anna Beck is a lucky girl.' Miriam's eyes gleamed. 'Can you imagine, waking up to a man like that?'

Grace knocked over her cup with a clatter, making them jump. They all stared in horror at the brown tea stain spreading over the snowy white linen tablecloth.

'Honestly, Duffield, do you have to be so clumsy all the time!' Miriam Trott snapped.

'Typical Duffer! We can't take you anywhere!' Mary Finnegan laughed.

'Let's get this mess cleared up.' Sylvia snatched up a napkin and began dabbing the stain.

Usually Grace would have been in there too, blushing like mad and stammering apologies while she tried to help, her long limbs and pointed elbows getting in everyone's way.

But this time she didn't move. She sat watching them, a dazed frown on her face. It wasn't until Miriam snapped at her that she finally galvanised herself and grabbed a napkin.

There was definitely something on her mind, Dulcie thought. But she didn't think any more of it until much later that evening, when they were walking from Walford House to the hospital building together to begin their respective night duties.

'Typical,' Dulcie moaned. 'New Year's Eve and I'm working. I swear Miss Sutton does it on purpose, just to spite me.'

Grace said nothing. She plodded next to Dulcie, her head down.

'I bet they'll be having a party in the Students' Union bar,' Dulcie went on. 'I know a lot of the doctors go. Perhaps Dr Logan will be there?' Although she couldn't imagine it. Robert Logan was proving to be annoyingly anti-social. He hadn't turned up to the Christmas show, or any of the festive parties and get-togethers that follow it.

At least it meant none of the other nurses had had a chance to get their claws into him, but neither had Dulcie.

Perhaps all that would change tonight? Perhaps he would turn up to a New Year's Eve party, and when midnight struck some nurse would seize her chance to grab him for a kiss . . .

Please God, don't let it be Miriam Trott, Dulcie thought.

'I hate night duty,' she muttered.

'So do I.'

Dulcie glanced at Grace in surprise. It wasn't like her to complain about anything.

'I'm not surprised,' she said. 'The shell shock ward gives me the creeps during the day, I certainly wouldn't fancy being alone with them after dark. I mean, they're so deluded they could do anything, couldn't they? Especially in the dead of night.' A thought struck her. 'What if they mistook you for a German spy creeping around their beds in the dark? You could be minding your own business and suddenly—'

'Don't!'

The forcefulness with which Grace spoke stopped Dulcie in mid-sentence.

'I was only joking,' she said.

'Well, don't. I don't want to hear it.'

Dulcie sent Grace a sidelong look. Her friend's expression was more troubled than she had ever seen it.

'Duffield, has something happened?' she asked.

'No. No, of course not.'

'Are you sure? You can tell me.'

'There's nothing to tell. Now just shut up about it, all right?'

Grace strode on ahead of her, her cape pulled tightly around her shoulders. Dulcie stared at her in astonishment. She wasn't sure she had ever heard Grace Duffield raise her voice before.

Fortunately, it looked like being a quiet night on Monaghan ward. Dulcie knew there was plenty she could be getting on with, like making splints and mending worn bed sheets and packing the sterilising drum ready for the morning. But then two of the medical students arrived and so she decided to have a cup of tea in the kitchen with them instead.

'It's a pity you can't come to our party,' one of them, Henry Davies, said. 'We're going to have a riot in the Students' Union bar.'

'If it's anything like last year, I'm sure you are.' The previous year a few of the students had decided to strip to their underwear and dance in the hospital courtyard on the stroke of midnight. All the nurses had found it hilarious, until Matron appeared in her nightgown and gave them a piece of her mind. Watching her frog-marching the students to the dean's office, still half naked, was one of the funniest things Dulcie had ever seen.

'It won't be the same without you there.' The other student, James Dillon, gazed at her with soulful brown eyes.

He had already told Dulcie several times that he was in love with her. He was very handsome, and his father owned a munitions factory. But James was barely twenty, far too young for her. Fun to flirt with, Dulcie had decided, but hardly a serious marriage prospect.

'Perhaps I could come back at midnight, and we could have a party of our own?' he suggested in a low voice.

Dulcie stared at him. Those deep brown eyes and declarations of undying love did not fool her for a minute. She knew exactly what James Dillon was after.

'I shall be far too busy,' she dismissed.

'Oh, go on. It'll be fun.'

'I told you, I—'

A roar erupted, ripping through the silence of the ward.

Henry turned pale. 'My God, what was that?' he cried. But Dulcie was already through the kitchen door.

She reached Sam's bedside, the two students at her heels.

'No, I won't. You can't make me!' He lay rigid in the bed, as if pinned down by invisible hands. He strained against them, the muscles and sinews in his neck, arms and shoulders taut with effort. 'Christopher, run for your life!' he roared. 'Run, boy!'

'Wake up, old man.' Henry put out a hand to shake him.

'No, don't—' Dulcie started to say, but she was too late. Sam's eyes snapped open, and a split second later he had Henry round the throat. The student gasped and choked, toes scrabbling uselessly on the polished floor.

'Let him go, you fool!' James Dillon fought to prise apart Sam's iron grip.

'Sergeant Trevelyan? Sam?' Dulcie cried out desperately.

The sound of her voice seemed to get through to him. Sam blinked, the life returning to his eyes. He looked at Henry, dangling like a puppet, and abruptly released his grasp. Henry collapsed, coughing and fighting for breath.

'My God, man, you could have killed him!' James turned to his friend. 'Are you all right, Davies?'

'I – I think so.' Henry massaged his throat. Even in the dim light, Dulcie could make out the dark marks of Sam's fingers on his skin. 'Just a bit of a shock, that's all.'

'You shouldn't have woken him,' she said.

Sam said nothing. He stared down at his hands, lying on top of the bed cover.

'She's right,' Henry said, in a croaking voice. 'It was a damn fool thing to do, grabbing him like that.' He turned to Sam. 'How are you feeling, Sergeant?'

'Better than you, I daresay,' James spoke for him. He looked at Dulcie. 'Shall I give him something to make him sleep?'

'No.' Sam's voice was a low growl.

James ignored him, still looking at Dulcie. 'Nurse?'

Dulcie glanced at Sam, then shook her head.

'Are you quite sure?' the student said. 'I don't like to think of you alone with him. What if he has another nightmare?'

'I'll manage,' Dulcie said.

'But all the same . . .'

'You heard her.'

James shot Sam a look of dislike.

'I'll come back later,' he said. 'Just to make sure you're all right.'

By the time the students left, Sam Trevelyan was already half asleep. Dulcie was about to go back to her desk but then she changed her mind and went to the kitchen. She made two cups of tea and brought them back to Sam's bedside.

'Here,' she said, placing one on his bedside locker.

'I'm asleep,' he said.

'You might have fooled Dillon and Davies, but you can't fool me.' Dulcie sat down in the chair beside his bed.

Sam opened one baleful eye. 'You don't have to watch over me,' he said. 'I'm not going to go berserk, whatever your friends think.'

'I'm glad to hear it.' Dulcie sipped her tea. 'Once is more than enough.'

He smiled slightly at that.

Encouraged, she said, 'What were you dreaming about?'

His face took on a closed look. 'I don't remember.'

'You mentioned a name . . . Christopher?' She saw him flinch. 'Who is that?'

'I told you, I don't remember anything about it.' He turned his face away from her. 'I want to sleep now, if you don't mind?'

'But your tea—'

'I don't want it.'

'I'll leave it here, just in case you change your mind.' Dulcie stood up. 'It might help to talk about it, you know,' she said. Sam said nothing. 'Dr Logan reckons—'

'Dr Logan! I might have known you'd listen to him.'

'Dr Logan says it's harmful to shut difficult memories away. He thinks we should get them out in the open, talk about them. It can't do any harm to try, can it?' she said. 'And you never know, it might help.'

Sam opened his eyes, and Dulcie was shocked by the depth of anguish and despair she saw in them.

'You wouldn't want to hear what I've got to say, Nurse. Believe me,' he said hoarsely.

Chapter Twenty-Eight

Anna's hands shook as she took out the pins from her hair and let it fall about her face. Outside, the clock was striking midnight, hailing in the year 1918. She could hear the shouts and laughter of revellers spilling out of the Angel and Crown. From the sound of it, the party seemed to be continuing on the street.

Anna sat still, listening for Edward's voice. When she had left him there an hour ago, he had been sinking pints at the bar with Mr Hudson and Mr Wheeler.

She hadn't expected them to spend all night in the pub, but Mr Hudson and the other men insisted on buying Edward one drink after another.

'It ain't often you have a drink with a war hero, is it?' Mr Hudson kept saying. 'You enjoy it, boy. After all, you've earned it.'

Anna had sat nursing her port and lemon for as long as she could. She had never liked drinking, and the heat and noise of the pub, with its stench of beer, stale sweat and cigarette smoke, was beginning to make her head ache.

But when she had suggested that they should go home, the men wouldn't hear of it.

'It ain't even midnight yet!' Mr Wheeler said. 'Let the lad see in the New Year!'

'She just wants to show you who's boss,' Mr Hudson agreed. 'Don't fall for it, Edward lad, or you'll be under the thumb forever!'

'Leave the girl alone, it's her wedding night.' Mrs Hudson

nudged Anna. She had been downing gins all night, matching her husband drink for drink, and now she was red-faced and slurring her words. 'I expect you'll be wanting to get him on his own, eh? Can't say I blame you, good-looking man like him!'

She couldn't be more wrong, Anna thought as she brushed her hair over her shoulders. The thought of the wedding night and what was to come terrified her.

She had little idea what to expect. Four years of nursing had taught her about male anatomy, and she knew how babies were born, but she had little idea how they got there. Even listening to the other girls' chatter had barely given her any answers; for all their talk, they seemed as clueless as she was.

Once again, Anna longed for her mother. She would have been able to tell her what to expect.

She shivered inside her lace-trimmed nightgown. She felt a little foolish when she looked at her scared, pale face in the mirror. She had chosen the gown especially, but now it seemed too sophisticated for her. She looked like a little girl in her mother's clothes.

She picked up the bluebell brooch from the dressing table, admiring the way the coloured enamel caught the light as she turned it this way and that.

'Something blue.'

Anna turned around. Edward stood in the doorway, looking slightly dishevelled. His suit jacket was missing, the top buttons of his shirt were undone and his tie hung loosely about his neck. But he was still the most handsome man she had ever seen in her life.

She smiled at him. 'I didn't hear you come in?'

'I'm not surprised, all that racket going on outside.'

Edward came over to stand behind her and slid his hands down her shoulders. His fingers felt warm through the thin silk.

'I've missed you,' he said.

'We've only been apart an hour!'

'If I'd known you were sitting here looking this beautiful, I would have come home sooner.' He bent down and nuzzled her neck. Anna squirmed with pleasure.

'And there was me, thinking you were going to spend your wedding night with Mr Wheeler!'

'I wouldn't want to spend it with Mrs Wheeler, let alone her old man!' His hands slid slowly down her bare arms, then slipped to cup her breasts. Her nipples hardened under the light graze of his thumbs.

Anna felt herself melting inside with a sweet heat she had never experienced before. She turned to face Edward, entwining her arms around his neck, surrendering to his kiss.

He pulled away from her, laughing. 'Blimey, girl, hold your horses! Let me get undressed first.'

Anna looked down, embarrassed, as Edward started to unbutton his shirt. Had she been too keen? she wondered. She had no idea what she was supposed to do.

She turned away and put the bluebell brooch back in her jewellery box. All the while, she was aware of Edward behind her, taking off his shirt. Even the scars from the gas burns on his chest couldn't mar the perfection of his body with broad, powerfully muscled shoulders tapering to narrow hips. His skin gleamed like gold in the lamplight.

'I don't think I've ever seen that brooch before. Where did you get it?' he asked.

'It's from France.'

Anna answered without thinking, her mind elsewhere. It was only when she looked up that she saw Edward's frozen expression reflected in the mirror.

'I don't remember sending it to you.' His voice was light, but his eyes were intent as they met hers in the mirror.

It was too late to lie now. Besides, she had nothing to hide.

'Tom sent it to me for Christmas.'

'Tom?' He bit out the word coldly. 'Tom Franklin?'

'I've been writing to him.'

'Have you now?' He tossed his shirt on to the floor. 'And how long has this been going on?'

'Since he was sent to France, three years ago.'

'You mean to tell me you've been writing to another man for three years?'

'Tom was good to us when you were away,' Anna said. 'I felt as if I owed him something.'

She looked into Edward's face. It was impossible to tell what he was thinking.

'I haven't done anything wrong,' she protested.

'Why keep it from me, in that case?'

'Because – I knew you wouldn't like it.'

Edward's brows rose but he said nothing. Anna watched him as he picked up the brooch and examined it.

'It's funny that you chose to wear this on your wedding day,' he said in a low voice.

'I wore it because it was pretty, that's all. Something blue, like you said.' Anna watched him anxiously. 'It doesn't mean anything, Edward.'

'Do you still have them?' he interrupted her.

'What?'

'The letters. Do you still have them?'

Anna nodded, not meeting his eye.

'And you say it doesn't mean anything.' Edward's smile was twisted with malice.

'But I keep all my letters,' Anna protested. 'Yours, and Liesel's, and my parents'.'

'That's different, isn't it?' Edward snapped. 'We're your family. You don't keep letters from someone who means nothing to you!'

'All right, perhaps he does mean something,' Anna said. 'Tom saved our lives, don't forget. Liesel and Mother and I wouldn't be alive now if he hadn't risked his life to rescue us. And we wouldn't have a roof over our heads if he hadn't rebuilt this place.'

'All right, all right! You don't have to go on about it.' Edward cut her off angrily. 'Christ, I'm sick of hearing what a bloody hero Tom Franklin is.'

'You're right, we don't have to talk about it.' Anna turned to him pleadingly. 'Can't we just forget all about it, please? This is supposed to be our wedding night.'

'Fetch the letters.'

'What? No.'

'Why not? What have you got to hide?'

'Nothing.'

'Then you won't mind me reading them, will you?'

Anna stared at his face, so cold and implacable she barely recognised him. Anger rose inside her.

'Actually, I do mind,' she said. 'Those letters are private.'

He looked coldly triumphant. 'So you do have something to hide?'

'No!'

'Then I want to see them.'

Anna sighed angrily. 'All right. If that's what you really want.'

She crossed the room and retrieved the box from the back of the wardrobe.

'There,' she said, dumping it in Edward's hands. 'These are all my letters. Now please, can we stop all this?' she begged.

'That depends, doesn't it?' He undid the top bundle of letters, holding up the red ribbon she had tied them with.

'On what?'

'On what you and Tom Franklin got up to while I was away.'

Anna gasped. 'Edward! You don't think—'

'I don't know what to think. You said Tom Franklin was good to you. How do I know you weren't good to him, too?'

'Edward!'

'He was always sniffing around you like a dog on heat, even when I was here. I wonder if you got bored of waiting for me and decided to give him a chance instead.'

Anna didn't know what she was doing until she felt her hand sting and saw Edward standing in front of her, one hand pressed against his cheek. The letters were scattered on the floor at his feet.

'I'm sorry,' she whispered. 'I – I just want all this to stop. Please, Edward,' she begged. 'Can't we forget everything and start again. It's our wedding night.'

Edward stared at her, his face expressionless. As he took his hand away from his face, Anna could see the reddened imprint of her palm on her cheek.

Then he smiled, a menacing smile that did not reach his cold blue eyes.

'So it is,' he said softly.

He took a step towards her. Anna backed away from him, colliding with the iron bedstead.

'What – what are you doing?' she said.

'Like you said, it's our wedding night. I'm only taking what's rightfully mine.'

He grabbed her by the shoulders. Anna fell backwards on to the bed, Edward on top of her.

'No!' She fought him off, her hands pushing hard against his bare chest. 'Not like this!'

'I bet you didn't push Franklin away, did you?' Edward pinned her down, his face leering above hers. His breath stank of cigarettes and beer. 'I'll bet you couldn't wait, could you?'

'I didn't, I swear.'

'Did you do it here, in this bed? Is this where he had you?' He was pressing down on her, making it hard for her to breathe. 'I bet he wasn't gentle with you, was he? I bet he was rough, like an animal . . .'

'No! Edward, please!' Anna fought to get herself free. But the more she squirmed, the more excited Edward seemed to be. 'I swear, I've never—'

'There's only one way to find out, ain't there? Believe me, I'll know if you've been with someone else!'

What followed was as brutal as it was shocking. After a few moments, Anna stopped trying to fight and lay still as Edward thrust into her, grunting like an angry beast. The burning, searing pain was almost unbearable, but Anna did not dare cry out. Instead she bit her lip, tasting blood, and prayed for it to end.

Mercifully, it didn't last long. Finally Edward rolled off her, and a moment later he was asleep on his back, his drunken snores echoing around the silent room.

Anna turned her head away from him and saw the shredded remains of what was once her beautiful nightgown lying on the rug beside the bed.

She swallowed back the sob that rose in her throat, too terrified even to cry.

Chapter Twenty-Nine

She woke up in darkness to the clatter and chink of the milk cart in the street.

'Happy New Year!' someone called out, and for a brief moment Anna felt nothing, until the blackness of what had happened engulfed her all over again.

She had been too terrified to go to sleep at first. She had lain there rigid, staring at nothing, her mind blank with horror. It hadn't happened, she tried to tell herself. It was nothing more than a terrible dream. But all the while the burning pain between her legs consumed her. She longed to get up and wash herself, but Edward's arm was flung possessively over her body, pinning her to the bed. Anna scarcely dared to breathe in case she woke him and he wanted to have his way with her again.

Somehow, finally, she must have fallen into a fitful sleep, because when she woke up the bed beside her was empty.

Still Anna lay for a while, too terrified to move. She didn't want to stay there, but she didn't want to get up either, because that would mean facing Edward and what had happened.

She looked to one side. The tattered remains of her nightdress had gone, and so had the letters.

Then she heard trays clattering in the kitchen below the bedroom, and Edward's voice.

' "I'm Burlington Bertie, I rise at ten-thirty, and saunter along like a toff . . ." '

He was singing. At first she could hardly believe it, but

there he was, actually whistling a merry tune as he went about his work.

Anna cautiously got out of bed. The burning throb between her legs had subsided, but she still felt sticky and sore, and when she went to wash herself she found a pattern of bruises at the tops of her thighs where Edward had forced them apart.

Her stomach lurched, and the next moment Anna was violently sick.

She bent over the basin, her head resting on the cold porcelain, the bitter taste of bile filling her mouth and throat. She wanted to stay there forever, never have to go out and face the world.

But then she looked up at her wan reflection in the mirror, and slowly but surely her good sense began to reassert itself. Why should she be the one to hide herself away? She had done nothing wrong. If anyone should be ashamed, it was Edward.

Besides, this was her home, her bakery. She belonged here.

' "I'm Bert, Bert, I haven't a shirt, but my people are well off, you know . . ." '

His voice drifted up from downstairs, rising over the clatter of tins.

Anna scrubbed her face, washing away all traces of tears. If she was going to show her face to the world, she would make sure it was a brave one.

But her nerve almost failed her as she went downstairs and headed for the kitchen. As she approached, she could hear Edward and Charlie laughing together like old friends.

They both turned to face Anna when she walked in.

'Here she is, Charlie. My beautiful bride.' Edward came to greet her, his arms open, a wide smile on his face. 'You should have stayed in bed, sweetheart. I would have come and woken you up with a cup of tea and a kiss later.'

Confused, Anna allowed herself to be swept into his warm embrace. All the while, her mind was racing. Was this really the same Edward who had forced himself on her so savagely, who had hurt and humiliated her and spat curses in her face while he was doing it?

Over Edward's shoulder she saw Charlie leering suggestively. Had Edward told him what had happened? she wondered. Hot shame washed over her.

She moved out of his arms, smoothing down her skirt with trembling fingers. 'I should give you a hand.'

'There's no need,' Edward said smoothly. 'Charlie and I can manage. Why don't you go back to bed? It's still early. I'll come up and join you when I've finished this next batch of loaves.'

'No!' Nausea lurched in her stomach. 'I'm up now,' she said, more calmly. 'Besides, I'd like to help.'

'And I've told you, we don't need it.' She flinched as Edward's hands came down on her shoulders, steering her towards the door. 'If you want to help, why don't you make us all a cuppa? Charlie and I are parched, ain't we, mate?'

As Anna went down the passageway to the smaller kitchen she could hear them laughing again. Were they laughing at her?

She was shaking as she filled the kettle under the tap. This was supposed to be a happy day, the start of her new life with Edward. She was meant to wake up feeling loved and cherished, not used and hurt.

And for Edward to act as if nothing had happened – she could scarcely believe it. It unsettled her, made her wonder if she had imagined the whole thing.

Or perhaps this was what it was supposed to be like? Was this how it happened? Did all brides wake up the following morning feeling as shocked and humiliated as she did?

Surely that couldn't be right. Anna had heard the women on the wards, laughing and nudging each other and making sly remarks about what happened with their husbands in the bedroom. They certainly didn't make it sound as brutal or as frightening an experience as the one she had suffered. And if it were, she wondered that they ever wanted to do it again.

Once again, she longed for her mother. Dorothy Beck would have been able to advise her, to tell her what was right and what wasn't.

Who else could she ask? she wondered. Mrs Wheeler, or Mrs Hudson from next door? Not unless she wanted her business broadcast up and down Chambord Street. Or perhaps Mrs Church? Anna shuddered at the thought. No, she decided, this was something she had to sort out on her own.

Edward came in as she was pouring the tea. For a long time he stood in the doorway, just watching her. Anna moved stiffly, her body rigid, every muscle tensed. If he touched her again, she would throw the scalding contents of the teapot over him, she decided.

Finally he spoke. 'I'm sorry,' he said.

Anna paused, the teapot in her head. She didn't turn round, or look at him.

'I should never have behaved like that,' he went. 'I know I was drunk, but that's no excuse for what I did. I hurt you, and I can't forgive myself for that. I feel so wretchedly ashamed.'

Anna said nothing. She thought about him laughing and singing in the kitchen that morning. He hadn't sounded like someone consumed with shame.

'I – I couldn't help myself,' Edward said. 'When I saw

that brooch, and those letters – I just saw red. I thought you were hiding something from me.'

'I wasn't.'

'I know that now. I should have trusted you. But I was a jealous fool.' He was quiet for a long time. When he spoke again, his voice was broken. 'I remember when I was away in the trenches, the men who got letters from their sweethearts telling them they had met someone else. I used to live in fear that one day I'd get a letter like that from you.'

Anna swung round to face him. Edward's handsome face was desolate, like a lost child's. She had never seen him so vulnerable, not even when he was poorly in hospital.

'I always knew Tom liked you – no, he did,' he insisted, as she opened her mouth to speak. 'You might not have been able to see it, but I could. It nearly sent me mad when I had to go off to France and leave you here with him. I felt sure he'd take you away from me. And then when you wrote and told me what a hero he'd been, saving you from the fire and rebuilding this place . . .' He lifted his gaze to meet hers. 'It should have been me here looking after you, not him.'

'It wasn't your fault you weren't here,' Anna said quietly.

'That doesn't matter. The point is, I wasn't and he was. And there was nothing I could do but watch and wait and hope that he wouldn't take you away from me.'

'No one could ever do that,' Anna said.

'I know.' Edward's mouth curved into the smallest of smiles. 'I suppose deep in my heart I always knew you weren't that kind of girl. But over there – well, your mind starts to play tricks on you. The day Tom Franklin got called up was a great relief to me, I can tell you.'

Anna had a sudden picture of herself saying goodbye to Tom at the station three years earlier, the look of wonder and disbelief on his face when he realised she had come to wave him off. He had no one else in the world who cared enough to see him go to war.

'And then I found out about the letters.' Edward's expression was bleak. 'Can't you try to imagine how I felt?' he pleaded with her. 'It was as if all my worst fears had come true, that you had feelings for him after all . . .'

'I felt sorry for him, that's all.' But even as she said it, Anna knew it wasn't true. What had started out as a gesture of pity had turned into a warm friendship. She wanted to be completely honest with Edward, but she felt wary of his rage.

'I know that now. I let my jealousy get the better of me, and I was cruel to you.' His voice faltered. 'I was hoping you might find it in your heart to forgive me, that we could make a new start this morning, pretend it had never happened. But I know now that's too much to ask. I could see it in your eyes when you looked at me this morning. I was a fool to think you could forget something like that. How can I expect you to forgive me when I can't forgive myself?' He dropped his gaze. 'I've ruined everything, and I'm deeply sorry. If you want me to leave, I'll understand . . .'

'No.' The word was out before she had even had a chance to think about it. Edward looked up, his blue eyes full of hope.

'I'm still angry with you,' she said. 'You hurt me, and you frightened me, and it will take a long time to put that behind me. But – I want to try,' she went on. 'I understand this must have been a lot for you, coming out of the army and getting married and moving back here. You need time and patience while you get used to it all.'

She thought about all the soldiers on the ward, their outbursts of temper and frustration as they slowly and painfully tried to adjust to their new lives.

She looked up at him. 'I want to make this marriage work, Edward. If you do?'

'Oh, Anna!'

Edward took a step towards her, but she backed away sharply. He stopped, crestfallen, his hands falling to his sides.

'Sweetheart, I'm sorry,' he said quietly. 'I just want to love you, that's all. I'll never hurt you again, I swear.'

Anna looked into his face and saw the tender sorrow in his eyes.

'I'm scared,' she whispered.

'I know, darling. But let me try again, please. It will be better this time, I promise.'

And it was. Anna was nervous as Edward led her upstairs to the bedroom. But this time he was different. He undressed her carefully, as if she was a delicate piece of china, trailing feathery kisses on her bare skin. His lips and fingers worked with infinite loving gentleness, so that by the time he laid her on the bed, Anna was trembling with anticipation and longing instead of fear.

Afterwards, she lay in his arms, her head resting against his broad, muscular chest. Her fingers traced the scars of the gas burns as she breathed in the clean soapy smell of him. Outside, dawn was breaking and the street was coming to life, the steady clopping of horses' hooves and the squeak of cart wheels mingling with the sound of Mrs Hudson berating Mr Hudson as he opened up the shop.

This was what it should be like, she thought. Her and Edward together, just as she had always dreamed they would be.

'You do love me, don't you?' Edward said suddenly.

Anna raised her head to look at him, surprised by the question. 'Of course.'

'I don't know what I'd do if I ever lost you.'

Anna saw the look in his eyes and realised with a shock how insecure he was, even now.

'Lucky you don't have to worry about it, then, isn't it?' she said, laying her head against his chest again. His heart beat steadily under her ear.

He curled his arm tighter around her, holding her close. 'And to think how close I came to losing you, all because of my stupid jealousy,' he said. 'I mean, what does it really matter if you write to another man? You're still mine, aren't you?'

Anna hesitated, then said, 'I won't write to Tom again if you don't want me to.'

She felt him turn his head to look at her. 'Do you mean that?'

'I've been thinking about it, and you're right. I shouldn't really be writing to other men now I'm married.' She reached for Edward's hand, pressing it against her own. His long fingers wrapped tightly around hers.

Even as she said the words, she felt her heart sink slightly in her chest. But it was the right thing to do, she told herself. Edward was her husband now, and she had to make him happy.

'I'll write to him this morning and tell him,' she said.

'Why can't you just stop writing?' There was an edge of impatience in Edward's voice.

'That wouldn't be fair. I need to explain, or he'll wonder what's happened to me.'

She felt his hand tense against hers, and for a moment Anna thought he might argue. But then he said, 'As you wish, my love.' He rolled over on to his side, propping himself up on his elbow to smile down at her. 'You can tell him to find himself another girl to write to, because you're taken. You're mine now. All mine.'

Anna flinched for a second as he bent his head to kiss her, but this time his lips were gentle against hers.

It will all be all right, she told herself. *From now on, everything will be perfect, just as it should be.*

As Edward moved on top of her, his weight pressing down, a flash of colour on the other side of the room caught her eye. It was a scrap of red ribbon, dangling from the fire grate.

Chapter Thirty

'You did what?'

'I wrote to your family.' Dulcie didn't meet Sam's eyes as she straightened his bedclothes. 'It was the right thing to do,' she went on quickly. 'They deserved to know where you are and what's happened to you. It seemed so unfair not to tell them . . .' she gabbled on, not daring to look up. 'And I was right, your mother was so grateful. I've got her letter here, if you want to read it?'

She took it out of her apron pocket and proffered it to him. Sam ignored it.

'You had no right,' he said, his voice soft with menace.

'I'll put it here, in case you want to read it later.' Dulcie placed the letter down on his bedside locker.

'I won't.'

'You might.' She hesitated for a moment, looking at the letter. 'Your mother says she can't wait to see you.'

'I don't want to see her,' he cut her off bluntly.

'But—'

'I mean it. You can write back and tell her that.'

Dulcie kept her head down, tucking in a corner of the bedclothes. 'It might be a bit late for that,' she said. 'She's on her way.'

Sam sat up straighter. 'My mother's coming here?'

Dulcie risked a glance at him. 'Not just your mother,' she said. 'She's bringing your children too.'

He stared at her. His face was impassive, but she could see a myriad emotions reflected in his green eyes.

'What have you done?' he murmured at last.

'They're your family.'

'You had no right to interfere!' He turned on her savagely, his voice rising. 'For God's sake, it's not as if you even really care.'

'Shhh!' Dulcie glanced around the ward nervously. 'Stop shouting, or you'll get me in trouble.'

'Get *you* in trouble?' He stared at her, his eyes black with anger. 'Christ, do you ever stop and listen to yourself, you stupid, stupid girl?'

'What's going on here?' Dulcie's heart sank as Staff Nurse Hanley bustled over. 'What's all this noise about, Nurse?'

'Nothing, Staff.'

'Well, it didn't sound like it to me.' Nurse Hanley turned to Sam. 'Sergeant Trevelyan, perhaps you'd like to tell me why you were shouting?'

Sam stared back at her, tight-lipped and silent.

Nurse Hanley sighed. 'Very well, if neither of you wishes to speak . . . Nurse Moore, please come with me. There are some linens in the store room that need counting. That should keep you out of trouble,' she muttered.

As she followed Staff Nurse Hanley up the ward, Dulcie took a quick glance over her shoulder. Sam's face was buried in his hands, his broad shoulders slumped in utter despair.

For the first time, it began to dawn on her that she might have been too hasty.

She stayed out of his way most of the morning. But as noon approached, she knew she would have to speak to him again. The visitors would be arriving at two o'clock that afternoon, his mother and children among them.

She got her chance just before lunch. Staff Nurse Hanley was taking her break, and Sister was doing bed seven's abdominal drainage behind the screens, assisted by Miriam Trott.

Dulcie crept over to Sam Trevelyan's bed. He was lying on his back with his eyes closed, but she could tell he was not asleep.

'I know you're upset,' she started.

'You don't know anything.' Sam kept his eyes closed. 'As far as I can tell, you don't give a damn about anyone's feelings but your own.'

'That's not fair!' Dulcie gasped. 'I did this for you.'

'No, you didn't. You did it for yourself, just like you do everything else.' He opened his eyes, his face full of contempt. 'Have you told Sister what you've done? Or how about Dr Logan? No point in doing a good deed if you don't get noticed for it, is there? So why don't you just run off and tell them? With any luck they'll transfer you to the shell shock ward and we'll all be better off!'

Dulcie stared at him, shocked by his bitterness. 'Is that what you really think?'

'It's the truth, isn't it?'

She was silent. He had a point, of course. Dulcie did usually have her own interests at heart. But to hear it exposed brutally like that . . . Was she really so calculating?

'Perhaps you're right,' she said. 'But I still think it would do you good to see your family again. You might not feel like it now,' she pressed on, as Sam opened his mouth to speak. 'But just imagine what it will be like to hold your children again.'

'You still don't understand, do you?' he cut her off, his face bleak. 'I don't want to hold my children again. I don't want to see them!'

'Why not?' Dulcie looked down at his chest. 'Is it that you're worried your wound will distress them? Because if that's it, I can—'

209

'It's nothing to do with the bloody wound!'

'What, then? What's so bad that it's keeping you from seeing your own children?'

'None of your business,' he bit out.

'But I want to know. Don't you love your children?'

He flashed her a look of pure dislike. 'Of course I love them!

'Then why don't you want to see them?'

For a moment he said nothing, his mouth a tight line. Then, quietly, he said, 'Because I'm—'

'What?' Dulcie prompted.

He turned to look at her, and she saw the depth of sorrow in his eyes.

'Because I'm too ashamed,' he said.

It was the last thing she had been expecting him to say. The words hung in the silence between them.

'Ashamed? You? But – but why? You're a hero, you earned a medal.'

'I followed orders and they gave me a piece of tin,' he snarled. 'What does that matter, compared to . . .' He stopped.

'Compared to what?'

Sam looked away. 'You wouldn't understand.'

'I'd like to try.'

'I don't want to talk about it.'

She recognised the stubborn lift of his chin. If Sam Trevelyan really did not want to speak then wild horses wouldn't drag it out of him.

'You'd rather just have nightmares about it instead?'

His mouth curled. 'So you're a psychiatrist now, are you? Have you been taking lessons from your friend Dr Logan?'

'I don't have to be a psychiatrist to know you've got a

secret,' Dulcie said. 'And I also know if you don't let it out, it's going to poison everything.'

'Too late for that,' he muttered.

'It doesn't have to be. You can still have a life, Sergeant Trevelyan. You can get out of here, and go back to your family, and be surrounded by people who love you.'

'Even if I don't deserve it?'

Dulcie sank down on the chair beside his bed. She knew she would get an earful from Miss Sutton if she were caught sitting down on duty, but she didn't care. At that moment it seemed there were bigger matters to worry about.

'What makes you say that?' she asked. 'What did you do that was so bad you can't face your family, Sergeant?'

He was silent for a long time. Dulcie was just about to give up when he murmured something under his breath.

She leaned forward. 'What did you say?'

He turned to look at her, his pupils so wide they turned his green eyes black.

'I said, I killed a man,' he said quietly.

For a moment she wondered if she had misheard him again.

She searched for the right words. 'All the men on this ward have killed someone, Sergeant. It's awful, but it's the war, isn't it?'

He sent her an almost pitying look. 'You don't understand,' he said. 'This wasn't some German in No Man's Land. This was one of our own.'

'He was only a kid. Sixteen years old, only four years older than my son. He lied about his age because he wanted to fight for his country.'

Sam spoke in a flat voice. He didn't look at Dulcie, but stared instead into space, as if he was describing a scene that was playing out in front of him.

'Trouble is, he didn't know what he was signing up for. No one did. You can't make people understand if they weren't there. You can describe the trenches knee-deep in water and running with rats, and the cold, and the noise of the shells, and the stink of dead bodies heaped up and rotting because no one has time or a place to bury them. But until you've lived through it . . .' He shook his head. 'It was too much for anyone, and too much for this lad. He'd just watched his best pal die, you see. Right next to him. One minute they were sharing a cigarette, the next a shell hit and this lad was picking bits of his mate's skull off his gas cape. And that wasn't even unusual, it happened all the time . . .'

He stopped for a moment, and Dulcie could see him struggling to gather himself.

'Anyway, this boy took fright. When we got our orders from down the line, he decided to make a run for it instead. He went into hiding, down in the sappers' tunnels. But they found him and brought him back.'

He turned to Dulcie for the first time. 'I couldn't blame him,' he said. 'When you get the orders to go over, you know that's probably it for you. You hear that whistle blow, and you know you have to scramble up that ladder and fight your way through the mud and barbed wire. And then you have to walk – actually walk – into the artillery fire, with shells exploding all around. No wonder half the men in here are doolally. And they're the lucky ones!'

He lit a cigarette and held it between his lips.

'What happened to the boy?' Dulcie asked.

'He was court martialled. Sentenced to death, just like all the other deserters.' Sam blew a steady stream of smoke up into the air. 'Death by firing squad.'

'And you were the one who had to shoot him?'

'Me and a couple of others. Early in the morning, they dragged him out. His knees were knocking so much he could hardly stand up, poor kid. He was sobbing the whole time, crying for his mother. That was the last thing I saw as I raised my rifle, the tears running down his face.' He drew hard on his cigarette. 'I wish to God they'd never caught the poor little sod,' he said in a low, angry voice.

Christopher, run for your life. Run, boy . . .

'You were only following orders,' Dulcie said.

'And that makes it all right, does it?'

'No, but—'

'No,' he cut her off bluntly. 'No, it doesn't.' He puffed angrily on his cigarette. 'I kept thinking about his mother and how she would feel when she got the letter saying her son was dead. Dead because of me.' He ground out his cigarette in the ashtray, forcing it down until the stub was nothing. 'You say it was only orders, but I was the one who pulled the trigger. I was the one who saw his face . . .'

Dulcie thought about his medal. *For bravery in the field.*

'Is that why you saved all those men from No Man's Land?' she asked. 'Because you wanted to make up for what you'd done?'

His mouth twisted. 'You really do fancy yourself as a psychiatrist, don't you?' He shook his head. 'Sorry to disappoint you, but there was nothing noble about what I did that day. The reason I kept going back, again and again, wasn't because I wanted to save lives. It was because I wanted to die. That was why I stood in that field and let all those shells explode around me. I wanted one to hit me, to end it all. Typical, isn't it?' he said. 'All those poor devils wanting to live but getting blown to pieces, and then there's me . . .' He looked disgusted.

'You didn't deserve to die.'

'Neither did that boy.'

For a moment their gazes met and held. Then Sister emerged from behind the screens around bed seven, breaking the spell, and Dulcie shot automatically to her feet.

'I'd better get on,' she murmured.

'You do that.' He wasn't looking at her anymore.

As Dulcie turned to go, she remembered something.

'Was his name Christopher?' she asked.

He frowned. 'Why do you ask?'

'That was the name you shouted in your sleep. You were telling him to run.'

Sam was silent for a while. Then he said, 'His name was Gerrard. Private Malcolm Gerrard.'

'Then who—'

He looked at her, his green eyes dark with anguish. 'Christopher is my son's name,' he said quietly.

Chapter Thirty-One

As two o'clock crept closer, Dulcie began to doubt herself more and more.

Sam Trevelyan looked sick with fear, and she felt sick too. She found it even harder than usual to concentrate on her work, and several times Staff Nurse Hanley had to take her to task about her 'daydreaming'.

'Sister wants you to prepare a cotton jacket for the pneumonia patient in room two,' she said. 'The doctor will be back to see him shortly.'

Dulcie glanced at the clock. It was a quarter to two.

'Can't one of the VADs do it?' She said the words without thinking.

'I beg your pardon, Nurse?' Veronica Hanley blinked at her.

'Sorry, Staff. I – I just wanted to be on the ward when the visitors arrived.'

'Oh, I'm terribly sorry, Nurse Moore. I'll ask Nurse Trott to do it instead, shall I?' Staff Nurse Hanley's broad face was mottled red with suppressed fury. 'I know you think everyone and everything was put on this earth for your convenience, girl, but I'm afraid that is not how we do things on this ward. If Sister wants you to prepare a cotton jacket, then that is what you must do. And be glad she hasn't got you scrubbing the toilets!' she added.

'Yes, Staff.'

Dulcie retreated to room two, one of the private rooms adjoining the main ward. The patient was young, an officer in his early twenties, but he gasped and wheezed like an old man. His body was emaciated, muscles wasted to nothing, and when he fought for breath Dulcie could see the rapid rise and fall of his ribcage clearly outlined through his translucent skin.

She got to work, spreading the rolls of absorbent cotton around his sunken chest and back, then fitting the flannel into place over it. It took all the young man's efforts to breathe, let alone talk, so she was able to allow her thoughts to wander back to Sam.

It would be visiting time soon. The families would be gathering outside the double doors, eager with anticipation to see their loved ones. And then the bell would ring, and one of the VADs would open the doors, and then . . .

'Nurse?'

Dulcie looked up sharply, surprised to see Dr Logan standing behind her.

'I'm sorry, Doctor, I didn't hear you come in.' She started to her feet, but he gestured for her to carry on.

'Please, don't let me disturb you.'

'Thank you, Doctor.'

Dulcie went back to her stitching, but it wasn't long before her thoughts strayed to Sam again.

What if she had got it wrong? She had been so sure of herself when she wrote to his mother, but now she could see she'd had no right to interfere. Sam had made a choice for himself; she should have respected that.

Now he had to face the consequences, all because of her.

'Isn't that stitching rather tight, Nurse?'

Dulcie looked up, surprised that Dr Logan was still in the room. It was the oddest thing – usually she was very aware of him when he was near her.

'It's not a straitjacket, Nurse. And Captain Waterford has enough trouble breathing, don't you think?' Dr Logan looked rueful.

Dulcie stared down at the needle in her hand. 'Sorry, Doctor. I wasn't paying attention.'

She started to unpick the stitches, her thoughts straying straight back to Sam.

What if he refused to see them? What if he turned them away, after they had come all the way up from Cornwall? Surely he wouldn't be so cruel . . .

Two o'clock struck and Dulcie was so nervous she jumped, pricking herself with the needle. She let out a yelp of pain.

'Are you all right, Nurse?' Dr Logan was staring at her. Even Captain Waterford turned his sunken eyes to meet hers.

'Yes. Yes, I'm sorry.' Dulcie sucked the end of her finger. Dr Logan's brows rose, but he said nothing.

She quickly finished fitting Captain Waterford's cotton jacket, then waited while Dr Logan examined him. All the while her gaze kept straying up to the clock on the wall.

Finally, Dr Logan finished writing up his notes and they were about to leave. Dulcie prayed he wouldn't ask her to make up an ice pack or anything. She wasn't sure her nerves could stand it.

As they left the patient's room, Dr Logan said, 'Do you have another appointment, Nurse?'

Dulcie looked round at him, startled. 'No, Sir.'

'It's just you kept looking at the clock. I wondered if there was somewhere you needed to go?'

Dulcie blushed. 'I'm sorry, Doctor. Sam – Sergeant Trevelyan – is expecting a visitor today, and I'm rather worried about it.'

'Worried? Why?'

Heat scalded her face. 'Because I organised it, Sir.'

Dulcie explained what she had done. Dr Logan listened in his usual careful way, his head bowed.

'And you say Sergeant Trevelyan didn't want this visit to happen?'

'No, Sir. But I thought it would do him good. I did ask you for your advice,' Dulcie reminded him.

'Good Lord. Did you?' Dr Logan looked startled. 'And what did I say?'

'You seemed to think it was a good idea.' She looked up at his grave expression. 'It won't do any harm, will it, Sir?'

Dr Logan shook his head. 'Time will tell, Nurse,' he said. But he didn't look very convinced.

So much for trying to impress him, Dulcie thought as she watched him striding away down the ward. She had been so preoccupied she had even forgotten to flirt with him.

There was no sign of Sam or his family when she returned to the ward. Dulcie was still staring at his empty bed when Nurse Hanley bustled up in a flurry of crackling starched linen.

'There's an amputation coming up from surgery,' she announced. 'Fetch Nurse Trott and make up bed eight, please.'

'Where is Sergeant Trevelyan?' Dulcie asked.

Nurse Hanley's face twitched with displeasure. 'Really, Nurse, I do wish you would stop answering all my instructions with a question,' she snapped. Then she added, 'As far as I am aware, Sergeant Trevelyan is on the terrace with his family.'

'On the terrace? But he never goes outside!'

She saw she had said the wrong thing when Staff's brows rose. 'I didn't realise you were such an expert on Sergeant Trevelyan,' she said. 'Why are you so fascinated by him, Nurse?'

'I'm not, Staff. I – I was just curious, that's all.'

'Well, kindly stop being curious and get on with your work.'

'Yes, Staff.'

She was aware of Nurse Hanley's gaze following her as she made her way down the ward towards the linen store. As she passed the French doors leading out to the terrace, she could see several men and their families sitting outside. She didn't dare stop to look because Veronica Hanley was still watching her keenly from the other end of the ward.

Dulcie quickly gathered up sheets and blankets for making up the bed. As she emerged from the linen store, she noticed Nurse Hanley berating a tearful VAD who had managed to drop a cup of tea all over the polished floor. While she was distracted, Dulcie darted to the French doors and peered outside.

It took her a moment to spot Sam among all the other men. He was surrounded by his family, half hidden from her view. He was in a wheelchair, which surprised Dulcie, since he'd always refused one before. His mother sat beside him on a bench, holding his hand. Two children, a boy and a girl, perched on his knees. The little girl had her arms wrapped around his neck, her face pressed into his shoulder. An older boy, tall and upright, stood before them, pointing out something a few feet away. Christopher, she thought.

He was only a kid. Sixteen years old, only four years older than my son . . .

'Nurse Moore?' Dulcie heard Staff Nurse Hanley's voice but ignored it, craning her neck to see Sam's face. He was in profile, so she couldn't read his expression.

'Nurse Moore! I hope you're not daydreaming again?'

Then Christopher must have said something because Sam threw back his head and laughed.

Dulcie stood rooted to the spot, watching him. Then, suddenly, she found she was filled with an absurd burst of happiness. It was all she could do not to laugh, too.

'Nurse Moore!'

She turned. Nurse Hanley was bearing down on her, face like thunder.

'Wipe that silly smirk off your face, girl. You won't be smiling when your name's in the ward book, I'm sure.'

But Dulcie was still smiling when she went to make up bed eight with Miriam Trott.

'You look pleased with yourself,' Miriam commented sourly.

'I am.'

'And why is that, may I ask?'

Before Dulcie could answer her, Dr Logan walked over.

'Well, Nurse, I see your experiment worked.'

Dulcie beamed at him. 'Yes, Doctor.'

'Keep up the good work, won't you?' As he turned to walk away, Dulcie could have sworn he winked at her.

Miriam Trott looked fit to burst. 'What was all that about?'

'I did a good deed.' Dulcie explained about writing to Sam Trevelyan's family. Miriam listened, eyes round with astonishment.

'You?' she said finally. 'You actually did that off your own bat?'

'There's no need to look so surprised about it,' Dulcie said defensively.

Miriam laughed. 'But I *am* surprised,' she said. 'It isn't like you to think of other people.'

'Hark at the pot calling the kettle black!'

Miriam ignored her. 'There must be a reason for it,' she declared. She thought for a moment, then said, 'Do you have a soft spot for Sergeant Trevelyan?'

'No!'

'Are you sure?' Miriam eyed her narrowly. 'You're blushing.'

'Don't be absurd.' Dulcie busied herself plumping a pillow with unnecessary force. 'If you must know, he's a means to an end.'

'What's that supposed to mean?'

Dulcie gave her a smile that she knew would infuriate her. 'You'll see,' she said.

By four o'clock visiting time was over. The families were all ushered out amidst lots of tears, and the nurses set about getting the ward back into some kind of order.

Dulcie made up her mind that she would not approach Sam. She could tell the visit had gone well, but she was still wary of what he might say to her.

Fortunately, Sister set her to work in the kitchen, preparing supper for the men with the VADs. Usually Dulcie would have balked at the task, but today she was grateful as it meant she could give Sam Trevelyan a wide berth.

But when it was suppertime, Miss Sutton insisted that Dulcie should be the one to serve Sergeant Trevelyan.

Dulcie approached him cautiously. Neither of them spoke as she pulled up the bed tray and placed the plate down in front of him.

Sam stared down at it.

'Did you help cook this?' he asked.

'Yes, why?'

'I can tell.' He poked at the grey slab of roast mutton with his fork.

Dulcie caught the amused glint in his eye and relief surged through her. She was forgiven.

'If you don't like it, you know what you can do,' she said shortly.

'Mend my boots with it?'

'If you're going to be rude about it, I'll take it back.' She went to whisk the plate away.

'No, don't.' He put out his hand to stop her. For a moment

they were both still, staring down at his fingers encircling her bare wrist.

Then, slowly, he took his hand away.

Dulcie cleared her throat. 'Anyway, you don't know what pudding is yet!' she said brightly.

He looked up at her from under lowered brows. 'Let me guess. Something unrecognisable with custard?'

'Jam roly-poly, actually.'

'Oh, God,' Sam groaned.

'I'll be sure to pass your compliments on to Sister.'

As Dulcie was walking away, Sam suddenly said, 'Thank you.'

She looked over her shoulder at him. 'For the food?'

'You know what I mean.' His eyes met hers, and suddenly Dulcie felt the imprint of his fingers again, warm and strong against her skin.

Chapter Thirty-Two

Once Edward had got up to light the ovens, Anna curled into the space on his side of the bed, still warm from where his body had been a few minutes earlier. She buried her face in the pillow and breathed in his clean, soapy smell.

Downstairs, she could hear him greeting Charlie at the back door, ready to start their day in the kitchen. Usually, Anna would be up and dressed herself by now, gulping down a cup of tea and pulling on her shoes ready to hurry out for another day on the ward. But today was a rare day off, and she looked forward to spending it with her husband.

Her husband. Anna held up her left hand, admiring the faint glint of her wedding band in the dim dawn light. She was Mrs Edward Stanning. Sometimes she had to say the name out loud just to make herself believe it.

Marriage suited her, she decided. After three weeks, she still woke up every morning feeling absurdly happy and content. This was what her life was supposed to be like, she and Edward together at last. It was everything she had ever wanted.

And, Lord knows, she had waited long enough for it. All those years of worrying that Edward wouldn't come home to her, of reading the casualty lists in the newspapers and fearing the worst. And then those dreadful, empty months after Papa and Mother had gone back to Germany, and Liesel was away and so taken up with Davy that Anna felt as if she didn't have another soul in the world.

But now she had Edward home again, running the bakery, just as her father would have wanted. And if only Mother and Papa could come home again, her happiness would be utterly complete.

Anna pushed the thought away. She shouldn't be greedy. At least she had Edward now, and that made her luckier than most. Only the day before, Nurse Pope had found out her fiancé, missing since Cambrai, had finally been declared killed in action. And now the Russians had laid down their arms, the newspapers reckoned the Germans would have even more forces to muster against their boys. Which meant the New Year would probably bring even more tragedy and lives lost.

She turned her face back into the pillow. She wouldn't think about that, not today. It was going to be a special day. She was looking forward to being back in the kitchen with Edward, working alongside him the way they used to when Papa ran the bakery.

When she arrived there half an hour later, she found Edward and Charlie already hard at work.

'There's no need for you to help out, love,' Edward said as she reached for her apron. 'Charlie and I have already done most of it. Eh, Charlie?'

He nodded. 'We have.'

'You enjoy your day off. You deserve it, after all those hours you put in at the hospital,' Edward said.

Anna looked at Charlie, watching her slyly from behind Edward's shoulder. 'But I want to help.'

'Listen to her, Charlie. I wouldn't say no if someone told me to go and put my feet up, would you?' Edward grinned. 'A glutton for punishment, that's what you are.'

Anna looked from one to the other. 'What am I supposed to do, then?'

'Whatever you like.' Edward shrugged. 'Why don't you

go out? Take yourself up West for the day. You used to like a trip around the shops.'

'I don't want to go up West. I want to stay here with you. I've been looking forward to us spending the day together,' Anna protested, but Edward was already ushering her out of the kitchen and down the passageway towards the shop.

'Tell you what, we'll go out together,' he said. 'When the shop closes for dinner, we'll have a walk around the park. Or we could go round to Wheeler's café for a cup of tea and a bacon sandwich, how about that?'

Anna pouted. 'I still don't understand why I can't help you.'

'Because you'd be too much of a distraction.' Edward's eyes glinted with meaning. 'Do you really think I'd be able to get anything done with you there? I'd just want to kiss you all the time. Like this . . .'

He pulled her into his arms for a demonstration. As his tongue plundered her mouth, Anna felt the heat rising, melting her from inside.

She pushed him away, laughing. 'Edward! Not here!'

'You see what I mean? We'd make poor Charlie blush.'

'I reckon it'd take a lot to make Charlie Atkins blush!' Anna glanced back at the door to the kitchen, now firmly closed. 'I suppose I could help Mrs Church in the shop,' she said reluctantly.

'Like I said, a glutton for punishment!' Edward rolled his eyes.

'Unless you think I'd be too much of a distraction for you there, too?' Anna teased him.

'You're a distraction wherever you are.' Edward wrapped his arms around her waist, scooping her into the air until her face was level with his. Next minute he was kissing her hungrily again, and this time Anna didn't try to push him away.

They were still locked in a passionate embrace in the passageway, oblivious to everything else, when a voice behind them said, 'Don't mind me, I'm sure.'

Anna swung round to see Mrs Church's thin shape in the doorway to the kitchen, bundled up in a heavy overcoat, a shapeless hat jammed on her head.

'Charlie thought you might be upstairs,' she said, looking from one to the other.

'Another five minutes and we might have been,' Edward said.

Anna nudged him sharply, glad that the darkness of the shop hid her blushing face.

Mrs Church looked from one to the other, her thin face tightening. 'You ain't at work today then,' she said to Anna.

'No, I've got the day off,' she said, fighting to stop herself from laughing. She didn't dare look at Edward behind her, his hands still encircling her waist.

'That's nice, ain't it?' Mrs Church addressed herself to Edward. 'Bet you'll be glad of an extra pair of hands, won't you?'

'Actually, Edward doesn't need me, so I thought I'd help you out in the shop.'

'Is that right?' Mrs Church fixed her gaze on him for a moment. Then she said, 'Well, I dunno as there's much work for two in the shop, either. But it'd be nice to have company.'

She turned away from them, unbuttoning her coat.

'It's another freezing cold morning,' she said.

'That'll be because it's winter, Mrs C,' Edward said cheerily.

'They're already queuing up at the soup kitchen, poor souls,' she went on, ignoring him. 'It breaks my heart to think of all those little mites going hungry. How can they go to school with nothing in their bellies?' She shook her head sadly.

'Perhaps we should take some of our stale loaves down there?' Anna suggested.

'Give away our stock, you mean?' Edward laughed.

'Only the ones we don't sell that day,' Anna said.

'Unless you can sell 'em the next,' Mrs Church muttered.

Anna shook her head. 'We'd never sell stale bread. Would we, Edward?' She twisted round to look at him. He was staring back at Mrs Church, his mouth a tight line. 'Edward?'

'It's better than wasting them,' he said.

'But you know Papa would only ever sell bread that was baked that morning.'

'Yes, well, he didn't have to deal with shortages, did he?' Edward snapped. 'You don't know what it's like. It ain't easy when you don't know when your next batch of flour is coming.'

'All the same,' Anna said. 'We don't want to get a bad reputation. It would be better to give the bread away, don't you think?'

She looked at Edward. He was staring past her, his gaze still fixed on Mrs Church.

'I'd better get back to work or there won't be any bread at all.' He turned on his heel and stalked back to the kitchen, slamming the door behind him.

'Someone's not happy,' Mrs Church observed.

Anna stared at the closed door. 'I'd better go and talk to him.'

'No, leave him for a bit. Least said, soonest mended, I always say. That's what I always did with my Ron, and it worked a treat.' Mrs Church rubbed her thin hands together. 'I'll put the kettle on, shall I?'

She made the tea while Anna lit the lamps in the shop

and pulled up the window blinds. Charlie appeared with a tray of loaves.

'I've been told to let you know they're fresh baked this morning,' he looked pointedly to Anna as he set them down on the counter.

'I should think so, too,' she replied pertly.

Ida Church was right, she thought. Let Edward sulk if he wanted to. She knew she was in the right. And Edward probably did too, which was why he was hiding away in the kitchen.

Chapter Thirty-Three

At eight o'clock they unlocked the shop door. But there were no customers queuing outside.

'It'll pick up,' Mrs Church assured Anna, as she stood at the window, peering out into the empty street. 'We're seldom busy first thing.'

'We used to be busy all the time,' Anna said. 'I remember when we had customers queuing outside for hot bread before the shop opened.'

'Times have changed.'

It was a slow morning. Anna swept the shop and polished the brass on the till, and rearranged the loaves and buns in the shop window twice to make them look more appealing, but still no one came in.

She stared at the window display. She was beginning to understand what Edward meant. She had imagined they might have a couple of loaves left over at the end of the day, two or three at most. It would be heartbreaking to have to throw away so much stale stock. No wonder he wanted to keep it to sell the next morning.

Finally, the shop bell clanged and a harassed-looking young woman came in, ushering three children before her. Anna recognised her right away as Mrs Burns, who lived round the corner in Gossett Street.

'Good morning, Mrs Burns,' she greeted her.

The woman looked up at Anna, her gaze narrowing.

''Morning,' she mumbled a half-hearted greeting, then turned to Mrs Church. 'I'll just take half a loaf, please.'

Anna watched as Mrs Church carefully sliced off half a loaf and wrapped it in brown paper. While her children were all bundled up against the cold in thick coats and mufflers, Mrs Burns' coat was thin and threadbare. Her ungloved hands were raw with cold as she counted coins out of her purse.

On impulse, Anna went to the counter and fetched three penny biscuits.

'Here, these are for you.' She went to offer them to the children but as they reached out Mrs Burns put out her hand to stop them.

'No,' she said. 'We can't afford them.'

Anna looked at the three forlorn little faces staring up at her, their eyes round. 'But they're a present.'

'We don't want your charity!' Mrs Burns snapped.

She stared at Anna, fire in her eyes. Then she turned back to Mr Church and counted out the last of the coins.

'There,' she said. 'That should be right.'

She snatched up the bread and stuffed it in her basket, then ushered the now tearful children out of the shop without another word.

'Mrs Burns—' Anna started to say but the door had already shut in her face, the sound of the bell drowning out her words.

Anna stared at the door. 'I don't understand . . . I was only trying to be nice.'

'Take no notice, love,' Mrs Church comforted her. 'She's had a tough time of it since her husband was killed. And then there was all the business about her credit being stopped.'

Anna turned to face her. 'What do you mean?'

'Oh, didn't you know? Your husband's told me I'm not to let anyone have anything on tick anymore.'

'Since when?'

'Since he took over this place. Caused a right ruckus, I can tell you. I had to go around asking everyone to settle up their accounts. 'Course, some of 'em just didn't have the money to pay, like poor Mrs Burns. But he wouldn't hear of it, said they had to pay up before they were allowed anything else.' She cocked her head. 'I'm surprised you didn't know about it? I thought he would have talked to you first.'

'No,' Anna said. 'No, he didn't.'

She looked back at the door, her mind racing. No wonder the shop was empty. At least half their customers bought on tick, paying up at the end of the week after they'd been paid. Not everyone could afford to settle their bills in full, and sometimes they would go weeks or months stacking up their credit, but her father never minded.

'They'll pay in the end,' he said, and they always did.

And now Edward had decided to put a stop to it.

'But I don't understand. Why would he do something like that?' she spoke her thoughts aloud.

'Same reason he's put the prices up, I daresay. To make money.'

Anna turned to her sharply. 'He's put the prices up?'

'Didn't he tell you that, either?' Mrs Church's brows rose. 'Seems like he's making a lot of decisions without consulting you,' she remarked.

'Yes,' Anna said, ignoring her sly look. 'Yes, he is.'

She went to the kitchen to look for Edward, but there was only Charlie in the kitchen. He was lounging against the sink, reading through the *Racing Post*. He glanced up at Anna, then went back to leafing through his newspaper.

'If you're looking for Eddie, he went out,' he said.

'Where did he go?'

'I don't know, do I?'

Anna glared at Charlie, but he didn't look up. 'When

Mr Stanning comes back, tell him I want to see him,' she snapped, and walked out of the kitchen.

She was restless all morning, waiting for Edward to come home. She did her best to help in the shop and keep up a cheery smile for what few customers they had. But all the time, she kept her ear cocked, waiting for his return.

They were shutting up the shop at noon for lunch when she finally heard his voice in the kitchen. Anna hurried down the passageway, Mrs Church at her heels.

Edward was laughing with Charlie about something as he took off his coat. He was still laughing when Anna walked in.

'All right, love?' He looked from her to Mrs Church standing at her shoulder. 'Charlie's just told me you wanted to see me. Is something wrong?'

'Why didn't you tell me you were putting up the prices?' Anna blurted out.

Edward's smile faded. He looked away, peeling off his gloves. 'I didn't think I had to,' he said.

'It would have been nice if you'd consulted me. This is my bakery, after all.'

Something in his expression changed, like a light going off behind his eyes.

'I had no choice,' he said. 'The suppliers put their prices up, we were barely breaking even—'

'Is that why you've cut off our customers' credit?'

Edward looked at Mrs Church. 'My, you have been busy, ain't you?' he said softly. 'Bet you couldn't wait to tell tales.'

'I'm glad someone's seen fit to tell me what's going on!' Anna shot back.

Edward's face was taut with anger. Even Charlie looked wary, his glance flickering from one to the other.

'I asked them to pay their bills, what's wrong with that?' Edward said.

'You know most of them can't afford it.'

'Exactly! They're in here every day, running up bigger and bigger bills they're never going to pay. Meanwhile, we're losing money. We might as well stand at the back door and give the bread away!'

'My father would never have turned anyone away.'

'Your father isn't running the business anymore!' Edward turned on her angrily. 'And perhaps if he'd been more of a businessman, we wouldn't be in the mess we're in now!'

Anna stared at him, stunned. The kitchen had fallen silent, except for the sound of Edward's heavy, furious breathing.

Then, suddenly, he was gone. They stood, frozen, listening to the sound of his footsteps thudding up the stairs, followed by the slam of doors overhead.

Anna glanced at Charlie. He scowled back at her from behind his newspaper. Mrs Church cleared her throat nervously.

'Give him time. He'll calm down soon, I expect.'

Another door slammed overhead, rattling the light fittings.

'I'd better go and talk to him,' Anna said.

Edward was pacing up and down in the sitting room like a caged tiger. As soon as Anna walked in, he turned on her furiously.

'How dare you?' he yelled. 'Telling me off like I was a child!'

'You're acting like a child, throwing a tantrum and then running off!' Anna threw back at him.

He ignored her and carried on pacing, as if he could walk off the heat of his temper. Then he stopped suddenly and turned on her.

'I bet you love it, don't you?' he sneered. 'Coming in and throwing your weight about, humiliating me in front of the staff.'

'I wasn't trying to humiliate you,' Anna protested. 'I was only asking why you'd made these decisions without talking to me first.'

'"It would have been nice if you'd consulted me,"' Edward mimicked her, his face twisting. '"This is *my* bakery, after all." As if we didn't already know that!'

'That's not what I meant,' Anna said. 'I don't think of myself as being in charge, you know that. It's your job.'

'Try telling that to Charlie and that old cow Mrs Church!' Edward turned on her, his face a mask of bitter anger. 'It's already difficult enough to get her to take orders from me as it is. She's always trying to put me in my place, telling me how Mr and Mrs Beck would do it.' His features twisted into a cruel parody of Mrs Church's thin, sombre face. 'Then you turn up, checking on me, questioning everything I do, asking to know where I am, like I'm still the apprentice. God, I bet the old bag loved that!' he scowled. 'I bet she's down there now, clapping her hands in glee.'

'Edward!'

He swung round to face her. 'You want to know where I was today? I'll tell you, shall I? Delivering stale loaves to the soup kitchen, like you told me to.'

Anna stared at him. 'I – I don't know.'

'No, because I didn't realise I had to ask your permission for everything I did.'

'You don't.'

'That's not what it feels like. I ask you, how am I supposed to run a businss when you're constantly undermining me?'

'I'm not.'

'Oh, yes, you are.' Suddenly all the anger seemed to go

out of him and he sank down on the moquette-covered couch, his head in his hands. 'Christ, don't you think it's hard enough for me, taking over from your father? Friedrich Beck, the best baker in Bethnal Green.' There was a bitter edge to his voice. 'Everyone loved him, didn't they? And everyone knows I'll never be as good as he is.'

'That's not true!' Anna sat down beside him and slipped her arm around his broad shoulders. 'Papa was very proud of you, he wanted you to take over the business.'

'But I'm making a mess of it, aren't I?' Edward turned his face to hers. 'We're struggling, Anna. Our costs have gone through the roof, we scarcely have any customers, and the ones we do have don't pay their bills. It ain't like the old days when they were queuing halfway down the street.' He shook his head. 'I'm sorry I didn't tell you when I put up the prices and stopped the customers' credit. But I didn't know what else to do.'

Anna looked into his face, and for the first time saw the despair in his blue eyes. 'You're doing your best. I know you are,' she said.

'But I ain't your father, am I?'

'Papa didn't always get it right, either. Remember how Mother was always telling him off about letting customers run up big bills on tick?'

Edward gave a crooked smile. 'I do remember that.' He held her hand. 'I just want to make you and your father proud.'

'I *am* proud of you.' Anna planted a kiss on his cheek. 'You're going to make a big success of our bakery, Edward Stanning.'

He sent her a teasing look. 'Don't you mean, *your* bakery?'

Anna felt herself blushing. 'I mean *our* bakery,' she corrected him. 'We're married now, remember? Everything I have is yours.'

'I do remember.' He smiled. 'So does that mean you'll trust me to make decisions?'

'Of course.'

'And I won't have to ask your permission?'

'Whatever you think is best.'

'And you won't listen next time Mrs Church goes telling tales?'

'I'll tell her to mind her own business.' Anna kissed him again. And this time he kissed her back.

Chapter Thirty-Four

The end of January brought a new intake of nurses to Walford House and as usual the residents had to shuffle around to make space for them. After escaping the Home Sister's eagle eye for more than a year, Dulcie's luck finally ran out and she was forced to give up the luxury of her single room to share with Grace Duffield.

Grace arrived on a damp, grey Sunday afternoon, dragging a trunk of belongings behind her.

'I'm sorry about this,' were her first words as she manhandled the heavy leather-bound trunk into the middle of the room and promptly tripped over it. 'It's an awful nuisance, you having to share.'

'It isn't your fault, I suppose,' Dulcie sighed. 'I've emptied the bottom drawer in the chest and cleared you some space in the wardrobe. Although goodness knows if it will be enough . . .' She eyed the trunk, squatting in the middle of the room.

'I'm sure I'll manage,' Grace said cheerfully. She bent down to unfasten the strap buckles on her trunk.

'I hope you don't snore?' Dulcie said, as she watched her unpack.

'I don't think so.'

'And don't break anything.'

'I'll try not to.'

Grace threw open the wardrobe door and gazed at the sliver of space Dulcie had grudgingly cleared for her.

'I didn't think you had that many clothes?' Dulcie said defensively.

Grace gave a little shrug. 'I'm sure I'll fit everything in somehow.'

She fetched an armful of clothes from her trunk and started arranging them on hangers.

'I must say, I'm very glad to be sharing a room again,' she said. 'I've been lonely since Anna Beck started living out.'

'I don't know why Beck is still working here,' Dulcie replied.

'I think she enjoys her work.'

'Then she must be mad!' Dulcie snorted with derision. 'When I'm married, I intend to be a lady of leisure – watch out!'

Grace swung round with an armful of clothes and knocked Dulcie's powder compact off the bedside cupboard. Dulcie made a grab for it just before it hit the floor.

'You clumsy goose! What did I say about not breaking anything?' she snapped.

'Sorry.'

'You would be, if you broke this.' Dulcie snapped open the compact and checked the mirror. The enamelled compact had been a gift from a besotted medical student. Dulcie had waited until he had presented it to her to tell him she wasn't interested.

She watched in fascination as her room-mate unpacked the rest of her belongings from the trunk.

'You have a lot of photographs,' she observed, as Grace arranged them carefully on her bedside table.

'They're my family.' She polished a gilt frame with her sleeve and smiled fondly down at the photograph. 'I like to see them when I wake up and say goodnight to them before I go to bed. A bit silly of me, I suppose.' She looked shame-faced.

238

Dulcie glanced at her own bedside table, empty but for her compact, her lipstick and a tattered copy of *Tatler*.

'Let me see.' She reached for one of Grace's photographs. 'Goodness, what a lot of children!'

Grace grinned. 'Those are my brothers and sisters.' She looked over Dulcie's shoulder, pointing them out. 'Those are my older brothers, Matthew and Mark. Those two are Luke and John. They're all away in France now. And those are the twins, Patience and Prudence, and the other girls, Charity and Mercy. And that's the youngest, Peter. Or he was the youngest,' she added as an afterthought. 'Mother has had Reuben since then. Oh, and that's me,' she said, pointing to a face nearly lost at the back, peeping out from between her brothers' broad shoulders.

Dulcie studied the couple seated in the centre of the family group and thought how much they reminded her of her own parents. The father, with his whiskery face and big rough hands, looking so ill at ease in his Sunday suit. And the mother, so proud and so careworn.

'And who's this?' Dulcie picked up another photograph. It was a dark-haired, bearded man in his late-thirties or early forties. Handsome, in a rough sort of way. He was also in his Sunday best, a Bible tucked under his arm.

'That's Mr – Noah – Wells,' Grace mumbled.

Dulcie looked at the piercing eyes staring back at her from the photograph. 'Is he a friend of yours?'

'He's my fiancé.'

Dulcie looked up sharply. Grace was blushing fiery red to the roots of her hair. 'Your fiancé? You're *engaged*?'

Grace looked away. 'I think I might be, but I'm not sure.'

Dulcie stared at her, stunned. 'How on earth can you not be sure?'

'It's hard to explain.'

'Has he asked you to marry him?'

'Sort of. But I haven't said yes yet,' Grace added hurriedly.

'And are you going to say yes?'

'I don't know. Probably. I don't know if I have much choice really.'

Grace took the photograph out of Dulcie's hand, glanced at it for a moment then shoved it away in the drawer. She looked rather wretched for a girl who might be newly engaged, Dulcie thought.

'I think you'd better tell me all about it,' she said.

Dulcie listened in growing astonishment as Grace explained what had happened to her at Christmas.

'So if I understand you, this man you scarcely know has just lost his wife and now he wants you to replace her?' Grace nodded. 'And your parents want you to marry him because he's rich and owns a lot of land.'

'That isn't the only reason,' Grace argued. 'They know he'll be a good husband. They want me to be happy.'

'But how can you be happy with someone you hardly know?'

Grace lifted her shoulders in a shrug. 'He seems nice. And I'll have a husband and a home of my own. And I'll be close to my family. It's everything I could want, really.'

'And what about love? Don't you want that, too?'

'I'm sure I could make myself love him in time.'

'You can't make yourself fall in love with someone, you know.'

Grace turned to her with a frown. 'But you said you could. You decided to fall in love with Dr Logan, didn't you?'

'That's different,' Dulcie muttered.

'How?'

Dulcie looked into Grace's face. She seemed genuinely perplexed. She opened her mouth to speak, then found she could not answer.

'Dr Logan is my type,' she said at last.

'How do you know that? You've barely spoken to him.'

'I just know, all right?' Dulcie snapped.

Dulcie was washing up the breakfast dishes in the kitchen with Miriam Trott when Nurse Hanley appeared in the doorway and said, 'Moore, you are to report to Matron's office immediately.'

Dulcie and Miriam looked at each other. 'Why, Staff?' Dulcie asked.

'I don't know!' Hanley snapped back. 'I daresay you're in trouble again.'

She left, and Dulcie reached for the towel to dry her hands. Miriam glanced at the clock and smirked.

'You haven't even been on duty half an hour and already you've been summoned to Matron. That's a record, even for you.'

Dulcie changed her apron, rolled down her sleeves and fastened on some clean starched cuffs. She checked herself in the bathroom mirror, making sure all her brown curls were tucked inside her cap, gave her shoes a quick polish on the backs of her woollen-clad legs, and headed down to Matron's office.

As she tapped on the door, Dulcie was still trying to work out what she might have done wrong. As far as she could recall, she hadn't been late for ages. She hadn't broken anything, her uniform had passed without comment, and once Miss Sutton had even commented in the ward book that she was 'sensible'. It was the highest praise Dulcie had ever received.

So she was completely mystified as she stood before Matron's desk, her hands clasped tightly behind her back.

'Ah, Moore.' Matron gave her a chilly smile. 'I have some good news for you.'

Dulcie warily tried to read her expression. Matron's idea of good news wasn't necessarily hers.

'As from next week, you are to be transferred to Wilson ward,' Matron went on.

'What?' Dulcie was so shocked she didn't realise she had blurted out the word until she saw Matron's brows rose.

'I think you heard me correctly, Moore.' Her smile became more strained. 'Although you might well be surprised,' she said. 'I certainly was, when the request came through from Dr Logan.'

'Dr Logan?' Dulcie echoed.

Matron nodded. 'He has asked for you especially.' She looked up at Dulcie. 'It seems you have particularly impressed him. Although I must say, I am at a loss to know why,' she added under her breath.

Dulcie was so overwhelmed, she barely registered the insult.

Matron was still speaking, talking about the shell shock patients and how nurses had to be particularly understanding of their difficulties. But Dulcie had stopped listening.

Dr Logan has asked for you especially.

It was a sign, Dulcie thought. Just as she was beginning to think Robert Logan was a lost cause, at last he had shown interest in her.

She had already impressed him with her compassion. Once she was working alongside him on Wilson ward, he would soon realise that she was the woman he had been looking for all his life.

She had been gone a long time, Sam thought.

He was annoyed with himself for noticing. But then he seemed to notice everything about Dulcie Moore. He noticed the soft brown of her eyes. He noticed the way her cap could never quite contain all her curls, and how, when she bent close, he could see a smattering of freckles covering her snub nose. The nurses weren't supposed to wear perfume on the ward, but Dulcie had a light, flowery scent, quite different from the usual nurse smell of starch and carbolic.

He told himself it was because he was bored. Watching Nurse Moore beat counting the panes of glass in the windows, or listening to Sergeant Patterson in the next bed relive his time in the trenches. But deep down Sam had to admit it was more than that.

'Where's the other one?' he asked Nurse Trott when she came round with the washing trolley.

'She's been sent to Matron.'

'Why? What's she done?'

'Heaven knows.' Nurse Trott shrugged. 'It could be anything with Moore.' She brandished a flannel. 'Now, shall I help you, or can you manage by yourself?'

It was all wrong, Sam reflected, as he washed himself behind the curtain. He didn't want to feel like this. He had shut down that part of him when his wife died.

And going off to war had killed the rest. He had returned from France an empty shell – shattered, cynical and devoid of feeling.

But seeing his family again had reawakened something in him. He had started to see the world as a less brutal place. He no longer dreamed of death and bleak, dark landscapes littered with corpses. Now he saw a place of possibilities, of life, and beauty, and kindness. He had even begun to imagine that he might deserve to find some happiness there.

But he was never going to find it with someone like Dulcie Moore.

He didn't even know why he liked her. She was self-centred, petulant, positively rude at times. But there was a spark about her that none of the other nurses had.

Besides, Sam was hardly perfect himself. He could be every bit as blunt, stubborn and selfish as Nurse Moore, as she had pointed out to him often enough. She was the only one who stood up to him, who gave as good as she got instead of offering simpering sweetness.

They were more than a match for each other.

And she wasn't all bad. She had, after all, given him back his family.

All right, she had done it for selfish reasons. Or so she said. But there had been a moment, just after the visit, when Sam thought he had glimpsed a genuine joy in her, the kind of pleasure that only came from doing something for someone else.

It had given him hope that perhaps Dulcie Moore had a heart after all.

She returned to the ward in time for the dressings round. She was grinning from ear to ear, Sam noticed.

The round took a long time. Usually the men did not mind having to wait for the Agony Wagon, but Sam was impatient by the time she reached him.

'You look happy,' he commented, when she finally arrived at his bedside.

'I am,' she said.

'Any particular reason?'

'I'm moving to Wilson ward.'

He twisted his mouth into a reluctant smile. 'You mean you managed to convince them you actually have a heart?'

'It looks like it.' Dulcie grinned back at him. 'And I believe I have you to thank for that.'

'They noticed your good deed?'

'I can't think of any other reason why they would

transfer me.' She leaned in, and once again he noticed her flowery scent. 'Matron said Dr Logan asked for me 'specially.'

A fist closed around his heart, squeezing it painfully. 'No wonder you're in a good mood.'

He watched her as she removed his dressing, her fingers dancing against his skin.

'When will you be leaving?' he asked.

'Next week, Matron says. Or possibly sooner, if they can find someone to take my place.'

'Now where on earth are they going to find someone like you?'

His words hung in the air between them, and for a moment Sam thought he'd said too much. Then Dulcie laughed.

'That remains to be seen, doesn't it?'

Sam gritted his teeth and fell silent as she cleaned his wound and replaced his dressing. It had healed enough to stop hurting a long time ago, but at least pretending meant he didn't have to find any words.

By the time she had finished dressing his wound, he had recovered himself enough to say, 'So I suppose you'll be picking your trousseau from one of those magazines of yours soon?'

Dulcie blushed. 'You never know.'

'Well done anyway.' He hated the gruffness in his voice. 'It looks like you finally got what you wanted, doesn't it?'

Dulcie looked up at him.

'Yes, it does, doesn't it?' she said quietly.

Chapter Thirty-Five

The dawn was breaking on another freezing cold morning as Anna plodded home from a gruelling night shift. February was almost over but still the weather had not turned, and she could feel the ice-covered puddles cracking under her feet.

There was an outbreak of dysentery on one of the other military wards, and Anna had been sent down there to help the nurse on duty. All night they had been on their feet, rushing up and down the ward with bowls and bedpans, applying stupes and fomentations, changing beds and soaking endless buckets of soiled sheets in carbolic.

By the time the day staff arrived to take over, Anna was utterly exhausted. As she trudged through the dark, cold streets, all she could think about was getting home to Edward and a warm bed.

Light spilled from the kitchen window into the yard. But when Anna let herself in through the back door she found the kitchen empty.

'Edward?' she called. There was no response.

She put her hand on the oven door. It was stone cold.

'Edward?' she called out again.

She swung round as the door opened. But it was only Charlie Atkins standing there, a steaming teacup in his hand.

'Oh, hello,' he said. 'I didn't hear you come in.'

Anna watched him set his teacup down on the wooden

counter, next to a folded copy of the *Racing Post*. 'Where is Mr Stanning?'

'I dunno. He wasn't in when I arrived.'

'Did he say anything to you about where he might be going?'

'Not a word, Missus. I thought you might know, since you're his wife?'

Anna stared at him. Charlie's face was blank, but there was a glint in his eye she did not trust. As if he knew more than he was letting on.

Then another thought occurred to her. 'How did you get in if Mr Stanning isn't here to open the door?'

'He gave me a key.'

'Why?'

'You'd have to ask him that. I s'pose he wants me to come and go as I please.'

His gaze held hers. Charlie Atkins was a bit too cocky for Anna's liking, but Edward reckoned he was a good worker and wouldn't hear a word against him.

'Did he also say you could wander about the house, making tea?' she asked.

'Eddie doesn't mind.'

'No, but I do. Upstairs is our private quarters.'

'I'm only putting the kettle on.'

'All the same, I don't want you going up there.'

Charlie looked sulky. 'If that's what you want.'

'And why haven't the ovens been lit yet?'

'I dunno, do I?' he grunted, bad-temperedly. 'Eddie usually sees to it before I get here.'

And where is Edward? The question gnawed at her.

'Go and see to it, please.'

'Righto, Missus.'

As Anna went to leave the kitchen, he muttered, 'It ain't my fault your husband keeps secrets from you.'

Anna turned to face him. 'What did you say?'

'I said, I wouldn't worry about him, Missus. Eddie generally turns up eventually. Wherever he's been.'

There it was again, that mocking gleam in his eyes.

'Just get on with your work,' she snapped.

Perhaps Edward had gone out early, Anna thought as she hurried upstairs. Although she couldn't imagine the kind of errand that would take him out of the house at the crack of dawn. And if he had gone out, surely he would have left her a note . . .

But their bed had not been slept in.

Anna stared at the pristine bedclothes, the plumped pillows, and panic rose in her chest.

Oh, Edward, where are you?

She heard the sound of the back door opening and hurried back downstairs.

'Edward?'

She pushed open the door to the bakery kitchen. There was Mrs Church, taking off her coat. Charlie was leaning against the counter, the *Racing Post* lying open beside him.

'Good morning,' Mrs Church greeted her. 'It's another cold one, isn't it? They say spring is on the way, but I can't see any sign of it – goodness, whatever is the matter, my dear? You look as white as—'

'Do you know where Edward is?' Anna cut across her.

'Well, no, I—' Anna caught the quick glance that passed between Mrs Church and her nephew. 'Isn't he here?'

'She wouldn't be asking otherwise, would she?' Charlie's voice was laced with sarcasm.

'He's been out all night,' Anna said, ignoring Charlie's sly look. 'Did he say anything to you about where he was going?'

'No one knows where he is,' Charlie interrupted. 'Ain't that right, Auntie Ida?'

Anna looked at Mrs Church. She was silent, her mouth a pinched line.

'What?' Anna looked from her to Charlie and back again. 'What's going on?'

Neither of them answered. Then Mrs Church said, 'I'm going to open up the shop,' and bustled out, her coat under her arm.

Anna looked back at Charlie. His expression was blank as he picked up his newspaper.

'Why are you reading that when you should be working?' frustration made her snap.

'I'm just waiting for the ovens to warm up – oi!' he cried in protest as Anna snatched the newspaper out of his hands. 'I was reading that!'

'Not on my time, you're not. I'm sure there's some work you could be getting on with.'

'We'll see what Eddie has to say about it,' Charlie muttered darkly as Anna left the kitchen, the newspaper tucked under her arm.

'You'll have to find him first,' Anna called back over her shoulder.

Mrs Church was pulling up the blinds when Anna walked into the shop. She glanced back and Anna saw her face fall. Then she turned away again.

'I hope you ain't going to be pestering me with questions about your husband?' she muttered.

'You do know something, don't you, Mrs Church? What is it? What won't you tell me?'

'I don't know anything.' Mrs Church kept her back turned, fiddling with the blind cord. 'I keep my eyes and ears closed, I find it's the best way. Don't want to be accused of *interfering*,' she added meaningfully.

Anna stifled a sigh. There had been a couple of times over the past month when Mrs Church had tried to tell her tales about Edward, but Anna had kept her promise to him and refused to listen. The last time Mrs Church had come to her, Anna had told her not to interfere.

Mrs Church had not taken it very well.

'Fine, don't tell me,' Anna snapped. 'I daresay he'll find his way home soon enough.'

'I daresay he will,' Mrs Church sniffed. Then, as Anna turned to go back upstairs, she added, 'But if you want to know where to look for him, I'd try the Fallen Angel.'

Anna looked back over her shoulder at her. 'The Fallen Angel? I don't think I know it . . .'

'No, you wouldn't. It's the other side of the park, near Hackney way. Not the kind of place a respectable person should know about.' Mrs Church looked disapproving.

'What would Edward be doing up there?'

'That's where his new pals hang out. So Charlie says, anyway. He often leaves the boy in the kitchen while he goes off there to play cards and – whatever else.'

So that was why he'd given Charlie a key. 'How long has this been going on?' Anna asked.

'I really couldn't say.' Mrs Church pursed her lips. 'I've been told to mind my own business, and that's what I'm doing.'

Anna could tell from Mrs Church's gloating expression that she was dying to say more. Edward was right, she really didn't have a good word to say about him.

'I daresay Edward misses his friends now he's out of the army,' she said. 'It will do him good to get out and about.'

'Even when he's supposed to be working?' Mrs Church's brows lifted.

'It's up to him, isn't it? Edward knows what he's doing.'

'Well, I hope you're right. Although I can't say I'd like the idea of my husband associating with the likes of Billy Willis,' she added.

Anna looked at Mrs Church's smug face. She was enjoying this, she thought. She was the kind of woman who loved having secrets and knowing all the gossip. Anna didn't want to give her the satisfaction of asking, but in the end she couldn't help herself.

'Who's Billy Willis, when he's at home?'

'Only the biggest villain in Bethnal Green. Honestly, I'm surprised you ain't heard of him. Billy and his gang run the betting at all the racecourses between here and Doncaster. And a lot of other things besides,' she said darkly. 'Believe me, your husband's doing himself no favours getting mixed up with the likes of them. I'd be worried, if I were you, Miss Anna.'

Of course she was worried. But she wasn't about to show Mrs Church that.

'I can't choose my husband's friends for him, can I?' she said.

'So you don't mind that they're leading him astray?'

Anna frowned. 'What do you mean?'

'Yes, Mrs C. What do you mean?'

They both swung round. Edward stood in the doorway to the shop. He looked tired and dishevelled in his rumpled clothes, his eyes red-rimmed from lack of sleep.

'Edward!' Anna ran to him, relief surging through her. 'Oh, thank God. I've been so worried.'

'I'm not surprised. It sounds like Mrs C's been filling your head with all sorts of stories.' He put his arm around her and planted a kiss on her forehead. He smelled of stale beer and cigarettes. 'I bet you thought I'd been locked up in Pentonville, didn't you?'

'I'm just glad you're home safe.' Anna clung to him. 'Where have you been?'

'I was playing cards with my mates until late. I'd had a few drinks and I couldn't get a cab home for love nor money, so I decided to kip on the floor. I would have walked but the weather was so filthy, I didn't want to catch my death.' He held her closer. 'I'm sorry, love. I didn't mean to worry you. I meant to be here when you got home but it took me ages to walk back from Hackney. Did Charlie manage to open up the kitchen all right without me?'

'Yes, he did.' Anna hugged him close, too overcome with relief to think about anything else.

'He's a good boy.' He released Anna and turned to Mrs Church. 'Sorry, Mrs C, I reckon I interrupted you when I walked in. What was it you were saying?'

Anna looked from one to the other. Mrs Church's face was a taut mask.

'It doesn't matter,' she said.

'No, come on. I'd like to hear it. Something about me being led astray, wasn't it?'

'I said, it'll keep,' Mrs Church bit out.

Edward smiled slowly. 'I'm sure it will,' he said.

Chapter Thirty-Six

Anna went up to bed but, exhausted though she was, could not sleep. Mrs Church had planted all kinds of ideas in her head that had left her feeling deeply unsettled.

Despite what she had said to Mrs Church, she didn't like the idea of Edward going off the way he had. She certainly couldn't imagine her father abandoning his work at the bakery to go off and play cards. He would never leave his apprentice to open up the shop, either. Friedrich Beck made sure he was the first to arrive every morning and the last to leave at night.

And that was when Edward had been his apprentice. If he'd had someone like Charlie Atkins working for him, Papa would never have trusted him to wash up a baking tray on his own, let alone run the kitchen. And he certainly wouldn't have given him a key to the place. It made Anna uneasy, knowing that Charlie could come and go as he pleased. How often did he go upstairs and poke around in their belongings while she and Edward were both out?

And as for this business with Edward's friends . . . Even though Anna had tried to pretend she wasn't concerned, her chest fluttered with anxiety whenever she thought about them.

She trusted Edward, of course. But she couldn't forget how he had almost been led into a life of crime before. He'd told her himself how he had got involved with the Franklin brothers when he was a boy, and had almost gone to jail for robbery.

He was a lot younger then. But Anna was still uneasy about the idea of him falling in with another bad crowd.

She wished she could have written to Tom and asked his advice. Tom was a Franklin himself, had grown up in that dark underworld and understood it better than she ever could. He would have been able to help her, to put her mind at ease about this Billy Willis character and his friends.

But she hadn't written to Tom since the day after her wedding, when she had sent her final letter to him. And she had heard nothing from him since, either. She knew she had done the right thing, but she still missed him.

At midday Anna went downstairs to find Edward shutting up the shop for dinner.

'Where's Mrs Church?' she asked.

'She had some errands to do, so I sent her off early.' Edward held out his arms to her. 'Are you all right, sweetheart? You still look tired.'

'So do you.' Anna hugged him, pressing her face into his chest.

Edward's laughter rumbled against her cheek. 'That's my own fault for staying out all night playing cards with the boys!' He held her closer. 'You're not upset about that, are you, love?'

For a moment she was tempted to speak up. 'No, of course not,' she said instead. 'You're a grown man, you can do as you like.'

'That's my girl.' He held her tighter, his arms wrapped around her. 'They're just ordinary men, you know,' he said. 'Whatever Mrs Church likes to say about it.'

'She made it sound like you'd spent the night in a den of thieves!' Anna searched Edward's face as she said it, but he only laughed.

'Did she now? I daresay she thought we were planning our next bank robbery.'

'Don't give her ideas!' Anna hesitated a moment, then said, 'She mentioned someone called Billy Willis?' Edward's expression was blank. 'Do you know him?'

'I've heard of him, of course. And I know people who know him. But I can't say I've ever met the man personally. Not sure I'd want to, either.'

'But Mrs Church said—'

'Mrs Church would say anything to make me look bad,' Edward cut her off. 'I can't do a thing right as far as that old cow's concerned.'

'Edward!'

'I'm sorry, but she's driving me barmy. She's always watching me, keeping tabs, waiting to tell you what I've been doing.'

'I don't take any notice of her, you know that.'

'Yes, but that doesn't stop her, does it?'

Anna sighed. 'I'll speak to her again.'

'I was hoping you'd do more than that.'

'What do you mean?'

Edward's expression softened. 'If anyone should be in that shop, it's you. You're Friedrich Beck's daughter, you'd be able to bring the customers in far better than Mrs Church can. Who wants to see her sour face behind the counter? And as for that sharp tongue of hers . . .' He looked down at Anna. 'It's what your father wanted, isn't it? You and me working together?'

Anna blinked up at him, realisation dawning. 'You want me to give up nursing?'

'Why not? It was never what you wanted, was it? You only signed up because of the war. You trained as a baker, Anna. It was always your dream, remember?'

He was right, she thought. It was her dream. And it was what Papa would have wanted, too.

She had a misty vision of herself and Edward working

alongside each other, laughing together in the bakery kitchen, just like her own mother and father had done. They might even be able to get rid of Charlie. His presence disturbed her more than she liked to admit.

'And just think, I won't be able to get into trouble with my new friends if you're there to keep me on the straight and narrow!' he said.

Anna shoved him playfully in the ribs. 'I trust you.'

'I'm glad to hear it.' He caught her hands in his, thumbs gently tracing circles on the skin. 'So what do you say? You and me, working together, just like old times?'

It sounded like heaven. But still something niggled at her.

'What about Mrs Church?'

Edward's blue eyes grew cold. 'What about her?'

'We can't get rid of her. She's been here for years. Besides, she's a widow, she needs the money.'

'We need the money!' Edward reminded her. 'Think what we can do if we save on her wages. We might be able to bring down our prices, or even start offering customers tick again.' He let her hands drop. 'Of course, if you don't think it's a good idea . . .'

'No! No, it's a very good idea,' Anna assured him hastily. 'I'm just a bit worried about telling her, that's all.'

'I'll tell her,' Edward said. 'Believe me, it would be a pleasure to give the old bag her marching orders!'

'No,' Anna said. 'I should be the one to do it. Promise me you'll leave it to me – please?'

'If I must,' Edward sighed. Then he smiled and grabbed her hands again. 'Just think, in a couple of weeks we'll be working together like we used to. How does that sound?'

For a moment Anna felt a pang, thinking of the Nightingale Hospital and all the good times she'd had there. She had made so many friends, it would be sad to leave them all behind.

Then she remembered the previous night, and all those buckets and bowls and bedpans. She certainly wouldn't miss nights like that.

She grinned at Edward. 'I think it sounds like heaven,' she said.

Chapter Thirty-Seven

'What are you supposed to be doing, Nurse Moore?'

Dulcie's heart sank at the sound of Sister's voice. She turned round, stifling a sigh, to see Miss Parker bearing down on her.

'I was going to take blood from the patient in bed fourteen, Sister.'

'And how do you propose to do that, Nurse?'

Dulcie looked down at the kidney dish in her hands, filled with the hypodermic apparatus and covered with a cloth. 'The usual way, Sister.'

Miss Parker gave an exaggerated sigh. 'How long have you been working on this ward, Moore?'

Too long, Dulcie thought. 'A month, Sister.'

'Then you should know by now that particular patient doesn't like needles.'

'Then what am I supposed to do, Sister?'

Miss Parker sighed. 'Ask Duffield, she'll tell you.'

'Yes, Sister.'

Dulcie walked away, quietly furious.

Ask Nurse Duffield. Nurse Duffield will show you. That was all she seemed to hear. She was getting sick and tired of it.

She watched Grace at the other end of the ward, laughing with a patient. That same man had glared at Dulcie in hostile silence this morning when she had tried to make conversation with him.

It was as if Grace had found her natural home, Dulcie thought. On Monaghan, she had always been so awkward and clumsy. And yet in the four weeks Dulcie had been on Wilson, she had not seen Grace drop or spill a single thing. She moved around the ward with assurance, perfectly content and untroubled by all the shrieking and moaning going on around her.

And of course she knew exactly what to do about the troublesome patient in bed fourteen.

'Oh, you mean Captain Dodds? Yes, he can be rather difficult,' she said cheerfully. 'But it isn't the needle he dislikes, it's the sight of blood. Just distract him and you should be fine.'

'And how am I supposed to do that?'

'I find a crossword usually works. Or else talk to him. Get him on the subject of motor cars. They're a bit of a passion of his. You could probably saw his leg off if he's talking about Aston Martins or Rolls-Royces.'

Dulcie stared at her. 'How do you remember so much about them all?'

'I take an interest.' Grace shrugged. 'Once you find out what kind of person they are and the way they think, it's really quite easy to work out what they need.' She smiled. 'I'm sure you'll get used to all their funny little ways in time. Take the new patient, Corporal Gates, for instance . . .'

But Dulcie wasn't listening. She was distracted by the sight of Sam Trevelyan, visible through the French doors. He was shuffling across the terrace, leaning on Miriam Trott's arm.

I'll bet he hates it, Dulcie thought. Sam Trevelyan was not the type of man to lean on anyone.

She watched them for a moment. Sam looked so tall and powerful beside Miriam's diminutive figure. She could see Miriam's mouth moving ten to the dozen as usual and wondered what she was talking to him about. Something tedious, no doubt. If she knew Miriam Trott, she was probably explaining the plot of the latest romance novel she had read.

They reached the end of the terrace and turned around. As they started back, Miriam caught sight of Dulcie watching them and gave her a mocking little wave. She must have said something to Sam, because he looked up too. Their eyes met and he gave her such a long-suffering look, Dulcie couldn't help laughing.

'You miss them, don't you?' Grace said behind her.

Dulcie turned around sharply. 'What?'

'The men on Monaghan? I think you enjoyed working there more than you do here.'

Dulcie turned back towards the window, but Sam Trevelyan had disappeared from view.

'I – understood it better,' she admitted slowly. 'I know where I am with bad chests and trench feet and missing limbs. But these men – they scare me.' She looked around her. She would rather dress gaping wounds all day than have to look into those lifeless, glassy-eyed faces. At least the men on Monaghan were predictable; the shell shock patients could be laughing one minute, and screaming in terror the next.

'You'll get used to them,' Grace said kindly.

'I'm not sure I want to.'

'Not even for him?' Grace nodded up the ward to where Dr Logan was approaching them.

Dulcie immediately straightened her cap and put on her best and most winning smile, but Robert Logan didn't even look at her as he addressed himself to Grace.

'How does Private Tennant seem to you this morning, Nurse?'

'Much better, Doctor.'

'Any hallucinations?'

'Not today.'

'Good, good.' Dr Logan pushed his spectacles higher on his nose and looked thoughtful. 'Let me know if there's anything you're concerned about, won't you?'

'I will, Doctor.'

Dr Logan gave Dulcie a brief nod and walked off.

'Good morning to you, too,' she muttered. 'Did you see that?' she said to Grace. 'He barely looked at me. Honestly, I don't know why he bothered to ask for me 'specially if all he's going to do is ignore me!'

'I expect he has a lot on his mind,' Grace said mildly. 'He has to prepare reports for the Medical Board next month. That always puts him in a bad mood.'

Dulcie knew all about the Medical Board. Every couple of months, the doctors had to submit reports on the men's progress so they could be put before the board. They would then decide who could be passed fit.

'It's always difficult on this ward because the men have no physical symptoms,' Grace explained. 'It's easy for the board to decide whether someone with a missing foot or a gunshot wound should be sent back to the Front. But if it's their mind that's been injured . . .' She looked down the ward to where Dr Logan was talking to Albie Sallis. 'A lot of the Medical Board still won't accept neurasthenia as a diagnosis. Dr Logan and Dr Carlyle have an awful job stopping them from being sent back to fight.'

'Have you heard about Anna Beck?' Dulcie changed the subject abruptly. She could see Grace was getting upset, and didn't want to have to listen to her complaining about how dreadful it all was. If Grace had had her way, no one would ever be sent back to France.

'What about her?'

'She's leaving.'

Grace looked dismayed. 'Why? What's happened? Is it her husband?'

'As far as I know, she's decided to go back to the bakery.' Dulcie frowned. 'Why did you ask about her husband?'

'No reason,' Grace mumbled. But Dulcie could see the colour flooding her friend's face.

'Duffield—'

'I'd better get on.' Grace rushed off, tripping over her shoelaces in her rush to get away.

Dulcie stared after her. What was that about? she wondered.

Chapter Thirty-Eight

On Anna's last day at the Nightingale, the other nurses surprised her with a tea party.

'You didn't think we'd let you go without a proper good-bye, did you?' Dulcie had said, as they marched her down to the local café.

All the girls from her original set were there – Dulcie, Grace, Miriam, even Sadie Sedgewick had taken time off to join them. She looked smart in her dark blue district nurse's uniform, her leather Gladstone bag at her feet.

The only one missing was Anna's former room-mate Eleanor Copeland, who was still serving with the Queen Alexandra's Imperial Military Nursing Service in Mesopotamia.

'Look at us, all together again.' Grace smiled around the table. 'Can you believe it's three years since we first started our training? I don't know about you, but I didn't think I'd make it through the first day, let alone six weeks of pre-liminary training!'

'I didn't make it, did I?' Dulcie said gloomily. 'I failed PTS and had to do it all again.'

'At least you came back,' Grace said.

'I was ready to go home that first day,' Anna remembered. 'I sat in my room at Porthleven House that first day and cried my eyes out. I think I would have run away if Sedgewick hadn't knocked on my door and asked to borrow a hairpin.'

'I'll let you into a little secret, shall I?' Sadie grinned. 'I heard you crying through the wall so I thought I'd better do something.'

'You didn't?' Anna stared at her friend's laughing face. 'I didn't know anyone heard me.'

'Blimey, girl, you were sobbing so loud I'm amazed they didn't hear you in the main hospital building!' Sadie grinned. She looked like a doll, with her honey-gold hair and wide green eyes. Until she opened her mouth. Her rough East End accent had only broadened since she had started district nursing on the streets of Bethnal Green.

Anna saw Miriam's mouth purse fastidiously. She and Sadie had clashed endlessly during their training – mainly due to jealousy on Miriam's part, she thought.

'Thank you for rescuing me, anyway,' she said to Sadie.

'Don't mention it, mate. That's what friends are for, ain't it?'

Anna gazed around the table. These girls truly were her friends, she thought. Or perhaps sisters would be a better description. They had not chosen each other, but fate had thrown them together in the same set, and they had become like an odd little family.

And God knows, they had fought like sisters sometimes. They bickered, and fell out, and said petty, spiteful things to each other. Anna could remember times when she could have cheerfully wrung their necks. But like sisters they had stuck together, defended and consoled each other.

It gave her a physical pain to think how much she would miss them.

'Who'd have thought we'd still be here, three years later?' she said out loud.

'Not me!' Dulcie grimaced.

'No, you thought you'd be married to a doctor by now.' Miriam gave her a malicious little smile.

'So did you,' Dulcie shot back.

'Hark at them,' Sadie said. 'Some things never change, do they? They were pecking at each other on that very first day, as I recall.' She winked at Anna. 'Bet you won't miss all the arguments, will you?'

Anna smiled. 'Actually, I think I will.'

'Get on with you! You'll be too busy with that handsome husband of yours to give us lot a second thought.'

She was right, Anna thought. She had been so caught up thinking about what she was losing, she hadn't really stopped to think about what she would gain.

Edward had certainly been a lot happier since Anna agreed to give up nursing and return to the bakery full-time. And he had been overjoyed when Mrs Church had left a few days earlier.

Anna still cringed to think about her last conversation with her. She had tried to be kind about it, but Ida Church took it very badly indeed.

'I suppose this is all his doing?' she had said, nodding towards the kitchen. The faint sounds of Edward's merry whistling came from beyond the door.

'We decided it together,' Anna insisted firmly.

'Don't give me that! It was his idea, and you went along with it as usual.' Mrs Church's eyes narrowed. 'He's been wanting to get rid of me ever since he moved in. He knows I'm wise to him.' She jabbed a finger at Anna. 'Well, I just hope you know what you're doing, my girl. You might think he can do no wrong, but you'll soon find out different, believe me!'

Anna stared at her. No wonder Edward didn't want her around!

'Please don't speak about my husband like that,' she said, fighting to keep the anger out of her voice.

'Listen to you, defending him again!' Mrs Church's thin lips curled. 'He knows how to charm his way round you, all right. God knows, I've watched him do it enough times.' She shook her head. 'Oh, he's clever, I'll give him that. But one day you'll wake up and see him for what he really is.'

'I think you'd better go,' Anna said.

'I'm going, don't you worry. I wouldn't stop here for all the tea in China. Not after the way you've treated me.'

Mrs Church went into the hall and unhooked her coat from the hallstand. Anna watched as she struggled to get into it, punching her arms through the sleeves in her agitation.

'I shouldn't think Charlie will be working here much longer, either,' she said. 'My sister reckons your husband's a bad influence on the boy. She's only allowed him to stay this long because I've been here to keep an eye on him.'

Good thing too, Anna thought as she watched Mrs Church jamming her hat on her head.

'You don't know the half of it,' Ida went on. 'But you'll find out soon enough. There'll be no more charm once he's got you where he wants you, you'll see another side to him then.'

Anna fought to control her temper. But her hand was trembling as she held it out.

'I'll have your keys, if you don't mind?' she said. 'You won't be needing them anymore.'

Mrs Church shot her a venomous look, then fished in her coat pocket. She drew out the jingling bunch of keys and slapped them into Anna's palm.

'Good luck to you,' she said. 'I daresay you'll need it.'

They lingered for as long as they could over their tea and cakes, laughing about the fun they'd had, and the dreadful ward sisters they had endured. They were having such a good time Anna didn't want it to end. But all too soon Miriam looked up and said,

'Gracious, look, it's gone four. Miss Sutton will have my guts for garters if I'm not back on the ward at five.'

'Me too,' Dulcie said.

Anna felt a sharp pang of regret as she watched them gathering up their coats and hats. She had only been away from the place for a couple of hours, but she already missed it.

There was a flurry of hugs and kisses and goodbyes. When it was Grace's turn she hugged Anna fiercely.

'You will be all right, won't you?' she mumbled into her friend's ear.

'Of course.'

'And you'll keep in touch?'

'I promise.'

'Oh, do stop being wet, Duffield!' Miriam snapped. 'Trust you to get all sentimental about everything. You'll be seeing her soon, anyway. Saunders' wedding?' she said, as Anna looked blank. 'You are still coming, aren't you?'

'You can't miss the social event of the year,' Dulcie put in dryly.

'If I get an invitation,' Anna said.

'Oh, you'll get one,' Dulcie predicted. 'Saunders wouldn't want anyone to miss the chance of seeing her walking up the aisle in white.'

'Whereas your wedding will be such a quiet, understated affair,' Sadie said.

'If it ever happens,' Miriam added acidly.

Sadie rolled her eyes at Anna. 'Here we go again!'

As they left, Grace suddenly turned back to her. 'I meant what I said about keeping in touch?'

'So did I.'

'Do you promise? And if there's ever anything you want, or you need to talk to someone . . .' There was a message in her eyes that Anna didn't quite understand.

'I'll remember,' she said.

267

Chapter Thirty-Nine

The following week there was an outing to the picture house for some of the men on Monaghan ward, and Dulcie was invited.

The sisters on the military wards often received free tickets to the pictures or the theatre or the music hall, from people keen to show their appreciation for the work they were doing with brave wounded soldiers. Usually they would hand the tickets over to one of the junior nurses and ask them to organise the outing.

This time the task had fallen to Miriam Trott, which was why Dulcie was so surprised to be included. As far as she was concerned, there was no love lost between her and Miriam. But the mystery was solved when Miriam explained that the nurse who was supposed to come with her, Hilda Wharton, had been confined to the sick bay with a bad cold.

'And everyone else was busy, so it was either you or Nurse Hanley,' she said.

Dulcie was thankful for a free night out, even if she did have to put up with Miriam Trott all evening. At least it was a chance to dress up. She chose her outfit carefully, picking out her favourite blue dress. Her mother had made it for her, copying the pattern carefully from a dress Dulcie had seen in Selfridge's.

It was a good match, she thought. Anyone seeing it would probably think it was the real thing.

She longed for the day she could buy anything she wanted. Being able to shop for a dress up west, having assistants fussing around you, commissionaires opening the door as you emerged with your purchases, that was as much a part of the pleasure for her as actually wearing an expensive dress.

But one day, she told herself. One day she would have an account in Selfridge's and then she would be able to buy whatever she liked and sign her name with a flourish.

Mrs Dulcie Logan.

And she would never have to wear a home-made dress again.

Home-made or not, the men waiting by the double doors to Monaghan ward certainly seemed to appreciate her as she walked towards them.

'Aye, aye, lads. Here's a sight for sore eyes!' One of the men, a burly corporal called George Yeoman, nudged the man next to him.

The others joined in, whistling their admiration.

'Don't you look nice, Nurse? Civvies suit you.'

'Blimey, you scrub up well, don't you?'

'If I'd known you were that pretty, I'd have asked you out earlier!'

Dulcie accepted their compliments with a smile. But all the while she was aware of Sam Trevelyan, standing silently to one side.

She hadn't expected him to be there. The sight of him standing in his hospital uniform, leaning on a walking stick, unsettled her for some reason.

'Listen to you all. Anyone would think you'd never seen a girl in a dress before!' Miriam Trott snorted.

'Not a girl like her we haven't!' Private Hobbs leered.

Miriam's pinched little face flushed. Dulcie guessed she hadn't received such an admiring reception.

'Shall we go?' Miriam said, her voice tight with annoyance. 'I'll lead the way.'

It was the middle of March, but there was still no sign of spring. The trees in Victoria Park were starkly bare against the dismal grey sky, and a bitter wind blew as they set off along Bethnal Green Road.

Dulcie stayed at the back of the group, helping Private Hobbs, a young man with an amputated foot. Sam Trevelyan was at the front, his limping steps at first keeping up with Miriam Trott's briskly tapping heels. But then, gradually, he fell back until he was level with Dulcie.

'Fancy seeing you here,' he said in a low voice.

'I could say the same about you. I didn't think you were the type to go on an outing?'

He sent her a sideways look. 'Am I that much of a misery guts?'

'Well, now you come to mention it . . .'

Sam shook his head. 'I'm a reformed character,' he said. 'I even played whist with someone last week.'

'You didn't!'

'I did.'

'You'll be joining in with one of Nurse Trott's sing-songs next!'

Sam grimaced. 'God forbid! I'd never go that far.' Then he paused and said, 'You do look nice, by the way.'

'Thank you.'

'That colour suits you. It matches your eyes.'

She could feel herself blushing. 'Two compliments, Sergeant? You really are a reformed character, aren't you?'

'You'd be surprised.'

For a moment they looked at each other, and Dulcie felt a tiny surge of something like panic. She broke the silence.

'Aren't you going to ask me how I'm getting on on Wilson ward?'

He looked amused. 'How are you getting on?' He looked at her left hand. 'Not engaged yet, I see?'

'It's only a matter of time,' she said lightly.

'I'm sure. You seem very determined.' The way he said it, she wasn't sure if it was meant to be a compliment or not.

When they reached Smart's Picture House, Miriam made them wait in the foyer while she went off to the box office to sort out the tickets.

'I wish people wouldn't keep looking at us,' Private Hobbs muttered.

Dulcie gazed around. She hadn't noticed it before but they were drawing quite a lot of attention in their hospital uniforms. Some of the crowd seemed friendly; others were gawping openly at the men's missing limbs and injured faces.

'Seen enough, have you?' Corporal Yeoman snarled, glaring round at them all. 'P'raps you'd like to pay for a ticket to see us instead of the film?'

'Corporal, please!' Dulcie begged, but Corporal Yeoman was already squaring up to one of the men, his one remaining fist raised.

'Come on, then,' he challenged him, but the man just laughed.

'You're joking, mate. I'd never hit a cripple. It wouldn't be a fair fight.'

Corporal Yeoman's face flushed red, but Sam Trevelyan stepped in.

'Leave it, George.' His voice was low but full of authority. 'He's not worth it.'

For a tense moment George Yeoman carried on squaring up to the man. Then he let his fist drop to his side.

'You're right,' he muttered, turning away.

'Coward,' the young civilian said under his breath. The sight of his jeering face brought a red mist down in front of Dulcie's eyes. Before she knew what she was doing, she had grabbed the man by the sleeve and wheeled him round to face her.

'How dare you?' she roared. '*You're* the coward, not him! What was your excuse, then? Short-sighted? Flat feet? I suppose you've ended up with some cushy office job? What a hero you are, shuffling forms all day. Takes a real man to do something like that, I reckon.' The man flushed deep crimson. 'And yet you dare to stare and call these men names? I'll bet the closest you ever get to Vimy Ridge or Cambrai is reading about them in the newspaper while you're safe at home.'

'Moore! What do you think you're doing?' Miriam had returned from the box office, a sheaf of tickets in her hand. 'Stop making a show of yourself at once.'

Dulcie looked round at the ring of wounded soldiers, all staring at her in astonishment, then back at the man in front of her. He seemed to have shrunk before her, shrivelling into his smart suit, his face puce with embarrassment. Even his lady friend was glaring at him as if seeing him for the first time.

'Come on!' Miriam Trott took her arm, leading her away. But Dulcie hadn't finished yet.

'You're pathetic,' she called back over her shoulder. 'Corporal Yeoman might only have one arm but I bet he'd still be able to knock you out with a single punch!'

'Really, Moore, don't you know how to behave?' Miriam hissed as they took their seats in the darkened picture house.

'I don't care. He deserved it,' Dulcie said.

'You'll soon care if someone tells Matron!'

'And who's going to do that? You?' Dulcie stared at Miriam, who coloured guiltily.

'No. Of course not,' she muttered. 'Is everyone here?' she changed the subject abruptly, standing up to count heads. 'Five, six, seven . . . there's one missing. Who's missing?'

'Trevelyan went to the kiosk to buy cigarettes,' Private Hobbs called out.

Miriam looked vexed. 'I do wish he'd told me. How am I supposed to keep track of everyone when—'

'Here I am.' Sam Trevelyan limped towards them. 'Sorry, Nurse.'

'I should think so. Sit down please, Sergeant, the film is about to start.'

As it happened, Dulcie was nearest the end of the row, and the only vacant seat was beside her.

'Did you get your cigarettes?' she whispered to him.

Sam nodded. 'And I got you these.'

Dulcie looked down at the box he had handed her. 'Violet creams,' she said.

'Sorry there isn't a private box to go with them. But I suppose it's the thought that counts, isn't it?'

Their eyes met again, and Dulcie felt a tiny jolt of sensation.

'Yes,' she said, gazing at the chocolates. 'I suppose it is.'

After the film had ended, they made their way back to the hospital. Some of the men wanted to go to the pub, but Miriam Trott was having none of it.

'I promised Sister I would have you all back before she went off duty,' she said primly. 'Besides, a public house is not the place for respectable young ladies,' she added, looking sideways at Dulcie.

'I know that, Nurse,' Corporal Yeoman said. 'It's the ones who're not respectable we're after. Ain't that right?' He turned to his fellow soldiers, who all laughed in agreement.

Dulcie thought they might have a riot on their hands, but then Sam said, 'Nurse Trott's right. We ought to be getting back. Unless you fancy facing up to Miss Sutton's rage, because I certainly don't.'

The men's laughter died.

'Come to think of it, I am feeling a bit tired.' Private Hobbs feigned a yawn.

'You could be right,' another of the men, Sergeant Silcott, agreed. 'Miss Sutton's got a worse temper than my missus, and that's saying something!'

'You're lucky you won't have to put up with it for much longer,' Corporal Yeoman said to Sam.

'Why's that?' Dulcie asked.

'Haven't you heard?' Sergeant Silcott said. 'He's got his marching orders. Ain't that right, Sammy lad?'

Dulcie looked at Sam. 'You're being discharged?'

He shook his head. 'No such luck. They're sending me to a convalescent home, to learn to make baskets with the other old codgers.'

'You're being sent for extended rehabilitation,' Miriam corrected him primly.

'Same difference.' Sam did not look thrilled at the prospect.

'When are you leaving?' Dulcie asked.

'Not for another month. End of April, if they can find me a place.' His mouth twisted. 'Why? Will you miss me?'

He made it sound like a joke, but Dulcie could feel the weight of meaning behind it.

'Promise me you'll come and said goodbye?' he said.

'Of course. I'll probably put out the flags, too!' She smiled, but Sam's face was serious.

'I promise,' she said.

Chapter Forty

Private Gordon was making real progress. His stammer had improved, he looked Grace in the eye when she spoke, and most significant of all, he had taken his first steps.

This morning he had managed to totter all the way out to the terrace, leaning heavily on his friend Albie Sallis' arm. He and Albie sat side by side on a bench in the cool March morning, Gordon listening as Albie chattered nineteen to the dozen, holding forth about what lay beyond the hospital railings.

'There's no place like the East End, mate, believe me,' he was saying. 'Once you're properly on your feet, I'm going to take you down Brick Lane for pie and mash. Maybe some jellied eels too, if you fancy 'em. Now don't pull a face like that, not till you've tried 'em.' He looked up at Grace. 'You ever had jellied eels, Nurse?'

'I can't say I have, Corporal Sallis.' Grace smiled back as she tucked in a rug around a patient in a wheelchair.

'Then you'll have to come with us. We'll have a proper beano. What do you say, mate?' He grinned at Gordon, who smiled vacantly back at him.

'I think jellied eels sound perfectly foul,' Dulcie announced from the other end of the terrace, where she was settling another patient.

'That's 'cos you're too lah-di-dah,' Albie called back. 'I bet you wouldn't say no to a plate of oysters at a fancy restaurant, would you?'

'Of course not. But that's different.'

275

'I don't see how. They both come out of the sea, don't they?'

'Well, I won't be coming on your outing if jellied eels are on the menu,' Dulcie announced.

'I don't recall you being invited.'

Grace looked from one to the other of them, and an idea occurred to her.

'Can you manage by yourself for a moment?' she asked Dulcie.

She looked up, a rug in her hands. 'Why? Where are you going?'

'I just have to talk to someone, that's all.'

'Can't it wait?' Dulcie said, but Grace was already heading for the French doors.

'Don't be long,' she heard Dulcie calling across the terrace. 'I don't see why I should have to do everything . . .'

Dulcie had been in a foul mood in the past few days. Grace thought it must have something to do with the fact that Dr Logan still hadn't noticed her, in spite of her best efforts.

Sometimes Grace cringed at Dulcie's determination to flirt with him. She seemed so desperate and heavy-handed. But then again, Grace had never flirted with anyone in her life, so she was hardly qualified to comment. For all she knew, it might be the right way to go about attracting a man's attention.

She thought about Noah Wells. Another letter had come for her the previous day, written in his careful hand.

Grace supposed they must be love letters of a sort, even though they were mainly about slurry spreading, and how he had finished sowing the sugar beet. She did her best to read some poetry and meaning between the lines, but in the end she had to admit that Noah Wells was too straightforward for all that nonsense.

And so was she, she reminded herself. There had been a time when she had measured her year by muck spreading and sowing, lambing and calving. It was the life she had been born to, and the life she enjoyed.

She would have preferred to speak to Dr Carlyle about her idea, but she was away on a walking holiday in Scotland with her fiancé Dr French. He was on leave from his posting in France.

Instead, she knocked on Dr Logan's door.

'Come.'

As Grace fumbled with the doorknob, she could imagine him sighing with impatience inside the room.

Robert Logan was sitting behind his wooden desk, a pile of papers in front of him. The reports for the Medical Board, Grace guessed.

He looked up at her. 'What is it, Nurse? Is it one of the patients?'

'No, Sir. I just wanted to speak to you about something.' She glanced down at the reports. 'But I can come back when you're not so busy . . .'

'No, stay. Please.' He sat back in his seat, took off his glasses and rubbed a hand wearily over his eyes. 'I would be pleased of the distraction, actually.' He replaced his spectacles and looked up at her. 'What was it you wanted?'

Grace looked around her at the book-lined walls, suddenly very nervous. She kept her hands clasped together, her elbows tucked in at her sides in case she knocked something over.

'I've been talking to Albie – Corporal Sallis.'

'Talking to him?' Dr Logan raised his eyebrows. 'I'd be very surprised if you got a word in edgeways, Nurse.'

Grace smiled. 'Very well, I was listening to him talking about London, and how much he loved it. And I wondered – might it be possible to organise an outing for some of the men?'

Grace risked a glance up at him. Dr Logan's dark eyes were fixed on her so intently behind his spectacles that she almost lost her nerve.

'An outing?' he said.

'We wouldn't have to go far.' Grace was gabbling now, the words tumbling over themselves. 'Just around the park, perhaps, or to a café? We might even go to a concert? People are always sending us free tickets.'

Dr Logan went on staring at her, and Grace felt her confidence start to crumble.

'On second thoughts, it might not be a very good idea,' she mumbled. 'It would probably be too much for the men. They need peace and quiet, don't they? The noise, the busy streets, the people . . . I daresay it would set them back in their treatment.'

'I think it's a capital idea,' Dr Logan said.

Grace stared at him. 'You do?'

He nodded. 'It would give them a taste of normality. Of course, we'd have to be careful which patients we took. They would have to be the more robust of the men, the ones who were responding best to treatment.' He looked up and gave her one of his rare smiles. 'Let me think about it, Nurse. But we will definitely organise something.'

Grace smiled back in disbelief. 'Thank you, Sir.'

'I would accompany the men, of course. But I assume you would be willing to assist me?'

'Of course, Doctor.' Then another thought struck her. 'And perhaps Nurse Moore could come, too?'

He frowned. 'Nurse Moore?'

'It was her idea.'

'Was it?' He looked surprised. 'But I thought you said

you thought of it? After talking to Corporal Sallis?' he reminded her.

Heat rose in Grace's face. She had never been very good at lying.

'Nurse Moore was there, too. And she has had experience with taking men on outings,' Grace added.

Dr Logan looked thoughtful. 'I suppose it wouldn't hurt to have an extra pair of hands.' He looked up at her. 'Leave it with me, Nurse. I will make the necessary arrangements.'

'Thank you, Sir.'

As Grace turned to go, Dr Logan said, 'Nurse Duffield?'

'Yes, Sir?'

'It was an excellent idea. Even if you didn't think of it.'

It might have been the lamplight reflecting off his spectacles, but Grace could have sworn there was a twinkle in his blue eyes.

'Thank you, Sir. I'll be sure to let Nurse Moore know.'

Grace was so pleased and flustered, she barely noticed the skeleton standing sentry by the door until she had collided with it.

Chapter Forty-One

Dear Mother,

Thank you for your letter. I'm sorry I haven't replied sooner but working in the bakery hardly leaves me any time, as I'm sure you well remember! But today is half-day closing so at last I can sit down and write a few lines.

I'm very glad to hear you have found a place to settle at last. Bavaria sounds beautiful – very different from Bethnal Green, but I know you will both be very happy there. And what good news that Papa is setting up another bakery in the village. I'm sure it won't be long before the customers are queuing up outside the door again, just as they used to here.

We're all doing well over here, too. As I mentioned in my last letter, I have given up nursing and now I am helping Edward at the bakery. Since Mrs Church left, her nephew Charlie has also gone (and I can't say I'm sorry about that!) so now there are just the two of us.

I know you were worried about me leaving the Nightingale, and I do miss my friends sometimes, but as Edward says, this is what Papa would have wanted. And I am very happy for us to be working together again at last. Sometimes it almost feels like the old days, when we were all together here . . .

Anna paused, her pen stilling on the paper, and took a moment to gather herself. Then she continued:

Working in the bakery has done wonders for Edward's spirits. He has settled back into life in London, and has even made some new friends . . .

Once again, her hand fell still and she had to force herself to continue.

Of course, he is still quite frail in some ways, but I truly believe that with love and patience, he will soon be quite back to his old self.

Love and patience. How often had she repeated those words to herself in the three months they had been married?

I must say, I am surprised that Liesel felt the need to write to you and complain that I never see her. Unfortunately, it just so happens that the last couple of times she has tried to arrange to visit, it has not been convenient for us. But if I went to visit her in Essex I would hardly expect her to abandon her work to see me, so why is she so upset? We are both busy, and it's nonsense for her to say I am avoiding her. I'm only sorry she had to trouble you with her silliness. Please take no notice – you know Liesel is only happy when she's making a fuss about something!

For a moment she heard Edward's voice in her ear. 'Why does she have to come? I prefer it when it's just the two of us, don't you?' And then: 'Sometimes I think you care more about her feelings than you do about mine.'

Anyway, I must end this letter as I want to catch the last post. Please give Papa my love and tell him that I wish he could visit the bakery in Bethnal Green again, and see that we are carrying on his good work. I miss you both very much, and long for the day we can all be together again.

Dashing away a tear, Anna signed the letter and sealed it in an envelope quickly, before she could change her mind.

It had taken her a long time to write the letter. She had started it many times, but it hurt her too much to lie to her parents. In the end she had managed to craft something that wasn't quite a lie, but wasn't quite the truth, either.

Edward appeared in the doorway to the bakery kitchen as Anna was slipping on her coat in the hall.

'Where are you sneaking off to?' There was a smile on his face, but his eyes told a different story.

'I'm going to post a letter.'

'Who to?'

'My parents.' Their eyes met for a moment. Then, without a word, Anna handed over the envelope.

Edward flicked a quick glance over the address and handed it to her, his smile back in place.

'I hope you gave them my love?' he said.

'Of course.'

She stiffened automatically as he came towards her, only to relax again as his arms went around her.

'Don't be too long,' he whispered. 'I love you.'

'I – love you too.'

He kissed her tenderly, and Anna tried to blank out the memory of the previous night, when he had come home from the pub in the early hours and drunkenly forced himself on her.

She had learned not to fight back anymore. Instead she submitted to him, lying as still as she could and trying not to breathe in the sickening stench of beer and cigarettes.

'Christ, it's like making love to a block of ice. You could at least try to look as if you're enjoying it!' he'd mocked afterwards.

Anna wondered if he even remembered it now. He

seldom seemed to recall what he said or did when he was drunk.

Love and patience, she reminded herself. The drinking, the uncontrollable rages, the lack of trust – they were all down to his terrible war experiences. If she just gave him enough time and enough love, one day she would cure him and then she would have her Edward back.

It was a blustery April day, but Anna could see the beginnings of spring. The trees in Victoria Park were cautiously unfurling their tender green leaves, and there was a slight warmth in the air that hadn't been there for months.

Perhaps it was a sign that things were changing, getting better, she thought.

Then she turned the corner and saw Ida Church hurrying towards her.

Anna turned away sharply to stare into the window of the draper's shop while she approached. But as the older woman drew level, she heard her say, 'Miss Anna?'

Anna forced herself to turn and look at her. 'Mrs Church. I didn't see you.'

'Didn't you? I saw you.' Ida Church pursed her lips. She looked Anna up and down. 'You're looking – well,' she said at last.

It was a lie. Anna had caught sight of her reflection in the draper's window on her way over and knew exactly what she looked like.

'How are you?' she asked.

'Oh, you know – fair to middling. I've been meaning to call in and see you, but I didn't want to run into *him*.'

Anna tensed. 'You mean my husband?'

'How are your mother and father?' Mrs Church changed the subject abruptly. 'Have you heard from them lately?'

'They're very well. Actually, I was just on my way to post a letter to them . . .'

'And your sister? How is she?'

'She's fine.'

Mrs Church paused for a moment, then said, 'Tell you what, why don't we have a cuppa together at Wheeler's? Then we can have a proper catch-up.'

'I don't have time.' Anna glanced furtively up and down the street. 'I promised I'd get straight back.'

'You can spare five minutes, surely?'

'No, really – I have to get home.'

Mrs Church's eyes narrowed. 'He's really got you under his thumb, hasn't he?'

'No!' Anna stared at her, shocked. 'No, not at all. Now if you'll excuse me?'

She started to walk away, but Ida Church's voice followed her down the street.

'Is he still taking money out of the till?'

Anna stopped in her tracks for a moment, then hurried on.

'It's a terrible shame,' Mrs Church called after her. 'After everything your father did, building up that business . . .'

Anna kept her head down, but she could still feel people turning to look at her, their gazes following her down the street.

'I'm only looking out for you,' Mrs Church shouted. 'I promised your mother I would!'

Anna ran the rest of the way home.

Thankfully, the kitchen was empty. Anna closed the back door and leaned against it, fighting to get her breath back.

'Is that you?' Edward called from the shop.

'Yes.'

'Did you catch the post?'

It took a moment for her to remember what he was talking about. She looked at the letter in her hand. She had been so desperate to get away from Mrs Church that she had forgotten all about it.

'Yes,' she said, slipping it into her pocket.

She heard the ring of the till, followed by the thunk of the cash drawer closing.

Is he still taking money out of the till?

Anna flinched as Edward appeared, smiling.

'What's up with you?' he said. 'Have you been running?'

Anna forced the corners of her mouth upwards. 'I wanted to get back to you.'

Edward grinned. 'That's my girl. Come here and give your old man a big kiss.'

As she moved into his arms, Anna tried not to notice the outline of a wad of banknotes in his pocket.

Why ask him, when there was bound to be an innocent explanation for it? she thought. And if there wasn't, she was too afraid to want to know.

Patience and love.

She would make him better, and everything would be all right.

Chapter Forty-Two

Sam slumped in the chair, watching as the VAD folded his belongings and packed them carefully into a small suitcase. She kept up a cheerful stream of chatter as she worked.

'I'm sure you'll love it at Hambleton Hall. My friend works there as a VAD and she says it's a wonderful place.' She was young, fresh-faced and enthusiastic, with a chirping little voice that reminded him of a budgerigar. 'Apparently they have all sorts of pastimes and activities there. They have several tennis courts, a swimming pool and a cricket pitch. My friend says they even have their own amateur dramatics society. Are you interested in acting at all, Sergeant Trevelyan?'

'I think I've had enough drama for one lifetime, don't you?'

'Oh, yes. Of course.' The VAD looked crestfallen. 'I suppose if you put it like that . . . But perhaps you could take up a sport, or learn a musical instrument?'

And then she was off again, chirruping away like a bright little bird.

Sam turned his gaze reluctantly to the clock hanging above the double doors. He had managed to restrain himself for several minutes, as if by not looking at it he could somehow stop the time from ticking by.

Finally, the VAD finished the packing and closed the lid of his suitcase.

'Right, that's all done,' she announced. 'I'll go and fetch Sister.'

'Can't you leave it a couple of minutes?' Sam said. 'I want another cigarette before I go.'

'Well, I don't know.'

'Go on. I need something to steady my nerves before the journey.'

'All right, I'm sure another couple of minutes won't hurt,' the VAD agreed reluctantly. 'But if I get in trouble with Sister I'm blaming you,' she added, wagging a warning finger at him.

Sam lit his cigarette and took a long drag, his gaze fixed on the double doors.

She wasn't coming.

He didn't know why he had ever believed she would. But she had promised, and like a fool he had thought she meant it.

But they were just words to Dulcie Moore. She had probably forgotten all about her so-called promise.

He wasn't even angry with her. He was more angry with himself for not knowing better, for daring to think that he might be more to her than just another wounded soldier.

He was a fool. Now all he could do was leave while he still had a shred of dignity.

And then Nurse Trott came hurrying down the ward, and he forgot all about his dignity and instead blurted out, 'I don't suppose you've seen Nurse Moore, have you?'

Nurse Trott frowned at him, her beaky little face pinched. 'Moore? As far as I know, she's gone up West with Dr Logan today. Apparently they're all on some outing.' She frowned. 'Why? Did you want her for something?'

'No. I just wanted to say goodbye, that's all.'

'I expect she forgot all about it,' Nurse Trott said. 'You know what Moore's like.'

'Yes,' Sam said. 'Yes, I do.'

At that moment Miss Sutton came plodding over.

'Ready to go, Sergeant Trevelyan?' she said.

Sam glanced at the double doors again.

'More than ready, Sister,' he said.

Dulcie was beginning to wish she had never come.

They were drawing quite a lot of attention from the other customers in the Lyons Corner House. One of the men, Lance Corporal Fletcher, kept laughing and pointing at nothing, while another, Private Walsh, rocked back and forth, tears running down his face. Two men sat absolutely still and silent, their plates untouched in front of them.

She looked up at the clock. Just past three.

Sam Trevelyan would be on his way by now.

She wished she had been there. She should have been there. As soon as she had found out the ward outing was planned for the same day as Sam was being discharged, she should have told them she couldn't come. They would have understood. God knows, it wasn't as if she was even really needed. Grace and Dr Logan seemed to be managing perfectly well between themselves.

She should have told them she had made a promise, and wanted to keep it.

But it was more than just a promise. Dulcie wanted to see Sam, to say goodbye.

And that was the problem.

She hadn't come today out of a sense of duty, or even because she wanted the excuse to spend time with Dr Logan. If she was honest, she had come because she was afraid. Her emotions were getting away from her, and if she was not careful she knew she might be tipped into a situation she could not control.

Far better to avoid it completely, if she could.

'Do you have another appointment, Nurse?' Captain Jeffers was smiling at her across the table. He always seemed out of place among the other patients, with his sleek fair hair and handsome looks. 'You've been staring at that clock on and off ever since we arrived,' he said. 'I wondered if you had somewhere else to go?'

'No, I don't.' *Not anymore.* Dulcie dragged her gaze away from the clock.

'I don't blame you for wanting to leave,' Captain Jeffers said. 'I'd go if I could. It's all rather tedious, isn't it? I could do without everyone staring, too. Still, it can't be helped, can it? I suppose we do look rather a sideshow.' He gave a dry smile. 'Christ knows why they made us wear these wretched hospital badges. I should imagine we'd be rather easy to spot without them, shouldn't you?'

Dulcie glanced up to the other end of the table, where Albie Sallis was talking nineteen to the dozen as usual. He was deep in conversation with Dr Logan while his friend Gordon sat beside him, trembling like a spaniel in a thunderstorm. Grace was with them, holding Gordon's hand.

'Do you think they're a couple?' Captain Jeffers asked.

Dulcie laughed. 'Duffield and Private Gordon? I shouldn't think so.'

'No, silly. I mean her and the good doctor.'

'No!'

'Why not? He obviously likes her.'

'No, he doesn't. How can you say that?'

'My dear Nurse Moore, I've spent months on that ward watching them. Believe me, I can tell. And you can see for yourself how close they are. I do believe Dr Logan trusts to Nurse Duffield's opinion more than he does Sister's.'

Dulcie turned back to study them at the other end of the table. As far as she could see, they scarcely seemed aware of each other.

'I think you're wrong,' she said. 'Anyway, Nurse Duffield is engaged to someone else.'

As soon as the words were out she knew she shouldn't have said them. Grace had sworn her to secrecy.

'Is she now?' Captain Jeffers looked intrigued. 'I wonder if Dr Logan knows that?'

'You mustn't tell anyone,' Dulcie pleaded.

Captain Jeffers' eyebrows rose. 'That sounds rather intriguing.'

'Please, don't.'

'Oh, don't worry, I'm not going to say a word. I probably won't be around for much longer, anyway.'

'Oh? Why's that?'

'I'm being boarded next week.' He blew a thin stream of smoke into the air. 'I daresay I'll be back on the boat to France soon.'

'Not necessarily.'

'What reason do they have to discharge me? As you can see, I'm perfectly fit. And thanks to the wonders of Dr Logan, I've recovered fairly well mentally, too.' He shook his head. 'No, I'm almost certain the Medical Board will send me back to the Front as soon as they can. God knows, they're running out of men over there. The buggers will keep dying!'

His face was bitter as he took another long drag on his cigarette.

'And how do you feel about that?'

'How do you think I feel?' His voice was suddenly sharp. 'I'd throw myself under a train before I let that happen.'

For a moment they stared at each other. The next minute Captain Jeffers was laughing. 'Honestly, Nurse Moore, don't look so stricken. I think you've been on Wilson too long. You've forgotten how to take a joke.'

They finished their meal and Dr Logan paid the bill. They caught the Underground back to Bethnal Green, but as they were emerging from the station Grace suddenly had the idea of walking to the pie and mash shop to buy some jellied eels for Albie Sallis.

Dulcie was against the idea; it had begun to rain and she could feel her hat turning limp about her ears. But Dr Logan seemed to think it was a capital plan, and so they all trooped down Vallance Road towards Mile End.

They hadn't gone very far when the air-raid warning bell sounded. Other whistles, horns and klaxons took up the cry and soon the air was filled with a jarring cacophony of wailing, hooting and ringing.

'This is your fault!' Dulcie turned on Grace. 'We could have been safely back at the hospital now if you hadn't decided to go and look for wretched jellied eels!'

'Don't you have a go at her!' Corporal Sallis jumped to Grace's defence. 'She was only being kind – you should try it sometime!'

'Stop it, both of you!' Dr Logan's voice rose over the wail of the siren. 'We've got to get these men back to the hospital.'

Chaos had broken out among them. Private Walsh and a couple of the others had thrown themselves to the ground. Lance Corporal Fletcher stared up at the sky, roaring with laughter, as people pushed past him, running for shelter.

'Where's Captain Jeffers?' Grace asked.

'I don't know.' Dulcie looked around. 'He was here a minute ago.'

'Did you see which way he went?'

'If I knew that he wouldn't be lost, would he?'

'Who's lost?' Dr Logan came up behind them, propping up Private Walsh with his shoulders.

'We can't find Captain Jeffers, Sir,' Grace said.

Dr Logan looked wildly around. 'What do you mean, you can't find him? Who saw him last?'

'I did, Doctor,' Dulcie said. 'We were walking along

together, but then the sirens went off, and he just – disappeared.'

Dr Logan stared at her. The rain was falling heavily now, soaking his suit and hat and plastering his white shirt to his torso.

'Here.' He lifted Private Walsh's arm from around his shoulders and across Dulcie's. She buckled under the sudden weight of him. 'You get the men back to hospital. I'll go and look for Captain Jeffers.'

He was off before Dulcie could reply, running down the street, looking this way and that.

'Come on,' Grace said. Dulcie could see her mentally bracing herself. 'We'd better do as he says. Sister will be furious if we all catch pneumonia!' She hauled one of the men up from the ground and linked her arm through his. 'Lance Corporal Fletcher, come out of the road, please. And, Corporal Sallis, will you keep an eye on Private Gordon? I think that's all of us . . .'

They started up the road. Grace was grimly silent, and Dulcie could tell she was punishing herself over Captain Jeffers' disappearance.

'I didn't mean it,' Dulcie said. 'It isn't really your fault.'

'But you're right, I was the one who insisted we should go to the pie and mash shop.' Grace's voice was choked. 'I wish I knew why he ran away.'

'I think I know,' Dulcie said.

Grace looked at her sharply. 'What?'

'It was the boarding. He was worried he was going to be sent back to France.'

'He said that to you? That he was worried?'

'He said he would throw himself under a train before he let it—' Dulcie stopped speaking abruptly. She could see the same realisation dawning on Grace's face.

They had reached the hospital gates.

'Get the men back to the ward,' Grace said.

'On my own?'

'The porters in the lodge will fetch an orderly to help you.'

She shifted the weight of the man she had been helping and propped him against the hospital railings.

'Where are you going?' Dulcie called after her.

'To find Captain Jeffers. And I think I know where to look . . .'

It took a long time to get the men back to the ward. Miss Parker was utterly furious, and because Dulcie was the only one there, she suffered the brunt of Sister's rage.

'Get these men into hot baths immediately,' she instructed the VADs. 'And I want dry clothes for them all, and hot water bottles in their beds.' She shook her head. 'I shall certainly be having words with Dr Logan when he returns.'

'He couldn't help the rain, Sister. Or the air raid,' Dulcie pointed out, then wished she hadn't as Miss Parker turned her icy blue gaze on her.

'And you say one of the men is missing?' she snapped.

'Captain Jeffers, Sister.'

Miss Parker gave a heavy sigh. 'It's too bad, it really is. I suspected this outing was a bad idea, and it looks as if I was right.' She glared at Dulcie. 'I just hope for all your sakes that this man is found soon, or Matron will have something to say about it. And the War Office too, I should imagine. And frankly, I don't know which I would fear most!'

Dulcie left her fussing over the men and trailed miserably back down the corridor. Her new shoes squelched unpleasantly with every step and cold rain dripped from the sagging brim of her now ruined hat, running down the back of her neck.

It never occurs to Sister that I might get pneumonia, she thought furiously. If anyone needed a hot bath, dry clothes and a warm bed, she did. As it was, she would probably get another telling-off from the Home Sister for treading mud on the parquet floor.

As she passed Monaghan ward, she heard someone calling her name. She turned to see Lottie Jones, one of the VADs, hurrying towards her.

'I thought I spotted you going by,' she said. 'I was clearing out Sergeant Trevelyan's locker earlier on and I found this . . .' She held up a small package, haphazardly wrapped in newspaper. 'I thought he might have left it behind but then I saw it had your name on it.'

'My name?' Dulcie looked down at the parcel.

'I don't know of another Dulcie Moore in this hospital.' Lottie Jones pressed it into her hand. 'I suppose he must have meant to give it to you before he left.'

Pain and guilt lanced through Dulcie. 'What is it?'

'You'll have to open it and see, won't you?'

Lottie craned forward eagerly as Dulcie started to peel away the layers of newspaper to reveal a small leather box.

As soon as she saw it, Dulcie slipped it in her pocket.

'Don't you want to know what's inside?' Lottie pouted.

'I already know.'

'But I want to see . . .' Lottie's voice, shrill with disappointment, followed her all the way down the passageway.

She didn't open the box until she was safely back in her room at Walford House. That was when she found the note, tucked inside.

I know I said I'd thrown it away, but I thought you might like it. It seems to mean more to you than it ever did to me.

Regards,
Sam Trevelyan

She picked up the Military Medal, feeling the warm weight of it in her hand, and turned it over to read the inscription.

For bravery in the field.

Oh, Sam, she thought, tears pricking her eyes. How she wished now she had been brave enough to deserve it.

Chapter Forty-Three

The air raid had stopped by the time Grace reached Bethnal Green Underground station.

Once the crowds and the noise of the big city would have terrified her but now she scarcely noticed them as she descended the steep flight of stone steps, pushing against the tide of people who had sought shelter there. She was too intent on finding Captain Jeffers.

The station platform was still full of people waiting for the next train. Grace pushed her way through them, searching this way and that. Then she saw him at the far end of the platform, sitting alone on a bench. He was a forlorn figure, fair head bowed, hands hanging limply between his knees.

Grace approached him cautiously but he barely seemed to register her presence. As she drew closer, she could hear him humming a tune under his breath.

' *"It's a long way to Tipperary, it's a long way to go . . ."* '

He didn't look up at her as she sat down beside him. Then he said, 'I've spent the past God knows how many months listening to Frost singing that damn tune, and now it's stuck in my head.'

'It helps calm him down,' Grace said.

'So I understand. Doesn't seem to be working for me, though.'

Captain Jeffers looked up at her for the first time. Beyond his rueful smile, Grace could see the fear in his pale blue eyes.

'I suppose you know they're sending me back?'

'Nothing's been decided yet.'

'Oh, I'll be going back, Nurse. I've seen men in a worse state than me passed fit.' He turned his head to stare at the railway line a few feet away. 'How did you know where to find me?'

'Something you said to Nurse Moore . . .'

'So I did. I meant it, too. I would rather kill myself than go back to France.' He paused, then said, 'I suppose you think I'm a dreadful coward for not wanting to do my duty?'

'Not at all.'

He was silent for a while. Grace looked down at his hands, clasping and unclasping. The skin around his nails was raw where he had bitten it.

How had no one noticed before? she wondered. Captain Jeffers always seemed to put up such a calm, urbane front, with his dry sense of humour and mocking observations.

Now she realised that it had been just that – a front.

'I wasn't always like this, you know,' he said suddenly. 'I was a captain of the cadets at school. A born leader, they called me.' His mouth twisted. 'If they could only see me now, eh, Nurse?'

Grace said nothing. After a moment, Captain Jeffers continued speaking.

'We practised endlessly for the war at school,' he said. 'We all knew it was coming, and we wanted to be ready for it. All those drills, learning how to march, how to strip and clean and fire a gun . . . Frankly, we couldn't wait. I don't think the war could come soon enough for us. Especially me.

'And then, when it did, I was first in line to sign up. Eighteen years old, and desperate to do my duty. If I'd known . . .' He shook his head. 'But I didn't. None of us knew. We all thought it was going to be a great adventure, like the stories we read in the *Boys' Herald*.'

He patted his pocket and drew out a packet of cigarettes.

'Twelve of us joined up from my form, all commissioned as junior officers. Eighteen years old, and we suddenly found ourselves in command of men twice our age.' He shook his head. 'God, what were they thinking?'

He lit a cigarette and took a long draw.

'I'm the only one left now,' he said. 'The last one to survive, Marshall, was killed at Cambrai. One of our tanks went over him as he was lying injured in No Man's Land. Not their fault, of course. They can't be expected to grind to a halt and sort out which men are theirs and which are ours in the middle of fighting, can they?'

He sat back, his head pressed against the tiled wall. 'Marshall,' he said. 'Now there was a hero. It was his twenty-first birthday when he led those men over the top. And when I say led, he would have been out there in front, believe me.' The captain took a vicious drag on his cigarette. 'God only knows what he would make of me if he could see me now.'

The train was approaching, a rumble in the distance from the mouth of the tunnel. On the platform, people were stirring themselves, ready for its arrival.

Captain Jeffers dropped his cigarette and ground it out with his heel.

'Well, here we go,' he said. He sounded almost cheerful.

Grace grabbed his sleeve. 'Please don't,' she said. 'There must be some other way. I could talk to Dr Logan, I'm sure he could do something . . .'

'There's nothing he can do, Nurse. There's nothing anyone can do.'

The train appeared at the mouth of the tunnel. Before she could stop him, Captain Jeffers had wrenched himself free from Grace's grasp.

'Captain Jeffers!' she called out to him, but he was already striding purposefully towards the edge of the platform, pushing his way through the throng of people.

Grace covered her face with her hands, her whole body tensing as she waited. The train brakes screeched, filling her head with sound . . .

And then it was all over.

When Grace looked up again, Captain Jeffers was standing alone on the platform's edge. He was sobbing.

'I couldn't do it,' he cried. 'Damn it, I really am a coward, aren't I?'

Grace rushed over to him and pulled him away from the edge of the platform.

'Listen to me,' she said firmly. 'There's nothing cowardly about wanting to live.'

'But why?' He stared at her, his face ravaged with tears. 'Why should I want to live? It's not as if I have anything to live for.'

'That's not true.' Grace guided him another few steps from the edge. 'Surely you have your family.'

He shook his head. 'My father is ashamed of me. Thinks I'm weak for letting my nerves get the better of me. He told me himself, he would have been happier if I'd died a hero's death.'

'No!' Grace stared at him, shocked.

'And my fiancée has broken off our engagement. She doesn't want to be with a coward, either.'

'Then she doesn't deserve you,' Grace said staunchly. 'You're a fine man, Captain Jeffers. You can't help being ill.'

'But I'm not ill, am I? That's the point.' He rubbed his eyes. 'God, I'm just so tired . . .'

There was another train coming. Grace could feel the rumble beneath her feet. She still had hold of Captain Jeffers' sleeve, the rough fabric of his hospital uniform gripped between her fingers.

A sudden thought occurred to her.

'What if you were to get on the train instead?' she said.

Captain Jeffers stared at her blankly. 'What?'

'Get on the train. I'll tell them I couldn't find you.'

'Desert, you mean?' He straightened up. Even through his tears, Grace could see a trace of affronted pride in his face.

'Why not? You said yourself you can't face being sent back to France.'

The train was coming closer. Captain Jeffers stared up the line towards the mouth of the tunnel. 'But where would I go?'

'Anywhere you like. Make a new life for yourself. Here.' Grace rummaged in her purse and pulled out a ten-shilling note. 'Take this. I know it isn't much, but if you write to me at the nurses' home, I'll send you some more.'

The train appeared at the mouth of the tunnel. Grace could see Captain Jeffers' expression change. He took a step towards the platform edge, but she held on to him firmly.

'Please, Captain Jeffers,' she begged.

He looked down at the money she had pressed into his hand. 'Why are you doing this?' he asked.

'Because you deserve a life.'

The train came into the station, and Captain Jeffers made his move.

Five minutes later, Grace ascended the flight of steps from the platform. She was still trembling with shock.

'Grace!'

She looked up to see Dr Logan running across the road towards her, dodging motor cars, heedless of their tooting horns.

She blinked at him in surprise. She wasn't even aware he knew her first name.

'Where were you? I've been searching everywhere.'

'I took shelter in the station.'

'But the all clear sounded ages ago.'

'We didn't hear it, did we?'

Grace looked at Captain Jeffers standing just behind her, his face pale and blank.

Dr Logan looked from one to the other of them. His expression was unreadable, but Grace knew his keen brain would be working, trying to fathom out what had gone on.

'Let's get back to the hospital,' he said.

They were all silent on the way back to the Nightingale. Grace tucked her arm into Captain Jeffers' for support, but he barely registered her beside him. She wondered if he was already regretting his decision.

Miss Parker was relieved to see them all, although she did her best not to show it.

'And what time do you call this?' she demanded. 'Honestly, if I'd known this outing was going to cause so much trouble, I would have had something to say about it! I will not have my ward disrupted in this way, do you understand?' She glared from Grace to Dr Logan and back again.

It wasn't until Grace watched the VADs guiding Captain Jeffers back to bed that she realised how very tired she felt. Her whole body ached with it, and all she could think about was getting back to Walford House, crawling into bed and pulling the blankets over her head.

But as she left the ward, Dr Logan said, 'A moment, if you please, Nurse Duffield?'

Grace followed him reluctantly into his office. He closed the door, then turned to face her.

'Right,' he said. 'Now perhaps you'll tell me what really happened.'

Grace composed her features into what she hoped was a picture of innocence. 'I don't know what you mean, Sir.'

'Oh, come on, Grace, I'm not a fool!' Dr Logan looked impatient. 'I saw your faces when you came out of that station. Do you really expect me to believe that you were only taking shelter from the air raid?'

Grace opened her mouth then closed it again. She couldn't lie to him, no matter how much she tried.

'He said he wanted to throw himself under a train,' she said.

Dr Logan didn't look horrified, or even surprised. He simply nodded.

'I was afraid of that,' he muttered. 'But you talked him out of it?'

Grace thought about it for a moment. Had she? It didn't seem like it. 'He couldn't do it,' she said. 'Not when it came to it.'

'Thank God for that.' Dr Logan sank down into his chair behind the desk. He took off his spectacles and rubbed his eyes, a gesture Grace had come to know well. He looked as weary as she felt.

'He's afraid of being sent back to France,' she said.

'Yes, I know.'

She paused. 'I told him he should get on the train and go.'

Dr Logan looked up at her sharply. 'Good Lord! Did you?'

'I tried to give him money. I thought he deserved a chance to make a life for himself.'

'You tried to encourage him to desert?' Robert Logan spoke slowly, his expression grave.

'Yes, and I'd do it again,' Grace replied defiantly.

He stared at her. 'And what did he say to that?'

'He wouldn't go.' When it came to it, he had decided it was better to do his duty than to take the easy way out. If nothing else, Captain Jeffers had proved to himself today he was no coward.

'Thank God for that,' Dr Logan muttered. 'You could

have both been in serious trouble if he was caught. He would have been court martialled, shot . . .'

'What does that matter? Either way, he knows he's going to die. At least with a court martial it would be quick. He wouldn't have to suffer like those poor men on the ward.'

'I'll pretend I didn't hear that, Nurse.' Dr Logan looked down at the papers in front of him.

'I don't care,' Grace said. 'It would be so unfair if he were passed fit when he's obviously still not well.'

'That's for the Medical Board to decide,' Dr Logan cut her off.

'Can't you do something?'

'I already do what I can.' His blue eyes flared behind his spectacles. 'I detest writing these reports. Sometimes I think I might as well be signing these men's death warrants. I seldom recommend a return to active service, but whether the board takes up my recommendation is another matter.'

'They should send the whole Medical Board to the Front and then see what they have to say about it,' Grace said.

Dr Logan's mouth curved in the smallest of smiles. 'I've often thought that myself,' he said. He leaned back in his chair. 'You look tired, Nurse. You should try to get some rest.'

'Yes, Sir. Thank you.'

As she turned to go, he said, 'Nurse?'

'Yes, Sir?'

They looked at each other, their eyes meeting across the office.

'I would have told him to get on the train too,' said Dr Logan.

303

Chapter Forty-Four

'You've had a wedding invitation.' Edward looked down at the card in his hand. 'Someone called Sylvia?'

Anna had to hesitate for a moment before the name fell into place. It felt as if it belonged to another world. 'Oh you mean Saunders.'

'Who is she?'

'A friend. We nursed together at the Nightingale.' Anna looked at the curling copperplate script on the invitation Edward had passed her. Hard to believe Sylvia's wedding was once all they had talked about. Now, after a couple of months, she had almost forgotten about it.

'There's another letter from your sister, too.' Edward tossed the envelope across the table.

Anna picked it up and looked at the ragged, torn edge. 'I wish you wouldn't open my post.'

'How else would I know who it was from?' Edward asked, as if it were the most obvious question in the world.

'You must recognise Liesel's handwriting by now, surely?'

'I recognise her handwriting on the envelope. But I don't know what's inside, do I? For all I know, she might be sending on messages from *him*.'

Anna forced down her rising irritation. 'You know I never write to Tom anymore.'

'I know what you tell me.' Edward sent her a suspicious look.

Anna sighed. 'How long will it be before you trust me?'

'As long as it takes.'

'We've been married for nearly five months and I've never given you cause to doubt me, have I?' *Unlike you*, whispered a voice inside her head.

'Not yet. But that's only because I've been watching you. How do I know what you'd get up to behind my back if I let you?' Edward put down his cup. He was smiling but his eyes were steely. 'I'm sorry, my love, but you really only have yourself to blame. If you hadn't gone sneaking about, writing letters to another man in secret . . .'

I didn't write to him in secret! Anna opened her mouth to argue, then gave up. She had learned the hard way that it was never worth trying to get the better of Edward. He had a way of twisting her in knots, making her think she had said and done things she hadn't.

And besides, she didn't have the energy for an argument. A disagreement that started at breakfast was likely to simmer on all day, or until she apologised and Edward decided to forgive her. All she wanted was some peace.

But deep down she knew it wasn't really Edward talking. Her Edward would never look at her so coldly, or say such hurtful things. Her Edward loved her, trusted her. He would have laughed off stupid arguments, put his arms around her and told her it didn't matter.

She looked across the table at her husband. He still looked like Edward. The months since leaving the army had restored his well-built frame and his fair good looks. But inside, Anna knew he was still fragile, wary, damaged. It would take more than a few months to put that right.

In the meantime, all she could do was try her best to put up with the barbs, and the mistrust and the cruelty, and trust that one day her Edward would come back to her and everything would be all right again.

Besides, what other choice did she have? This was her

dream, to be with Edward at the bakery, and she had to make it work.

'I see your sister is still on about wanting to come for a visit?' Edward's voice broke into her thoughts. 'Honestly, they can't work those Land Girls very hard if she has time off to visit every five minutes!'

'I've only seen her once since we got married,' Anna pointed out quietly.

'Yes, well, I don't like her sniffing around. This isn't her home anymore. It's ours.'

'Edward!'

'It's true. Your father left this place to us, not to her.'

He left it to me. Anna bit back the comment. 'But I'm sure he knew we would always welcome her . . .'

'She's had her money,' Edward cut her off. 'That's all she can expect.'

'She's still my sister. I want to see her.'

The words hung in the air between them. Anna saw Edward's face tighten, and started to regret what she had said.

'Then of course you must.' The words came out from between taut lips. 'I'm sorry, I didn't realise I was keeping you from her.'

'You're not,' Anna rushed to reassure him.

'I just know how much she upsets you,' Edward went on. 'I'm only thinking of you, Anna.'

'Liesel doesn't upset me.'

'You know what she's like. She always stirs up trouble when she comes to visit. She's bound to say something cruel or hurtful. I don't know why you'd put yourself out for someone who doesn't care about you.'

'She does care!'

'Remember how she abandoned you on Christmas Day and left you all alone?'

Anna was silent.

'But of course you must see her if you want to,' Edward said. Then he smiled. 'Forgive me,' he said, reaching for her hands. 'I suppose I'm just too protective of you. I can't bear to see my little Anna hurt.'

She squeezed his hands. 'That's what sisters are like,' she said. 'We fight and squabble, but we don't mean it.'

'Perhaps I don't understand.' Edward's gaze fell to his plate. 'Having no family of my own, I don't know what it's like to feel close to someone. The only person I have is you.' He looked up at her, and for a moment she saw her Edward in his pleading blue eyes. 'You can't blame me for wanting you all to myself, can you?'

Anna looked down at the letter in front of her. 'I'll write to Liesel,' she said. 'Perhaps it might be better to put off seeing her until the summer.'

'Whatever you think best,' he said.

She picked up Sylvia's wedding invitation again and studied it. 'But I think I will go to the wedding,' she said. 'It will be nice to see everyone again.'

'When is it?'

'The twenty-ninth of June.'

'A Saturday?' He shook his head. 'I'm not sure we'd be able to spare you.'

'Surely we could manage? After all, we have some help in the shop now . . .'

After sacking Mrs Church, a couple of weeks ago Edward had changed his mind and decided that perhaps they could do with some help after all.

'It isn't fair to expect you to manage all by yourself,' he had said to Anna. 'Besides, you're far more use to me in the kitchen.'

Anna had agreed it made sense. But before she had had a chance to advertise the position, Edward had turned up with Nellie Madigan in tow. She was an Irish girl with flaming red hair, a barmaid at the Fallen Angel, he had said. She had lost her husband in the war and she needed the extra money.

'She'll be good with the customers,' he had told Anna. 'And she might be company for you, too. I know how lonely you've been since you left the hospital.'

Anna wondered if she and Nellie Madigan would ever be friends. Nellie was an abrasive girl with a loud laugh and a vulgar sense of humour. Anna doubted her mother would ever have entertained the idea of someone like her working behind the counter. But Edward wouldn't hear a word said against her, so that was that.

Now Anna put down the invitation and looked back at her husband. In the months since their marriage she had learned to read his expressions, and the frown on his face now made her feel wary.

'What is it?' she asked.

Edward looked at the invitation, then back at her.

'So do you want to go to this wedding?'

'I'd like to.'

'Are you sure she's not just being polite?'

Anna stared at him, taken aback. 'What do you mean?'

'You've been gone a while now. And it's not as if you see any of your old friends anymore, is it?'

And whose fault is that? Anna wanted to say. She had turned down their invitations to meet for tea or for an outing to a concert because Edward made it clear he didn't like her going out without him. After a while, they had stopped asking.

It was a relief when they did, in a way. At least she no longer had to make up excuses.

But she missed them desperately.

'But Sylvia sent me an invitation . . .' she insisted.

'Yes, but I don't suppose she expected you to accept.' Edward tilted his head and smiled at her. 'I'm only thinking of you, my love. I don't want you to make a fool of yourself.'

Anna looked down at the card in her hands. 'Is that what you really think?' she asked. 'That she didn't want me to accept?'

Before he could reply, the back door opened downstairs and Nellie Madigan's voice rang out.

'Eddie?'

Anna winced. 'I wish you wouldn't let the staff call you that.'

'The staff?' Edward mocked her.

'You know what I mean. Charlie used to call you Eddie, too. It doesn't seem right.'

'It's how she knows me from the pub.' He shrugged. 'I suppose it's hard for her to remember to call me anything else.'

'I still don't like it. You wouldn't have called Papa Friedrich, would you?'

She knew it was the wrong thing to say when she saw Edward's face stiffen.

'Yes, well, I don't have to do everything the way your papa did, do I?' He stood up. 'I don't mind what she calls me, so I don't see why you should, either.'

At that moment Nellie appeared in the kitchen doorway. 'Oh, beg pardon. I didn't mean to disturb you.'

But there was a glint in her green eyes as she said it. She was a big, brassy girl, her wide, smiling mouth painted scarlet even first thing in the morning. She was only twenty-one years old but already had two small children, so Eddie said.

Anna surveyed her critically, noticing her grubby blouse and the way her skirt strained over her rounded hips.

Edward checked his watch. 'Is it that time already? I should be getting the next batch in the oven.'

'You mean you haven't done it?' Nellie shook her head. 'You're slacking, Eddie Stanning.'

'I can't help it if I wanted to spend time with my wife,

can I?' Edward leaned over and planted a kiss on Anna's cheek. 'No, you finish your breakfast, sweetheart,' he said, as she started to rise. 'Nellie and I can open up the shop. It's about time she started earning her living!'

'Cheeky beggar!' she laughed.

Anna felt a sudden stab of jealousy.

'Nellie?' she said. The girl turned around. 'Make sure you fasten your hair up. You need to look tidy for the customers.'

Nellie glanced at Edward, twisting a red curl between her fingers. Then she gave an insolent little smile.

'Yes, Mrs Stanning.' She bobbed a curtsey and left the room, her hips swinging.

Edward went after her. Anna heard their murmuring voices as they descended the stairs, followed by a sudden burst of coarse laughter from Nellie.

She sat very still at the table, looking down at her hands.

They must have thought she was very stupid. Or perhaps they just didn't care enough to try to hide their dirty little secret.

It hurt that she wasn't enough for him. But at least it meant he left her alone in the bedroom, and Anna was grateful for that.

She finished her tea and went to the sink to wash up the breakfast dishes. Nellie and Edward's voices drifted up to her from downstairs, laughing and joking together.

That was what really hurt, more than anything. It should have been her and Edward laughing together, working side by side, just as they had once. That had always been her dream and now it felt as if someone had stolen it.

If Edward had deliberately set out to hurt her, he couldn't have picked a better way.

But it wasn't his fault, she reminded herself. He was sick, he didn't know what he was doing. If anything it was her fault for not being the wife he needed.

Chapter Forty-Five

Dear George,

As I write this letter to you, I am sitting at the French windows looking out over the garden. How beautiful it all looks now it is starting to flower again. It has been such a long, dreadful winter I began to wonder if we would ever see spring. But now the cherry trees are heavy with blossom, and even the roses are starting to bloom . . .

Dulcie looked up at Sub Lieutenant Hawkins. He was slumped against the pillows, his eyes half closed. She didn't blame him for his lethargy; his mother's letters were enough to send anyone to sleep.

She let the letter drop into her lap and turned her attention to the commotion going on at the far end of the ward.

Private Gordon was staggering down the centre of the ward, clinging to his friend Albie Sallis' arm, Albie was egging him on every step of the way, while Grace and Dr Logan stood at the end of the ward, beaming like proud parents.

Dulcie watched them, lanced with jealousy. She had tried her best to dismiss what Captain Jeffers had said to her about them. But she couldn't ignore what her own eyes were telling her.

She could see it now, in the sideways glances Dr Logan kept giving Grace. He couldn't seem to take his eyes off her for a second.

Grace, of course, seemed utterly oblivious. All her attention was fixed on Private Gordon's progress down the ward. Her hands were clasped together, willing him on with every step.

Gordon finally reached Dulcie's end of the ward.

'Well, done, mate! You did it!' Albie Sallis clapped him on the shoulder, nearly knocking him off balance. 'I told you, didn't I? You can do anything you set your mind to.'

At the far end of the ward, Grace and Dr Logan had burst into spontaneous applause. As Dulcie watched, Grace turned around and grinned at Dr Logan. It was the widest, least flirtatious smile Dulcie had ever seen, yet Dr Logan gazed at her as if she were Pearl White or Mary Pickford.

It couldn't be, she told herself. She had lost men before, but never, ever to a goose like Grace Duffield.

'Nu – nu—' George Hawkins made a strange grunting sound at the back of his throat. His hand pawed at hers on top of the covers, silently urging her to finish reading. Dulcie sighed resentfully and snatched up the letter.

'Now where was I? Oh, yes, the blooming roses . . .'

Dulcie was still sulking when they all met in the nurses' common room that night. Sylvia had handed out her wedding invitations, which of course prompted yet another tedious discussion about arrangements.

'I'm going for my final dress fitting in a couple of weeks,' she said coyly. 'I wondered if anyone would like to come with me?'

She was looking straight at Dulcie, but she ignored it. Let the other girls twitter with excitement if they wanted. Dulcie refused to give her the satisfaction.

Thankfully, the conversation changed to another outing to the picture house Miriam Trott was planning for the men of Monaghan ward for the following evening. For some reason she was asking Grace to come this time, instead of Dulcie.

'Don't ask her.' Jealousy made Dulcie waspish. 'Last time she took the men on an outing she managed to lose one of them!'

It was supposed to be a joke, but no one laughed.

'I can't come anyway,' Grace said. 'I've already made an arrangement for tomorrow evening.'

A shocked silence fell. The other girls all turned to stare at her.

'You have a date?' Miriam spoke for all of them.

'I wouldn't call it a date, exactly.' Grace blushed. 'Dr Logan has invited me to a lecture he's giving on shell shock.'

Another shocked silence, then Sylvia Saunders hooted with laughter. Mary Finnegan and Miriam Trott joined in, and soon they were all laughing. Except Dulcie.

Grace looked around, genuinely baffled. 'I don't understand,' she said. 'What's so funny?'

'Oh, Duffield!' Sylvia shook her head, wiping tears from her eyes. 'And they say romance is dead!'

'There's nothing romantic about it,' Grace insisted, turning redder. 'He had a spare ticket and thought I might be interested.'

The other girls laughed even more.

'Oh, Duffers, what are we going to do with you?' Hilda Wharton shook her head pityingly.

'Don't you know when a man is showing an interest in you?' Mary Finnegan put in.

'Showing an interest? But I don't—' Realisation dawned on Grace's plain face. 'But it's nothing like that! Honestly, it isn't.'

But the more she tried to insist, the more the other girls laughed.

'You ought to be careful, Moore,' Miriam Trott put in with a malicious little smile. 'It looks as if you're going to lose your Dr Logan.'

'No, really. He'd never look twice at someone like me. He was probably just being polite . . .'

This last comment was aimed at Dulcie. She could sense the pleading look Grace was sending her, but refused to look her in the eye.

Dulcie couldn't bring herself to speak to her room-mate for the rest of the evening. She made an excuse to go to bed early and was under the covers, pretending to be asleep, when Grace came to their room later.

Dulcie heard her blundering around in the dark, knocking things flying.

Finally, as she got into bed, Grace whispered, 'Moore? Are you awake?'

Dulcie thought about not replying. But then she hissed back, 'Not much chance of sleep with you acting like a bull in a china shop!'

'Sorry.' There was a pause, then Grace whispered, 'I just wanted you to know – you've got nothing to worry about.'

'I don't know what you're talking about.'

'You know – what the other girls were saying. About Dr Logan and me? I'm sure he didn't mean anything by it when he offered me that ticket. It was just a kind gesture, that's all.'

Dulcie burned with fury. She didn't need pity from the likes of Grace Duffield!

'I know there's nothing to it,' she snapped back. 'How could there be, when you're engaged to someone else?'

Grace fell silent, and Dulcie knew her barb had hit home.

She threw off her covers and sat up, staring at Grace in the darkness. She could make out her tall, gawky shape sitting on the edge of her bed, her head hanging low.

'I just wonder that you decided to accept the invitation, that's all,' she said.

Grace's head lifted. 'What do you mean?'

'I mean it's hardly right for a girl to be seen around town with another man when she's supposed to be marrying someone else.'

'But it's nothing like that. I told you—'

'I know what you said. But I'm not sure what your fiancé would think about it.'

Grace was silent for a moment. Dulcie could almost picture her furiously blushing face in the darkness.

'So you think – I shouldn't go to the lecture?' she said slowly.

'That's up to you.' Dulcie shrugged. 'But if it was me, I don't think I'd care to get myself a reputation.'

Another silence. Then Grace said, 'You're right. It – it wouldn't be fair to Noah.' Her voice was flat when she said his name, Dulcie noticed. 'Thank you,' she said.

'What for?'

'For giving me good advice. Honestly, I'm such a fool, I don't know what I'd do without you helping me.'

Now it was Dulcie's turn to blush.

'That's what friends are for,' she said.

'Look at him go! He'll be tripping the light fantastic next.'

'Y-you're p-putting me off,' Private Gordon grumbled. He was hanging on to Grace's arm, his fingers biting into her flesh through the thick cotton. Close to, she could see the beads of sweat standing out on his brow at the sheer effort of putting one foot in front of the other.

'I mean it, mate. I can see you now, doing the foxtrot round the dance hall, all the ladies lining up . . .'

'Shhh –' Gordon turned around, lost his footing and stumbled, taking Grace with him. They fell in a tangle of limbs on the floor.

'Now see what you've done!' Gordon shouted, but Albie only laughed.

315

'He did that on purpose, Nurse, just to get you in his arms!' Albie stepped forward. 'Come on, mate, let's get you back on your feet.'

He hauled Gordon upright. Dr Logan put out his hand to help Grace but she scrambled to her feet before he could touch her.

'I beg your pardon, Nurse,' Gordon mumbled, glaring at Albie.

'No harm done, Private Gordon.' Grace brushed down her apron. 'It was probably my fault anyway. I never look where I'm putting my feet.'

'I think that's enough exercise for one day.' Dr Logan made a note on Private Gordon's chart and hung it back on the hook at the foot of his bed. 'Get some rest, man. You've earned it.'

'I could've gone a bit further if you hadn't put me off!' Gordon muttered to Albie as Grace helped him back into bed and pulled the covers over him.

Albie shook his head. 'I saw you wrestling on the floor with poor Nurse Duffield. Any further and it wouldn't have been decent!'

Grace was aware of Dr Logan watching her as she finished making Private Gordon comfortable. Usually she wouldn't even have noticed, but since hearing what the other girls had to say, she had started to feel very aware of him.

When she walked away, he fell into step beside her.

'I'm sorry you couldn't come to the lecture last night,' he said.

Grace was surprised. 'I didn't think you'd notice if I wasn't there?'

'Of course I noticed.'

There was something about the way he looked at her

that made the breath catch in her throat. No man had ever looked at her like that.

'Talking of tripping the light fantastic,' Dr Logan changed the subject, 'are you going to this wedding?'

Grace nodded. 'Are you?'

'I'm the best man.'

'I didn't realise Roger – I mean, Dr Wallace – was such a friend of yours?'

Dr Logan looked rueful. 'To be honest, I scarcely know the chap. But I get the impression that most of his friends have been called up, so I was the only one available. The last man standing, as it were. It's a bit awkward, really. I haven't been very sociable since I came to the Nightingale, so I don't think I'll know anyone at this wedding.'

'You know me,' Grace said.

Dr Logan swung round to face her. 'Would you go with me?' he asked.

'I—'

'It would make such a difference if I had someone I knew by my side. Someone I felt comfortable with.'

'I can't,' Grace blurted out. 'I'm engaged.'

Dr Logan's features froze. 'You're – engaged?' he repeated slowly.

'Yes. So, you see, it wouldn't be appropriate for me to go with you?'

'No. No, I see that.' He looked lost. 'I – I'm sorry, Nurse Duffield. I didn't mean to offend you. I would never have suggested it if I—' His voice trailed off. His face was suffused with colour.

'Why don't you ask Dulcie?' Grace said.

'Dulcie – oh, you mean Nurse Moore?'

'I'm sure she would love to go with you,' Grace said encouragingly.

'Right. Yes.' He went on staring at her. Behind his spectacles his blue eyes were clouded with confusion. 'Engaged, you say?'

Grace gave an embarrassed laugh. 'Is it that hard to believe, Doctor?'

'No!' His colour deepened. 'Not at all. I just thought – but it doesn't matter.'

She had done the right thing, Grace thought, as she watched him hurrying away from her down the ward. Thank God for Dulcie, setting her straight before she made an utter fool of herself.

Chapter Forty-Six

'Any headaches?' the doctor said.

'Sometimes.'

'Lethargy? Depression?'

'Yes.'

'Insomnia?'

Anna looked back at him across the desk as he scribbled his notes. *Only if you count the hours I've lain awake waiting for my husband to come home.*

'Yes,' she said.

She shouldn't be here, she thought. She had only come because Edward had said she must.

'You're not yourself,' he'd said. He was in one of his solicitous moods. It always astonished Anna how he could swing from cruelty to kindness, almost as if he was deliberately trying to unbalance her. 'You need to go to the doctor, get something for your nerves.'

He had been so loving, so concerned, that for a moment Anna had almost believed he truly cared.

'And how is everything at home?' the doctor asked.

'What?' Anna stared at him, startled. It was almost as if he had read her thoughts.

The doctor looked up at her, his eyes kindly behind his spectacles. 'I know it can be very difficult, looking after a home and family under the circumstances in which we find ourselves. Would you say you are under particular strain?'

He looked so sympathetic, Anna thought about telling

him the truth. That her husband was stealing money from their business and gambling it all away with his friends night after night. She could even tell him about Nellie Madigan too, and all the whispered conversations and laughter she pretended not to hear.

But she still had a shred of pride left, so instead she pasted on a smile and said,

'I wouldn't say so, Doctor.'

Half an hour later, she was lining up at the pharmacist's with a prescription for an iron tonic in her hand.

Seeing the doctor's scrawl on the paper made her think of all the Latin instructions she had had to decipher at the Nightingale. *Donec alv. sol. fuerit, Per. op. emet, Omn. hor* – she had learned them all during her training. She knew from the words *Noct. Maneq.* on her prescription that the tonic was to be taken morning and night, even before the chemist told her.

Once she had been the one dispensing the medications. She had a sudden picture of a very different Anna, doing the drugs round, measuring out medicines and administering pills and injections, utterly sure of her own ability.

Now she could barely get dressed in the morning without doubting herself.

'I hope it does the trick.'

Anna caught the look of pity on the chemist's face as he handed her the brown paper bag. She knew what he was seeing. Not the proud, confident young woman she had once been, but the thin, washed-out wreck she had become. Anna could scarcely bear to look at herself in the mirror anymore. She could not face the drawn, pale face under lank brown hair, or those hollow, desperate eyes.

She trudged home slowly, taking the back streets, clinging to the brick walls like a shadow. There was a time when she would have greeted everyone and stopped to chat.

Now she kept her head down and prayed that she didn't see anyone she knew.

As she approached Chambord Street, the old familiar dread began to uncurl inside her. What would be waiting for her at home? Would Edward be in a good mood? Would he take her in his arms and tell her he loved her, or would he snarl at her?

Worst of all, he might be in one of his difficult moods. This was when Anna could sense a storm brewing, and had to pick her way carefully around him, knowing that any wrong word, or even an unguarded look, could cause him to erupt.

Sometimes she could tell what the day would bring from the night before. If Edward had won on the cards, he would probably be laughing and joking in the morning. If he had lost – which was the case more often than not – he would be surly and snappish.

Last night he hadn't returned until the early hours. Anna had lain rigid, pretending to be asleep. But she could smell Nellie's cheap scent coming off him as he undressed and got into bed beside her.

She turned the corner and stopped in her tracks. There was a man up a ladder outside the bakery, a paintbrush in one hand, pot of paint in the other.

Anna ran down the street, pushing past the late-afternoon shoppers.

'What are you doing?' she called up to the workman.

'What does it look like?' he shouted back.

The words 'Beck's Bakery' were already half obliterated under a thick coat of black paint. 'Who told you to do it?'

He jerked his head towards the shop. 'Better ask the boss.'

Anna stood her ground. 'I want you to stop,' she said.

'Can't do that, Missus. I've got my orders, y'see.'

321

Anna stormed into the shop. It was empty, except for Nellie half-heartedly organising jam tarts on a plate. She looked up as Anna came in, slamming the door behind her.

'Afternoon,' she said with that sly little smile of hers. Anna ignored her, lifting the flap in the counter to go through to the back.

'Edward!'

He emerged from the kitchen, wiping his hands on a towel.

'Hello, love,' he said. He was all smiles, but for once that hardly mattered to Anna.

'What are you playing at? You can't paint over my father's name.'

His face darkened, like clouds passing over the sun. 'I can do what I like.'

'But this has been Beck's Bakery for the past twenty-five years!'

'And now it's mine.' His chin lifted. 'I can't wait to see my name up over the door, where it belongs.' He held up his hands, as if he was picturing it. 'Stanning's. It's got a nice ring to it, don't you think?'

Anna was half aware of Nellie, standing in the doorway, watching them with interest.

'You must tell the signwriter to stop.'

Edward folded his arms across his chest. 'Says who?'

'Me.'

He smiled nastily. 'Ah, but I don't have to take orders from you anymore, do I? I ain't the apprentice. I'm the boss now. And once my name's over the door, everyone will know it.'

She looked at him and felt a searing rage that burned away her fear.

'Do you really think you can take my father's place just

by painting out his name on a sign?' She spat the words out scornfully. She saw Edward's eyes narrow but she was too angry to stop. Seeing him trying to obliterate her father's memory had unleashed a fury in her that she'd thought was long gone.

'I know why you're doing this,' she said. 'You're jealous. That's why you want to wipe out Papa's name, because you know you'll never be half the man he is.'

'That's enough!' The stinging slap caught her off guard. Behind her, Anna heard Nellie hiss with shock.

She put her hand up to her cheek, feeling the jarred bones. Edward towered over her, tall and threatening.

'I'm sick of listening to you going on about your father as if he was some kind of hero!' He grabbed her by her shoulders, shaking her like a rag doll. 'When are you going to face the fact that he's gone? He's scuttled back to his little German rat hole, and good riddance to him.' Edward's mouth curled into a sneer. 'Christ, all those years I had to kow-tow to that self-satisfied little German, not to mention your snobbish cow of a mother!'

Anna stared up at him in horror. 'You – you don't mean that. My father loved you, he treated you like a son.'

'He treated me like a bloody servant!' Edward cut her off. 'I had to go cap in hand to them for everything, to be grateful for his charity. The only time he started to treat me with any respect was when I decided to take up with you. But even then your mother and sister still looked down their noses at me. As far as they were concerned I was the kid from the orphanage. I should have known my place.' He looked around with a self-satisfied smirk. 'Well, I know my place now, don't I?'

But Anna wasn't listening. Her mind had snagged on a few words.

'You – decided to take up with me?'

'How else was I going to get my hands on this place?' He sent her a pitying look. 'What? You really believed I'd fallen in love with you? Do me a favour! I could have done a lot better than you, believe me. I even thought about trying my luck with Liesel, since she's prettier,' he said casually. 'But she's a high-handed bitch like her mother, and I knew she wouldn't look twice at me. But you,' he sneered. 'You were desperate, weren't you? Poor, plain little Anna. I could see it written all over your face, you couldn't believe your luck when I showed an interest in you. And neither could your precious papa.' He gave a snort of laughter. 'God, the relief on his face when he found out about us! I daresay he was wondering if he'd ever be able to marry you off.'

This time it was Anna who lashed out. Her hand connected with Edward's cheek, but with nowhere near as much force as he'd struck her.

'Get out!' she hissed.

Edward laughed, nursing his jaw. 'I ain't going anywhere. This bakery was mine the day I married you. But you're welcome to go if you want. I certainly ain't going to stop you. It would be a blessing if you did go, then at least I wouldn't have to put up with you whining about your bloody father!' He leaned closer, his blue eyes glacial with anger. 'But that sign over the door is there now, and there it will stay. I'm telling you, I'm in charge here. And there's nothing you can do to change that!'

Chapter Forty-Seven

There was a week to go until Sylvia's June wedding, and this time it wasn't only the bride who couldn't stop talking about it.

'Do you think I should wear my hair up or down?' Dulcie pushed her brown curls on top of her head and turned this way and that, admiring her reflection in the dressing-table mirror. 'Up shows off my face more, don't you think? But then I suppose it all depends which hat I'm wearing . . . Duffield, are you listening to me?'

Grace looked up vaguely from polishing her shoes. Dulcie had twisted round from the mirror to look at her.

'You haven't heard a word I've said, have you?' she accused. 'Mind you, I don't even know why I'm bothering to ask your opinion. I've never seen you do anything to your hair but pin it out of the way.'

Grace put up her hand to touch a strand of her light brown hair. 'It's practical.'

'Who wants to be practical?' Dulcie turned back to face her reflection. 'I'd rather be pretty any day.' She teased a couple of curls to frame her face and smiled coquettishly at herself.

Grace watched her wistfully for a moment. It had never occurred to her she could even try to be pretty. Her mother had certainly not put such ideas in her head. As far as she was concerned, clothes only needed to be warm and practical enough to withstand the rigours of farm work.

Dulcie had grown up in the country too yet she knew all

about the latest styles and fashions. From what Grace could tell, her mother had encouraged her interest, sewing her copies of the dresses she had seen in magazines, teaching her how to do all kinds of fancy things to her hair.

Sarah Duffield had never encouraged Grace to think much of herself. In her opinion time spent in front of the mirror was time wasted, especially where her daughter was concerned. As she had said to Grace often enough, 'You'll never make a silk purse out of a sow's ear.'

'Anyway, you could be more interested,' Dulcie said. 'This is my big chance, remember?'

'How could I forget?' Grace murmured. She went back to polishing her shoes.

'Of course, I knew Robert would notice me in the end,' Dulcie said. 'Although I must say, I didn't think it would take this long.' She giggled. 'It sounds funny to call him Robert, doesn't it? But I suppose I shall have to get used to it. I mean, I can't call him Dr Logan when we're married, can I?'

Grace said nothing. She kept her eyes fixed on her polish brush, going back and forth across the toes of her shoes.

'I wonder why it took him so long to ask me out? I daresay he's just shy, don't you think?' she answered her own question. 'I mean, he can still scarcely get up the nerve to speak to me. Have you noticed that? It's so sweet, don't you think? Duffield?'

'Hmm?'

'Don't you think it's sweet that he can hardly dare to speak to me? Mind you, I hope he plucks up some courage at this wedding,' she laughed. 'I shall be very disappointed if he doesn't kiss me before the evening is out.' She leaned forward, pouting her lips to kiss her own reflection. Then she looked at Grace in the mirror. 'Careful, Duffield, you'll polish the leather away if you keep scrubbing at them like that!'

Grace was aware of Dulcie watching her as she put down the cloth and started buffing her shoes with a cloth.

'You seem very agitated today,' Dulcie commented at last.

'Do I?'

'Yes. And I think I know why, too. It's him, isn't it?'

'What?' Grace looked up sharply.

'That soldier – what's his name? Gordon. He's being discharged today, isn't he? I bet that's what's upset you. I know how attached you get to them all,' she said.

'Yes.' Grace set down her shoes. 'Yes, that must be the reason.'

Perhaps she was right, Grace thought. As it happened, she *was* upset at the thought of Private Gordon leaving. He was being sent to a convalescent home up in Scotland, close to where his family lived. Grace was pleased for him, but knew she would miss him.

The first person Grace saw when she walked on to the ward was Dr Logan. He was at the far end of the ward, talking to Private Gordon.

Try as she might, Grace's gaze still seemed to seek him out. And his seemed to do the same, head lifting the moment she walked in. For a moment they stared at each other down the length of the ward.

'Look at him,' Dulcie said beside her in a thrilled whisper. 'He can't take his eyes off me. Do you think I should go and say hello to him?'

'Not if you want to stay out of trouble with Sister,' Grace whispered back.

'And I fully recommend you do stay out of trouble, Nurse.' Sister's brisk Scottish voice rang out behind them, making them both jump. Miss Parker was so slight, she constantly managed to creep up on unsuspecting nurses, unlike Miss Sutton's heavy, ponderous tread that could be heard like distant thunder.

As ward sister, Miss Parker was not supposed to come on duty until eight o'clock, but had a nasty habit of arriving an hour early, just to catch out any nurses who trailed in a few minutes late, or who didn't help out the night staff.

'Nurse Duffield, I want you to pack up Private Gordon's belongings for him,' she said.

Grace opened her mouth to speak but Dulcie got there before her.

'I'll do it, Sister.'

Miss Parker frowned at her. 'You, Nurse? I don't think I can ever recall you volunteering for extra duties before?'

'I just want to help, Sister.' Dulcie lowered her eyes demurely.

Grace glanced at Dr Logan, still deep in conversation with Gordon and Albie Sallis. She knew Dulcie was anxious to help Private Gordon for exactly the same reason as Grace was anxious not to.

'That's very commendable of you, Moore.' Miss Parker did not look convinced. 'But I think this is best left to Duffield. She has more of an affinity with Private Gordon. You can help with the bedpan round,' she added as an afterthought.

'Well, I like that!' Dulcie stared after Miss Parker as she marched off down the ward. 'You'd think she'd be happy I was showing an interest. Affinity, indeed!' she huffed. 'As if I can't throw a few belongings in a stupid old suitcase!'

Chapter Forty-Eight

'All right, Nurse?' Albie Sallis hailed Grace with a smile as she approached Private Gordon's bed. 'Come to see him off, have you?'

'Yes, indeed, Corporal Sallis. And to pack his belongings.'

'You hear that, mate? You've got your own batman.' Albie grinned at Gordon. 'And there was us thinking only the officers had those privileges!'

Grace glanced at Dr Logan. He was studying a chart, his back half turned to her.

'Mind you, you're a lot better-looking than most of the batmen I've ever met,' Albie went on. 'Don't you reckon, Doctor?'

Dr Logan did not respond. He went on staring at the chart as if his life depended on it.

Albie winked at Grace. 'Look at him, he's in a world of his own. You want to watch out, Gordon lad. The way he's looking at your chart, I reckon he wants to find an excuse to keep you in here a bit longer!'

Private Gordon sent them a sheepish look. 'I wouldn't mind if he did.'

'Listen to that, Nurse. Reckon our Gordon's got a soft spot for you!'

Grace jumped as Dr Logan slammed down the chart. Then he stalked off without a word.

'Someone got out of bed the wrong side this morning,' Albie commented. 'And he's usually such a friendly sort, too. What's got into him, I wonder?'

'I've no idea, Corporal Sallis.' Grace watched Dr Logan until he disappeared into Sister's office. Then she fixed a bright smile on her face and turned back to face Private Gordon. 'Right, let's see about packing up this bag, shall we?'

All too soon, it was time for Private Gordon to leave. Albie Sallis fell silent for once as Grace helped Gordon into the wheelchair that was to transport him to the waiting ambulance.

It wasn't until they were ready to leave that he spoke again.

'Well, all the best, mate.' He shook Gordon's hand. 'Have a good time at the convalescent home, won't you? And remember – just because you can walk again it don't mean you can go running after all them nurses!'

Gordon gave him a lopsided grin. 'I r-reckon they'll be r-running after me.'

It was the first time in a long time that Grace had heard him stammer, a sure sign he was nervous.

'Listen to him, Nurse!' Albie crowed with laughter, but his eyes glistened with tears. 'Talk about big-headed! Have you ever heard the like?'

Just then Sister appeared, accompanied by an orderly. 'Ready, Private Gordon?'

'As ready as I'll ever b-be,' Gordon replied. He turned back to Albie. 'Take care of yourself. And thank you,' he said. 'If it hadn't b-been for you taking me under your w-wing, I don't think I would have ever p-pulled through this.'

'Oh, stop it! Don't get all soppy on me now, for gawd's sake!' Albie looked away, his voice gruff with emotion.

He didn't look back until Private Gordon had gone. He kept his gaze fixed on the ward doors all the while Grace was stripping Gordon's bed.

'He will be all right, won't he, Nurse?' he said finally.

'Of course he will, Corporal Sallis.'

'And they'll look after him properly?'

Grace looked at Albie. His voice was flat, less ebullient than she had ever heard it.

'They'll take good care of him,' she said.

'I hope so. He can be a funny bugger, y'see. If you'll pardon my French. Bit too quiet.'

'I'm sure he'll make friends soon.'

'Yes.' Albie looked troubled by the thought. 'He's asked me to write to him, but I dunno if I'll bother. I ain't really much of a one for letters.'

'I'm sure he'd be disappointed if he didn't hear from you.'

'D'you think so?' Albie looked up at her.

'I'm sure of it.'

'But like you said, he'll make new friends.'

'That doesn't mean he'll forget you. You heard what he said, your friendship means a great deal to him.'

'I s'pose so.' Albie paused for a moment, taking it in. 'I won't know what I'm going to do with myself now he's gone,' he said at last. 'It gave me a sort of purpose, looking after him. And now . . .'

Then his grin returned and he said, 'Hark at me, I must be going soft in my old age! Take no notice of me, Nurse. I dunno what I'm saying half the time.'

Grace finished stripping the bed and put the dirty sheets in a bag, ready to go to the laundry. As she returned from the sluice, she noticed Albie sitting forlornly on his own, staring into space. He looked so lost, her heart went out to him.

Sister was at her desk in the middle of the ward, deep in conversation with Dr Logan. Grace promptly changed her mind about approaching them. She had just turned away when Miss Parker called after her, 'Was there something you wanted, Nurse?'

Grace turned back reluctantly to face them. 'I wondered, Sister, whether it would be all right to spend some time with Corporal Sallis? He was such good friends with Private Gordon, it's going to be difficult for him now.' She risked a glance at Dr Logan. He had his back to her, ignoring her presence.

'I think that would be an excellent idea, Nurse. What do you say, Doctor?' She turned to Dr Logan.

His shoulders lifted in a non-committal shrug that made Grace's blood boil in her veins. Why was he being so childish? It wasn't as if he didn't have anyone to take to Sylvia's wedding, after all.

'Certainly you may spend time with him, Nurse, if you truly think it will help.' Miss Parker looked at the clock. 'But aren't you supposed to be off duty from ten o'clock until two? It's twenty to ten now.'

'I won't spend too long with him, Sister. I just want to make sure he's all right.'

Grace stared at Dr Logan's turned back as she said it. The tips of his ears glowed scarlet through his neatly trimmed dark hair.

Grace had only intended to spend a short while with Albie Sallis, but was so engrossed in their game of whist, she didn't notice the time until Dulcie came up to her.

'What are you doing?' she hissed. 'We're supposed to be off duty now. We're meeting the others by the gates at half-past ten, don't forget.'

'I'll be there soon,' Grace said.

'But we'll be late.'

'Then you go without me,' Grace cut her off. 'I'll join you as soon as I can.'

'What's this?' Albie asked as Dulcie stomped off. 'Got a date, have you?'

'Hardly,' Grace smiled. 'Sylvia – Nurse Saunders – is

having a wedding dress fitting and she's invited some of us to go with her.'

'Then why are you still here? You should go.'

'I'm sure they won't miss me.' Grace laid down a card.

'All the same, you should be there. It ain't fair that you're always the odd one out.'

Grace looked up at him. Was that really how people saw her, the odd one out? 'I really don't mind.'

'No, but I do.' Albie gathered up the cards, ending the game. 'You don't have to sit here and keep me company,' he insisted. 'I'm old enough and ugly enough to look after myself. Besides,' he added, his eyes twinkling with mischief, 'it looked like you were going to win that round!'

Grace laughed. 'I think I was, for once!' She stood up. 'Are you sure you'll be all right?'

'I'll be fine. You get off to your wedding dress fitting.'

Grace turned, just in time to see Dr Logan standing behind her. He stared from Albie to her and back again, then turned on his heel and walked off.

'Not again! He's really got the hump today, hasn't he?' Albie commented.

'Yes,' Grace sighed, watching him go. 'Yes, I'm afraid he has.'

Dulcie, Miriam and Mary Finnegan were already at the dressmaker's when Grace arrived. As an assistant opened the door to her, she could hear them in the waiting room, twittering excitedly together like birds.

'There you are!' Miriam looked up at her accusingly. 'We were beginning to think you weren't coming.'

'Where's Saunders?'

Mary Finnegan nodded towards a door. 'Through there, getting dressed.'

Grace sat down on the end of the row as the other three

all turned towards each other to resume their giggling conversation. They were discussing which men were going to be at the wedding, and who might invite them to go as their escorts.

Grace concentrated on taking off her gloves and smoothing them out in her lap. She was used to being left out of such conversations.

Dulcie, of course, was very smug, since she already had an escort for the wedding. She made sure she kept mentioning it too, just to irritate Miriam. Grace couldn't help smiling at the other girl's tight-lipped expression.

Suddenly, Mary Finnegan turned to Grace and said, 'Do you have your eye on anyone, Duffield?'

Miriam Trott gave an unkind snort. 'What are you asking her for? She's never even had a boyfriend.'

'Neither have you,' Dulcie pointed out. Then, to Grace's dismay, added, 'Anyway, Duffield will probably be married before any of us.'

'Oh, yes? And how do you work that out?' Miriam asked.

Grace sent Dulcie a pleading look, which she ignored.

'Because she's engaged.'

Grace's heart sank. The other girls immediately turned to her, mouths agape.

'Engaged?'

'Never!'

'But you're not wearing a ring?'

'That's because it's not true,' Miriam declared. 'Moore's having us on.'

'I'm not,' Dulcie insisted. She looked at Grace. 'Go on, tell them.'

Grace stared down at her ringless left hand. 'It is true,' she said. 'And I do have an engagement ring, I just – don't like to wear it.'

Noah had not seen anything wrong with giving her his dead wife's ring, and her mother thought it a very practical idea.

'Why go to all the expense of buying a new ring, when you've got a perfectly good one lying in a drawer?' she said. 'Besides, it's not as if his wife's going to need it, is it?'

But somehow Grace could not bring herself to put it on.

'So why haven't you told us this before?' Miriam wanted to know.

'There isn't much to tell.'

Mary laughed. 'Oh Duffield, that's typical of you! Of course there's a lot to tell. What's his name, for a start? Where did you meet him?'

'Is he handsome?' Miriam put in.

Grace stared at them, perplexed by their questions.

'He's an old friend,' Dulcie said. 'You've known him years. Isn't that right, Duffield?'

Grace nodded dumbly.

'How did you know he was the one for you?' Mary asked.

Grace looked at her friend's eager face. Mary Finnegan was already smiling brightly, expecting to hear some romantic love story.

'I—'

She was saved from answering when the door to the fitting room opened and Sylvia Saunders stepped out, a vision in white lace.

'Well?' She looked at them shyly from beneath her lashes. 'What do you think?'

'Oh, Saunders!'

They all joined in the chorus of admiration, telling her how beautiful she looked. Even Dulcie couldn't help complimenting her.

All the while, Sylvia gazed at herself in the mirror, as if she couldn't quite believe what she was seeing.

'Do you think Roger will like it?' she asked, biting her lip.

'He'll love it,' Miriam said.

'He already adores you,' Mary added. 'This will make him adore you even more.'

'I bet you can't wait to see his face when you walk down the aisle?' Miriam said.

'No, I can't.' Sylvia looked back at her reflection, her face suddenly wreathed in smiles, as if she was picturing that wonderful moment. She looked so radiantly happy, Grace felt a lump rise in her throat.

Mary Finnegan nudged her. 'Just think,' she whispered. 'That will be you soon!'

Grace looked back at Sylvia, still twirling in front of the mirror, admiring herself from all angles.

No, it won't, she thought. She tried to imagine herself standing in front of a mirror in a white dress, so in love and excited to be getting married she almost couldn't wait for her wedding day to come. But every time she pictured it, all she could feel was dread settling in her stomach like a cold, hard stone.

But it was time to change that, she thought.

Chapter Forty-Nine

It was the day before Sylvia's wedding, but Anna had already decided she would not go.

The invitation had been sitting on her dressing table for weeks, and every time she looked at it Anna felt herself wavering.

Sometimes she thought she would go. Sometimes she managed to convince herself she had not been forgotten, that Sylvia had sent the invitation because she genuinely wanted her there, and not out of politeness as Edward had said.

And then, at other times, her confidence would wane and she knew she had sunk too low to face any of her old friends. She could not bear to see the shock on their faces when they saw the wretched creature she had become.

But this morning, seeing the invitation propped up against the mirror, it felt as if it was mocking her. She snatched it up and ripped it into pieces, letting the fragments drift to the ground like confetti around her. How could she possibly go and celebrate someone else's future happiness when her own was full of nothing but bleak bitterness?

She threw back the curtains. Even the mornings felt as if they were making fun of her now. It was another beautiful June day, the sun already warming the window pane even though it had barely risen. Anna yanked the curtains closed, unable to look at a day so bright and full of promise.

She looked back at the bed. Edward had not come home

again. But instead of panic, these days she felt only relief. At least it meant a few hours' respite from the heavy, dark cloud that seemed to hang over them when he was at home.

Anna dressed quickly. Her clothes felt even looser today, her skirt hanging off her hips. She could hardly bear to look at herself in the mirror because the sight of her sharp bones protruding from under her skin repelled her so much.

The only saving grace was that Edward showed no interest in her anymore.

She went downstairs to light the ovens, out of habit as much as anything else. Keeping to the steady routines of the day was a comfort to her, giving her an anchor to a past when things were less fearful and uncertain.

But as she took down Papa's battered old tub from the shelf, ready to weigh out flour, the now familiar feeling of dread and shame rolled over her and she remembered what she had done.

She had lost Papa's business.

Everything he had achieved, everything he had worked so hard for, was all gone. It belonged to Edward now. His name in bold gold letters over the door reminded her that on the rare occasions she dared to venture outside.

It was the insult to Papa that hurt her, even more than her own wounded pride. The knowledge that Edward had never truly loved her, that their marriage had all been part of a plan to further his own ambitions, barely registered compared to knowing that her father's legacy had been lost.

And yet part of her could still hardly believe it was true.

She looked around the kitchen, remembering all the times she and Edward had worked here alongside Papa. She could picture her father, painstakingly teaching Edward how to knead dough and fold cake batter and how to roll and twist pastries into all kinds of intricate shapes. She remembered how Edward would look up and catch her eye across the kitchen, and how they would smile at each other, speaking without words . . .

Could he really have done that and not loved her? It seemed impossible to think that all that time the only thing in his heart was greed and ambition.

And how would things have worked out if the war hadn't happened? she wondered. Would he have married her and bided his time for years, just waiting for her father to retire and leave the business to them?

The war had done him a favour, she thought. He probably hadn't been able to believe his luck when her father was sent back to Germany, leaving the way clear for him to take over.

And yet . . . She remembered Edward in his hospital bed, just after he had been sent home injured. He had been through so much, Anna still clung to the forlorn hope that he was sick, that the war had turned his mind.

She had just put the first batch of loaves in the oven when she heard footsteps crossing the yard. Anna's whole body stiffened, thinking it was Edward. But when the back door opened it was Nellie Madigan who stood there.

'Oh. Hello.' She looked around. 'Where is he?'

'I thought he was with you.'

At least Nellie had the grace to blush at that. But Anna didn't care. She turned her back on her, reaching up to fetch another baking tray. She could feel Nellie watching her.

'I dunno why you bother,' she said at last. 'After everything he's said and done.'

'I'm doing it for my father, not for him.'

'It ain't your father's place anymore though, is it?' Nellie pointed out.

Anna said nothing.

'You must have been close to him?' Nellie said at last.

Anna paused, her hand stilling as she dusted the tray with flour. 'He was a good man,' she said.

'My pa reckons the only good German is a dead 'un. But then again, he ain't much to write home about himself,' she added, her lip curling with disdain.

Anna ignored her and carried on with her work. But still Nellie stood in the back doorway, watching her.

Finally, Anna looked over her shoulder and said, 'Are you going to open the shop, or aren't you?'

'In a minute.'

Anna looked her up and down. Nellie was still a mess, her blouse grubby and rumpled, as if she had picked it up off the floor and put it back on. But there was a wantonness about her, with her tumbling red hair, full mouth and husky voice, that Anna could imagine men found appealing.

Edward certainly did, at any rate.

'I expect he's gambling again,' Nellie said.

'Who?'

Nellie gave one of her earthy laughs. 'Eddie, who d'you think?' She pushed a stray lock of hair behind her ear. 'I happen to know Billy Willis had a game going last night. I daresay that's where Eddie will be, sitting round the table with his new pals, acting like the big shot.' She shook her head. She might have been younger than Anna, but life and experience had made her older than her years. "Course, he's in over his head with that lot. He might think they're all pals together, but I know Billy Willis' crew. They're taking him for a fool. They'll string him along until they've had every penny he's got, then they'll be done with him.' She looked around. 'I wouldn't be surprised if Billy ended up owning this place.'

Anna let the tray fall with a crash. 'Over my dead body!'

Nellie laughed. 'Don't speak too soon, love.'

Anna was silent, taking it in. She could only hope Edward didn't try to treat Billy Willis the same way he treated her.

'Why don't you leave him?' Nellie asked, surprising her.

Anna turned on her. 'So you can move in, you mean?'

Nellie laughed. 'Oh, no, love. I wouldn't take your place for all the tea in China. Listen, I've had an old man who knocked me about, and I ain't interested in going back to that, believe me. Besides, Eddie's worse than my Frank ever used to be. Frankie used to use his fists, but Eddie – well, his sort of cruelty don't leave a mark, does it? Except up here.' She tapped her temple. 'I've seen what he's done to you. He's a nasty swine, and no mistake.'

'That hasn't stopped you wanting him, though, has it?'

Nellie smiled knowingly. 'We're different, you and me. I've got the measure of him, and he knows it. We're just a bit of fun for each other, that's all. I ain't so foolish as to fall in love with him like you did.' She paused. 'You ought to leave him, y'know,' she said at last. 'It ain't going to get better for you, believe me. Now he's got what he wants, Eddie ain't got no use for you. He'll keep on being cruel to you until he drives you out.'

'Is that what he told you?'

'Not in so many words, but it don't take a genius to work it out. I reckon even you must have an idea what's going on in his mind.'

Of course she did, but she didn't want to admit it. She turned away, back to her work.

'I'm just worried about you,' Nellie said.

Anna laughed, a harsh sound that filled the kitchen. 'You didn't feel sorry when you were down here kissing my husband!'

Nellie's cheeks turned red. 'Like I said, it was a bit of fun,' she mumbled. 'But believe me, I ain't the reason your marriage is in trouble. You should never have wed him.'

'You think I don't know that?' Anna snapped.

'Then you should leave him.'

'You didn't leave your husband.'

'I didn't have to, in the end. An artillery shell at the Somme did for him before he did for me. Good riddance, too.' Her mouth curled. 'Pity you weren't so lucky.'

Anna turned on her. 'Edward wasn't always like – he is now,' she protested. 'He used to be so kind, so loving—'

Then she saw the look of pity in Nellie's eyes and remembered that it had all been a lie. Nellie was silent for a moment. Then she said, 'there was a fire here, wasn't there? You nearly died, didn't you? You and your family.'

Straight away Anna felt the searing heat on her skin, her eyes stinging, the thick smoke in her lungs, making it hard for her to breathe. Even now, four years later, just thinking about it was enough to take her back to that terrible night.

'How do you know about that?'

'Eddie told me. He knows all about it.'

'Edward was in France.'

'He still knows all about it. He says the Franklin boys started it.'

'The Franklin boys?' Anna stared at her.

Tom's brothers.

'He's never said anything to me about it.'

'Well, no. He wouldn't, would he?'

Anna stared at Nellie, itching to slap the smug expression off her face. She looked almost pleased with herself, as if she enjoyed knowing something Anna didn't.

She turned away. 'If Edward knew the Franklin boys were behind that fire he would have gone to the police. He hates the Franklins. There'd be no reason for him to try to cover for them.'

'That's what you think.'

Anna swung back to face her. 'If you've got something to say, then you should come out with it. I'm sick and tired of your stupid games!'

'Ain't you worked it out for yourself? And you think

you're so clever.' Nellie sent her a pitying look. 'It was your precious Edward that put them up to it, you silly mare.'

The floor seemed to give way beneath her feet and Anna had to clutch the edge of the kitchen table for support.

'That's not true,' she whispered.

'He told me himself.'

Nellie was still speaking, but her words were lost in a rush of sound that filled Anna's brain.

Just when she didn't think her life could unravel any further, suddenly there were yet more loose threads she knew nothing about.

But still her mind rejected it. Not Edward. Not her Edward. He might not love her, but surely he would never wish her harm.

'He hates the Franklins,' she whispered. 'He hasn't spoken to them in years.'

'I've seen him drinking with them at the Fallen Angel.'

'No.'

'Wouldn't be the first time he's lied to you, would it? I know there was a falling out when they were kids, but Eddie ain't daft. He knows when people can be useful to him, and he don't mind taking advantage to get what he wants. I mean, look at you.'

Anna flinched at the casual insult, but Nellie went on, 'Mind you, he weren't pleased that they went too far. Silly buggers nearly burned the place down with you in it. That would have been a thing, wouldn't it? He would have ended up with nothing.'

Anna was silent for a long time. She didn't want to believe it, but at the same time she knew there was a tiny spark of truth in what Nellie was saying. She had no reason to lie.

Unlike Edward.

No. No, it couldn't be. She thought about his jealous rage

over Tom's letters. He hated the Franklins, he always had . . .

Or perhaps it was just Tom he hated? The thought came to her, crystal clear. He hated Tom because he was the one Edward could not control, the only one who saw through him. He was the only one who stood between Edward and his ruthless ambitions.

No wonder he had wanted her to cut off all ties with Tom. And Anna had gone along with it, out of blind, foolish love. She had allowed herself to turn her back on the one man who might have saved her.

'Why would he do it?' Dry-mouthed, her voice came out as a whisper. 'If he wanted the business, why would he try to destroy it?'

'Like I said, they went too far. I suppose he wanted to teach you a lesson, to frighten you. He told me he wanted to marry you before he was called up, but you wouldn't do it. And you know Eddie don't like his plans going wrong, does he?'

She knew too much about it to be lying, Anna thought. How could she have known Anna had turned down Edward's plan for a quick wedding because she was so desperate for her father to give her away?

'You need to leave him,' Nellie's urgent voice broke into her thoughts. 'Leave him while you've still got the chance.'

While you've still got the chance. The words fell ominously, like leaden drops.

'What do you think will happen to me?' said Anna in a small voice.

'I dunno,' Nellie admitted. 'Nothing, while I've got anything to do with it. I like you, believe it or not,' she said wryly. 'And I reckon you deserve better than you've got. But sooner or later Eddie is going to want you out of the way. At the moment, he's hoping he can make you walk out on him. But I couldn't imagine what he's got in mind if you don't.' Nellie laid her hand on Anna's arm. Her nails were grubby and bitten, Anna noticed. 'You've got to leave him,' she pleaded.

Anna saw the urgency in her eyes. If she didn't know better she could almost believe that Nellie truly cared.

She turned away, shaking off Nellie's restraining hand. 'I don't have a choice,' she said. 'This is my father's bakery, and I have to hold on to it for his sake.'

Nellie sighed. 'Hasn't it sunk in yet? It's a bit late for that, girl. It's your old man's business now.'

'I don't care whose name is over the door!' Anna's temper flared. 'It's my father's business, he built it up from nothing.'

'It's just bricks and mortar, girl.'

Nellie's words stopped Anna in her tracks.

'Listen to me,' she said. 'If your father's half as good a man as you reckon he is, do you really think he'd want you to put yourself through this? I bet if you asked him he'd tell you to get yourself out of it while you still can.' Her face softened, her green eyes turning gentle. 'Face it, your dad's long gone. And if you've got any sense, you'll go too. Before Eddie's taken away your last shred of self-respect and you're too ashamed to try to leave.'

It's too late for that, Anna thought bleakly.

'Well?' Nellie prompted her.

Anna looked back at the other woman standing in front of her, a shimmering blur of red hair and creamy skin through her tears. She had no idea how long they had both been standing there, but suddenly she felt deeply weary, right down to her bones.

'Go home,' she said.

Nellie blinked at her in surprise. 'But what about the shop?'

345

'We're not opening today.'

'Eddie won't like that.'

Anna felt her temper flare again, a spark igniting in her chest. 'Eddie isn't here, is he?'

Nellie stood her ground, arms folded over her ample chest. 'What about my money?'

'You'll get it.'

Nellie didn't look convinced until Anna found her purse and took out a ten-shilling note. Nellie grabbed it and rooted around for a moment, arranging it inside her grubby blouse.

Anna turned away and opened the oven door. The delicious aroma of warm baking bread filled the kitchen. Nellie breathed in deeply.

'Lovely,' she sighed. She looked at Anna. 'You're a better baker than he is, you know. Eddie knows it, too.'

Anna held herself rigid, her back turned. She tipped out the first loaf and tapped the base, listening for the hollow sound.

'You've still got friends, you know. You might not think it, but you have. Including me,' she added quietly.

Anna ignored her. She turned out another loaf and tapped it.

'Suit yourself,' Nellie sighed. Anna heard the back door open, then Nellie said, 'But I'll prove how much of a friend I am. Look in the back of Eddie's wardrobe. There's something in there that might cheer you up.'

The back door closed, and all Anna's fragile strength seemed to seep out of her body. She slumped forward, curling her fingers around the wooden counter top for support.

Nellie was wrong, so wrong. Anna did not have any friends. She was utterly, utterly alone.

And that was the way Edward had wanted it. Anna could see it now, as plain as day. All the time he had supposedly been protecting her, convincing her that he had her best interests at heart, that he was the only one she could truly trust, he had been planting seeds of doubt in her mind, isolating her from her friends and family.

And now she had no one to turn to, no one to help her out of her misery.

Her only 'friend' was apparently Nellie Madigan, the woman who had helped plunge her into despair and misery in the first place. It was so pathetic Anna would have laughed if it hadn't been so terribly sad.

But Nellie wasn't really responsible for the ghastly predicament she found herself in. That was all Edward's doing. And her own, of course.

She looked around the kitchen. She had had such high hopes for her marriage. She had wanted Edward and herself to be like her parents, close and happy, living and loving and working side by side in utter contentment.

And when it had all started to go wrong, she had blamed herself. She had spent months feeling like a failure, wondering what was wrong with her that she couldn't create the same happy, loving relationship with her husband.

But it took two to make a marriage. Now she realised she had been the only one trying to make it work, while all Edward had wanted was to destroy her.

And she had been too blinded by her dream to see the reality.

A customer was rapping on the shop door, but Anna ignored them. She stood at the counter, staring at the neat line of loaves she had just baked. What was the point of it all? she thought. Nellie was right, why should she bake bread and open up the shop just for Edward's benefit? Especially when he wasn't even there to see it.

The customer rapped again, more loudly this time. Anna thought about answering the door, but her limbs suddenly seemed to be filled with lead, making it hard to drag herself along. Her head ached, a rim of pain around her crown from ear to ear.

Slowly, she dragged herself upstairs to the bedroom to fetch her nerve tonic. She helped herself to two spoonfuls, then lay on the bed.

Edward's wardrobe loomed over her in the corner of the room, wide and solid, with curved doors of polished walnut.

There's something in there that might cheer you up.

It took a moment for Anna to rouse herself enough to stand up and walk across the room. She threw open the wardrobe doors and peered inside. Immediately Edward's scent wafted across the room and for a moment she was filled with panic that he was there with her.

She steeled herself and rummaged among his clothes, wondering what she was looking for.

Something that might cheer you up . . .

She could scarcely imagine what it might be. Surely there could be nothing in Edward's wardrobe that might make her feel better . . .

And then she saw the box.

Chapter Fifty

By the time Edward came home, Anna was ready for him. She had made an effort to tidy herself up; she had washed her hair, put on her best dress, and cheered up her wan face with some make-up.

From time to time, she'd heard customers tapping on the shop door downstairs but had ignored them. She was too busy preparing herself.

Just putting on lipstick transformed her and made her feel more powerful. Now, when she looked in the mirror, she could almost see the old Anna staring back at her.

But that didn't stop her from jumping nearly out of her skin when she heard the sound of the back door opening just before noon.

Anna steeled herself as she listened to him calling out her name, the sound of his footsteps up the hall going into the shop.

'Anna?' His voice was louder now, a rough edge to it. She clasped her hands together to stop them trembling as she heard him coming up the stairs.

He threw open the bedroom door. She was sitting before the dressing-table mirror, pinning up her hair. She saw his quick frown behind her reflection.

'There you are. Why's the shop closed?'

'It's your shop. You tell me.'

His brows lifted. Then he looked her up and down, his mouth twisting.

'You're very dolled up, I see. I hope it ain't on my account?'

'I wouldn't waste my time.'

'Someone's in a mood today,' Edward commented. But he was rattled, she could tell. And no wonder. He must have got used to coming home to a cringing, submissive wretch over the past few months.

Anna turned away from him and finished doing her hair in the mirror. There was no fear in her eyes anymore, she noticed. Only stone-cold resolve.

She wondered if Edward had noticed it too.

'Aren't you going to ask what I've been doing with myself all day?' she said.

'I'm not particularly interested.'

'I'll tell you anyway, shall I? I've been reading.'

'And why do you think I care what—' As Anna stood up and stepped to one side, Edward's gaze fell on the box sitting on the dressing table.

His face tightened and for a moment Anna tensed too, wondering what he might do. He was capable of anything, she realised that now.

His fiery gaze rose to meet hers. 'Where did you get that? You have no right to go through my things.'

'And you had no right to keep Tom's letters from me,' Anna shot back.

Edward pulled himself upright, towering over her. 'I told you I didn't want you writing to him.'

'But they were my letters.' No wonder he had run to meet the postman every morning. It all made sense to her now. 'You let me think he hadn't written to me. You made me think he didn't care.'

But Tom did care. Anna had spent all morning reading the letters he had sent to her since her marriage, letters Edward had carefully intercepted.

Every week he had written to her, even after she had told him not to. He had somehow read between the lines of her last message, put two and two together and realised what was happening to her, even before she knew herself.

And why wouldn't he? After all, he understood Edward better than she ever had. Tom had seen him for what he really was while she was still blinded by love. He had even tried to warn her before he left for France. But she wouldn't listen. Anna felt ashamed of the way she had rejected his advice.

But Tom had remained her steadfast protector. Reading his letters, Anna had felt the warmth of his affection, his genuine friendship, coming through each scrawled line, each page of tissue-thin blue paper. He was the only one who had ever truly cared enough about her to tell her the truth. And he still cared now, even after she had shunned him. She felt warmed by his friendship, like the flowers in Victoria Park, tentatively emerging from the winter cold to show their faces to the sun.

You've still got friends, you know. You might not think it, but you have.

All this time she had had a friend. Knowing that gave her the strength to face Edward. To do what she had to do.

Her husband sneered, 'You really think he cares about you? He's only out for what he can get.'

'Like you, you mean?'

Fire flared in Edward's eyes. 'Don't you dare compare me with him. I'm nothing like Tom Franklin!'

'No, you're right,' Anna said calmly. 'You're not half the man he is.'

For a moment she thought she had gone too far, but she no longer cared. The days had gone when she would tread carefully, living in fear of upsetting him. He could do what he liked to her, but she would never fear him again.

She could see him now, fighting for control of his temper, his mocking smile reasserting itself.

'Maybe you should have married him, then,' he said.

'Maybe I should.'

He laughed. 'Your father would never have allowed it. You, marrying the messenger boy!'

'Why not? He let me marry the apprentice.'

Her barb hit home. Edward flinched. 'I was different.'

'You were both nothing!' Anna threw back at him. She could feel her own anger unfurling inside her, rising to match his. 'What makes you think you were so special? You were just another orphanage kid until my father took you in and gave you a start.'

'You know nothing about me!'

He was furious, his fists balling at his sides, his lips turning white. Anna cautiously circled the room, putting the bed between them.

'You think I'm not special?' he raged. 'You didn't see the kind of hell I was brought up in. Thrown away by my own mother, chucked into the workhouse when I was just a baby. You don't survive that without having something about you. Christ, even your precious bloody Tom had some kind of family! I had no one. I watched the other kids sink into nothing around me, dying because no one cared. I had to learn to fend for myself just to survive.' He looked her up and down with contempt. 'But you'll never understand that, will you? You and your sister, with your charmed lives and your loving parents. You think you've had it hard these past few years? You don't know the meaning of the word. Try being a kid of six years old, going to bed hungry, too frightened to go to sleep in case you get another beating.'

Anna stared at him, realisation dawning. 'Is that why you resent me so much? Because you think my life has been too easy?'

'Hasn't it? You've never had to worry about where your next meal was coming from, have you? Your future was all settled for you, from the moment you came into this world. You and your perfect family.' Edward's eyes were like chips of ice. 'I used to watch your father fussing over you, praising you for whatever you did. His *liebling* – "Such a talent! Just look at her sugarcraft, Edward, have you ever seen such a delicate touch?"' He cruelly mimicked her father's German accent. 'And there was me, working twelve-hour days for him with scarcely a word of thanks for it.'

'Papa loved you,' Anna said. 'He thought of you as a son.'

'He thought of me as a skivvy!' Edward shot back. 'At least until the day he realised his precious daughter had fallen for me. Then, suddenly, everything was different. Suddenly he was welcoming me into the family with open arms, telling me how I'd run the place one day.'

'Which was what you wanted all along.'

'It was what I deserved.' His mouth curved in a cruel, cold smile. 'Don't look so shocked, Anna,' he mocked her. 'You have to learn to take in this world. That's what growing up in the workhouse taught me.'

'But Papa welcomed you into our family,' Anna said. 'And you repaid his kindness by taking everything away from us.'

'Kindness is a weakness,' Edward said.

Anna shook her head pityingly. Looking at him now, she wondered how she had not seen what he was really like. 'You've got a black soul, Edward Stanning. I feel sorry for you.'

His eyes flared with rage. 'Don't you dare feel sorry for me!' Edward hissed. 'I've got everything I ever wanted.'

'Have you? Is this really all you've ever wanted?' Anna curled her lips. 'Then I really do pity you.'

He glared back at her, his fists clenching, and for a

353

moment she thought he was going to hit her. But to her surprise she did not care. Nothing he could do to her now was as bad as the torture he had put her through already.

'I want a divorce,' she said flatly.

His eyes flickered with surprise. Then he shrugged.

'Suit yourself. You can go whenever you like.'

'But this is my home.'

'It's mine now.'

She was disappointed but not surprised. She had hoped that there might have been some shred of decency left in him – but no. He was too consumed with greed.

The war hadn't changed him, she thought. She had tried to use it as an excuse, but the reality was he had always been like this. She had never allowed herself to see behind the mask he wore.

Her suitcase was already packed. Edward watched her out of the corner of his eye as she retrieved it from under the bed.

'You're leaving?' He sounded uncertain.

'One of us has to go. And you've made it very clear that you won't, so it will have to be me.'

She could feel his gaze on her, wary as an animal. 'You ain't getting this place,' he said. 'It's mine now, all of it.'

'So you've said.'

His eyes narrowed, still sensing a trick.

'There's no catch,' Anna said. 'I'm moving out. You can have it, all of it.'

She had wondered how she would feel, saying those words. But she was amazed to feel a real sense of peace and calm settling over her. None of it mattered, she realised.

It's just bricks and mortar. Nellie's words had been the key, unlocking Anna from the miserable prison she had placed herself in. Suddenly, she had been able to see it all clearly for the first time. What was she fighting for? A few poky rooms over a shop. And the bakery itself, a sink and a set of ovens. There was no real value in it, not the kind that was truly worth anything.

Nellie was right; the bakery wasn't her father. All this time, Anna had been clinging on to it, thinking she was holding on to him, too. But she didn't have to fight for it any longer. Friedrich Beck's spirit was alive and well and flourishing in Germany.

And he would want her to be happy. He hadn't opened up the bakery to fulfil any greedy ambition. He had opened it to provide a home and a life for his family. Because that was what was really important to him.

Nellie was right about that, too. Friedrich would never have wanted her to spend the rest of her life living in misery, just for the sake of a shop in a back street of Bethnal Green.

She could almost imagine him now, smiling at the very idea.

Her only sadness was in letting go of her dream to have the kind of life her parents had had. She had tried so hard to make it work, blaming herself when she failed.

'I wish you luck,' she said, and was surprised to realise she meant it. 'I hope it makes you happy. But I don't think it will. I don't think you'll ever truly be happy, Edward. Because you'll always know in your heart of hearts that this place isn't really yours. You can paint your name over the door as big as you like, but everyone will still know you didn't build it up, you didn't work for it. You stole it. And I'll tell you something else, too,' she added. 'No matter how much you have, it will never be enough. Because in your heart you'll always be the kid from the workhouse who never feels good enough.'

He flinched, but didn't say a word. Anna knew she had

wounded him as surely as if she had taken a knife and stabbed him to the heart.

'I made a mistake,' she said. 'Not just marrying you, but thinking you could ever be like my father. You're not, and you never will be. My father is a wonderful man, honest, kind and gentle. Everyone loves him. But you?' She looked him up and down. 'You're not fit to lick his boots, Edward Stanning!'

She picked up her case. Edward stood stock-still as she moved past him. But as she reached the door, he suddenly found his voice.

'You'll be sorry,' he called after her.

Anna turned to look at him.

'No,' she sighed. 'You'll be the one who's sorry, not me.'

Chapter Fifty-One

'What do you mean, you don't want to marry him? It's all arranged.'

Grace's mother confronted her across the kitchen, barely paying any attention to the infant screeching in the crook of her arm. This was Grace's youngest sibling, a boy called Reuben.

Grace tugged at the collar of her dress. It was a warm June day outside and the back door was open, but the sticky heat of the kitchen was still making her feel faint.

This wasn't going as well as she had hoped. The elegant speech she had rehearsed on the train down to Devon had stuck in her throat, until all that emerged was a confused jumble of words that even she scarcely understood.

'We haven't set a date,' she pointed out quietly.

'That doesn't matter,' her father dismissed. 'You've promised to marry Noah Wells, and that's that. We Duffields never break our word.'

'We're talking about my marriage, Pa, not trading a pig!' Grace protested.

'Sounds the same to me!' her sister-in-law Jessie said, and both she and Eliza sniggered.

'It's just nerves, that's all,' her mother said to her husband. 'All brides get them, it's nothing to worry about. She'll come to her senses and do the right thing in the end.'

Grace turned on her. 'That's just it, don't you see? I'm tired of coming to my senses all the time. Good old Grace, always doing the right thing. But not this time. I don't want to be the sensible one anymore. I don't want to wear practical shoes, or clothes that don't show the dirt. And I don't want practical hair, either! I want dainty dancing shoes, and – and curls!'

She finished her outburst to see a ring of astonished faces staring back at her.

'Have you gone quite mad, Gracie?' her mother asked.

'Dainty dancing shoes!' Eliza spluttered with laughter. 'There's nothing dainty about those great big feet of yours!'

'I know what's wrong with her.' Jessie sent her a sly look. 'She's in love.'

'I am not!' Grace felt the heat rising in her face.

'I knew it!' Jessie crowed. 'Look how she's blushing. She reckons she's going to get a better offer.'

'Don't be silly,' her mother said, 'Grace knows very well that will never happen.'

'Why not?' Grace turned on her mother. 'Is it really such a silly idea that someone might fall in love with me?'

'Especially with her curls and her dainty dancing shoes!' Eliza chimed in, still laughing.

Grace ignored her. 'I mean it,' she said to her mother. 'Why shouldn't I be like all the other girls? Why shouldn't I be like Sylvia Saunders?'

'And who's Sylvia Saunders when she's at home?' her mother wanted to know.

'One of her London friends, I daresay,' her father said. 'Led her astray, no doubt, and made her forget her duty to her family.'

'Why should I be the only one with a duty to the family?' Grace asked him. 'Matthew and Mark were allowed to marry whoever they liked. Why do I have to marry a dull old man I hardly know, just because—'

She caught the appalled looks on the faces of her

sisters-in-law and turned around slowly. Noah Wells stood in the doorway.

Only the sound of little Reuben howling in his mother's arms broke the silence. Grace closed her eyes and wished the stone flags would open up and swallow her.

At last Noah spoke. 'Your father told me you were visiting. I thought I'd come over and say hello,' he said gruffly, not meeting her eye.

Grace was utterly mortified. Poor Noah. She didn't want to marry him, but she didn't want to hurt him, either.

'The girl didn't mean it, Noah,' her father stepped in to smooth things over, but Noah cut him short.

'I reckon that's between me and Grace, don't you?' He glanced at her. 'Shall we go outside and talk where it's quiet?'

He turned on his heel and went outside. Grace hesitated.

'Well? What are you waiting for?' her father said. 'You go out there and talk to him. See if you can put things right before it's too late.'

Noah was waiting for her in the middle of the sunlit farmyard, tamping down the tobacco in his pipe.

Grace took a deep breath. 'Mr Wells—Noah, I—' she started to say, but Noah shook his head and nodded towards the farmhouse behind her. Grace followed his gaze and saw her sisters-in-law both crowded at the window, watching them avidly.

Noah took Grace's arm and steered her across the yard and round the side of the milking sheds, into the cool shadows.

'That's better,' he said. 'Reckon we can do without an audience, don't you?'

Grace watched him lighting his pipe and waited for him to speak. She was afraid to say anything herself; she had already put her foot in it more than enough.

'So,' Noah said finally. 'You don't want to marry me.'

'I'm sorry, truly I am.' Grace opened her mouth and the words tumbled out again. 'I know I should have said something sooner . . . I didn't mean to hurt you . . . It all happened so fast . . .'

'So you need more time, is that it? Because I don't mind waiting.'

He was being so kind, Grace felt utterly helpless.

But then he gave a sad little smile and said, 'But I can see from the look on your fact that won't do, will it?'

'No,' Grace said unhappily. 'No, it won't.'

He paused for a while, puffing on his pipe and gazing into the far distance.

'I can't say I blame you,' he said finally. 'After living in London these past years, the idea of coming back here to live must seem very unappealing to you.'

'No, it's not that.'

He smiled wryly. 'So it's me that's unappealing, then?'

Grace felt herself blushing. 'I'm sorry,' she started to say, but Noah shook his head.

'I was only teasing you, girl. You don't have to explain yourself to me. I've been half expecting you to change your mind, if I'm honest. I mean, what would a young girl like you want with a dull old man like me?'

Grace felt her blush deepening. 'I shouldn't have said that. It was very cruel.'

'Why? You're quite right. I thought the same thing myself when your father first mentioned the idea to me. But I was so lonely after my wife died, I was willing to give it a try.'

He looked so forlorn, Grace's heart went out to him. 'I'm sorry.'

'Will you stop saying that? You're a young girl, you're entitled to go off and get giddy over a fellow. Just like your friend – what's her name?'

360

'Sylvia Saunders,' Grace said miserably.

He laid his hand on her shoulder. 'Don't look so sad, Gracie. I've got no hard feelings against you. I wish you well.'

He tapped out his pipe on the side of the milking shed. 'Well, I don't suppose we've much more to say to each other, have we?'

'No,' Grace said.

He jerked his head towards the farmhouse. 'I daresay you'll be wanting to go back inside, to your family?'

'Actually, would you mind giving me a lift to the station? If I hurry I might catch the last train back to London.'

He frowned. 'But you've only just arrived. Aren't you staying for a visit?'

Grace looked back at the house. 'I was going to travel tomorrow morning, but I'd rather go tonight. I don't think I'm going to be very welcome after this,' she said.

Noah regarded her with sympathy. 'I could talk to them if you like, explain what's happened? I'm sure I could make peace with them for you.'

'Would you do that?'

'Of course.'

Grace looked back at the farmhouse, then shook her head. 'No, I'd like to go back tonight. If I wait until tomorrow there's a chance I'll miss my friend's wedding.'

Noah smiled. 'That wouldn't be Sylvia, would it?' Grace nodded. 'You can't miss that, can you?'

Grace had a sudden vision of Dr Logan coming in to the wedding with Dulcie Moore on his arm.

'I suppose not,' she said.

Ten minutes later, Grace was sitting up on top of Noah's cart beside him, lurching along the country lanes. Her parents had been happy enough to wave them off. Grace wondered if they were hoping that Noah might use the time to change her mind.

'So you were planning on going home in the morning?' he said. 'It's a long way to come for a flying visit.' He sent her a sideways look. 'You could have written me a letter?'

Grace shook her head. 'That would have been a horrible thing to do. You deserved to hear from me in person. And I wanted to give you this back.'

She delved into her bag and pulled out the box containing the engagement ring he had given her.

Noah flinched at the sight of it. 'Keep it,' he said gruffly.

'No, I couldn't. It wouldn't be right.' Grace dropped it into his pocket. 'You must save it for when the right woman comes along.'

'*If* she comes along.'

'Oh, she will. I'm sure of it.'

Noah sent her a sidelong look. 'You're a good girl, Gracie.'

Grace folded her arms around herself and stared out over the fields. She didn't feel like a good person. If this was what breaking someone's heart felt like, she never wanted to do it again. She couldn't understand why the other girls bragged about it so much, as if it was something to be proud about.

Not that Noah Wells seemed too heartbroken. He whistled a little tune between his teeth as he jingled the reins.

'So have you got your sights set on someone else?' he asked.

Grace thought of Dr Logan again. She was too late there, she decided. By tomorrow he would well and truly belong to Dulcie.

'No,' she said. 'Not anymore.'

At the station, Noah came round to help her down from the cart. 'Well, take care of yourself,' he said.

362

'You too.'

On impulse, Grace reached up and planted a kiss on his cheek. Noah touched the spot, rubbing his hand over his bristled jaw.

'What was that for?'

'For being so kind.' She looked up at him. 'You're a good man, Mr Wells. I hope you find someone who deserves you.'

He smiled, a warm, rare smile. 'You too, Gracie,' he said.

Chapter Fifty-Two

Having hurried back from Devon the previous evening so as not to miss Sylvia's wedding, Grace woke up the following morning to the news that Celia Padgett, the nurse who had been brought in to cover on Wilson ward, had been struck down by a summer cold. No other nurses could be spared, so Miss Parker had insisted that either Grace or Dulcie had to cancel their day off.

Naturally, Dulcie wasn't having any of it.

'You can't ask me to do it, Duffield,' she had wailed in their room that morning. 'You know how important today is for me. Besides, I'm a bridesmaid,' she added as an afterthought. 'Go on, please. No one would miss you.'

For a moment, Grace was sorely tempted to refuse. But then she realised Dulcie had a point. Poor Sylvia could hardly walk down the aisle without one of her bridesmaids. And at least this way Grace would be spared the misery of watching Dulcie work her magic on Dr Logan.

'All right, I'll do it,' she sighed. 'I'll go and tell Miss Parker before breakfast.'

'Oh, don't worry about that. I've already told her you'd do it.' Dulcie had turned away to inspect her bridesmaid's dress hanging on the wardrobe door. 'I do wish she'd chosen a different colour,' she complained. 'Eau de nil always makes me look so washed out . . .'

As soon as Grace went on duty she went to check on Albie Sallis. He had been tired and listless since his friend Gordon had left. Grace missed his jokes and his cheery laughter ringing down the ward.

As usual, the first thing Albie did was to ask her if she had heard anything of his friend.

Grace shook her head regretfully. 'I'm sorry, Corporal Sallis. No one's told me anything.'

'I hope he's all right.' Albie Sallis' brow was furrowed with concern. 'I haven't had a letter from him yet.'

'It's only been a couple of days. I expect he's still settling in.'

'I expect you're right, Nurse.' But Albie did not look reassured. 'I worry about him, y'see. He's a shy lad, needs someone to bring him out of his shell. And I worry how he'll manage with his exercises if I ain't there to nag him. You know he has to practise his walking every day . . .'

'Rest assured, Corporal, your friend is doing very well.'

Grace swung round to see Dr Logan standing behind them. She glanced at the clock. It was only just turned seven. It was very unusual to see a doctor on the ward so early. But then she remembered the night sister had summoned him to attend to a new patient who wouldn't settle.

Albie Sallis sat up, propping himself against his pillows. 'You've heard from him?'

'I knew you were concerned, so I telephoned the convalescent home. They say Private Gordon has settled in very well. His condition is improving, and he has started to make friends.'

The doctor didn't glance Grace's way at all as he spoke. It was as if she was invisible.

Albie looked back at him intently. 'You're sure?'

'I spoke to the medical officer myself.'

'And he's doing his exercises?'

'At least twice a day, so I understand.'

Albie's face relaxed into a smile. 'That's all right, then.'

Dr Logan drifted off, and Grace set about making Albie comfortable.

'That's good news, isn't it?' she said as she straightened his bedclothes. 'I daresay you'll get a letter from him soon.'

'Oh, I don't mind about that,' Albie dismissed with a wave of his hand. 'I told you, I ain't really one for letters. So long as I know he's all right, that's all that matters.'

Grace finished tucking in his bedclothes and looked down at him. Albie's face was haggard and grey against the snowy pillows. Worry had obviously taken its toll on him.

'Try to get some rest,' she said.

'Oh, I will. I daresay I'll be able to get some proper kip now.'

'Perhaps we could have a game of whist later, if you feel up to it?'

He smiled. 'I'll only beat you.'

'You never know, I might surprise you.'

Grace turned away to see Dr Logan still lingering nearby. He was studying the chart of a sleeping patient.

Grace straightened her shoulders and went to pass him. As she drew level, he suddenly said, 'I'm surprised to see you here this morning.'

'Nurse Padgett has a cold.'

He sent her a sharp look. 'So you aren't going to the wedding?'

'It doesn't seem like it. Although Miss Parker has already told me she'll try to arrange my off-duty hours for the middle of the day, so I might be able to get to the ceremony. At least I'll see them married.'

'But you won't come to the reception?'

Grace had a sudden vision of Dulcie, whirling around the dance floor in his arms.

'No,' she said.

'That's a pity.'

'Oh, I don't mind, really. I'm not a very good dancer. Two left feet!' She smiled ruefully.

For a moment they stared at each other. Grace opened her mouth to speak, then closed it again.

'What?' Dr Logan said.

'Nothing.'

'You were going to say something. What was it?' His eyes were suddenly very bright and intent behind his spectacles.

She was going to tell him about her broken engagement, but what was the point?

'I was going to thank you – for checking on Private Gordon,' she amended herself. 'It means a great deal to Corporal Sallis to know he's doing well.'

'Ah.' Dr Logan nodded.

As he went to walk away, Grace called after him, 'Enjoy the wedding.'

But he didn't respond.

Miss Parker was as good as her word. At ten o'clock, she told Grace she could go off duty.

'But I'll need you back at two,' she reminded her. 'I'm sorry, Nurse Duffield. I know you had other plans.' Her blue eyes were genuinely regretful.

Before she went off duty, Grace checked on Albie Sallis. He was still fast asleep, snoring gently. Poor man, she thought. He had a lot of catching up to do.

She hurried back to Walford House. It was hardly the perfect day to get married. Yesterday's blue sky had turned a sludgy grey, with the kind of half-hearted damp drizzle that lowered everyone's spirits. But Grace was sure Sylvia and Roger wouldn't allow a spot of rain to spoil their big event.

The wedding was at eleven, which should have given Grace enough time to get ready, if she hadn't managed to lose one of her shoes and put a hole through her only pair of stockings while rushing to put them on. Then she accidentally sat on her best hat, squashing it flat.

It took her ages to push it into shape again. She had her head down, still trying to tweak the artificial roses back into shape as she hurried down the gravel drive towards the hospital gates.

'Duffield?'

She looked up sharply. There, standing by the gates, was the forlorn figure of a young woman. She was shivering in the rain.

'Beck?'

It took Grace a moment to recognise her. Anna had always been slight, but now her coat almost swamped her fragile frame. Even under the careful powdering, Grace could see the pallor of her complexion and the purple shadows that circled her eyes.

There was a suitcase at her feet. As soon as she saw it, Grace realised what had happened.

'Come with me,' she said.

Grace took Anna to the café around the corner where she ordered tea for them both, and eggs on toast for Anna.

'But I'm not hungry,' Anna protested.

'You have to eat something.' Grace looked at her friend's fleshless face, her skin drawn over sharp bones and shadowy hollows. Underneath the lipstick, her lips were chapped and bitten. It was obvious she hadn't been looking after herself.

Their tea arrived and Grace poured it. She added three spoons of sugar to Anna's cup, then pushed it across the table towards her.

Anna stared down at it, her brown eyes troubled. 'I'm sorry, I'm being a nuisance,' she said. 'I don't want you to miss the wedding.'

'The wedding doesn't matter,' Grace dismissed. She reached for Anna's hand. 'Now, tell me what happened.'

At first Anna couldn't speak. She sat with her head down, her shoulders shaking with silent sobs.

Grace waited patiently, still holding on to her friend's hand. The skin was dry and papery, like an old woman's.

Then, gradually, between sobs the story began to emerge.

It was exactly as Grace had feared, ever since the day she'd read Edward's notes. She had tried to tell herself it might be different with Anna, that he loved her and would never hurt her. But as her friend tearfully unfolded her story, it became clear that Edward Stanning was not capable of loving anyone.

Grace could only imagine how frightening it must have been for Anna to live with someone like him. Constantly tiptoeing around his moods, never quite sure what was going on behind that smiling face. He wielded his cruelty like a knife – not stabbing, but inflicting a thousand tiny wounds that seemed like nothing on their own, but that gradually ate away at her confidence, her self-esteem.

'He was so clever,' she said, sniffing back her tears. 'He always made me believe he was doing things out of love, because he cared about me and wanted to protect me. I couldn't argue with him. And if I tried, he'd twist my words around and make it seem as if I was the one being unreasonable.'

Grace remembered the night Edward had confronted her on the ward. The way he had begged and pleaded with her, convinced her not to deny him his chance of happiness.

And she had believed him, even though she had read his notes and knew exactly how manipulative he could be.

Anna was right – he was dangerously clever.

'I wish you'd come to us,' she said.

Anna shook her head. 'I couldn't. Edward made me feel as if I didn't have a friend in the world.'

'You know that's not true.'

'I do now.' Anna looked around her. 'The last time we sat in this café was the day I left the Nightingale. We had tea and cakes. Do you remember?'

'Of course.' Grace silently cursed herself. 'I'm so sorry, I should've thought – this is probably the last place you'd want to come.'

'It doesn't matter,' Anna said. 'It's over now.'

Grace looked at her friend's troubled face. She hoped she was right.

The waitress brought the eggs on toast, and Grace encouraged Anna to eat. At first she could only pick at it, but after a few minutes her appetite resurfaced and she began shovelling food into her mouth as if she had been ravenous for weeks.

Grace watched her, satisfied. A quick look at the clock told her that the wedding had ended a long time ago, but she didn't mind at all.

'So what will you do now?' she asked.

Anna paused, her expression darkening. 'I don't know.'

She let her fork fall back to her plate. Anna could see her mood sinking and knew she had to step in.

'You could come back to the Nightingale,' she said.

Anna blinked at her. 'What? I couldn't!'

'Why not? I bet you if you went to see Matron she would give you a job on the spot. We're desperate for trained nurses, especially with all the men coming in from France.' The latest German offensive, combined with an influenza epidemic at the Front, meant more convoys were arriving every day.

'Yes, but – I couldn't.' Anna looked around her desperately. 'What if I've forgotten everything?'

'In three months?' Grace laughed.

Anna looked thoughtful for a moment, then shook her head. 'I'd feel too ashamed.'

'Ashamed? Why?'

'It would be like admitting I'd failed, wouldn't it? What would people say?'

'If they're your friends they won't say anything. And if they're not your friends . . .' Grace shrugged. 'Why would you even care what they say?'

That brought a smile to Anna's face.

'Dear Duffield,' she said. 'You always know the right thing to say.'

Grace blushed. 'I don't know about that!'

'You do. I'm glad you were the one I met at the gates. I don't know what I would have done if I'd run into Moore, or Trott!'

Grace looked at her, intrigued. 'Why did you come here?' she asked. 'Of all the places in London, why did you decide to come back to the Nightingale?'

Anna looked down at her plate. 'I don't know,' she admitted. 'I suppose it was the last place I felt happy and safe.'

Grace smiled. 'Well, then. That must tell you something, mustn't it?'

'I suppose it does,' Anna agreed.

By the time they had finished talking, it was nearly two o'clock, and Grace was due back on duty.

Rain was falling steadily as they emerged from the café.

'Where are you staying?' Grace asked.

'I found a boarding house last night.' Anna grimaced. 'It's not very nice, but it's cheap. The landlady won't let me back in until four, though.'

'What will you do until then?'

Anna shrugged. 'I don't know. I'll just walk the streets, I suppose.'

Grace looked at her, shivering inside her coat, and made up her mind.

'Come with me,' she said.

'Where are we going?' Anna asked, as she followed Grace back through the hospital gates and up the wide sweep of gravelled drive.

'To the nurses' home. You can use our room to rest and keep dry. It's the Home Sister's day off, so you'll be quite safe,' she added.

Anna did not protest as Grace helped her off with her damp coat and laid it out to dry. She pulled a spare nightgown out of her drawer for her to put on, and carefully folded up her clothes.

'Try to rest,' she said. But Anna's eyes were already closed as her head touched the pillow.

'I'm sorry you missed the wedding,' she mumbled, half asleep.

Grace looked at the clock. They would be in the middle of the wedding breakfast by now. She could imagine Dr Logan standing up to make his speech, Dulcie beside him, looking up at him adoringly . . .

'It's probably for the best,' she said.

She left Anna sleeping and headed back to the main hospital building.

Now she had started thinking about the wedding, she couldn't seem to stop. She kept torturing herself with images of Dulcie and Dr Logan together. She could imagine her charming him, looking up at him through her lashes in that way she had. She had once told Grace that whenever she spoke to a man she liked, she always pouted her lips slightly.

'It puts them in mind of a kiss,' she had said.

Grace could imagine her pouting up at Dr Logan now,

372

and him accepting her unspoken invitation, his head lowering to meet hers . . .

And then she walked on to the ward, saw the curtains drawn around the bed at the far end, and all thoughts of the wedding, Dulcie and Dr Logan went right out of her mind.

Chapter Fifty-Three

Dulcie was having a wonderful time. At least, that was what she kept telling herself.

She and Robert Logan made the perfect couple, she decided. She could see the envious looks the other girls were giving her as she entered the wedding reception on his arm. Miriam Trott looked as if she might expire with jealousy.

Even the bride looked slightly put out at the amount of attention Dulcie was getting, she noted with sly satisfaction.

The only one who didn't seem to be looking at her was her own partner.

Robert had been a dutiful escort, opening doors and pulling out chairs for her, complimenting her dress and making polite conversation when they sat down for the wedding breakfast. But dutiful was the word; Dulcie sensed his heart wasn't really in it.

Even now, as she was doing her utmost to flirt with him, his gaze was straying around the room, pulled towards the doors.

Finally, she could stand it no longer.

'Are you looking for someone?' She smiled when she said it, but her voice was laced with irritation.

She expected him to apologise, but he said, 'I thought Grace – Nurse Duffield – might be here.'

'She's on duty,' Dulcie replied, tight-lipped.

'Yes, but she said she might come to the ceremony, at least.'

She whipped her head round to look at him. 'You've seen her?'

'This morning, on the ward.' Once again his gaze strayed to the doors. 'I hope nothing's happened to her . . .'

Dulcie tapped him playfully on the arm. 'Really, Robert, it's hardly gallant of you to be thinking about another woman when you're supposed to be with me!' she reminded him.

'Oh!' Dr Logan turned red. 'Yes, of course. I do apologise.' He looked down at her empty glass. 'May I offer you another drink?'

'Thank you.'

She watched him making his way across the floor. He was so handsome, she thought. Her perfect man. She tried to think about them on their own wedding day, standing at the altar, making their vows to each other . . .

She closed her eyes to picture it, then opened them again.

Nothing.

She closed her eyes again, and concentrated hard. She could see herself in her dress, an elegant silk creation, her hair threaded with pearls, a bouquet of fragrant lily of the valley, her face delicately veiled.

She saw herself walking up the aisle on her father's arm. She could see Robert in the distance, standing with his back to her, tall, dark and handsome in his smart suit. As she approached, he turned to look at her, and Dulcie felt her heart leap with—

Nothing.

She could see him there, watching her, his face suffused with love, eyes misty behind his spectacles. But her heart lay like a stone in her chest.

She screwed her eyes shut and tried to think about their lives after marriage. They were living in a big house, an Edwardian villa in Hampstead. They had a servant – no, two servants, a maid and a housekeeper. Dulcie spent her days on charity committees, or shopping in the West End.

Sometimes she would deign to meet one of her old friends for tea at Fortnum & Mason, just so she could show off. And then, in the evening, Robert would come home, and she would greet him, and—

'Dulcie?'

She opened her eyes, startled to see Robert Logan standing over her, a glass in each hand.

'I'm sorry,' he said. 'Did I wake you up?'

'No. Not at all.' Dulcie felt the heat rising in her face. 'I was just . . .'

She stopped. What was she doing? It hardly felt like daydreaming. Daydreaming usually lifted her up, filled her with happiness and excitement. But this time it felt more as if she was watching someone else's life than her own.

You can't help who you fall in love with.

She snatched the drink out of Robert's hand, annoyed with herself. This would not do, she decided. She had to try harder.

As he went to sit down beside her, he knocked her bag off her lap. It fell to the floor, spilling its contents.

'Oh, I beg your pardon. Here, let me help you . . .'

'It's all right.'

'Allow me.'

They both stooped to pick up her belongings at the same time. Dulcie moved quickly, but not quickly enough.

'What's this?' Robert held up the medal. It glinted silver in the low lights.

'It's mine.' Dulcie took it from him. 'It was a gift from – someone.'

'It's a Military Medal, isn't it? That's quite something to give away.'

'Yes.'

'He must have meant a great deal to you for you to carry it with you.'

Dulcie looked down at the medal, heavy in her palm.

For bravery in the field.

The inscription seemed to mock her.

Perhaps that was why Sam had given it to her, she thought. Because he knew she was a coward.

Or perhaps he had meant it as a challenge? If so, she had failed it.

Her mind went back to the day Sam left, when she had stayed away rather than say goodbye. She had bitterly regretted it since, but deep down she knew that if she had her time all over again she would probably do the same thing.

She was not brave enough to face him, in case she was forced to admit how much she truly cared.

You can't help who you fall in love with.

'Yes,' she said quietly, realisation dawning.

'Yes, I think he was.'

She stuffed the medal back into her bag and closed the clasp with a snap. This would not do, she chided herself. Every time she thought about Sam she could feel all her carefully made plans starting to unravel, and she could not allow that to happen.

The band struck up, and she grabbed Robert's arm. 'Come on, let's dance.'

'Must I?' Robert held back. 'I'm really not much of a dancer.'

'It doesn't matter. Come on!' Dulcie dragged him determinedly to his feet.

Robert was right, he wasn't a very good dancer. But that didn't matter. What mattered was that he was holding her close, breathing in her perfume. What mattered was that he was falling in love with her, and she with him . . .

'Sorry, was that your foot?' Robert's apology broke into her thoughts.

Dulcie sighed. 'It doesn't matter.'

She pressed herself closer to him, gazing up into his

face. His chin was lifted away from her, his eyes staring off into the middle distance.

This was all wrong, she thought. She had assumed that by now she would be melting into his arms, that once she was close to him it would all come naturally.

Her mind went back to another moment. Two hands brushing by accident, and the jolt of electricity that had gone through her then. The melting sensation she'd felt when she looked into those green eyes, caught a reluctant smile . . .

You can't help who you fall in love with.

Then she thought about the medal she carried everywhere, that she kept under her pillow at night.

For bravery in the field.

She stopped dead in the middle of the dance floor. 'This is all wrong,' she said.

Robert looked down at her, startled. 'I'm sorry. I did warn you I had two left feet . . .'

'Not your dancing. This. Us.'

'I don't understand?'

'We shouldn't be doing this. We're not supposed to be together.' She looked at him. 'You're supposed to be with Grace.'

Robert's expression darkened. 'Surely her fiancé would have something to say about that?' he muttered.

'There is no fiancé. Not anymore. She's broken it off with him.'

'She – broke it off?' Robert said slowly.

'She should never have got engaged in the first place. She only did it to please her family. Thank God she came to her senses in the end!' Dulcie looked up at Robert's bewildered expression. He was struggling to take it all in, she could tell. 'Although she might never have found the courage to end it if it hadn't been for you,' she said.

'Me?'

'She likes you, you dolt!' Dulcie sighed. For a doctor he could really be rather dim, she thought.

The music stopped and the couples began to leave the floor. But Robert stood rooted to the spot.

He stared at Dulcie, his eyes owlish behind his spectacles. Then he shook his head. 'That can't be true. She's never given me any indication . . .'

'That's because she's too nice and kind-hearted for her own good!' Dulcie said. 'You know what she's like, she always puts other people before herself.' *And we've all let her*, she added silently. *Especially me*. 'She's never thought of herself as special, or expected anyone to love her. But she deserves to be loved. And it's about time someone did.'

She looked up at him. He was so handsome, she thought. They would have made a perfect couple, if only . . .

If only they weren't both in love with other people.

She released him. 'Well? What are you waiting for? Go and find Grace and tell her how you feel. But I'm warning you, she might take some convincing.'

'Thank you.' Robert smiled down at her, such a heart-breaking smile that Dulcie began to feel herself weaken.

'Just promise me you won't hurt her,' she muttered. 'Grace Duffield has a good heart, and it doesn't deserve to be broken.'

'I won't,' he promised. He started to walk away, then turned back. 'But what about you? It's hardly right to leave you standing on your own in the middle of the dance floor.'

Dulcie looked around her. She had completely forgotten where she was until she saw Miriam smirking at her.

She thought of the medal, nestling in her bag.

'I'll just have to be brave, won't I?' she said.

Chapter Fifty-Four

'He's gone, Nurse. There's nothing more you can do for him.'

Florence Parker looked down at Grace Duffield, sitting at the side of Albie Sallis' bed. It had been half an hour since Dr Carlyle issued the death certificate but still Grace sat there, holding on to his lifeless hand.

'I can't believe it, Sister,' she kept saying. 'I keep thinking he's going to wake up any minute and smile and everything will be all right.'

The poor girl looked dazed, as well she might. No one had expected someone as full of life as Corporal Sallis to die. But as Kate Carlyle said, the shard of shrapnel was like a ticking time bomb lodged in his brain.

'I know, Nurse.' Miss Parker looked at Grace with sympathy. She had been sitting at Albie's bedside for most of the afternoon, talking to him in a gentle whisper as he drifted in and out of consciousness. She'd refused to leave his side.

'He needs me here, Sister,' was all she would say whenever Miss Parker suggested she should talk a break.

Now, as she watched the girl weeping silently, Florence Parker knew she should take a firm hand with her. After all, it wasn't the first time Grace Duffield had witnessed the death of a patient. All nurses accepted it as part of their job.

But somehow she could not bring herself to chastise her. Grace was generally a sensible girl – a little clumsy at times, but not usually given to silliness or sentimental outbursts like some of the other nurses. But she had developed a particular fondness for Corporal Sallis.

They all had, in their own way. Miss Parker had liked him a great deal, even though he could be a handful at times. She would miss his jokes, and his laughter. It wasn't a sound they often heard among the traumatised men on Wilson ward.

She looked back at Grace who was pale with exhaustion.

'Come along, Nurse.' She forced herself to sound brisk. 'Let's leave him now, shall we?'

'What about last offices, Sister?'

Miss Parker shook her head. 'I'll find someone else to do it.'

'But there are no other nurses here . . .'

'Then I'll find someone else,' Miss Parker cut her off. 'Go to my sitting room, Nurse. I'll get a VAD to bring you a cup of tea.'

'But—'

Miss Parker sent her a severe look. 'I hope you're not going to argue with me, Nurse Duffield?'

'No, Sister.'

Florence Parker watched her making her way unsteadily down the ward. She was an ungainly girl at the best of times, and her limbs were stiff from sitting for so long.

Ten minutes later, Miss Parker herself carried the tea tray into her sitting room. Grace was perched on the edge of the settee, arms wrapped around herself, perfectly still as if she was trying to stop herself from knocking something over.

She jumped to her feet when she saw Miss Parker, ran to take the tray from her and promptly upset a small vase of flowers.

'It doesn't matter,' Florence kept saying as Grace fell to her knees, desperately patting the rug with her apron to try and soak up the spilt water. 'For goodness' sake, girl, stop fussing! It's only water, it will soon dry. Come and sit down.'

She set the tray on the low table between them and took her seat in the armchair opposite Grace.

'I'll pour, shall I?' she offered. The last thing she needed was a pot of hot tea spilled in her lap.

'I'm sorry, Sister,' Grace said, as she took the cup from her. 'I know I shouldn't have made such a fuss. It was just so sudden.'

'We knew it could happen at any time, Nurse.'

'Yes, but he seemed so well.' She looked up. 'Do you think it had anything to do with Private Gordon leaving?'

The same thought had occurred to Florence, too, but she kept her expression bland. 'In what way, Nurse?'

'I'm not sure – it was just something he said to me, the day Gordon left. About not having a purpose anymore.' She chewed her lip. 'I wonder if he felt he had outlived his usefulness once he didn't have to take care of his friend.'

Miss Parker considered the question. 'I think it may more likely be the other way around, Nurse,' she said at last. 'It's possible that Corporal Sallis only stayed alive because of Private Gordon. He was in a great deal of pain, although he didn't like to show it. Perhaps he felt, with Gordon gone, he could finally be at rest?'

Grace was silent for a moment, and Florence could see her taking this in.

'I hope so,' she said finally. 'He was very brave, wasn't he, Sister?'

'Yes, he was.' Miss Parker took off her spectacles and wiped them on her apron. Goodness, she must be going soft in her old age, she thought. She had no idea what the other ward sisters would make of her, shedding a tear over a patient. Let alone allowing a humble nurse to take tea in her private sitting room.

But then, Florence Parker had always prided herself on being different from the others. She liked to think she was more modern and forward-thinking in her ways.

And besides, she had a soft spot for Grace Duffield. She was one of Miss Parker's best nurses, and yet she was so often overlooked by everyone.

She left Grace sipping her tea and went outside to supervise the laying out of Corporal Sallis. She was glad she had not allowed Grace to perform last offices; no matter how brave and committed she was, it would have been a task too far for her.

As she emerged from behind the curtains, Dr Logan was waiting for her. He looked towards the curtains, then back at her.

'Is he—?'

Miss Parker shook her head.

He swallowed hard. 'When?'

'Just over an hour ago.'

'Do you want me to do anything?'

'There's no need, Doctor. Dr Carlyle has already issued the death certificate.'

He was silent for a moment. Then he seemed to remember something.

'Where's Grace – I mean Nurse Duffield?'

Miss Parker decided to ignore this slip. 'Nurse Duffield is in my sitting room. I'm afraid Corporal Sallis' death has hit her rather hard.'

'I can imagine.' Dr Logan looked towards her sitting-room door, then back at Miss Parker. 'Perhaps I could go and see her?' he ventured.

She saw the wariness in his eyes. He was waiting for her

to say no, to bridle at the impropriety of his suggestion. It was a strict rule of the hospital that nurses were not allowed to be alone with men, even doctors.

Of course, it was always being broken. The ward sisters were forever finding staff nurses and probationers closeted in kitchens and sluices and linen cupboards with young doctors and medical students.

But for a ward sister to condone such a thing – well, that was an entirely different matter.

'I think that would be a very good idea, Doctor,' said Sister Parker.

The younger nurses always thought ward sisters were made of stone. Or iron, at any rate. Most of them would never have believed that their superiors were young too, once. They had flirted with doctors, crept back to the nurses' home with their shoes in their hand after lights out, and even fallen in love a few times.

Of course, most of the ward sisters had forgotten their own ill-spent youth, but not Florence Parker. Even though her salad days were long gone, she still enjoyed watching romances blossom on the ward – so long as the nurses didn't allow it to interfere with their work, of course.

And she had watched the tentative romance between Grace Duffield and Dr Robert Logan with particular interest. She had willed them both on from the sidelines as their friendship slowly developed, and silently cursed when Dulcie Moore decided to interfere.

There had come a point when she had begun to despair that they would ever find their way to each other. Dr Logan was far too shy for his own good, and as for Grace – well, she wouldn't have known a man was interested in her if he'd carried a banner.

But now, seeing the keen look on Dr Logan's face as he

headed for her sitting room, Florence Parker began to hope that love might at last have found a way.

Then perhaps the doctor would stop behaving like a lovesick puppy, and they could all get on with their work.

She turned away with a smile. She was definitely going soft in her old age.

Chapter Fifty-Five

'Don't you want to go outside, Sergeant Trevelyan?'

Sam looked up at the nurse hovering beside his chair. She never seemed to be far from his side.

Her name was Nurse Bright, and it really suited her. She was always irritatingly perky and full of good ideas about how he could fill his days. Even her voice grated on him.

'Some of the men are organising a cricket match on the front lawn. Perhaps you'd like to join them.' She beamed, showing off a mouth full of over-large teeth.

Sam pointed to the wound in his side. It was healing well, but the muscles were still weak. 'I reckon my days as a spin bowler are probably over.'

'I didn't mean join in, silly!' Nurse Bright brayed with laughter. 'But you could watch?'

Sam looked at her. He knew she was doing her best, but she was far too sweet for him. He missed having someone he could spar with, someone who could give as good as they got.

'Perhaps you might like to do something else then?' Nurse Bright suggested. 'The singing group are practising in the dining room?'

'That's the singing group, is it? I thought it was a bunch of tom cats fighting over the bins.'

Nurse Bright's smile hardened. 'Well, what would you like to do?' she asked.

'I'd like to sit here in peace, if you don't mind.'

'But you can't.'

'Why not?'

'You need to get better. You need to be rehabilitated.' There was a desperate look in Nurse Bright's eyes.

'I'm sure I'll get better faster if you just let me alone.'

'But—'

Then a voice said, 'Take no notice of him, Nurse. He was just as grumpy when I was nursing him.'

Sam's whole body went rigid at the sound of her voice. He did not dare turn round. He had pictured this moment so often, he was worried it might be his mind playing tricks on him.

But then he heard Nurse Bright reply, so he knew it couldn't have been his imagination.

'You nursed him?'

'I looked after him when he first returned to England. Believe me, he was worse-tempered then than he is now.'

'I find that hard to believe,' Nurse Bright muttered.

'I am here, you know,' Sam snapped. 'I can hear what you're saying.'

He kept his back to them, staring out of the French windows. But he could imagine them exchanging exasperated looks.

'I'll leave you to it,' Nurse Bright said. 'Perhaps you can cheer him up?'

'I doubt it,' Dulcie replied.

Sam heard Nurse's Bright's footsteps receding, but still he didn't turn around. He watched the men in their cricket whites gathering on the lawn.

'You took your time.' His voice sounded gruff. 'I thought you were never going to visit.'

'If I had known I was going to receive such a rapturous welcome I would have come sooner.'

Sam turned slowly to look at Dulcie, savouring the

387

moment. She was wearing that beautiful blue dress again. A fashionable hat was pulled low over her curls.

She looked nervous, he thought. He wondered if her heart was racing as fast as his.

'How are you?' she asked, sitting down in an armchair opposite him.

'Oh, I'm leading a very exciting life. Between the endless exercises and resisting Nurse Bright's efforts to bring me out of myself – it's all go.'

Dulcie smiled. 'It sounds as if you're winning that particular battle.'

'Don't I always?'

He glanced down at her hands folded in her lap, trying to see if she was wearing a ring on her left hand. It was hard to tell through her lacy gloves.

'How are you?' he asked.

'Very well, thank you.' Then she paused and said, 'I've moved back to Monaghan ward.'

'Why's that?'

'Various reasons. I'm happier where I am.'

She didn't look very happy, Sam thought. He searched her face, looking for clues.

'I was sorry I wasn't there to see you off,' Dulcie said.

Sam stiffened, remembering his disappointment. 'I daresay you had better things to do.'

'It wasn't that.'

'What was it, then?'

'It doesn't matter.'

Oh, but it does, Sam thought. Suddenly her answer seemed to be the most important thing in the world to him.

They sat in silence for a while, both watching the cricket match.

'Why did you leave me your medal?' Dulcie asked.

So you wouldn't forget me. Sam thought about saying the

words, but his pride wouldn't let him. Instead he shrugged and said, 'I thought you might like it. You were always more impressed by it than I was.'

'Was that the only reason?' Her voice was quiet, almost disappointed.

Out on the front lawn, the players were tossing a coin to see who went in to bat first. Sam stared at them, tussling with his emotions, unable to say the words he knew she wanted to hear.

He was a fool. He was going to lose her. He had waited all this time and now he was going to let her slip through his fingers, all because of his stupid pride . . .

'I wanted you to remember me,' he managed finally.

'I didn't need a medal for that.'

He saw the wry smile on her face and his heart lifted. But still he couldn't allow himself to hope. Not until he knew for sure.

'How is Dr Logan?' he asked.

'He's well, I think.' Dulcie's smile faltered slightly. 'Engaged.'

Sam took a deep, steadying breath. So that was why she had come.

'Anyone I know?'

'Nurse Duffield, would you believe?' Dulcie's smile was fixed.

He could believe it. He had always thought Dr Logan had a soft spot for the delightful Nurse Duffield.

'You must be very disappointed?'

'Actually, I was the one who gave him a bit of a nudge in her direction.'

Sam stared at her. 'You?'

Dulcie laughed. 'Don't sound so surprised. Am I really that selfish?'

'Well—'

'All right, perhaps I am. I probably wouldn't have done it if I hadn't . . .' She stopped talking.

'If you hadn't what?' he urged.

She looked at him. 'If I hadn't fallen in love with someone else.'

The door opened and Nurse Bright appeared. Sam flashed her a look. If she approached them now with another of her suggestions, he would not be responsible for his actions.

Thankfully, she seemed to understand and left the room again, closing the door behind her.

He turned back to Dulcie. 'Someone nice, I hope?' he said.

'No,' she said. 'He isn't very nice at all. He can actually be downright rude at times.'

'What an unpleasant man.' He raised his eyebrows. 'I hope he showers you with gifts, at least?'

'He bought me a box of violet creams once.'

'Sounds very generous. So I'm guessing it won't be long before you move in to your fancy London house?'

'I don't think so.' She gave a martyred sigh. 'The way things are going, I think I may well end up living in some muddy old farm in the middle of nowhere.'

'Would you mind that?'

'Not in the least.' Their eyes met.

'All the same,' Sam said, 'he doesn't sound like much of a catch to me.'

'You're right.' Dulcie smiled. 'But you can't help who you fall in love with, can you?'

Chapter Fifty-Six

Dulcie had never seen a place like Grace's home.

Ramshackle wasn't even the word for it. Water dripped from cracked guttering, the kitchen range belched black smoke, and the whole place smelled of wet dogs and dirty nappies. It was the middle of winter, and a damp cold seeped through the thick stone walls.

And the noise . . . dogs barking, babies crying, and children everywhere. They rampaged around like an army of little hooligans, diving under furniture and jumping on beds.

Grace shared her room with at least five of them. But Dulcie had insisted they should move somewhere quieter after she had found one of the younger girls smearing the baby's face with her best lipstick.

They ended up in Grace's mother's room. There was no fire lit, and Dulcie could see her breath curling in front of her face as she set about doing Grace's hair.

Just to make matters worse, Grace's sisters-in-law insisted on joining them. Dulcie had taken an instant dislike to Jessie and Beth when she met them. Grace had always told her they were the prettiest girls in the village, but Dulcie couldn't understand why she was so in awe of them. Beth was passable, in a blowsy, overblown kind of way, but to Dulcie's mind Jessie looked like a wiry little ferret.

They were certainly not endearing themselves now but kept trying to push Dulcie and Grace out of the way so they could admire themselves in the tiny dressing-table mirror.

'Isn't there somewhere else you two can get ready?' Dulcie asked Jessie pointedly when she thrust her face close to the glass yet again.

'Grace wants us here, don't you, Gracie?' Beth said.

'Well . . .'

'We're family,' Jessie put in.

Dulcie caught Grace's eye in the mirror. She shrugged helplessly.

Dulcie did her best to ignore them as she pulled the rags out of Grace's hair and twisted the curls around her fingers.

'Thank you for helping me,' Grace said. 'I'm sure I'd be all fingers and thumbs otherwise.'

'She's right,' Jessie chimed in. 'She's ever so clumsy.'

Dulcie caught Grace's eye in the mirror. 'I'm glad to help you,' she said. 'And your hair curls really well.'

'Do you think so?' Beth leaned her fat face in to inspect it. 'Looks a bit limp to me.'

'Grace's hair never looks right, no matter what she does to it,' Jessie agreed.

'Like rat's tails,' Beth said. 'But as Ma always says –'

'– you can't make a silk purse out of a sow's ear!' they chorused in delight.

Dulcie felt the anger rising inside her. She was just about to open her mouth and stick up for her friend when Grace beat her to it.

'If you can't think of anything nice to say, you can go away.'

It was the mildest of rebukes, but her sisters-in-law could not have looked more shocked if Grace had turned around and struck them.

Jessie found her voice first. 'You can't tell us what to do in our home!' she protested.

'Actually, it's more my home than it is yours,' Grace

392

pointed out. 'You two only live here because you're married to my brothers.'

Dulcie cheered silently as Jessie and Beth stared at her, open-mouthed.

'You can't talk to us like that,' Beth said.

'Can't I?' Grace turned her head slightly to look at her. 'I'd choose a different dress if I were you. That one might have suited you five years ago when you were May Queen but now it just makes you look fat.'

The girls gaped at each other. Then Jessie burst out laughing.

'She's right, you do look like a heifer!' she screeched. 'You tell her, Gracie!'

Grace turned on her calmly. 'And I think you should stop laughing,' she said. 'No one wants to see all those missing teeth.'

Dulcie ducked her head so they would not see her giggling to herself. She had never heard Grace stand up to anyone before. Now she seemed to be growing in confidence before Dulcie's eyes.

'Well, I like that!' Jessie's little face screwed up in fury. 'If that's the way you feel then – we won't come to your wedding!'

'That suits me perfectly,' Grace said.

They stomped off, slamming the door behind them. Grace raised her gaze to meet Dulcie's in the mirror.

'They will come,' she said. 'They would never miss a party. Let alone a chance to criticise.'

'All the same, I'm glad you stood up to them.'

'You don't think I was too harsh?'

'Not at all. They deserved it.'

Grace smiled reluctantly. 'I must say, it's something I've wanted to do for a long time. But I've never had the courage before.'

393

'Why not?'

Grace shrugged. 'I thought everyone was better than me.' She lifted her chin and met her reflection with a smile. 'But that's not true, is it? I'm just as good as everyone else.'

Dulcie looked at her friend's reflection, and a lump rose in her throat. Dear Grace, she was simply the purest and biggest-hearted person Dulcie had ever met. There was not a shred of malice in her.

If anyone deserved to be happy and loved, she did.

'No,' she said. 'You're not just as good as everyone else. You're far, far better than that. Now come on, let's get you into your dress.

It took a long time to get Grace dressed. She was trembling so much Dulcie could scarcely do up the tiny mother-of-pearl buttons. But once it was finally fastened, they stood back to admire her reflection.

'It's perfect,' Dulcie said. She had only ever seen anything like this delicate creation of fine lace and pearls in the pages of *Vogue*. 'It must have cost a fortune,' she said without thinking.

'Don't say that!' Grace cried in dismay. 'What if I tear it or spill something down it? You know what I'm like.' She gazed back at her reflection, her eyes round with wonder. 'I told Robert I would have been happy to make do with my mother's old wedding dress, but he insisted I should have one of her own.'

'And quite right, too,' Dulcie said. 'You deserve it.'

She waited for the jealous pangs to kick in. Here was Grace, living Dulcie's dream, getting married in her perfect dress and marrying her perfect man. Once upon a time she would have been so enraged with bitterness and spite she would not have been able to look at her.

But now she realised that wasn't what she wanted at all.

All the stylish dresses and smart addresses in the world simply didn't matter.

Now she had Sam, she couldn't imagine wanting anything more.

Grace turned to her, eyes misty with tears. 'Thank you,' she said. 'You've made me look beautiful.'

Dulcie smiled at her friend, genuinely happy for her. 'You *are* beautiful,' she said. 'Come on, now. Let's go and get you married.'

The morning after the wedding, Anna, Dulcie, Miriam and Mary caught the train back to London together. The glorious wintry sunshine that had shone down on Grace's big day had given way to a dreary dark sky and an icy wind that lashed the train windows with sleet.

'I'm so glad it wasn't like this yesterday,' Mary said, pressing her nose against the glass. 'It would have spoiled Duffield's day.'

'I don't think anything could have spoiled her day,' Anna said. Grace's smile as she walked down the aisle could have lit up the dullest weather.

'You're right.' Mary sighed. 'Wasn't it a beautiful wedding? That little chapel was exquisite, didn't you think?'

'It was a bit small,' Miriam said.

'And such a good idea to have those garlands of evergreen everywhere instead of flowers,' Mary went on, ignoring her.

'I'd never get married in the middle of winter,' Miriam declared. 'It's far too dreary.'

Anna caught Dulcie's eye across the train carriage and they both smiled.

'Come off it, Trott. You'd get married in the middle of a snowstorm if it meant you ended up with a ring on your finger!' Dulcie said.

'Duffield looked beautiful, didn't she?' Anna put in quickly, sensing an argument looming. It was a long way back to London and she didn't particularly want to listen to their bickering.

'Until she tripped over her train and went flying!' Miriam snorted.

'But did you see how Robert caught her in his arms?' Dulcie said. 'It was so romantic.'

Miriam turned to Dulcie, her mouth pursing. 'You know, you're taking it very well, considering Duffield has married your man,' she said.

Dulcie blushed. 'He wasn't my man,' she mumbled.

'Really? It wasn't so long ago that you were telling everyone you were going to marry him!'

'Why does she need Robert Logan when she has a fiancé of her own?' Anna said.

'Exactly.' Dulcie looked down at the engagement ring on her left hand, as if to reassure herself it was still there.

Miriam looked at the ring. 'Duffield's was twice as big as yours,' she commented unkindly.

'At least I've got one,' Dulcie snapped back.

Anna stifled a sigh and let her gaze drift towards the water drops streaming down the window as the sniping commenced. In spite of her best efforts, it seemed as if Dulcie and Miriam were determined to argue all the way back to London.

The flags were still flying proudly in Paddington station when they arrived. Two weeks after the Armistice had been declared, there wasn't a building in London that didn't have a Union Jack fluttering from its roof. Strings of bunting sagged, exhausted, between lamp posts, a reminder of the parties that had spilled out onto the streets the day the ceasefire was declared.

There had been so many celebrations on that day. Maroons exploded from the roofs of police and fire stations, church bells pealed, hooters blasted out from factories. Thousands poured on to the streets, waving Union Jacks and French flags. Bands played, and people sang and danced, all day and all night.

They had celebrated on the ward, too. The orderlies had brought in beer, and Miss Sutton had been in such a good mood that she had permitted the men to take a drink. Later, she had led a few rousing choruses of "Keep the Home Fires Burning" and "When the Boys Come Marching Home". But the party had really got started when another of the orderlies arrived with his accordion. Some of the more able-bodied men had got out of bed to dance with the nurses. Anna did not think she would ever forget the sight of Nurse Hanley being whirled around the ward by a burly lance corporal.

Now, two weeks on, the city was slowly beginning to recover – unlike Hanley, who still seemed to be in a state of shock after her ordeal.

At the station in London they said goodbye to Dulcie, who was catching another train down to Surrey to see Sam Trevelyan.

'Isn't it funny to see her so giddy?' Mary observed, as they watched her hurrying down the platform. 'I don't think I've ever seen her so head over heels for a man. Have you noticed how she blushes whenever she says his name?'

Even Miriam had grudgingly to admit she had never known Dulcie so happy or in love.

'But, of course, it could all change,' she added sourly.

'You know what Moore's like. She's never been able to keep a man.'

'I'm sure she'll keep this one,' Anna replied.

Anna, Miriam and Mary travelled together on the Underground to Bethnal Green. There Anna said goodbye to them.

'Aren't you coming back to the Nightingale?' Miriam wanted to know.

'I'm not on duty till five. There's somewhere I need to go first.'

'That sounds very mysterious.' Miriam's sharp little nose twitched, as it always did at the first hint of gossip. 'Where are you off to?'

'None of your business,' Mary cut in swiftly. 'Leave the girl alone, Trott.'

'All right, keep your little secrets,' Miriam huffed. 'But you needn't think I'm covering for you if you're late back. I shall tell Sister you said to mind her own business.'

Anna stood for a moment outside the station, watching the others go. When they were safely out of sight, she turned and headed towards Chambord Street.

She didn't know why she felt she had to see it again. It was like a wound she couldn't stop picking at, despite the fresh surge of pain it brought her every time.

As she turned the corner the sight of the bakery windows all boarded up gave her a painful jolt. The windows above the shop were blackened, gaping hollows, the brickwork charred.

Anna fumbled in her pocket for a handkerchief, feeling foolish. It had been nearly a month since the fire, and she had been coming at least once a week to see it ever since.

And every time it made her cry.

'Back again, love?' Anna started at the sound of Mr Hudson's voice. He had come out of the shop next door, wiping his hands on his stained apron.

'Yes.' Anna quickly stuffed her handkerchief back in her coat pocket, determined not to let him see her weep.

Mr Hudson came to stand beside her, looking up at the roof. The last few remaining slate tiles clung precariously to the soot-blackened skeleton of the rafters. 'I daresay it must be a shock for you, seeing it like this again.' He shook his head. 'And they say lightning doesn't strike twice, eh?' He paused, and Anna felt his sidelong look. 'I don't s'pose there's any word on . . .'

'No.' Anna cut him off abruptly.

'Well, you know what they say. No news is good news. I'm sure he's safe and sound somewhere.'

'I hope so.' She meant it, too. In spite of everything he had done to her, she would never want Edward to suffer what she had gone through.

Even now, just thinking about it made her heart drum again her ribs in fear. She could almost feel the burning heat in her throat, her eyes stinging, the terrible panic as she fought to breathe in the choking smoke . . .

No, she wouldn't have wished that on her worst enemy.

'And to think young Tom Franklin went to all that trouble to rebuild it after the last time,' Mr Hudson was saying. 'A crying shame, I call it. What does your father say about it? I daresay he's heartbroken, ain't he?'

'I haven't told him.'

'But surely you should?'

'Why? It was Edward's shop.' Anna glanced at the sign over the door. She could only make out the letters 'S' and 'G' in the blistering paintwork.

'Yes, but—'

'You said yourself, Mr Hudson, my father would be heartbroken if he knew. And since he's so settled in Germany now, I see no reason to upset him. I think he's been through enough, don't you?'

But Mr Hudson wasn't listening. He was looking past Anna's shoulder, a broad grin on his face.

'Well, I never! Look who it is. We were just talking about you, young man.'

Anna froze, every muscle tensing like a hunted animal's. Edward.

She didn't dare turn round. She couldn't trust what she might do if she had to look into his face again, not after everything that had happened . . .

And then she heard his voice, a voice she'd never thought she'd hear again.

'Is that right? And what would you have to say about me?'

Chapter Fifty-Seven

Anna turned around slowly until she was looking into the face of the young man standing behind her.

Tom Franklin was thinner than she remembered him. He leaned heavily on a stick, his suit hanging off his gaunt frame. As he took off his cap, she saw that his dark curls had been cropped close to his head in regulation Army style. But she would have known that lean face and those black, wolfish eyes anywhere.

A jolt of emotion ran through her. For a moment they stared at each other, neither of them speaking. In the end, it was Mr Hudson who broke the silence.

'You made it, then?'

'Just about.' Tom's gaze was still fixed on Anna as he spoke. 'Had a few close calls, mind.'

'When did you get back?'

'In the summer. Caught a lump of shrapnel in my leg, and that was it for me. Been convalescing on the coast ever since.'

'All right for some.'

Tom dragged his gaze away from Anna to fix Mr Hudson with a look so dark with meaning the older man's face coloured.

'Yes, well, I'd best get back to work,' he mumbled, turning away. 'It's nice to see you back, son. Well done for getting through it.'

Tom didn't reply. He took a cigarette from his pocket,

clamped it between his lips. He lit up as he watched Mr Hudson's door close behind him.

'Four years ago he wouldn't have given me the time of day,' he muttered. 'Now suddenly I'm a hero.'

'They'll be putting out the flags again, just for you.' Anna tried to smile but her mouth wouldn't work.

'I wouldn't bet on it.' Tom nodded towards the burned-out bakery. 'What's been going on here, then?'

'There was a fire, about a month ago.'

She saw him fighting for control, and knew he was thinking about the last time it had happened. 'Were you in there?'

Anna shook her head. 'No. But we think Edward might have been.'

'Is he—'

'No one knows,' Anna cut him off before he could say the word. Even now she didn't like to hear it. 'He's not been seen since. We don't know if he escaped or not.'

'I'm sorry.'

'Are you?'

He looked at her sharply. 'What?'

'There was never any love lost between you, was there?'

Tom sent a long stream of smoke into the air. 'No,' he said at last. 'But I'm sorry for you. For your loss. You loved him.'

Anna stole a glance at his hawkish profile as he looked up at the charred remains of the bakery. There was so much she wanted to say to him, but she couldn't find the words.

His presence confused her. After staring at her so hard at first, now he couldn't seem to bring himself to look at her.

'What are you going to do?' he asked.

'Pull it down, I suppose. I can't afford to rebuild it.'

'But surely there's insurance?'

'They won't pay out. They reckon it wasn't an accident.'

If Tom was surprised, he didn't show it. He took another long drag on his cigarette. 'And what do you reckon?' he asked.

'I reckon they're right. Edward owed money to the wrong people. Gambling debts, mostly. He took as much as he could out of the business, and then when all that was gone he borrowed from Billy Willis.' She couldn't look at Tom as she spoke. Strange as it seemed, she felt a kind of shame, as if Edward's downfall had somehow been her fault.

'And let me guess. He was arrogant enough to think he could get away without paying back his debt?'

Anna nodded, her gaze still fixed on the pavement. 'But I'm told Billy Willis always collects his debts, one way or another.'

'That he does.' Tom paused for a moment, then said, 'What's he said to you? Do you still owe him?'

'No, thank God. It was – made clear to me that Edward's debts died with him.' She suppressed a shudder, remembering the menacing-looking man who had appeared from the shadows one night when she was returning to the nurses' home after a late shift three weeks earlier. He had told her he meant no harm, but Anna had still been terrified.

Tom nodded, taking it in. 'That's something, at any rate.'

Anna hesitated, wondering whether to speak. Then she said, 'We weren't together. When it happened.' She stared straight ahead of her at the bakery as she spoke, but she could feel Tom looking at her. 'We'd parted,' she said quietly. 'In the summer.'

He didn't ask why, and she was thankful for that. Perhaps he didn't need to ask.

Anna looked at her watch. 'I should go,' she said. 'I'm due back at the hospital by five.'

'The hospital? You're back at the Nightingale?'

She smiled sadly. 'I had nowhere else to go.'

'I know the feeling.'

'Is that why you came back here?'

Tom looked around. 'I'm not sure why I came back, to be honest with you.'

They lapsed into silence. Anna found herself waiting, hoping that he might say something else. She wasn't even sure what she wanted him to say, but still she found herself teetering on the edge of hope.

But no words came from him.

'Well, it was nice to see you,' she managed at last. 'I'm glad you came home safely. I suppose we might meet again, if you're staying in the area?'

She looked at him hopefully. Tom dropped his cigarette butt and ground it into the pavement with the heel of his boot.

Anna turned and had started to walk away when he suddenly called after her,

'I'll walk with you.'

She looked over her shoulder at him. 'Isn't it out of your way?'

He ignored the question, falling into step beside her. All around them there was the rumble of barrows on cobbles as the costermongers closed up their stalls. Horses' hooves clopped, dogs barked and men shouted to each other, but Anna and Tom walked on, locked in a bubble of silence.

'I wrote to you,' Anna said at last. 'After Edward and I – but I suppose my letters must have missed you.'

'I was back in England by the summer. I didn't expect to hear from you, anyway. Not after the last letter you wrote to me.'

Anna felt herself blushing. 'I'm sorry,' she said. 'I should never have stopped. But I thought it was the right thing to do . . .'

'I understand,' Tom said. 'I probably should have stopped writing to you, too, but I couldn't bring myself to do it. Even if you never replied, I didn't want to lose touch, just in case.'

'Just in case what?' Anna prompted him.

'In case you ever needed me.'

Dear Tom, she thought. He had known what Edward was like, even if Anna hadn't. And all those miles away, with his own life in danger, he had still thought of her, sought to protect her.

She held herself rigid to stop herself from reaching for his hand.

'I didn't know you'd been writing to me,' she said. 'Edward hid your letters.'

She heard Tom's angry, indrawn breath.

'I was a fool,' she said, her words escaping in a rush. 'I know you tried to warn me about Edward, but I wouldn't listen.'

'I didn't expect you to,' Tom said. 'You were in love. People in love don't always see sense.'

Anna sneaked a sideways look at him, but his expression was impassive.

'I found out Edward started the fire that nearly killed me and my family,' she said.

'Did he tell you that?'

Anna shook her head. 'Someone else did.' She looked at him consideringly. 'You don't seem very surprised about it? But then, I don't suppose you would be, would you?'

To his credit, Tom didn't insult her by denying it.

'I tried to stop them,' he said flatly.

'I know. And you wrote that note warning me.'

'I wish I could have done more.'

'I wouldn't have listened. Anyway, you made up for it by rebuilding our home for us.'

He stopped dead and turned to stare at her. 'Is that what you think? That I did it to make amends?'

'What other reason would there be?'

Say it, she pleaded silently. Tom said nothing. But the answer she needed was there, in his yearning eyes. Just as it had been in every line of every letter he had ever written to her.

It was something they both felt, but neither had the courage to express.

Once again, she fought the urge to reach for him, but kept her hands rigidly at her sides, terrified to make the first move.

They carried on walking, neither of them speaking. Then suddenly Tom said,

'I could rebuild it.'

'What?'

'The bakery. I did it before and I could do it again. We could have the place open again by the spring. What do you say?'

For a brief moment she was tempted to say yes. To go back, to open up the bakery, to paint the name Beck's above the door, to put it all back together the way it once had been.

She shook her head. 'No,' she said, 'it wouldn't be right. We can't go back, Tom. We mustn't. We have to look to the future. Everything has changed now. Mother and Papa have their new lives in Germany, and Liesel is getting married to Davy in the New Year. They've all moved on, and now it's time I did the same.'

'So what will you do?' he asked.

Anna shrugged. 'I suppose I'll carry on working at the Nightingale.'

'And then?'

'I don't know.'

They had reached the hospital gates. She turned to him, forcing a smile.

'Well, I suppose this is where we part company. I'll be seeing you, Tom.'

He nodded. 'I daresay you will.' Once again, she caught the look of yearning on his face, as if he was fighting some inner battle.

She went through the gates and had nearly reached the Porters' Lodge before she heard his voice behind her.

'Your letters . . .'

She turned. 'What about them?'

'They kept me going when I was in France.' Deep colour suffused his face. 'There was something in them – like you felt something for me?' He lifted his gaze to meet hers, his black eyes full of a vulnerability she had never seen in him before. 'Am I wrong? Tell me if I am and I'll walk away.'

'No, Tom, you're not wrong.'

Anna walked back to where he stood. It was only a few paces, but it seemed to take forever.

She looked up into his narrow face; his black eyes fixed on hers intently. His years at war had left him battered and walking with a limp, but all his scars were on the surface. When she looked into his eyes, she saw none of the darkness she had seen in Edward's. She saw only love.

But it wasn't that simple. Tom had offered to rebuild her home for her, but to rebuild her shattered trust was what she really needed.

'I don't know if I'm ready,' she said. 'What I went through with Edward – it's going to take me a long time to get over it.'

'Then I'll just have to wait, won't I?' Tom squared his

shoulders. 'I've loved you all these years, I reckon I can wait a bit longer for you to love me back.'

This time Anna didn't try to stop herself from reaching for his hands. His fingers curled around hers, not seeking to possess her as Edward had, but making her feel cherished and safe.

Perhaps it wouldn't take her such a long time to regain her trust in love after all.